I, IAGO

Also by Nicole Galland

I, IAGO

NICOLE GALLAND

WILLIAM MORROW
An Imprint of HarperCollins*Publishers*

I, IAGO. Copyright © 2012 by Nicole Galland. All rights reserved. Printed in the United States of America. No part of this book may be used or reproduced in any manner whatsoever without written permission except in the case of brief quotations embodied in critical articles and reviews. For information address Harper-Collins Publishers, 10 East 53rd Street, New York, NY 10022.

HarperCollins books may be purchased for educational, business, or sales promotional use. For information please write: Special Markets Department, Harper-Collins Publishers, 10 East 53rd Street, New York, NY 10022.

FIRST EDITION

Designed by Diahann Sturge

Library of Congress Cataloging-in-Publication Data has been applied for.

ISBN 978-0-06-202687-3

12 13 14 15 16   OV/RRD   10 9 8 7 6 5 4 3 2 1

For Billy

An hour before the devil fell, God thought him beautiful in Heaven.

—*The Crucible*, Arthur Miller

I, IAGO

Before

Paterfamilias

Prologue

hey called me "honest Iago" from an early age, but in Venice, this is not a compliment. It is rebuke. One does not prosper by honesty. One does not rise in the social ranks. One does not curry favors. Honesty causes upset, and Venice is serene. The Serene Republic. It says so right there on the seal of state, which I could read when I was two, or so claimed the governess who struggled to keep up with my precociousness.

I am the fifth son born into a family where even a second son is redundant. My eldest brother, Rizardo, learned the family business, which he would inherit someday, along with the family home and the family riches. The second-born, lacking all imagination, of course became a priest. The third and fourth did not amount to much: one died in infancy; the next made it to maturity with military aspirations, but when I was ten years, he wounded himself so severely in cadet training that he bled to death. An artillery man, he had been cleaning his ceremonial sword when it slipped from his grasp, and the blade gouged him deep near his groin.

A tragedy, of course. But young as I was, I found in it a poignant irony, and said so one too many times in father's hearing. I was whipped for my candor. And then I was informed that it fell to me to restore the family's military honor. Clearly I would never make it as a courtier, a merchant, or any other trade that required me to don a false front. I was, said father irritably, too blunt and honest for anything but warfare.

Chapter 1

IN VENICE, EVERYTHING is a competition. The higher up the social scale you climb, the more rarefied the competition becomes. Thus among the upper echelon, whose houses are all equally gaudy and overdecorated, whose wives are all equally lamed by the weight of their jewels and gowns and hairstyles and footwear . . . among this circle of dandies, the prosaic is glorified beyond all reason. At the time of my brother's demise, the rage among these fine gentlemen was the owning of hens.

There were any number of categories for competition, in this scintillating hobby: how many hens, how lovely, how large, how small, how cute, how ugly, how elaborately gilded the coop, how pristine the pedigree, and so on. But the ultimate glory of the hen-keeper was the aphrodisiacal potency of his hens' eggs. The master of all egg maestros, one Pietro Galinarion, possessed one hen whose ovum, eaten raw and singly, accomplished things that gentlemen spoke of only obliquely, with knowing, pleased expressions. These eggs were too precious to sell. Galinarion occasionally doled them out as treasured gifts, and even used them in lieu of money at cards. I overheard of their existence in the late-night chatter among my eldest brother and his companions.

I knew the word *virility* and I was almost certain I understood the premise of the eggs. That "almost" fueled a burning curiosity. Roderigo understood only that the eggs were coveted—but that was enough to make him curious too.

Poor Roderigo. He was so earnest, and trusting, and he adored me. We'd met in the crib. Our mothers shared a wet nurse: his family was too poor to keep a nursemaid, even for their sole offspring; mine was rich enough, but by the time the fifth son came along they could not be bothered to spend the money. His father was a failing spice merchant, mine a *setaiòlo*, a thriving silk trader.

Roderigo and I did nearly everything together.

"BUT WHY AM *I* the one who must steal all the supplies for the break-in?" he demanded, wiping his nose with his sleeve. His legs hung over the side of the paving, and his feet dangled a foot or two over grey-green canal water by the Saoneri bridge. "Why don't you have to do any stealing?"

"It's not stealing," I reminded him. "It's borrowing things under a false pretense, but you're returning all of it. It's not stealing, it's lying."

"Why must I do all the lying, then?"

"Because you are an heir," I explained patiently, brushing aside my envy of this title. Drawing on what I had observed passing between my father and my eldest brother, I explained, "Heirs must be able to lie convincingly, so that when they are grown men, they will be able to operate smoothly in good society. This is important practice for you. There is no need for *me* to learn to lie. I would not rob you of an opportunity to practice an important skill that will be valuable to you when you're a great Venetian merchant."

He considered this for a moment, then nodded, satisfied with my reasoning.

"So after we get up there, then what?" he asked.

"We'll eat the egg, of course. We'll crack it open and split it," I said. "Or if you're too chicken, I'll do it."

Roderigo's face broadened with a huge grin. "Too chicken to eat an egg! That's funny, Iago! You're so clever." He punched me on the arm. He was the only boy my age whose punches didn't make me wince. I smiled and punched him back.

"So you'll eat it with me?" I pressed. "And then we'll keep the shells as proof we did it."

"And then we'll start a secret fellowship!" he announced, leaping up with excitement. The slime of Venice stained his already stained breeches; he did not notice. "And the only ones who may join are the ones who can accomplish what we did!"

We agreed upon a time the next day to do it, and swore each other to silence with our secret handshake, invented by me and known only to the two of us. Then we parted ways, each terrified and eager to embrace the hardened life of a juvenile criminal.

THE NEXT DAY we approached the tall iron gate built into the fence that surrounded the Galinarion garden. It was latched on the inside but not locked in daylight hours; by perching on Roderigo's shoulders I was easily able to reach up, slip my slender hand and wrist through the rails, and unlatch it. Roderigo knelt, and I climbed off his shoulders; we each carried a coil of hempen line that he had borrowed from the stores his uncle sold to mariners. To the end of each line we tied another borrowed item: a small grappling hook, the sort used by the navy to teach maneuvers in mock battles out in the lagoon. Emulating the champions of classical romances, we intended to hurl the grappling hooks up the full height of the building and scale the walls.

Inside the gate, we found ourselves in an unoriginal, but sumptuous, garden. It contained statues depicting pagan gods and fountains depicting pagan Venetians, and a few actual plants. In the center was a well.

Roderigo stared about with a slack jaw and glazed eyes.

"Come along," I said urgently, heading straight toward the tall stone house. There was a wooden staircase obtusely zigzagging up the right half of the three-story building. It led straight to the roof. We would not even need the lines and grappling hooks!

It was about dinnertime, and nobody was out here. We climbed a short flight of steps, which took us to the first elevated floor, and heard through the closed door the clanking efficiency of a kitchen. Up the next set of steps, to a heavier and more ornate door to the main hall, where Galinarion would be dining. The next flight went up to the bedrooms, and the final one—more of a ladder than a stairway—took us straight to the roof. The hardest thing about getting to the top was keeping the coils of line neat upon our shoulders.

A usual Venetian roof is shallow gabled, tiled with tight red brick. There is commonly a cistern in one corner, with pipes running down to the kitchen. I have been on our own roof (smaller than this one), and I thought I knew what to expect.

But this roof was flat, canted slightly to slough rainwater into the canal below. It was laid out just like the garden beneath, in miniature, with small wooden statues in lieu of the large stone ones below. The central well's rooftop equivalent was a round storage bin, by the smell of it containing dried corn. Directly across from us was the henhouse. It was designed to be a perfectly scaled miniature of the house upon which it sat. One half of this henhouse was made of wood, but the other half was made of glass, creating an outrageously expensive solarium for a single hen. There were wire-covered vents in the glass, but there was no open-aired coop for the legendary fowl at all.

We trekked gingerly across the roof, not wanting to alert whoever might be on the floor below. The henhouse waited quietly. We flicked the latch open and invaded.

"We've made it!" Roderigo whispered gleefully.

"It should have been more difficult," I countered. "That was too easy to give me any sense of accomplishment."

"Don't cheapen the pleasure, Iago," Roderigo begged. "Who cares if we've earned our success, or merely lucked into it?"

I care, I thought, but said nothing lest I sound like a moralizing parent.

The hen—the most famous hen in all of Venice, perhaps the world (considering the relative anonymity of domestic fowl outside of Venice)—was sitting in a nesting box covered with gold leaf and ornate arabesque decorations about two feet off the ground. Given the famed magnificence of her ovulations, she was not especially feminine. Her eyes were cold and dull, her feathers were a mottled grey and white. There was no fancy or no finery to her. I respected her simplicity. It was not her fault that she'd been made the heroine of a bored patrician's farce.

For the first time I was a little nervous. We had a clutch of hens, each nearly identical to this one, but the cook always collected the eggs. Would she peck at me? Would she cluck and squawk and make a fuss when I reached in for the egg?

"Shoo," I said and waved a hand at her. She made a wonderfully guttural sound, delicately grouchy, and settled farther into the box.

"She doesn't want to move," Roderigo said with spectacular powers of observation. "You can take the egg out from underneath her, and she'll let you. I've seen my mother do it all the time at home."

I reached under her, enjoying the silky softness of her warm feathers. I could feel the structure of her body—bones? sinews?—against the back of my hand as my fingers tentatively groped beneath her. She allowed me the grope and complacently repeated her guttural hum as she felt me under her.

And then I was holding the famous egg. It was warm in my palm, as I was not used to feeling eggs. I felt a strange thrill in the pit of my gut.

"Shall we eat it here? Or shall we go someplace public so people may watch us?" asked Roderigo, wide-eyed.

"It's just a regular egg," I said.

He pulled his head back a little and tried to stop gaping. "If we want to prove that, surely we need witnesses?"

"Who is going to believe two boys?" I asked. "We're just proving it for ourselves. Isn't that enough, Roderigo?"

This, I think, had not occurred to him, but dutifully he fell in line. "Well of course it is," he said, with a frowning nod. The eager beam returned to his face; he even rubbed his hands together. "All right then," he said. "Let's have at it."

There was a gold-embossed drinking bowl for the little fowl. I reached over with both hands and cracked the egg on the side of the bowl. The hen watched me, disinterested. Roderigo watched me, fascinated. The shell broke neatly, and a drop of transparent sludge ran down the side, the tiniest sliver of eggshell clinging to it. The jelly of the egg white glistened like molten glass in the dappled light of the solarium.

Roderigo imbibed first and announced "uck" from his throat. I dumped the rest of it down my own throat and swallowed as quickly as I could, thinking intensely about candy. It wasn't as bad as I'd feared.

Roderigo wiped his mouth and fingers on his clothes; I used a handkerchief with my eldest brother's mark upon it. I had set the shell aside; now I picked each half up and daintily wiped them clean, then couched one half-shell within the other, and lay them in the center of the kerchief. Carefully, I tied the corners together and lifted the small bundle by this lacy knot.

"And so, that is that," I said.

"That is that, indeed," he agreed.

WE DESCENDED JUST as uneventfully as we had climbed. Perhaps because we had now actually committed the act, my pulse was quicker and my hearing more acute as we stepped down into the garden. Roderigo, out of habit, glanced at me for guidance before beginning the obvious next step, which was to walk straight across, past the well, to the still-unlatched gate. I nodded and gestured; he nodded and smiled. He began to walk. I followed, shells cupped gently in the handkerchief, which was cupped in my left palm.

Roderigo approached the well, and my gaze flickered ahead to the gate, briefly. As I looked away, my mind registered that the gate had been relatched, and alarmed, I instantly looked back.

"And here are the little varlets left my gate open," growled the craggy-faced stranger, erupting from the far side of the well. He grabbed Roderigo by both arms, and Roderigo screamed.

I leapt back, startled.

"You're going nowhere," the fellow warned me. He was dressed as a gardener. He was glowering but not really threatening, and so clumsy-looking that I knew I could outrun him. Leaving Roderigo in the lurch would have been dishonorable, which does not mean I didn't consider it.

But I had a better idea: "Glad you caught us," I declared, defiantly. "We almost got away undetected. That would have been quite bad for you later on, when we reported to your master that we successfully broke in."

"Well now I'll be reporting to my master that you *unsuccessfully* broke in."

"Of course you will," I said. "Roderigo, calm yourself. The fellow's only doing his duty. Let's get it over with."

I RECOGNIZED PIETRO Galinarion by sight but did not know him so well as Roderigo did; Galinarion did business with Roderigo's father. He was rotund but he was handsome, and perhaps the bulk was muscle. His hair was curled and nicely styled; powder paled his face and hands; he had delicate fingers for his size, with fingernails exactly long enough to keep him from the sort of escapade we had just been caught at. He was eating in his grand hall, replete with chandeliers descending from a painted ceiling full of naked angels. The walls were of marble-painted panels largely covered with Persian tapestries, the floor of real marble laid out in a serpentine motif.

Galinarion's fellow diners were imitations of him but generally more wan, or in other senses diminished: one was shorter, one thinner, one less ribboned in his costume. There were five of them. As if they had been practicing synchronized feasting, every man of them held a knife with a bit of meat stabbed on it near his mouth, and froze like that as we were brought in. They lowered these utensils, the morsels untouched, again in unison, and watched the gardener triumphantly and indignantly present us.

"Roderigo," Galinarion huffed, astonished. "Tell me what mischief you've been up to, son."

Roderigo gaped as if at indoor lightning. He opened his mouth. No sound came out.

"Roderigo!" Galinarion repeated, plucked brows crinkling over powdered nose. "Answer me, boy. Or I'll summon your parents and ask them to tan your hide in front of me."

The other men around the table hummed with laughter, and—again, synchronized—finally put the meat into their mouths and began to chew. Roderigo still could not speak. I feared he had wet himself, but I did not wish to add to his humiliation by checking.

"You there, then!" Galinarion snarled, pointing at me with his knife. I must have jumped, or looked alarmed—something to afford the table mirth. *What cretins*, I thought, *to find amusement in the terror of those smaller than yourselves.*

"Yes, sir," I said smartly, and executed a courtly bow. This made the gentlemen of the table nearly choke on their meat, they were so amused.

"Who are you?"

"My name is Iago, sir."

"What were you doing in my garden without my permission?"

The table quieted itself in anticipation of the answer. Roderigo squinted and appeared to be praying silently.

"We were just coming down from your rooftop, sir, where we had stolen an egg from your hen," I said.

Galinarion sat up very straight, and his eyes opened very wide; the other men made amused *ooooo*-ing noises until he held his hand up, commanding silence.

"Those eggs are priceless, boy." He held his hand out. "Return it to me at once."

I held up the handkerchief with the shells in it. "I'm afraid this is all I can give you now, sir. We ate the raw egg between us, because we'd heard your eggs were special. I suppose we heard wrong."

Galinarion went red beneath the dusting of powder on his face, and his guests banged the table with the meat of their fists, howling. Roderigo made a small noise, and I felt him gaping at me, terrified. His breath began to shake, and I feared he would burst out sobbing.

For what felt like eternity, Galinarion glared at me, furious accusation on his face. The fury was so venomous that the table spontaneously quieted itself, sensing something hideous about to happen, hideous beyond the scope of even their perverse and petty mirth.

Suddenly, this was no entertaining escapade, but a catastrophe. It was within this patrician's rights to beat me savagely or imprison me, and my parents did not know where I was. He raised his impressive bulk out of his chair and took a threatening step in my direction.

Then abruptly, he sat back down . . . and burst out laughing.

His laughter was forced, like water through a fountain. It was so intense that his guests responded to it as to an order; they all laughed as well, although with less intensity and much bemusement.

"You little liar!" Galinarion harrumphed. "This is some prank one of my rivals has set up to discredit the worth of my hen!" He looked around the table, pointing at each of them in a grand, nervous gesture. "Which of you did this? Confess now! A very worthy prank, and neatly done, but you cannot unman me with it! Come now, which of you has set these boys on me?" They all continued guffawing, pointing at one another with good-natured accusation, shaking their heads in good-natured denial. Finally Galinarion turned back to me, still trembling with furious laughter. "Well, boy, tell me, don't be afraid, which of these gentlemen bribed you to try to make a fool of me? What are these then, the shells of some other eggs, eh?" He reached out for the kerchief, and I gave it to him.

"None of them bribed us to do anything," I said, raising my voice to be heard above the raucous chuckling. "We did it ourselves. We're boys. It's the sort of thing boys just *do*."

This brought a new wave of louder and more genuine laughter from the group.

"Precocious little whoreson, isn't he?" one cheered as two others echoed me, using a childish lisp I did not have.

"Well if it's none of you, it must be that whoreson da Chioggia! He is always trying to start a feud with me, he is so hopelessly jealous of my hen and all my other treasures. Admit it, boy, was it da Chioggia?"

"No," I said, impatient now that I realized we were out of danger.

"Of course it was. Well, never mind, this will yield a ducat for you each. Go back to him and tell him that you've failed. Give him my heartiest congratulations, though, for it was quite a good idea." He turned back to the table. "Have boys eat such eggs as those! One wonders what he does with his own boys when the lamps are low!"

This signaled the greatest laughing swell of all. Reassured that none of his guests now believed we had eaten his eggs without being transformed into young satyrs, he summoned his steward to hand us each a ducat from a velvet purse, and then shooed us away.

"May I have my handkerchief back, sir?" I asked.

He chucked it at me as if we were bosom chums.

The gardener, annoyed that his arrest had come to nothing, grabbed us each by the collar and trundled us through the great house, down the stairs, deliberately trying to take us off our balance, which he managed to do with Roderigo several times. We went through the kitchens and out into the garden, where he'd apprehended us. He expelled us from the back gate as if we were rodents.

Finally Roderigo and I looked directly at each other. "You are the most remarkable person I know," he said in an awed whisper.

"All I did was tell the truth," I said.

"And we got ducats for it!" Roderigo said, brandishing his.

"So the maxim is true: it pays to be honest," I said. I untied the kerchief and shook out the eggshells, then folded it up and tucked it into my belt. I'd have received a cuffing if I'd lost it.

I glanced at Roderigo. He was still staring at me as if I had performed a miracle. His clothes were dirtied from our adventure, and I knew he had little else to wear at home. I had the rummage of two surviving elders, so my wardrobe, although faded, was ample.

"Here," I said and handed him my ducat. "I could never have got this without you."

He blushed. "But you're the one who earned it!" he stammered. "If anything, I should give you mine."

"I don't need it, Roderigo," I said with the kindest bluntness I could manage. "And I know you do. Take it. Let it help your uncle buy new line and hooks, to make up for the ones we left back there. Or perhaps your father might purchase better clothes for you."

He started blubbering then and grabbed me in a tight embrace. "You are the best, most righteous fellow I have ever met or can imagine on this earth," he declared. "I don't know why Providence has blessed me with such a remarkable friend, but I shall always try to be worthy of you."

"Thank you," I said awkwardly. He smelled of barley, for some reason. I took a step backward, and he relented his grip. I patted his arm and held out my right hand, palm up, to initiate our secret handshake. "Let's be getting home now."

A fortnight later, the craze for hens in Venice was passé.

Chapter 2

BOYS GROW INTO YOUTHS, and youths to men. There are other tales of Roderigo and me, all conforming to pattern: Iago dreams up something clever to pass the time; Iago invites Roderigo to join him; they are nearly triumphant but in the end foiled; Iago gets them out of the scrape, and always by a blunt honesty that so embarrasses whoever apprehends them, that the apprehender would rather let them free than face the consequences of pursuing anything Iago is saying.

* * *

BUT THEN I became a man, and I put away childish things—for example, Roderigo. Our friendship faded without rancor. There were no fallings-out, no betrayals or public humiliations. We reached an age at which our time went into our emerging vocations, and here we differed so profoundly we simply had no chance to fraternize.

RODERIGO NOW SPENT his days by his father's side, a spice merchant acolyte. And I? I craved a life of the mind. I wished to be a scholar—a professor or at least a teacher. I was an insatiable reader and from the age of ten used my small allowance to buy the octavo size of every book published by the Aldine Press. In their original languages, I devoured Aristotle, Sophocles, Euripides, Aristophanes (although humor is too topical to age or translate well), Homer, Herodotus, Thucydides, Demosthenes, Hippocrates, Plato, Dante, Pindar, Virgil, Horace, Ovid, Plutarch, Pliny, Cicero . . . and, of course, Machiavelli, even though he was from Florence. My room, lacking shelf space, was filled with piles of books, every one of which I'd read and some of which I had nearly memorized. The Aldine Press's invention of *italics* delighted me: I loved that *passion* and *intensity* could be expressed with such a subtle alteration from the norm.

But for all my love of learning, I had known from the age of ten, from the day of my brother's funeral, that my future was to be a military one. I had no passion or interest in the military arts. In fact, given how little interest most Venetian families had in military reputations, I suspected my father, in declaring I must become a soldier, was merely being punitive. But he was still my father, and so his word was law.

Having exhausted the best teaching minds of Venice, I was declared (by father) to have finished my education, abruptly, one day in high summer. I had learned everything he felt I needed to know, from fencing to dancing to grammar to mathematics, history, classical languages, and philosophy. Now I faced my life's most defining decision: to which branch of the Venetian armed forces should I devote myself? There were four:

Cavalry. Navy. Artillery. Infantry.

I closed myself in my bedroom and languidly paced, then settled onto my uncurtained bed, then rose and paced again, then stared out the window at the rooftops of lower surrounding houses, then threw myself faceup onto the bed, then rose to pace again, all the time chewing my lower lip until it was swollen, playing out various scenarios regarding the remainder of my life.

I might become a horseman on the mainland cavalry—the best in Italy. Or I might be an officer in the ranks of Venice's fabled naval forces. I decided within the first hour of deliberation that I had no interest in the artillery, for they simply blew things up. I also had no interest in the infantry. Nobody had any interest in the infantry.

After a few more hours of pacing and fidgeting, I determined that between cavalry and navy, I preferred the navy. It would allow me to get farther away from Venice, a place full of people whom I felt compelled to try to impress even while I knew I never would—most notably, my father. Further, it seemed to me that in the navy, skill mattered more than privilege. In the cavalry, a rich man could afford a better mount than could a poor man, and therefore accomplish more. I did not want to rise because of the horse my father's money could buy; I wanted to *earn* what I became. I did not want people whispering what my own inner demons whispered to me: you are nothing at all, only your father's unloving wealth gives you the right to exist. On your own, you're nothing, because you are uncouth.

And so in the swampy height of summer, ruminating languidly upon my summer bedding, I chose the way of the sea. I had a weakness for the romantic: I liked the notion of continuing the ancient tradition of ruling the waves. I was, of everyone I knew (possibly excepting Roderigo), the least capable of filling the boots of the ancient mariners who went before me—and yet I committed to it in my heart. That commitment, once made privately, filled me with a giddy expectation. I stood and looked about at my piles of books, then selected Herodotus and resettled beneath the bare canopy frame, to revisit the Battle of Salamis with a new appreciation now knowing that I might someday find myself in straits similar to Xerxes'.

But my reading was interrupted by a tentative rap at my door. "Come," I said. A pretty, plump servant girl, whom I suspected my father was sleeping with, pushed open the door just enough to glance inside.

"If you please, master, your father has called for you," she said, with lowered gaze.

"Thank you," I said and set Herodotus aside, glad of the summons. I would have made my way down to his office soon anyhow, to share with him my vocational intentions.

Father was a silk merchant—or more precisely, an entrepreneur, a *setaiòlo*. He bought raw silk, oversaw the production without dirtying his own hands, and then traded the finished product at a profit. He was an officer in the Silk Guild and often took his dinner at the Silk Office in Campo San Giovanni Crisostomo, across the Grand Canal.

His storeroom was the first floor of our home, but his office was one broad flight of steps up from there, the marble burnished bright from so many feet trampling on it over centuries. Our bedrooms were all one floor above that; I descended briskly, affecting an energy I did not really have in the oppressive heat. I felt a happy nervousness; as I descended the steps, I anticipated Father's reaction to my decision. I knew he would agree with it, as it would save him the cost of a horse, but since he never outright approved of anything about me, I wondered how he would manage to express his approval in a disapproving manner.

The heavy oak door to his office was standing ajar, and I stepped through.

Father had a very comfortable chair in his office, of dyed leather rigged on a wooden frame. The seat was permanently concave from decades of taking the imprint of his buttocks. It was the only chair in this room; all other seating consisted of floor cushions around low tables, a custom borrowed from our one-time trading partners far to the east.

I was in my favorite *ormesini* summer wear. (The youngest son always gets the cheapest weave.) Father, in his black silk cap, in his unadorned red broccatello doublet, his samite breeches, his eyes glancing over an invoice from one of his shops, gestured me to sit on a fat cushion on the rugs. I did so, bowing first.

"And so," Father began, his eyes still on his work. "The da Cremona Artillery School starts next week."

I blinked in confusion. "I do not know anything about that, Father. I have decided on a naval career," I said.

He glanced up briefly as he transferred the invoice to a pile on his left while taking a new invoice from a pile on his right. I tried to ignore the sudden sinking feeling in my gut.

"A naval career for whom?" he asked.

"Myself," I said.

An expression crossed his face as if a bug was worrying his ear. Then the expression softened and he said, with a small cough, "No, you're going into the artillery. I have already enrolled you at the school."

"Father—"

"I have given this more thought than you have, Iago. Every member of the navy must be in top fighting form at all times. You would fail at that. The artillery has excellent placement and also gives you an inside advantage for a civilian office in the infantry later."

I stared at him, flummoxed.

"I do not need you making a fool of yourself or bringing embarrassment on our family name by being inadequate. I did not call you in here to discuss which branch of the military you prefer."

Swallowing a stomachful of bile in total silence, I managed to ask, "Then why did you call me in here, Father?"

His voice almost muffled behind the new invoice he was purposelessly staring at, he replied, "To remind you to pay your respects to your mother before you depart. She gets sentimental about these things, and I do not have the energy, in this heat, to soothe her. Make sure to leave her contented. And take this," he said, picking up a leaf of paper from his desk and holding it out to me without looking at it, or at me. "It details your training program. You're dismissed."

TOO FURIOUS TO be stunned, too stunned to be furious, I slumped on my bed and read the leaf he had given me.

The state-sponsored Artillery School, I learned, had once been based in the campo of Santa Barbara, Barbara being the patron saint of things that explode. The school's official quarters had moved to Campo Santa Maria Formosa, but there was a particular intensive training program based within the Arsenal. "Our three-month-long sequestering is meant as much to induct participants into military life as to teach artillery skills" I read. "This includes living as members of a company, specifically mess and bed in a dormitory built 350 years ago, when the entire Republic gave herself over to the creation of a Crusader fleet."

That fleet, by the way, besieged and defeated Constantinople, the greatest city in the world. You never see Venice attempt such heroics nowadays.

Chapter 3

ON THE APPOINTED DAY, my father's servants packed a leather satchel for me with the few requisite items that the Academy had advised. I was so disinterested in my imminent career that I did not even bother to examine the contents of the satchel. I added only a small blank parchment and a stub of lead, to capture interesting thoughts, if I should happen to have any.

Possibly the only issue about which my father and I were in agreement (although for different reasons) was that I should carry my own satchel to the Arsenal, rather than be escorted by a servant. I liked the notion of appearing self-sufficient from my first moment there.

Father liked the notion that he would not be inconvenienced by the lack of a servant for the afternoon.

I LEFT THE house on the fifteenth of August. This was the eve of the feast of San Rocco, when the doge would make a pilgrimage to our neighborhood church. I was glad to miss the pomp of that. There were no emotional leave-takings, not even with my mother.

To avoid the crowded Rialto, I took a gondola across the Grand Canal and then serpentined through the narrow alleys of San Marco until they opened up into the Piazza. Fabric stretched on large wooden frames had been erected to afford some shade to all the ministers and commissioners and aides and clerks who were trying to conduct business among the peddlers and fortune-tellers and flower sellers and notaries. The cloth frames had crowds beneath them; the rest of the Piazza was baking, heat rising in mercurial shimmers for two hundred paces.

I skirted the edge of the Piazza, asking pardon of the young gentles who were grudgingly trying to impress the older gentles in a game of patrician politics that I, by birth, would never be allowed to join. I turned right into the Piazzetta and, by the two columns, considered a second gondola. I decided that was a choice for weaklings. I was a man, and strong, and self-sufficient. I would walk. Laden with satchel, I strode the length of the Riva degli Schiavoni, growing sticky and then slick with sweat in the sultry breeze meandering in from the lagoon.

Near the Arsenal—a part of the city I had never ventured into—a series of side streets led me to a goodly campo, beside an inn called the Dolphin. Off the far right corner of the campo was the Arsenal's water gate. But directly ahead of me, the paved yard led to the

Arsenal's sole doorway: a large iron gate in a brick wall, with stone lions flanking either side of it.

For centuries, this has been the most guarded door in the entire Venetian empire. Citizens have easier entry to the Doge's Palace than to the storehouses of the Republic's armaments. Beyond that wall lies all the munitions of our state, from rifle shot to warships. And gunpowder. Lots of gunpowder. I was about to be among the favored few allowed within. This was something most of those young gentles hobnobbing in the Piazza could not claim.

With clammy palms clinging to the satchel as if for comfort, I crossed the sun-baked campo. My heart beat harder with each step. Finally I reached the steps leading up to the door. I took a deep breath, heaved a steadying sigh, and climbed the steps, feeling my garments sucking at my skin with sweat.

A young guard in a red-and-white jerkin brusquely asked my name and I gave it, surprised to hear my voice tremble. The Arsenal entrance swung open to receive me.

The guard, not much older than myself, and proudly hefting an arquebus as well as sword and dagger, squired me over the high-arching Arsenal Bridge. There were large, intimidating guards posted in pairs on either end of it. We crossed between two tall brick buildings; when we emerged from the shaded canyon between them, to our left opened out a huge man-made boat basin, at least ten times the size of Piazza San Marco. My jaw fell slack. About a dozen galleons sat moored in there; they looked like sparrows in an enormous puddle, so vast was the basin.

To our right, fronting this basin, was a row of enormous brick buildings full of men, lumber, and loud mechanical devices: they were actually *building ships*!

I tamped down my eagerness, because I was a man now, and men do not get giddy about such things.

We walked to the end of the basin past the different groups of men who were *building ships*, then turned left to skirt the basin, and then shortly after that, turned right across a small wooden bridge into a walled triangle of brick buildings and open courtyards. From reading father's educational leaf, I knew that this was to be my home for the next three months.

The barracks was the least ornate building I had ever entered in my life. There was not one decorative flourish to the architecture, no devices anywhere to suggest that those associated with the building had time or money to waste on nicety. It was functional, and nothing else. I noticed this detail with unexpected pleasure, almost a thrill. This building, like myself, had no time for artifice. For certain, military life would be likewise, and however dilatory, I would finally feel at home somewhere.

Inside, a corridor led down to a mess hall, but to our immediate left there was a spiral stairway—spiral! Small, compact, efficient, no broad swaths of carpeting, no murals, no alabaster handrails, no broad concourse to accommodate womanish costumes. Climbing that stairway, I fell in love with military life.

Briefly.

My enthusiasm was dampened immediately by what awaited me in the dormitory. Perhaps because I did not have a servant to help me with my load, I had arrived last, and there were nine other youths my age making up their sleeping cots.

". . . just a bit trashy, isn't it?" one snickered to another. "They might have warned us of that."

They all wore brightly dyed silk jerkins—*canevazze* mostly, by my guess—and breeches; jerkin and breeches slashed with crosses or stars, showing white taffeta beneath. I, in sharp contrast, wore a jerkin with a better weave than theirs but of much simpler tailoring, and no slashes at all. I looked, almost literally, like the black sheep of the herd.

I glanced quickly at the faces and realized at once that I would make no friends here. Not that I would have known what a friend's face looked like, but I know complacency at a glance, and these fellows fairly radiated it. At a guess I'd say that all of them had come

from families like mine—well-off merchants—although I was mystified why so many well-off merchant families would send their sons,
in peacetime, to become artillerymen.

They all glanced at me with passing interest and then returned
to carping about the state of our lodging. The room was small and
high ceilinged, which made it seem even smaller. Lacking windows,
it was lit by stinking pitch-torches and one oil lamp. As well as the
cots, there were two tables, one with jugs lined up on it, the other
with stacks of paper. There were no stools, chairs, chests, or closets,
no tapestries or carpets—it was completely naked of decoration.
And it was blessedly cooler than outside, but I was the only one who
seemed to appreciate that. The rest of them looked sullen.

Eventually one of my fellow students, whom I mentally titled
Brawny Lug (for he was brawny, and a lug) pointed out that this was
an excellent chance for us all to live like Real Military Men, and
we should welcome the opportunity to prove that we were tough
enough to survive without drapes and plaster and upholstery.

If I had made this observation, I'm sure I'd have been sneered
at, reviled for preachiness, and so on. But Brawny Lug was just the
fellow to make the point, and from his mouth this suddenly became
a brilliant idea, one to be embraced.

I rolled my eyes and set about to make up my hard little cot. I
knew how to do this no better than any other youth there, and my
cot looked just as lumpy as did theirs.

As I finished, the Campanile bells tolled from afar, by the
Doge's Palace, and within a minute after that, a handsome, broad-
shouldered man in his prime years came up the stairs, an attendant
youth to either side. They stood at sharp attention by the doorway
as he stepped farther into the room. All three wore red-and-white
jerkins, with the winged lion of San Marco, emblem of our Republic,
sewn over their heart. Between the thumb and first finger of his left
hand, the captain fidgeted with a stone about the size of a peach pit.

"Attention," he said.

He did not speak it in the smart speech of childhood military play-acting. He said it rather almost as a casual suggestion. Expecting a different demeanor, none of us leapt to obey.

"*Attention!*" he repeated, loud and fierce. Instantly we all stiffened and attempted sundry awkward shows of obeisance—one put his hand on his heart, several bowed, I saluted, and four who were clumped together scrambled to present themselves in a straight line.

His green eyes glanced coldly over all of us. "From now on," he informed us, resuming the quiet tone, "you will listen and attend me without my having to shout at you. It is a waste of my energy to shout. I am here to make you expend effort, not the other way around, is that clear? Say *yes, Captain*, if it is."

"*Yes, Captain!*" we all shouted in unison.

"Don't yell at me," he said calmly. "That is equally a waste of your own energies. Speak at a normal level, but clearly and respectfully. Do you understand?"

"Yes, Captain," we all said at once, with half the volume.

He nodded, his finger still worrying the stone. "Better. On behalf of the Alberghetti family, I welcome you to the Bartolomeo da Cremona training program. You will practice in the ranges here in the Armory, and four times a month you will muster with trained militia on the Alberghetti estate on Giudecca. Otherwise, for the next three months, except on Friday evenings, you are not to step foot off the grounds of the Arsenal unless in formation in this unit, and your presence is to be known to me or my attendants at all times. There is another unit being trained as you are, here in the Arsenal, so you will see other young men like yourselves attending to business like yourselves. You are to ignore them. You will have no time at all for anything but your own development, the development of your weaponry skills, and your understanding of what it means to belong to the military. Do you understand?"

"Yes, Captain," we said.

"Two units of ten young men apiece, and that is just this quarter; there will be more coming through soon after, and there have been plenty before you. If you understand the most basic mathematics you will know that there are more of you—budding artillery officers—than the state will ever need. I expect that most of you will come to nothing, despite the excellent training I am about to give you. I expect that half of you will not even last the first week. I have no interest in helping you to last here, I am only interested in making sure that if you do, you have come by it honestly. Do you understand?"

"Yes, Captain," we said. I liked this kind of talk, even though it frightened me to wonder how Father would receive me if I did not last the week. But the captain's speech was honest, blunt, and practical, and it encouraged bluntness. It had no connection of any sort to Venetian culture outside the walls of the Arsenal.

"We will now introduce ourselves, and I will assign each of you a daily task for the week, and then we will repair to the mess hall," said the captain. "I am Master Gunner, Captain Alvisio Trevisan."

Immediately after that my attention wandered. I did not care what the names of my fellow students were; I was bad at names and doubted I would ever call out to them anyhow.

Because I had been the last to arrive, I was also in the farthest cot, and so the last to present myself. Several of the young men received some ribbing or even rebuke from the captain as they announced their family name. No doubt the military, like the frivolous social culture my mother so adored, was full of family insiders, and everybody probably knew everyone else's second cousin. I was glad my eldest brother had worked on the civilian side of the army, and so there was no risk that my family name would mean anything to anybody here.

Or so I thought. "Iago Soranzo," I said, briefly pressing my right fist against my heart, as I'd seen others do.

I was nonplussed when four of my fellow students exchanged surprised looks, and then turned in my direction tauntingly. I glanced, trying to hide sudden nervousness, at Captain Trevisan, but he looked even nastier than they did. "Soranzo?" he repeated, archly. "As in Paolo Soranzo?"

My brother. The dead one. The one who had lethally wounded himself right here, in the Arsenal, six years back.

"Yes," I said stonily. "He was my brother."

The captain stared at me a moment blankly, his fingers neatly shuffling the stone. Then a cruel smile curled his lips. "When I said I doubted all of you would last the week, I did not literally mean I expected anyone to self-expire. Need I change that assessment?" He strolled in my direction along the row of youths.

"No, sir," I said, teeth clenching. The entire line was openly leering at me now.

"May I assume you are apter than your brother was?" the captain asked, moving closer still.

"I hope so, sir," I said, feeling my face turn red.

No sooner were the words off my lips than he chucked the stone at me. He was close enough to me that even if I'd been expecting it, I would have failed to catch it. As it was, it hit me in the ribs; I winced and let escape a pained sound.

The others laughed.

"That is no way to convince me you are apt," said the captain. "Pick it up."

I bent over to grasp the stone straight-legged, which brought more blood rushing to my face. Without his asking, I offered it to him, and he took it from me as if I might have a skin disease.

"Apparently it takes more than stone to destroy one of your family, it takes an actual blade," he said. "Luckily this is the artillery, and blades are not in common usage here. Not that that stopped your brother, of course."

This was permission to the entire group to cackle overtly. A few of the youths leaned in toward one another whispering, as the ones who did not know the story of my brother's embarrassing demise got some version of it—accurate or not, it did not matter—from the ones who did. The newly informed ones laughed even louder. And the captain let them.

This was appalling. On the one hand, of course, my very blood cried out to defend a kinsman; on the other, what the captain said about poor clumsy Paolo was true, and it would be insincere of me to proclaim otherwise. And then on the third hand: whether it was true or not, why was I to be punished for Paolo's mistake? Especially since his mistake had no guilt associated with it but acute humiliation; why was I to be held accountable for it? Is it inhuman of me to feel that I should not be held accountable for my older brother's haplessness? I did not make him hapless. God did. Or if anyone on earth did, surely it was our parents. They were never held to account for it—but somehow, I was.

I said nothing. The captain kept looking at me, as if expecting me to say something. I continued to say nothing. Finally he turned away from me and continued to stroll past us all. He began a new speech.

"We will begin the walking tour of the grounds, and I will assign tasks to each of you as we go. In Iago's case it is clearly important to keep him from sharp objects"— here of course another swell of nasty snorts—"so he will be the company's lamplighter. Iago, you will learn where the lamp oil is stored, and you will see to it that there is always enough oil in all the lamps in this building." He pointed to the table on which sat a row of jars. "You will begin by filling those lamps. I assume you know that oil is extremely expensive and should be used sparingly, and only when and where absolutely necessary."

"My father is a lamp oil merchant," offered a youth who looked even snottier than the rest of them. "He supplies the oil for the whole of the Arsenal."

"That's why you are not being given this assignment," the captain said dryly. "We would not trust *you* to be economical in the burning of oil." Laughter from the group, finally not aimed at me. "All right, then, you have now seen the room where you will sleep and store your clothes. Before the bells strike again you will have learned where you are to bathe, eat, shit, and receive your requisitioned weapons, powder, balls, and match, and most important, of course, you will see where you shall practice. You are expected to become master gunners in time, but most of you will fail and return to your father's trades, which I gather from your presence here none of you find interesting. In which case you are welcome to remain here as custodians, or perhaps young Iago will simply kill himself off."

Again the laughter. It was worse than Father's silence.

Chapter 4

"I HEARD HE cut his cock off," Brawny Lug said. "Heard he was trying to get the sword out of its case and *shwoosh!*"—here there was an illustrative gesture that actually implied flattering things about my brother's anatomy—"sliced it right off!"

"I don't believe you heard correctly," I said as calmly as I could. We had finished the tour of the grounds; I had been given, with a flood of forms and receipts, a large jar of oil that I had to carry with me for most of the tour. The others had been assigned their tasks—food preparation, foundry cleanup, sweeping the captains' quarters, managing the laundry—and we were now back in the dormitory, waiting to go down for our first shared mess. "If you will excuse me, I must light the lamps now," I muttered, to avoid any actual conversation. I picked up the jar of oil and turned back to the table.

"Of course, once he'd castrated himself, he better resembled the rest of his family," Brawny Lug continued. He was more than twice my body mass.

"How did you come to be so familiar with my family's private parts?" I asked, reaching for one of the lamps. "And, for future reference: do you swallow?"

That was foolish—because now, of course, he would have to

break my head against the wall. "You half-witted little ninny!" he hollered and threw his weight forward to rush me.

I looked up sharply and stepped away from the table with an expression of blank terror, resigned to be smashed straight into the solid rock wall behind me. The guttural gibberish of our spectators grew more guttural and more gibberish. He lowered his head as he approached, a charging bull, his crown aimed right at my belly.

I took one step to the side.

He did not notice. He threw himself, magnificently, crown first, straight into the unadorned stone wall. There was a *thwack*, a groan, and a group intake and exhalation as he slammed to the floor, stunned, at my feet.

I risked the tiniest cocky grin. "You missed," I said sympathetically. I shifted the oil jar to my right hip with a conclusive flourish. There was a round of chuckles, and for a moment I knew what it must feel like to be the person my father wanted to turn me into.

But Lug, it was clear, was about to rise again, and he was going to be furious. I knew this, and so did the octave. They also knew that they'd be sharing mess and dormitory for weeks to come with both the Lug and myself.

"Get him, lads!" somebody shouted, as if they had all said it at the same time. Before I had a chance to comment on their lack of both originality and spine, eight young men were reaching, even leaping for me. It was cowardly for eight to jump one, but this was not a matter of courage, it was a matter of self-interest, and each wanted to be able to tell Brawny Lug that he had done his share of vengeance on Brawny Lug's behalf.

I was cornered, so I used the only thing I had to hand: I hoisted the ceramic jar up off my hip and slopped the lamp oil over all of them. Being slopped this way surprised them; they turned to one another in confusion, as if by seeing another doused youth they might better understand what had just happened to them.

I reached for the smoky rush light on the wall behind me. "Now you're inflammable," I warned them, waving the fiery stubble in front of them. "Come one step closer and you'll light up like black powder."

Eight overexcited, mortified young men stared in outrage, afraid to move toward me, unwilling to back off. There were curses, and then all eyes fell floorward to Brawny Lug, who now was trying to sit up, groaning. I immediately splashed oil on the top of his head. He did not notice, but the others did. For a moment I thought they would all explode at me, torch be damned, and with incendiary panache send us all to purgatory.

But one of them made a calming gesture, and the others paused. The clump of angry, hostile, male adolescence disbursed, disbanded, and in various stages wandered out of the room for dinner. The bringer of calm helped Brawny Lug to his feet and checked his crown for broken skin.

I WENT DOWN to the mess and sat alone in the reverberate, dull room, willing myself calm enough to bring bread to my mouth without trembling. Whatever I ate had no taste at all. I only ate because I knew they were staring at me and I wanted to show them I was unaffected by what had just happened. But that was not true, of course, and I did not like to counterfeit.

After I finished pretending to eat, I walked slowly, with forced calm, back across the hall, up the stairwell, and into our dormitory. I checked the floor for signs of spilled oil, but there was none; my targets had all been packed together tightly. I took the jug of oil, lighter now, and continued to fill the lamps that were arranged on the wooden table. The more I concentrated on not trembling, the more I trembled. This was hell. I would have been less miserable trying to pass myself off as a fop among rich Venetian merchants.

As I worked, I heard and then saw the octave return, and after them Brawny Lug, with a poultice tied atop his head.

Behind him was Captain Trevisan.

Out of the corner of my eye I watched them all line up expectantly, as if for an inspection. I continued to fill the lamp wells, forcing myself to breathe slowly. The captain nodded to them once they were all in formation, and then coughed pointedly in my direction. I looked up, and he gestured to the line with his eyes.

I set down the jar, and with a curt nod, stood at attention at the near end of the line.

"Is it true?" the captain asked me, with a gesture to the rest of the youths. "What your colleagues have told me?"

"What have they told you, sir?" I asked.

I was treated to a slightly exaggerated depiction of my exploit. It did not seem worth it to explain away the exaggerations.

"That is true enough, sir."

"How much oil did you pour on these men?" the captain demanded coldly.

I opened my mouth to explain it had been merely *splashed*, not *poured*, but before I had uttered a syllable, a triad of the octave insisted, "It was more than that, sir!"

I looked at the captain and blinked a few times.

"Shut up," the captain said to them. "How much?" he demanded, back to me.

I considered the triad. "Half a jar," I said, which was more than it had actually been. That undermined their protestation.

"I will have the supply clerk calculate how much you owe the state of Venice for unauthorized use of lamp oil," the captain said. "Beyond that, you are to be commended for your excellent handling of a difficult situation."

I blinked again. So did the others. "Excuse me, sir?"

"You've not been properly trained yet and you efficiently contained a volatile option," the captain said, ignoring everyone else in the room. "An option I myself initiated. I am impressed."

"Thank you, sir," I said, saluting. I felt the blood in my cheeks. My dormitory mates were dismayed. "Sir, may I complete my assigned task?"

"Yes, soldier," the captain said.

It was our first day, and he had called me soldier. I could not have *invented* a better story to be told about myself.

* * *

FROM THAT MOMENT ON, I was treated with something that might pass as respect. It was a cold respect, but it was better than what I had feared would be the sum of my days at the Arsenal.

I had a small allowance from my father. It would cover the "unauthorized use of lamp oil" but leave me with no other spending money. I heard heartily whispered rumors that at the end of this first week, there would be a bacchanalian outing to foster our herd instinct. Now I understood the need for that instinct; I was determined to take part in the ritual, even though I considered myself more Apollonian than Bacchanalian.

DAILY TRAINING WAS intensive and exhausting. The matchlock rifle was our primary weapon. But we were taught how to load, aim, and shoot a variety of guns both heavy and light, and also cannon. We were trained to fire at targets while running and while crouching; these targets were forty paces away from us when we trained with arquebuses and eighty paces while running with muskets, which were lighter. We learned how to shoot at bobbing targets four hundred paces off the shore of the Lido. We learned command terms, drum signals, and how to run a quarter of a mile in formation. We learned how rust-free artillery was made within the Arsenal, and that iron was purchased primarily for mountings and for shot, which came in ten different calibers, each of which we learned to identify by touch. We learned that bullet-deflecting helmets, armor, and swords all came from Brescia, and we learned how to use everything that came from Brescia. We were each assigned a musket from the two thousand kept in stock by the Arsenal. We learned how the cannon foundry operated; we learned how to make gunpowder from the saltpeter of Trevisano, Friuli, and Istria, mixed in lime and boiled with ashes. We learned that as soldiers in the Artillery we took our orders from the secretive Council of Ten—not the Senate or the Great Council.

* * *

BRAWNY LUG BORE the Christian name Bucello; the fellow who had comforted him, Zanino. Having recovered, Bucello was devoted to proving himself to me. He was amazed that I had bested him, and with such a simple contrivance. Rather than acknowledging himself rash and foolish, he instead saw me as enormously clever and shrewd—so shrewd, I could outmaneuver *him*, the great Bucello! He never convinced me to engage in active competition with him, but I let him carry on as if we were deliberate adversaries. I let him attribute my small accomplishments over that first week to my attempts to match his muscle. When he did something clever, and then commented loudly that he was encroaching upon my mental abilities, I employed benign silence, which he considered agreement. I would have preferred to tell him honestly what I thought of his mental abilities, but I was also becoming a reluctant student of pragmatism.

As well as general training, that first week was spent on matchlock drills. The other trainees liked the matchlocks because they were guns—because, when handled correctly, their use resulted in loud noises and then something far away blowing up or shattering. I liked them because the contrivance of them, the way they worked, the science of them, was to me a thing of beauty.

A matchlock gun is a work of delicately deadly craftsmanship. The "match" is a slow-burning wick made of hemp, which is clamped to the gun by a spring-loaded serpentine lever. Pulling the free end of the lever drops the match end of the lever down into a flash pan, into which the shooter has placed priming powder. The smoldering match ignites the powder; that ignition flashes through a touchhole into the gun barrel, where gunpowder ignites and propels a ball out of the barrel with extraordinary speed in one direction, while kicking the gunner (at least, the novice gunner) stumbling backward and landing inelegantly on his backside as his fellows snort with laughter.

The final well-thought element within the firearm is that when the lever is released to its original position it sweeps backward, clearing the flash pan of any remaining powder. This greatly reduces the likelihood that the novice gunner will, while falling on his backside, also blow his face off.

BUCELLO DECIDED EARLY on that my regard for the mechanics of the matchlock was actually a feint, and that all I really cared about was how fast I could reload and shoot. I have no idea what gave him this impression, but he was invested in it. In the enclosed shooting yard outside the barracks, he always chose me as the man to outshoot—and he always did, which made him very fond of me. I endured this, but on our first Friday before the much-anticipated bacchanalian break, I made a bet with him. It was afternoon on a hot, hazy day, and we were still in our training gear.

"It is a shame our duels are always hampered by other men. Let's return to the range after the regular drill," I suggested. "We will come here after mess, before we go into town, and see which of us can hit the target more times within a turn of the glass." The time-glass measured off a period during which a rapid shooter should be able to load, shoot, reload, and shoot again. "Whoever wins must treat the other to all expenses when we rove tonight."

Even if I lost this bet, the arrangement benefitted me: although I would go into debt to fund the jaunt, I'd still be seen in Bucello's close company all evening. By the week's end he was clearly the Brawny Lug not only in our company but possibly of the entire Arsenal. A good ally to have, I decided, even if I lost the bet.

But I did not intend to lose the bet.

ON THAT FINAL AFTERNOON, we were given one hour of leisure time. Bucello chose to nap, because he wanted to have stamina for a good hearty bacchanalian sort of evening. I immediately corralled Zanino and the others, and suggested that the nine of us use this precious opportunity to practice shooting, so that we might eventually have a hope in heaven of coming anywhere close to Bucello's speed and accuracy.

The excellent thing about a matchlock is the slow-burning

match. This means that once one has loaded the priming powder into the pan and the rest of the powder and shot into the barrel, one can fire the gun *eventually*. Over the past few decades, since the match-lock was introduced as standard equipment, thousands of miles of hemp-wick have burned across Europe to no end at all, except to keep muskets available for shooting when the need might arise.

This means that if one convinces one's fellow cadets that they must practice shooting their guns, and then offer to clean their guns for them after, one suddenly has access to a group of rifles that one may load and prepare with slow-burning fuses ready to be fired, at one's convenience, later on.

My offer to clean the guns was explained as my wish to make up to all my mates for having splashed the lamp oil on their hair and clothes. That had been a time-consuming nuisance for them to clean, after all. They accepted my offer, gave me ritual permission to handle their weapons, and thought the world of me for it.

Then they all went over to mess to eat and fortify their bodies for the orgy to come.

I lay their weapons close together on the ground by my own. I doused my own hemp cord on both ends but did not load my gun. I loaded and lit a slow match on half the other guns, then scrupulously cleaned the remaining five of powder, but put slow-burning fuses on them anyhow, and these smoldering but impotent five I set at the end of the row.

There were a series of straw bales at one end of the gunnery range; from the small wooden shed beside them I grabbed two paper targets, and tied them around two of the bales. I thanked Minerva several times that Bucello had a poor sense of smell, because burning fuses have a distinct odor, and there was nothing in the yard to disguise it.

"There you are, fellow!" Bucello's bullish voice erupted from a corner between two buildings and echoed briefly around the yard. "Missed you at mess!" He was carrying his assigned firearm in one hand.

"Good evening. I've set up the targets. Let's shoot from over there where my gun is lying."

"What's all the rest of that, then?" he asked, pointing vaguely to the row of firearms lined up neatly close together.

"It seems I am to clean everyone's guns for them."

"Bad luck at dice, was it?" he said, assuming that it was and therefore not caring that I did not answer him. He laughed. "Can't say I see any sign of your luck improving now."

"My luck? No," I agreed. "You won't find me relying on luck any time again soon."

"Well, let's at it, then," Bucello said as we arrived beside the string of weapons. "I received permission from the captain for a round of target practice, so he will understand why our powder is short tonight. Have we a time-glass?"

I had one by my gun, the sand emptied into the lower chamber. I gestured to it.

"And just to be thorough about it, let's show each other that our guns are in an equally unready state," he added.

I immediately picked mine up and offered it to him for his inspection. He gave me a good-mate smile and handed his to me. I accepted it and glanced at its works cursorily. There was no powder in the flash pan, no powder nor projectile in the barrel, and no hemp cord in the serpentine.

Having established that each other's gun was as far from battle-ready as it could be, we swapped the weapons back. We shifted them to our left hands and inverted the time-glass together, then sat it on the ground. Bucello's demeanor immediately shifted to focused, precise, humorless soldier. He grabbed for his supply of cord in the pouch at his hip.

I lay down my weapon on the paving stones, reached for Zanino's gun—the closest preprepared one in the row— and raised it up. These were light muskets, to be shot without support. I rested the butt against my shoulder and pulled the serpentine down, touching the hemp into the flash pan. With a sizzle, the powder lit; Bucello looked up from cutting his hemp, surprised; his eyes widened as he saw I was already taking aim at my target. The musket kicked back against my shoulder as the ball erupted from the barrel with a roar; a blink later, before the bouncing echo died, it scorched a hole into the straw bale on the far side of the courtyard.

I smiled, lay down the heated gun, and raised up the one lying next to it. Bucello wore amazed confusion on his face as his hands expertly, automatically cut his hemp cord and began to thread the cord into the serpentine, even as the rest of his attention was distracted. "What . . . ," he began, then stopped; he could not manage speech.

I flipped the lever on this musket too and aimed. A second explosion shredded the late afternoon peace, and a second hole scorched my straw bale. As I set the second gun down on the paving stones, I explained politely, "We never specified we had to use our own guns to shoot." After the briefest pause, I added, to be precise, "Or use the same gun for all the shots." I picked up the third gun and steadied it against my shoulder.

Bucello's face darkened. "You conniving devil!" he shouted as I fired. He tossed his half-prepared gun to the ground and furiously crossed past me, to grab the next gun in the row. I did not stop him; I wanted him to have one round. He glared at me, stomped back to his position, and aimed the weapon as I picked up the fifth—and last—fully loaded musket. My fourth shot followed so near on his first, it could have been an echo.

I bent, as if to reach for the next gun, the first of the powderless and shot-less ones, but he shoved me aside and snatched it up instead—and while he was there, he grabbed the next one too. That left three unarmed weapons in the row. I turned back to my own assigned weapon, the nuances of which I was more familiar with, and with my adequate but unremarkable skills, I prepared it for a shot. As I was recapping my powder horn, Bucello gave up trying to fire the gun he held and finally thought to check its readiness. With a disgusted grunt he hurled it clattering down beside his own, picked up the other gun he'd grabbed, and checked it for a wick. It had one, but no powder or ball. By the time he'd discovered that, however, I was ready to fire my own weapon, making it my fifth shot.

"Time has run out," I observed laconically, in the silence after the explosion.

"You devil!" Bucello shouted at me, red-faced.

And then, to my immense relief, he burst into laughter. "You *devil*, you!" He slapped me on the shoulder so ferociously I nearly dropped my gun, and I had to stagger to keep from falling to my knees. "I knew you could not beat me honestly, but that's a very clever way to beat me with a trick!"

"What trick?" I demanded innocently. "We both had naked muskets. We both fired from the preloaded stash—you are as complicit as I am there. In the end, I am the one who fired the most, and the only one who fired his own gun."

"Yes, and all because you're a conniving bastard," Bucello said heartily.

"Bucello, call anyone to view the evidence," I said, straight-faced. "Your gun is clean. Mine has just been fired. So clearly, you fired a gun that was not yours into your target, while there is no proof I used any but my own weapon."

"The other guns are warm!" Bucello laughed. "Their fuses are lit. They have clearly just been fired, and there are balls lodged in your target to prove it!"

"But, Bucello, the guns will be cool soon. Perhaps they were shot this afternoon, then left untended by their neglectful owners. All those balls *could* have come from my own gun. While the ball in your target *clearly* came from not-your-gun. Did one of your fellow soldiers give you permission to touch their weapon, or must I turn you in for unauthorized use of a firearm?"

Bucello laughed harder, his face approaching the color of his maroon breeches. "You are wasted in the military, fellow!" he declared. "You really should become a lawyer!"

"Do you concede the match, then?"

"I do on one condition," he said, containing himself. "That we tell nobody else what you have done here. Do not worry, I'll cover your expenses tonight," he said quickly. "This is very clever, what you've done. If we tell the others, you will never get away with it again. If we do *not* tell the others, then it is our secret, and you can try this prank on someone else, but I'll be in on it, and I shall put a wager on your head and make a lot of money from it. Which I'll share with you, of course."

If he'd demanded I keep it secret to save his pride, I would never have agreed, but amused by his suggestion, I offered him my hand, and even joined with him when he laughed again. His slight to my brother's haplessness, I decided then, was slight enough.

And so I set off for my first night of debauchery arm in arm with my bosom friend, Bucello the Brawny Lug, who treated me to everything a young soldier in training might ever fantasize about.

PARDON, ARE YOU expecting me to *describe* the debauchery? But a gentleman does not do such things.

Perhaps a little bit.

Donning the clothes we'd been wearing the day of our arrival, we all went to a house near the Arsenal that did not front on any canal. On the main floor there was presented to us overpriced turgid wine, bad instrumental music, and flamboyantly clad women with breasts exposed to below the nipple who danced about the room, and sang, and then sat on men's laps for a few moments, before taking them upstairs to very small rooms, doing their business, and sending them on their way.

The city of Venice boasts approximately one whore for every seven male citizens. Of course, many of their clients are foreigners, traders, or sailors; and many of the prostitutes are mistresses who live better than proper wives. In other words, we were doing something common, regular, and normal. However, it was something I had never yet done. And I suspected this was true of most of my fellow cadets, although all of them were determined not to be perceived as virginal.

Bucello most definitely *had* been to brothels; we'd heard stories all week about it after curfew. The stories were boring. I was libidinous as any youth my age; I hoped the act of fornication would be at least as tremendous as my elaborate self-abusing fantasies. And yet Bucello's coarse depictions of the women, their body parts, his body parts, their body parts together . . . it aroused no envy or licentiousness in me at all, only a peculiar sense of embarrassment for *him*. He lacked the poetry to appreciate the greatest mystery of life, which he seemed to consider just a pleasurable mechanical exercise. Listening to his tales of whoring was like listening to a description of a thunderstorm by a person who is both blind and deaf, but who happened to be standing outside and therefore got wet somehow.

Too poor to enjoy the pleasures of the properly licensed whores of the Rialto, we made do with this small brothel in the Castello district. The room stank from the New World weed, tobacco. The smoke left a sticky residue, looking almost occult in the lamplight.

Bucello sat at the head of a creaky wooden table; sensing he was the captain for the evening, the women clustered to him, dressed almost exactly like patrician ladies, except for the exposed nipples. The other cadets angled to sit close to Bucello. I remained standing, watching them. To cover my awkwardness, I imagined myself a tactician, reading my fellows and their behavior. By the time they settled, there was only one stool left, and it was at the foot of the table. All the cadets leaned away from it, toward Bucello and the women.

"Come, friend, sit by me!" Bucello said buoyantly. He bodily lifted one of the bawds from off her stool and placed her on his own lap, to much delighted yelping from her and envious clucking from the others. "Here is a free seat! Put your buttocks here!" He patted what had been her perch. The others in our party exchanged glances, surprised and put out that I had somehow, since dinner, earned Bucello's affection. With my arms crossed and an expressionless face, I sat beside him. I did not like the smell of the place. This was not what I had been expecting of a brothel.

One of the women, wearing white ceruse with vermillion cheeks and lips, her eyelashes fashionably thinned and trimmed so that she resembled a painted fish, leapt at the opportunity, quite literally: she placed herself on my lap in imitation of her friend's position on Bucello's. I was less ample of lap than he, and so she balanced herself by throwing one arm around my neck. She was doused in a suffocating perfume, a cheap imitation of the suffocating perfumes my mother and her kind wore. Reflexively I pulled my head back, which tightened her grip around my neck.

"Shy one, are you?" she asked with a leering smile. The other males, wanting to put me in my place, assured her that I was not only shy but also other things that were not manly. She tipped her head to grin sassily at them from one corner of her eye but returned her cooing attention to me. "You from Terraferma, then? Never seen a city girl?" She winked and ran a plump pink tongue over painted lips.

Acutely nervous, I retreated to the only mental safety at my disposal: words. "A city girl? I rather think you are more of *cunt*-ry girl, no?" I said.

The bawds giggled; the young men cackled in their velvet jerkins, suddenly looking stupid.

"As a matter of fact"—she grinned—"I do know a little of country matters."

"Clever boy," said one of the older whores; another snorted, "Not that clever. He's not the first to jape that way."

"Excuse my lack of originality," I said to my detractor. It was bizarre to have captured the attention of the table, given as I was the least groping or eager-faced of any man there.

"I think he *is* shy," my lap-perch insisted.

"I am not shy, I'm just not *forward*," I corrected politely. And then added, as the words occurred to me (with some amazement at myself), "I prefer to come in a more *rearward* fashion."

The bawds all exchanged looks and then burst into hilarity. The youths, who had yet to manage to say anything directly to the women they intended to ride, looked almost scandalized.

"Where did you learn to talk like that?" the woman on Bucello's lap gushed.

"In the Low Countries, of course," I said, which delighted them all over again.

With that reference, I had now exhausted my repertoire of euphemisms for nether regions and sexual matters in general. However, emboldened by their approval, I decided to risk invention. "A cunning little wench there worked me stiff as we groped for trout in a peculiar river."

What in hell did that mean? Yet it was welcomed as though it were fraught with especially filthy innuendo. The bawd on my lap ground herself against me, bare nipples and all—the perfume really was atrocious—and moaned suggestively. "This fellow is a catch," she informed her cohorts. "And tonight . . ."—here she pressed her face right up into mine until I could see the places where the white paint creased—"tonight he is all mine to *dance* with." On the word *dance* she thrust her hips yet farther into my lap, which was frankly quite uncomfortable.

Still, it was enthralling to have such power. The bawd who'd settled on Bucello's lap, realizing she had not, in fact, picked the leader of our pack, sidled until she was nearly at the end of his knees and put a proprietary hand on my bawd's shoulder. "Surely you'd like to *snatch* more than one dance," she purred at me.

"Hey, I thought you were dancing with *me!*" Bucello complained. Immediately, she turned her tinted, ringlet-framed face back to him and smiled reassuringly.

"Of course, darling, but a quiver can hold many arrows."

"I've got the biggest arrow here," Bucello said, defensively, and the fellows round the table all laughed and hear-heared him, relieved the lecherous talk was finally comprehensible to them.

"I rather think I'd like him all for myself," said my aromatic lapweight, eyeing me. "You're a rare horn to catch, fellow. You've got a special something—" and again she leaned in toward me; her breath, at least, was not so bad; I think she had recently been chewing mint leaves—"worth *dying* over," she said suggestively, pretending to whisper but really speaking very loudly. "Or even dying *under*." As before, the bawds all giggled knowingly; the youths all sniggered with a rising level of awkwardness.

Despite my lack of sexual desire for this woman, the energy of the moment was addictive, and I decided to swim with the current.

"So you want to be buried with your face upward?" I asked her archly and actually dared put a finger on her left nipple.

God in heaven, that changed everything. Now I had to have her.

"Unless, as you said, you prefer the rearward fashion," she said breathily.

"Not necessarily between the sheets," I said. "There I prefer more standard entrances and exits."

"And exits and entrances," she said, quickly, rocking her hips toward mine with the syllables. Suddenly it was not nearly so uncomfortable.

"And entrances and exits," I said, encouragingly.

"And exits and entrances," she said more quickly, rocking still.

"Enough of this!" Bucello bawled, interrupting. "No pleasure listening to dirty talk—I'd much rather dirty action! So, Iago, my friend, either you must do it to her here on the table, or take a room upstairs and let the rest of us get on with our own dirty work!"

Before I could even think to answer, the white-faced whore had jumped off my lap and was tugging at my hand to make me rise. "Come along, then, darling," she crooned. "Time to make the beast with two backs."

Chapter 5

TRAINING TO BE a bombardier verged on blissful.

For three months my life consisted of daily musters, rising

before dawn, marching in formation, learning strategy, endless practice sessions (although not so endless, really, as they rationed our gunpowder almost to the grain). I was a talented student of the academic elements of warfare; I was natural at strategy and tactics; I could decipher some of the greatest battles Venice had ever won; in class exercises I made the same decisions that, it turned out, the best generals in our history had made.

I came to know and understand this about Our Serene Republic: having expanded our holdings to nearly infinite multiples of our original landmass, both to the west on Terraferma and of course east across the Empire da Mar, we were now simply trying to maintain said holdings, and keep them safe. We were conquerors until we'd conquered all we needed; now we were trying to protect and preserve it. In becoming a military man, I was promising to quietly guard all that my forefathers had not-so-quietly conquered. There would be no glamour to the profession, despite the romantic patina the Republic invested in our military glory.

And that sat fine with me. I loved what I was doing, and I loved that I could do it *well*. I wished to join an artillery unit on Terraferma or better yet da Mar, perhaps Corfu or Cyprus; I wished to practice what I'd learned until I was invincibly talented, and then (full-time bombardiering being hard to come by in times of peace) become a master teacher. I grew fond of my own instructors, basking in their approval, especially that of Alvisio Trevisan; approval of any sort to me was both alien and thrilling. Crowing reports of me had been sent home by my superiors. I never crossed the city to go home myself; I wanted to return fully fledged, entirely reborn into this new identity of mine: Iago Soranzo, Master Gunner.

And then, too soon, I was a formal graduate of the Alberghetti Family's Bartolomeo da Cremona training program at the Arsenal. I was now a qualified artilleryman. My captain declared I had great potential as a future commander.

* * *

VENICE IS A PLACE of pomp and circumstances, where every possible opportunity for ceremony is studiously observed and acted on, but there was little fanfare when we graduated from our training. Soaked by sheets of cooling rain, skirting the flooded Piazza of San Marco, I returned home, lugging my leather satchel—the weight of which was much less burdensome to me than it had been three months earlier.

A servant at the water gate took my soaked cloak and offered me a cloth to dry my head. I was summoned instantly to Father's study, that same study where there was only the one chair, and cushions at his feet. I did not sit. I was pleased, excited, and most of all relieved: I had done our family proud, and I'd done it in the most exciting branch of the military. The cavalry, even the navy, now paled in comparison.

Father, dressed as usual in black velvet with a surcoat to ward off the damp, somehow managed to look up at me as if he were looking down at me. "Welcome home, son," he said, without sounding welcoming. His grey eyes turned to scan a piece of paper. When he set it on the desk, I saw the state seal printed on it in red and, feeling strangely nostalgic, I recognized the personal insignia of Captain Trevisan. It was a letter of commendation.

Father, having read it, did not look impressed or even interested. My stomach clenched a little. Somehow, I thought my transformation would have effected a transformation within him too. But he was the same cold man who did not know quite what to do with this extra son he'd spawned.

"I am glad," he said, "that you have redeemed the memory of your brother's life. You were worthy of that task, from all that I have read in reports home from your instructors. Indeed, your gun-master seems to think you have some kind of genius."

I flushed with pride. That Captain Trevisan had described me thus, and my father was forced to acknowledge, to my face, that it had been said about me—this was enough. It made me Somebody. To dismiss me, now, was to dismiss the judgment of an expert.

But Father was not dismissing anything. "This esteem of your instructors is a good thing," he allowed, instead. "It may help the master plan."

Oh, dear. "What . . . master plan?"

"It will make it easier to place you well when you transfer to the army," Father said.

I had to repeat this phrase to myself at least twice to make sure I understood it. The army—by which he meant the infantry—and the artillery are two different branches, and the army is essentially a standing guard. There is no glory or excitement in it; members of the army simply guard what our more ambitious predecessors won for us. The artillery, although likewise a defensive force, at least teems with innovation.

"Why on earth would I leave the artillery to join the . . . heaven help me, the *army*?" I demanded, feeling my hands clench without my permission. I crossed to a window and looked out at the dismal rain. "Perhaps the cavalry, if you'd loan me the money to buy a horse, or better yet the navy, but if you will excuse me, Father . . . the army? The infantry? The infantry is nothing but garrison guards. Their very goal is to *not* be useful. I would end up guarding some half-remembered castle on some half-remembered hill town on the mainland. Why would I want that, when I have a signed letter from the captain of the—"

"Because it will be seen as a gesture of great loyalty to the Republic," Father said. "The infantry is desperately in need of recruits. You are a bit of a hero this week. Temporarily, of course, but enough so that if you enlist, and we make sure others hear about it, you may start a current flowing, and increase the rolls—a turnabout in the army's fortunes that will be forever associated with Iago son of Niccolo Soranzo."

Now I saw what this was about: Father was boot-licking someone in the Senate whose duty was to increase infantry recruitment. What better offering to make than his own son?

"But, Father, there are no *need* of more recruits," I argued. "The enlisted soldiers spend their lives standing about doing absolutely nothing but holding pikes and asking *who goes there* at some fortress gate. We have a hard time hiring *mercenaries* to do something so dull. What does it profit me, or Venice, for me to spend my life like that?" I took a deep breath, heart pounding, and declared firmly, "I am ambitious for a better lot."

Father sighed and gave me a long-suffering, oh-but-you-are-petulant-Iago look. "We have friends in places that matter, you know," he said. "I will ensure you are positioned to become a petty officer in no time at all."

I bristled. "I thank you, Father, but as I have now proven, my own abilities mark me. I do not *need* political favors to rise in life."

"I have already spoken to the commisioner of Tirano on Terra-ferma, and he has agreed to tell the captain that you will be joining their company," Father continued, as if I had said nothing.

For a moment I was speechless. "You cannot make me do that," I finally said. And then, outright defiance for perhaps the first time in my life: "I will not do it."

"They are relying on you, Iago. If you don't go, I will look foolish and unreliable in the eyes of Senator Brabantio, who is not only my most indulgent customer but also particularly good at sending new business my way. If I look foolish or ungrateful to him, it will have immediate and profound effects on the fortunes of our house. Frankly, it could ruin me. You will obey this plan or you will be disowned."

Hardly recognizing myself in my behavior, I laughed scornfully and met his eye. "Are you telling me you've placed your future in my hands?" I said. "I don't believe that. You have given me the power to destroy your industry? I'll pretend for a moment that you mean it, and so I must ask: why would you do something so rash, Father?"

Astounded by my resistance, he looked angry—a rare show of any emotion from him. "Because I wished to bask in the pride of knowing you would do the right thing. I wished the satisfaction of believing that were I ever to be in a position to depend upon you to look out for my interests, you would do so. It breaks my heart to see that I am wrong."

I considered this a moment, then announced: "That is twisted beyond all reason." My heart was pounding; no member of our family had ever censured him this way.

"Is it?" Father challenged. "To test one's son's character as he enters into manhood? How is that twisted? Is that not rather a commendable and affectionate action for a father?"

I collected myself. "You have exaggerated the danger you would be in, were I to disobey you. I do not know why. You have invented high stakes, to play some mental game with me. It's like something that Florentine writer liked to gush about."

"All the more your goodness in obedience, then," Father said. I blinked, trying to make sense of this. This must be dotage.

"Very well," I said with a grim sigh. "Tell me what brainless blind obedience I must honor, to keep intact your years of meticulous industry and skill."

Father's mood was instantly reformed, which further suggested to me this was the infirmity of an aging mind. "There is a ball tomorrow night," he said. "My good friend the senator will be there. He will introduce us to the regional commissioner, who will in turn introduce you to the regional captain, and you will discuss with him your future. As I understand it, the pope is far too interested in Tirano, and we are trying to raise a standing army at the border."

I barely suppressed a groan. The pope! Not even an interesting adversary like the Turk! This was why I had decided never to join the infantry: I would be guarding some place on the edge of civilization that Venice had once conquered and now needed to keep docile, in order to support our extravagant life at home. It was hard to imagine anything less noble. But: the patriarch was still the patriarch, however much I wished he wasn't. The fear of bringing shame upon the family stifled my will to resist him further.

* * *

THE BALL WAS being thrown in honor of someone I did not know, who was being feted by someone else I did not know. After months of dressing myself in simple cadet's garb, I found it irritatingly fussy to be trussed up by a servant in velvet and silk. I refused wearing a ruff, declaring it un-Venetian. I also resisted the slashed breeches; the servant protested, first to me and then to my father. Father did not care about my lower limbs, as long as I covered my torso with a silk shirt and my red-and-white jerkin bearing the winged lion of Venice. I was happy to comply.

My mother was striking in her vermillion pearl-encrusted *buratti* skirt and black French hood. With her feet strapped into eight-inch-high chopines, she towered above Father. She looked gorgeous as she always did, but—as always—she looked nothing like herself. It had been years since I'd seen my mother without tint of some kind on her face, but I remember clearly from childhood that she was beautiful. I could not understand why a creature of natural beauty, gifted by God, would create a new face for herself, a face identical to all the other painted faces of Venice. As she aged, the lead in the white ceruse had eaten away at her skin, and so more paint was required to hide the damage, and so she resembled my mother less and less. Still I bowed respectfully and offered her my arm; chopines are notoriously difficult to walk in (besides looking ridiculous).

She took my elbow. But then, as if I had suddenly vanished, she turned away from me to instead accept my older brother's arm.

Rizardo was dressed handsomely, although he looked as if he could not breathe, so tightly was he trussed in a bombastic black slashed doublet, red shirtsleeves showing beneath it. He was father's full partner in the business now but had yet to understand the silk trade with profundity. He had a poor grasp of geography and entomology, both of which happened to be interests of mine; I understood his product and his purpose more than he did. Entomologically, Rizardo did not know a *doppi* from a *galletta*; technically, a *mangle* from a *filatoio*; chromatically, *kermes* from *woad*; the raw silk might be *Ardassa* from Persia or *Ciattica* from

Spain, it was all one to him. He could barely tell the difference between taffeta and *straze*.

But he had been born first, so the burden was on him to make good of it all. Seeing him stand there dressed so handsomely, I felt a pang of envy of which I was not proud. I wished I had his opportunity, for I knew I was prepared for it.

Although, as I thought more on it, perhaps that was not true. Most likely, given the opportunity, I would have made a dreadful *setaiòlo*. I recalled suddenly an event when I was seven: Father had received a shipment of *bavelle*, the worst kind of waste-silk, lower quality even than the local Germans' *drappi da fontego*. To his clerk, in my hearing, he groused, "This shit will be good for nothing but stuffing codpieces. I must find some clever way to market it."

Moments later, a buyer's agent came into the storeroom; desperate even then to prove my usefulness, I eagerly informed the man that we had a warehouse full of shit for stuffing codpieces. I was whipped for this transgression. Rizardo would never have made such a blunder. So it was good he was the one who would inherit the business, and not myself. This was true, although mostly what he knew of silk was how to wear it well.

AS HE WAS doing this evening. He resembled our father greatly—tonight he was a taller, fitter, younger copy of father, from cool grey eyes to black duckbill shoes. I must have seemed a well-dressed servant in comparison, my hair uncoiffed, my face sunburnt from afternoons out shooting in the Arsenal.

So thanks to me, we were a motley assortment in the gondola, approaching the water gate of Ca'Whomever on the Grand Canal, just north of the Rialto Bridge. It was explained to me on the way, as the gondoliers rowed us through the filthy water of a side canal, that Father had made sure my name had been on everybody's lips for the past few days—my presence was anticipated at this gathering, and that is why he had "allowed" me to appear "unkempt." He wanted the shock effect of a "real soldier" at the party.

"If I handle myself well, I might start a mania for swarthiness among Venetian dandies," I said sardonically.

Father did not grasp the humor; my brother did, but did not approve it. My mother looked thoughtful; I suspected she was busy deciding which senator to flirt with first. So there was no further conversation in the gondola.

At least it was no longer raining.

Chapter 6

WE WERE ADMITTED at the water gate by a gaggle of well-dressed servants, all in high-waisted suits made of a black silk tabby that my father had sold their employer earlier that year. Although it did not look like much, I knew its worth, and it staggered me that so much would be spent on downstairs servants' garb. My father gave me a meaningful look, an eyebrow cocked at one of the servants. I nodded to acknowledge the significance: these were immensely wealthy patrons of Father's.

A resplendent, broad set of stairs, coated with gold leaf, led up to the main hall, which was easily four times the size of ours. It was warm from the heat of so many bodies; it smelled of clashing perfumes; the lamplight was too uneven to flatter anybody. Musicians were playing some piece by Francesco Landini in a corner, but it was not yet the time to dance. People were mulling, so that they could show off their finery and jealously eye one another as romantic rivals.

Near to our entrance, I saw Roderigo's mother. She was usually inclined toward older gentlemen in her flirtations, but this evening found her hand in hand with a fresh-faced youth. He was young enough to be her son.

In fact, he was her son.

I hardly recognized Roderigo. We had been out of each other's sights for not so very long, but he had made a stylish and successful transition to young Venetian foppery. I mostly recognized him by his stance: his neck pulled slightly in, like a nervous turtle, gave him an elegantly long, even regal, bearing from the back, but from the side it had provided him with double chins from about the age of twelve. Nonetheless, he'd always been a handsome boy, and now he was a handsome youth. One of those who had no need of styling, his hair was so naturally of the perfect kind of curl. He wore an outfit whose fabric I recognized as waste silk from my father's stores. His family was in the spice trade, but they had never been prosperous, and now they were surely short of cash, if that is what they dressed their only son in.

Still, nobody but their family and ours knew the silk was waste, and it had been cleverly cut so that he looked well dressed, almost as well as my brother (which is no small thing—all of us, as a family of silk merchants, were expected to use our haberdashery as advertisment). Roderigo's doublet ran to a low point in front, and the tight sleeves, in signature Venetian style, had stripes running in circles down his arms.

I could not decide whether or not I wanted to speak to him. The boy in me rejoiced at a familiar face, but the man I was becoming, especially tonight while still fuming about Father's actions . . . I would spare Roderigo my foul mood. So I thought perhaps I would not call out to him.

However, immediately upon arrival, I received the attention of the entire room, for I was the only sun-kissed guest; had I painted my face in streaks of green and orange I would hardly have been more alien to them.

Roderigo's face lit up. He cried out, "Iago! My dear Iago! What a soldier you've become!" and was already toward me, his suddenly-long legs halving, quartering, eighthing the distance between us until his hands were around my shoulders embracing, a kiss on either cheek. On instinct, as he released me, I offered him my right hand palm-forward, and he (with a delighted little vocal tic) responded with our secret handshake.

"How do you, Roderigo? You look remarkably well."

"Do you think so?" he said, sounding pleased. He had the look of a spaniel in his eye, and I realized, with a sinking feeling, that he still worshipped me as if we were boys. I did not want that responsibility; I was not worthy of it.

"What are you doing with yourself these days?" I asked. I glanced around, hoping to see people drinking, so that I might ask them where they'd found libations. But Roderigo seemed able to block my view no matter which way I turned.

"I have started working with Father," he said proudly. "I have convinced him that we should not simply sell at retail the wholesale pepper we buy so dear, but we should enter into the trade itself and become partners with a larger venture. I have a scheme to monopolize the Tellicherry pepper crop, which is superior to the Malabar pepper that the Portuguese have been cultivating on Java." Lowering his voice: "I have made connections with some Arab heathens to help me smuggle it from India by way of Alexandria. As long as none of those accursed Florentines outbid me for the Egyptians' loyalty, I am a made man."

For a moment I was speechless. Speechless. This was infinitely beyond the ambition of the boy I had grown up with—or for that matter, almost anyone I knew. He beamed at me, seeking my approval.

"Good heaven," I said. "That would be a most remarkable undertaking."

"Would be? No, it *is*—we are now six months into it, and already we have earned back the money we borrowed—including the atrocious interest Tubal charged us. We are being very thrifty—perhaps you recognize the fabric of my coat—but I expect that by the end of Advent, we will be well enough along in our profits that I may buy my own house."

I blinked. "Here in Venice, you mean?"

He nodded with delight. "Possibly even build a new one. I have a canny instinct to judge the pepper harvest, even though I have never been to see it myself. And I am learning how to speculate fearlessly. You would not believe how much I have learned since we last played our pranks together, Iago." This was not bragging—he was yearning to impress me.

He succeeded. My mouth had fallen slack with astonishment. Here was I, thinking myself so mightily changed because I knew how to shoot a musket, while little Roderigo was becoming Pepper King of the Mediterranean.

"So this spice trade," I said, trying to reclaim my calm, "it seems you have a nose for it."

His face wrinkled with laughter. "Oh, you are such a witty fellow, Iago! How I have missed your wit! I know all about your great adventures, lately and to come, but tell me—while you are back at your parents' home, before you go off to guard our borders, we must get together and have a drink and catch up on old times. I am sure that we could entertain each other mightily."

"I am not remotely entertaining," I assured him. "But it sounds as if you are, so I will willingly get drunk with you. As long as you get a little sun on your face. I cannot have a serious conversation with a man so pale. Roderigo, my friend, you look like a prostitute."

He laughed sheepishly. The partygoers around us pulled their lips back into transparently fake smiles. Then they moved away, perhaps afraid they might be commented upon with equal frankness.

As a space cleared around us, a new look came into Roderigo's eye. He lowered his voice and leaned in close to me. "I really do crave a word with you. It has to do with your new skills, in fact."

"What new skills?" I asked. He gestured to my face, which only confused me further, until I realized this was a reference to my "rough soldier" appearance. "You need a good artilleryman?" I jested.

He leaned in closer, his eyes darting nervously about the room. "In fact, my friend," he whispered, "that is exactly what I need."

For one fantastic moment I thought he was going to ask me to lead a raucous expedition into the land of pepper trees, shooting

all his adversaries as we went, and offering me a share of his great
empire as recompense.

But no. "You see," he said, "I am now of an age when I may be
called up for militia duty," he began. I nodded; this was true for
every citizen. "And I am an absolute catastrophe at shooting. I make
a damned fool of myself every first Sunday, when compulsory practice is summoned. I haven't the knack for it. I am a fine dancer, so it
is not a lack of coordination, just a lack of that *kind* of coordination."

"I'm sorry to hear it," I said.

"I want to hire you to tutor me," he said.

A tempting offer, but impossible to follow through on. "Gunpowder is extremely expensive, Roderigo; it is rationed by the Council of Ten."

"I can pay for it," he countered instantly. "I have been squirreling
money away for this exact purpose."

"It's not a matter of money," I explained. "It just isn't *done*. Letting private citizens buy gunpowder would be like letting them buy
state secrets. Even if I were in charge of the magazine dispensary, I
could not give you any. It is not available for private use. And"—for
I could see this idea already forming in his face—"if you were to try
to either make it yourself from scratch, or buy it from some foreign
source, you'd find yourself in dreadful trouble. You would probably
be put in prison for suspected sedition."

His handsome face puckered into a frown. "Then what am I to
do?" he lamented. "Every month I pray the campo will be flooded
and the muster cancelled. It's not my fault that I'm inept, but I am
punished monthly for my ineptness by all our neighbors, at the
drills! I am tormented by some of them with looks and comments
almost daily. It's humiliating, but more than that: if I am ever called
up for active duty, let God watch over our Republic while the likes of
me are on call to protect her."

"Hear, hear," said a sarcastic voice behind me. Roderigo's face
pinkened.

"Iago, this is Tasso," he said without enthusiasm, pointing to someone approaching from behind me. "The subcaptain of our neighborhood militia training. Tasso, this is Iago, who has just graduated from—"

"I know where he's graduated from, and it is an honor to meet you, sir," Tasso said, as if Roderigo had just evaporated. He was as tall as Roderigo but twice his weight; his eyes were close-set and he was fashionably pale. "I have heard about your inspiring decision to throw yourself in with the infantry. I can't say I would have the humility to do such a thing in your place, especially if I had your tremendous skills in gunnery."

"I'm not sure I have the humility myself," I returned. "I seem to be doing it anyhow."

"I mean, if it were Roderigo here, it would not be such a loss, eh?" the fellow continued, elbowing Roderigo as if it were a drollery they shared. Roderigo's expression revealed he did not find it droll. "Poor fellow was born without a feel for a musket."

"So he says. We were seeking solutions to that when you interrupted us," I said. "Would you like to help us seek a solution, or are you merely here to mock someone whose skills, in one arena, do not measure up to yours? If you believe this gathering should be to mock those of lesser abilities in gunmanship, then I offer to mock you."

Tasso reddened. "Oh, no," he said with a forced chuckle. "Totally at your disposal to assist our mutual friend here."

"Can you buy your way out of it?" I asked, returning my attention to Roderigo. By the way he was looking at Tasso, this man must be among the worst of his harrassers. A protective tribal instinct forged of childhood bonds welled up in me.

Roderigo shook his head. "If my circumstances were different, I would not care so much; I can endure being made to look a fool. But my life, Iago, my life is such that I *must* not appear foolish now, for the sake of a particular young lady."

Added Tasso, with a nasty little smile, "It is a most unfortunate coincidence for Roderigo that the young lady's brother is captain for our militia unit."

"Ah," I said. How humiliating for Roderigo that his infatuation was so public. I kept my expression carefully neutral.

But not as neutral as I meant to. "Wipe that look off your face!" Roderigo hissed in a horrified voice. "They'll be able to tell we're talking of them."

My eyes widened. I glanced around the party. "Where's the girl?" I asked as the cornet sounded the start of some quaint *estampie* dance.

"Do not look about like that," Roderigo ordered through clenched teeth. "They are eyeing us right now—I am sure it surprises them that I am friends with a soldier. Do not let them see you looking."

Another reason he had been so glad to see me: reflected credibility. I had no idea I was so useful. I wished I could have somehow aided him, but what could I do? "I would offer to speak to your captain and try to get your name out of the duty roster, but since that captain is the brother—"

"Oh, heaven, don't do that!" He made a wincing face, blinking very nervously toward Tasso. "No, Iago, I have no interest in shirking my duty. I ask only that you would help me to learn to be a better shot. I'd pay you very well."

"Oh, is *that* what you are pestering him about?" Tasso said. "Rigo, my dear friend, *I* can help you out with that. I would be happy to give you private lessons. I know the people to talk to, to get gunpowder on the sly."

Roderigo's face expanded with amazement at this announcement. "Really?" He breathed out, willing to immediately forgive whatever injustices the fellow had done him. I was angered on his behalf but forced myself to smile.

"Now you see, if I were a typical Venetian," I said, "here is what I would shift to do. I would tell Roderigo that he was like a brother to me, perhaps even call him a nickname I had never thought to use before. Say, *Rigo*. I would promise him that I knew the right people, and I had merely to grease a few palms, and we'd end up with the gunpowder, the gun, the match and balls, and permission to practice someplace private. Roderigo would ply me with gifts of thanks. Then, over the course of the next few weeks, I would go to fewer parties where he might be a guest, but each time we interacted, I would maintain a hint of a promise—enough to ensure his continued material show of gratitude—but each time slightly less so than the last time. And eventually I would simply vanish from his sight for a while, until he understood that there was nothing I could do for him, and he would be too shamed to ask again. Then—keeping the gifts I'd earned with all my promises—I would once again brazenly frequent the same gatherings as he, only this time I would somehow never manage to find time for him." I smiled warningly at the red-faced Tasso. "But I am not a typical Venetian," I went on, "and so instead I told him immediately that I cannot help him, because that is the only honest answer to be given here."

I had, despite my attempts at calm, raised my voice while I was speaking, and now there were a number of people listening. The blushing Tasso tried, with a spasmodic inconsistency, to presume some offhand gesture that would appear to make light of the whole thing. He finally said, in an extremely choked voice, "Of course, that is another way to manage it," and excused himself artlessly. I glanced at Roderigo. He looked both crushed and grateful, as he had frequently when we were six.

A dozen faces watched Tasso stagger off; another dozen stared daggers at me. I ignored them and thought how happy I would be when I was back in barracks, any barracks, even in the outlands of Terraferma spending my life playing chess and shadow boxing.

Chapter 7

MY FIRST POST was in Tirano. The Adda River flows through Tirano, on the westernmost boundary of Terraferma, Venice's mainland territory. It is a walled town, with nothing much to recommend it. In September of '04, the Blessed Mary had appeared to a local fellow named Omodei, and so there was a steady trickle of pilgrims to the area hoping they too would see the Madonna of Tirano.

Living in much greater comfort on the hill across the border were the monks in the town of Brusio. It had been founded five hundred years earlier as a monastery, and not much had happened there since. Heaven knows why we had to patrol it, but patrol it we did. We saw to it that those crafty monks never had a chance to frolic with the Madonna of Tirano.

I made my garrison life agreeable. I was the youngest of a band of rugged men, most mercenaries, most from foreign lands, and most from rough-hewn cultures. I was glad to be free of the insincerity and false laughter of Venice—but I did miss the clean sheets and the decent music, the casual ability to find something both man-made and beautiful. Still, I found the physical reality bracing: the hard mats, the dirt floors of the towers, even the flies and fleas and mud.

The towns we garrisoned were small and poor. There was little to do. We rotated guard duties, one week on, one week off; a week at the gate, a week on the wall, a week guarding munitions, a week in the piazza. After a few months, I was sent to another town, and some few months later, to another. Sometimes I was with the same group of men, sometimes not. I met a few fellow Venetians along the way, and each one of them gushed over me and cited me—and by association, of course, my family—as their inspiration to enlist. So my father had made much hay out of a little weed. I hoped the senator whose boots he had been licking sent plenty of wealthy customers his way.

I cannot say what my fellow soldiers did in their time off. I yearned for scholarship, and so to keep my wit sharp, I read and translated whatever I could get my hands on: bad poetry written by a mayor's wife; archived reports of skirmishes at the larger fortress postings; the Bible. I played cards and chess with elder statesmen of the towns where I was stationed, and so had access to their books. I was the only soldier, to my knowledge, so keen on this kind of entertainment.

Within the meager rations of gunpowder allotted any garrison in peacetime, all soldiers study shooting—and here, at least, a small fantasy of mine came true: I was the best gunner of each place I was stationed, and not a man of them but was improved under my tutelage. I found this satisfying—although I was admittedly (at first) the least distinguished swordsman.

Gunpowder and its possibilities had changed the face of battle, but gunpowder was hard to come by, guns expensive and too cumbersome for a free lance to carry comfortably about with him, so blade against blade was still the common conflict. Realizing this, I made it my ambition to excel the most accomplished mercenaries I was stationed with. One such German had assisted Paulus Hector Mair to perfect the techniques of his recent fencing compendium. The man was pleased to take me as a student; to his credit, he was delighted when, after months of being fiercely humiliated by him, I bested him for the first time.

I had been taught the rudiments of fencing growing up, just as one is taught how to move chess pieces around the board without really being *taught chess*. I'd received further training at the Arsenal, but it was only here in the outlands that I became truly skilled. Thanks to my German tutor, I was soon known to be "good for a Venetian." By my third year of practice, I was simply known to be good.

My reputation was not really deserved. Having no active enemy, soldiers sparred exclusively against one another; blood was rarely drawn, and nobody's life was ever nearly in danger. I was not prideful of my skills. I was more talented than a few, more industrious than many, and more intelligent than most, but it was the world I knew, and after five years of it, I could imagine no other.

IN FACT, BY the time five years had passed, I was grown so skilled at fencing that I began to teach others the rudiments of the Bolognese style, especially the northern *condottieri*, who were relatively new to

Italy. They presumed I was among the masters in the field despite my youth (I was not yet five and twenty), and thus a prodigy.

One afternoon, I was back in Tirano, site of my first posting, but now I was one of the veteran soldiers. It was a rainy day, which was not common; I was not on duty, I could not rouse anyone to dagger work, and outside exercise was impossible in the deluge. I found myself playing *primero* with some of the younger men, two of them from Venice—that was a rare thing indeed, for three native sons to be stationed together as infantry in the same godforsaken town. We were speaking of swordplay, as we often did, and these young colts were particularly taken with the theories of Camillo Agrippa.

In truth, Agrippa is among the best there is. As partial as I am to Marozzo, I know Agrippa is a practical improvement on him, simplifying Marozzo's eleven guards to four. But I like the Marozzo training, for it offers subtle variations, while Agrippa, although pragmatic, lacks Marozzo's artistry and adaptability. This would never carry as an argument with earnest young lugs, however, so I never tried to change anybody's mind about it.

But this particular cluster of lugs was being disrespectful: they were extolling the virtues of Agrippa by denigrating Marozzo, oblivious that without a Marozzo, there could be no Agrippa. It is a particular gripe to me, when worthiness is denigrated in this fashion, and I was about to scold them for it.

But instead, on a whim, I decided to attempt something that was, for me, extremely novel: a harmless counterfeit. It was unlike me to counterfeit anything, ever; the inspiration caused me nervous amusement, as though I were about to perform before an audience. As I was studying my four cards, I scoffed, "Camillo Agrippa . . . That whoreson."

They all glanced up, startled from their own cards. "You speak as if you know him," one of the young colts said, almost rebukingly.

I shrugged. "We dueled when he was last in Venice." The words came out of my mouth as smooth as silk drapes over alabaster. It was probably the first deliberate falsehood of my entire life, yet I found it effortless to keep a casual, even dismissive, expression on my face.

To a man, they all dropped their cards onto the wooden table. "*What?*" they gasped in unison, mouths hanging slack like fish, their faces sharply shadowed in the lamplight. The windows were all shut against the rain.

"The man is a buffoon," I said contemptuously, examining my hand. I had a *fluxus* of hearts. I decided to discard the deuce, and reached for it.

One of the pack put his large paw over mine to keep me from continuing the game. "Come now, Iago, you cannot make a comment like that and not expect us to want to hear the story. You *dueled* with the *master*? The master of all masters?"

I sighed, as if annoyed the game had been interrupted. "Only because he was a prideful ass. I would not have chosen to waste my time on him."

"Waste your *time*?" one of the other soldiers squeaked.

"He is a worthy strategist," I allowed, wondering what story I would end up telling them if they did not call me out. "But I believe the purpose of a duel is for two honorable men to meet, for honorable purposes, to determine who is the better swordsman. You would certainly think the creator of the greatest school of fencing ever conceived would, himself, hold such a position, but he challenged me for the most insipid of reasons."

They were all still slack-mouthed. It reminded me of that childhood moment in Galinarion's dining hall, when Roderigo and I had been caught during the egg incident. But then I had been telling the truth; now I was blithely inventing. I expected one of them to accuse me of gulling, but apparently the thought did not occur to a one of them.

Finally: "What was it, then?" somebody demanded in a hushed voice. "Why did Maestro Agrippa challenge *you*?"

Oh, dear. Now I must invent in detail. I decided to invent something ridiculous, so that one of them would call me out, and we could all have a laugh and return to our card game (which incidentally I was winning).

"We met at a party and he asked me what I thought of the cut of his beard. I thought it looked ridiculous, and I told him so," I said. "He was offended."

The foreign soldiers exchanged looks of astonishment, and a pale-haired youth opened his mouth, obviously about to accuse me of a falsehood. But one of the Venetians immediately declared, by way of explanation, "Iago is known in Venice for his bluntness. He really does say things like that." The other Venetian nodded gravely in support of this. The towheaded foreigner closed his mouth, uncertain now.

I did not realize until that moment that I had a reputation. I had not been home for five years and assumed I was forgotten by everyone, except (perhaps) my immediate family.

The foreigner opened his mouth again. "You said you didn't like his *beard*, so he *challenged you to a duel*?" he demanded. As if one unit, all leaned in a bit closer to me.

So they all believed there had really been a conversation. I could at that moment have told them I was lying, and we could have laughed, and returned to our card game, and I could have won a tidy sum. But now I was intrigued to see how far I could push their credulity.

"Even Agrippa is not so crude as that," I offered. "I said I did not like his beard, and he, after a moment of astonishment at my rudeness, informed me that he considered it extremely well styled. To which I said, 'You are of course entitled to your opinion, but I am entitled to mine as well, and since you asked me, I don't like it.' He said, with a forced laugh, 'Well, I did not cut it to please *you*, anyhow,' and I replied, 'That's good, because you have not pleased me at all, I think it looks ridiculous.'"

I paused a moment, to allow one of them to have the insight that not even Blunt Iago would really have had this conversation with one of the most famous military geniuses of our century. But not one of them considered I was counterfeiting.

"Then what happened?" a black-haired brute from Normandy demanded in hushed awe.

"He churlishly informed me that I had absolutely no taste or judgment in such matters," I continued. "And I agreed with him, earnestly and proudly, explaining that I would not *want* to be an expert on the matter of absurd facial hair. At this point the fellow was near to apoplexy. He screamed that he'd never been spoken to so rudely in his life, and that if I did not renounce what I had said, he would force me out to the courtyard of our host, and measure swords with me right there."

"What did you say?" the fair-haired youth demanded. By now they were all leaning Iago-ward on their stools.

I shrugged defensively. "I told him there was nothing to take back, I had spoke truth, and it would be dishonorable to now pretend it was an untruth."

"So you went down into the courtyard right there, and dueled? In the midst of a party?"

Good heaven, they were actually going to make me invent a duel with Camillo Agrippa. I tried to think if I had any scars that I might pass off as remnants of the altercation. I recalled a faded scar on my right shoulder blade, a result of tumbling off a bridge railing while playing cavalry years ago with Roderigo. (He had been the horse.) I was not sure whom I should have win the duel, or under what circumstances it could have ended in a draw.

"I wanted to decline," I said. "As I told you, I considered that a most improper reason to duel with anyone, especially a man who is supposed to be the living embodiment of military honor. But on the other hand, I could not imagine passing up an opportunity to duel with a master, so I accepted, and with tremendous fanfare and the entire population of the party following us, we stepped down into the torch-lit courtyard." I glanced at the two youths from home. "You have never heard of this in Venice?" I asked, with the barest hint of a smile—something I hoped would trigger them to consider my words false.

"Whose house was it?" one of them demanded breathlessly.

"It was Pietro Galinarion's," I answered. "His courtyard is full of statuary, and guests, so we agreed that we would engage according to the rules of battle, rather than a private duel."

A long pause. I stared at them; they stared at me. A similar expression on each face: on the one hand, this tale was incredible beyond incredible, but on the other hand, it must be true. As I held the gaze longer and longer, the Norman's face expressed a hint of uncertainty, and I smiled at him with conspiracy, which I hoped he would take as an invitation to call me out. No such luck; he rather looked reassured, taking the smile to mean I was utterly confident in the tale I was telling.

"We drew, and measured swords," I said. "And then—"

The sharp knocking startled all of us. The fair-haired soldier, closest to the door, jumped up and went to answer it.

Standing outside, rain streaming off his oiled canvas mantle, was a sodden man wearing the red-and-white livery of hired messengers from Venice. I recognized his face, for he was my father's most regular and trusted courier. He recognized me too, for he stepped into the room with an authority that forbad anyone asking who he was; he crossed straight to me and bowed.

"Master Iago," he said somberly, "it is my grievous duty to escort you home to Venice. Your honored father has just passed away."

Emilia

Chapter 8

n the few hours between the messenger's arrival and my departure back to Venice with him, I received my commission, hastily and without ceremony. I was now an officer. A low-ranking one, an ensign, but still—*I was an officer.* This elevation, anticipated for a year, should have overwhelmed me. But compared to a patriarch's death, it seemed almost a quaint distinction.

If Father had lived long enough to know I'd earned it, it would have meant much more.

I DID GRIEVE for Father's passing, although in a sense it felt almost as if he had not departed from us, so fully had Rizardo taken his place by the time I arrived home. Rizardo had married in my absence, had already spawned one son and had another child on the way. His wife, Marta, was classically Venetian—attractive, painted, silly, superficially well educated, and prone to insincere laughter. From the moment I arrived, I sensed my mother resented the presence of another woman in the house; they did not once address each other the entire week that we, the family, sorted out the funeral arrangements.

Besides the funeral itself, that week included a tearless reunion with my second brother (the priest) and my mother's shameless use of public mourning as an opportunity to attract new paramours.

There followed several weeks of airless, respectful mourning and moping. I was relieved when Carnival arrived.

Every civilized culture in the world has some kind of gallimaufry of gambols, a bacchanalia that it cleverly justifies through history or myth. Venice attributes Carnival to Doge Michieli's triumph over Ulrich II of Aquileia in 1162. Ulrich's ransom was an annual tribute of one bull, twelve pigs, and twelve loaves of bread—quite a bargain for Ulrich, by my estimation, but Venice perceived herself as getting an excellent deal. In commemoration of this event, every year from Santo Stefano's Day until Lent, the entire city of Venice dons masks and costumes, overindulges in food, wine, and other friendly vices, and enjoys all sorts of spectacles. It climaxes with a bull being slaughtered in the Piazza of San Marco on Fat Thursday—and when Lent begins a week later, we are all so overstuffed and exhausted from forty-odd days of debauchery that the deprivations of Lent are something of a relief.

As a youngster, I was fascinated by the mechanics of the spectacles: the War Machines, Neptune's chariot, the fireworks, the quick-change artists, and the magician's tricks. And I loved the *battagliole*—what boy wouldn't? These were staged fisticuffs between two territorial gangs. I lived in San Polo, which meant I should have rooted for the Nicolotti, who were mostly fishermen. But I preferred the Castellani, sailors and shipbuilders from the Arsenal: the Arsenal, that magically forbidden fortress that as a child I could not have imagined ever entering. The two gangs would fight on designated bridges at designated times; Father would take us in a gondola to watch. Carnival to me meant exuberance, joyful fun, and freedom from convention.

As a child, that is.

As an adult I faced a very different Carnival. My brother announced that it was time for us to don costumes and masks and attend a ball. This was to demonstrate that we, The Family, had recovered from our loss and were still hearty enough for the rigors of Venetian socializing and commerce. (It was often difficult to distinguish between these two.)

The evening of the masque, I wore my military jerkin. Father, for all of his indifference to me, would never have thrown his son out of his house; I was not sure I could trust Rizardo to be so tribal, so I gave in to his instructions regarding masks and wore a papier-mâché *Bauta*, which covered my entire face.

The ball was in the San Croce district, at the home of Hieronomo Capello, a wealthy merchant but no patrician; at first glance, there was nothing at all to distinguish it from every average ball in the history of Venice. Having arrived, I was recognized despite my mask, because I did nothing to disguise the rest of me: no black cape, no cloak, no hat. A mask on its own does not hide much. It covers nothing but the face. I can recognize a man by his gait, his girth, his standing; so can anyone. I could sense people whispering and pointing me out as I walked through the grand hall. Ignoring the comedy being performed in the center of the room, I pulled the mask up and nibbled pistachios, sweetmeats, sugared fruit, and marzipan, all laid out on a side table in a pattern the shape of Venice.

The first person to actually approach me was Roderigo, who rushed to me at once and repeated the welcoming embrace of five years earlier. He lowered his mask a moment to reassure me it was he, and damned if the fellow had not grown even more handsome than he'd been at twenty. I had lost my deftness at discerning fabric, but he seemed to be better dressed than my brother, the great silk merchant. His maroon doublet and breeches were high-and-low velvet, the best kind, I am sure processed from true silk. There was slashing and puffing to show off the taffeta below; even his duckbill shoes were slashed to show the patterned stockings beneath. It was the fussiest outfit I'd ever seen him in.

"Roderigo, I am pleased to see you," I said heartily and held out my hand for our secret handshake. "How have the years been treating you?"

Here I was exposed to a lengthy, happily nervous monologue about Roderigo's excellent fortunes, a monologue that lasted until the comedy was concluded and was replaced by a group of young men, dressed as women, dancing a ballet. Roderigo was, among our peers, easily the richest nonpatrician merchant, the king not only of pepper but also of nearly any spice used in a Venetian kitchen. His only concern was a Florentine family who was trying to buy the loyalty of his Egyptian connections, but his agents had so far managed to stymie the Florentines. He had not snagged that ginger-haired young lass whom he'd been so enamored of; but since then he had suffered through several other fascinations, none of which had led to marriage. By the time he'd finished the recitation of his thoroughly Venetian life, I was almost through being pleased to see him.

"And now you must tell me the details of what you've been doing," he finished, slightly breathless. "Beyond what has been reported back to us all over the years by your proud father, of course."

I blinked to hide my bemusement at that declaration. My father, proud of me? "I have been soldiering," I said simply.

My disinclination to say more than that made my life fascinating. To everyone. Over the course of the next hour, with Roderigo following me as ever like a faithful spaniel, I slowly strolled one side of the hall and was dazzled by the number of gentlemen and even ladies ogling me, to the point of ignoring the transvestite ballet taking place in the center of the room. I heard from all of them how proud my father had been of me, how they'd heard I had mastered both German and Bolognese swordplay, how I had protected our fragile borders while asking nothing in return but the honor of serving my state—an almost inconceivable action for any of them to consider themselves; therefore, all the holier was I, for having volunteered such an unusual course for my life.

I could not bear the attention and was glad of the mask, even if it failed to hide my actual identity. "This room is so airless," I whispered to Roderigo, "and I cannot bear the stench of all the perfumes. Is there at least some balcony to retch from?"

Immediately Roderigo led me past the curtsying male dancers, who were now clearing the floor as a buffoonish master of ceremonies introduced a juggling act. The other side of the hall opened onto a broad balcony overlooking a canal. It was winter, so the canal did not smell, and there was a breeze that cleared my head. Relieved to be out of the crowd, I removed my mask. Roderigo likewise untied his.

Near us on the balcony was a small flurry of Venetian dandies, also temporarily bald-faced in the moonlight. Beneath their long black robes, their doublets and breeches were as outlandishly slashed up as Roderigo's, the taffeta and linen as outlandishly puffed out through the slashes. Trying to remember how to behave in polite company, I attempted to take an interest in their conversation. This was a chorus of complaints about a young lady at the party. Roderigo gestured me over to the group, whose members he knew, and was beamingly proud to introduce his soldier-friend.

The first statement that caught my ears was one of furious indignity: "She'll never get a husband with that tongue of hers."

"I told her that," complained another. "She said that was fine with her—if she never has a husband, she will never be cheated on."

Several laughed; a third man added: "She told *me* she prefers the company of bachelors, not wooers, because with bachelors she can be as comfortable as she is with all her friends."

I smiled to myself. It was obvious what was happening here: the lady in question was a high-class prostitute, trying to find a man to take her as a mistress, and these young dolts had not yet figured it out.

"She told *me*," said a fourth dejectedly, "that men are made of clay and she was not of a mind to be lorded over by a clod of dirt."

"She told me," said a fifth, "that since we're both descended from Adam and Eve, we must be relatives, and didn't I think it sinful to proposition my own cousin?"

I laughed at that. I did not have the money to support a mistress, but this harlot's banter would be more entertaining than another hour like the one I'd just spent. I wanted to meet her.

"And what is it about this young lady that so inflames you all to want to wed her?" I asked.

They all shrugged a foppish Venetian-style shrug.

"We're practicing our wooing," one said, as if it should be obvious. "On all the young ladies here. We practice on them, they practice on us. It's delightful, harmless, and useful—but this one is so *contrary*. It's well known she is a pretty piece of flesh. Why does she even show up at a place known to be a site for flirtation, when she will not flirt?"

"What you have just described sounds exactly like flirtation to me," I said knowingly.

They gave me looks of disapproving disbelief. "Well, she's right over there. Have at her!" the first complainer suggested. He pointed. I looked.

A young woman was wearing a black velvet *Moretta* mask, with a pile of auburn hair coiled on her head. She glanced briefly toward our little group as she exited from the hall. Then she most pointedly took no further interest in us. She crossed past us to the far side of the balcony for air. The men all snickered and energetically gestured me in her direction.

If you placed me in a room with a Venetian lady my own age and told me to be gallant toward her, I doubt I could do it for a thousand ducats. I'd have no idea what would be considered rude, or why; what would be considered humorous, and why. But from that first week in the Arsenal, I knew that I could banter with a bawd. I decided I would banter with this one, in their hearing, and make her laugh not *at* me but *with* me. With much hand-clasping and false merriment and several bets placed, I received useless information from them— her name, her father's name, her father's family's name, her father's family's business, all of which I was sure was just a front, to disguise the fact that she was a courtesan.

I retied my mask and brushed imaginary dust from off my soldier's jerkin, and shared a friendly obscene gesture with the lads, which brought cackles of approval. Then, without the slightest subtlety, walked energetically right toward her.

She stood serene at the far corner of the balcony, in a funnel-sleeved bodice and red woolen skirt. She wore no pearls nor strands of jewels, nor any of the other fineries outlawed by the state's sumptuary laws and therefore worn only by the wealthy. There was an elegant simplicity in her dress compared to every other woman at this ball. That was unusual for a prostitute. So was the absence of chopines, those absurd cork-soled shoes that raise a woman a foot above her natural height.

She heard my approach, of course, and watched me. We had a chance to appraise each other fully from behind our masks, as I took a dozen strides. I could not see her face, and even in moonlight her silhouette was muted, but she had a most impressive shape. Most women present themselves either for the advantage of their curves, or the advantage of their slimness. She had both, and showed off both, yet her gown revealed very little flesh.

She put her hands on her hips as I stopped beside her; the tilt of her head suggested she was waiting for me to start bantering.

"Good evening, Emilia," I said. "That's your name, I hear. They spent so much time complaining about your behavior that they only thought to mention your name but the once or twice."

"*They?*" she replied in an arch voice. "Do *they* have names of their own?"

"I think they would prefer me not to tell you their names," I chuckled.

"Then they're cowards," she said, matter-of-factly.

"Well of course," I agreed. "That's why they don't want you to know who they are. I myself am not a coward, and therefore, if I were to defame you, I would not mind if you knew my name."

After the slightest appraising pause, she asked, "What *is* your name?"

"I don't need to tell you that, since I'm not defaming you."

"Yet," she amended.

"Oh, I think I can refrain indefinitely. The other fellows over there, who do not want me to name them—they've already complained about you so thoroughly, I cannot imagine there'd be any new complaints to register."

She removed her hands from her hips and now crossed her arms over her chest. These were not the gestures of a high-born lady, and neither were they the manners of a prostitute on the prowl for a gentleman. She had, even in these simple movements, a natural grace, but she moved without any pretensions of femininity. "You really will not tell me the names of the men who defame me?" she asked.

"Pardon me, but no, my lady."

"Then will you tell me, at least, who *you* are?"

"Not at the moment, my lady," I said. I finally grasped an oddity about her: she was speaking without holding her mask. The *Moretta* mask—commonly worn by women, as it allows a peek at the outline of their face—is usually held in place by a small button clasped between the wearer's teeth. This allows a lady both hands free for dancing and yet does not muss up her coiffure and cap with a tied ribbon. Which means that when a *Moretta*-masked lady actually speaks, she must hold her mask up with one hand. Or ideally, she simply must not speak.

This young woman, however, had tied her *Moretta* with a velvet ribbon that was close in color to her hair, and then arranged her tresses to cascade over it. Like myself, she wore nothing on her head at all.

We had been standing in silence as I noticed all this.

"Are you planning to flirt with me, sir?" she asked, polite but matter-of-fact. "If you intend to, please begin, so we may get it over with."

"I hear you are not interested in wooers."

"I'm not interested in fools," she corrected pleasantly.

"Then what are you doing at this party?" I asked.

"Possibly the same thing you are," she replied. "Wishing I had something more fulfilling to do."

"You might try a brothel," I said in a meaningful tone. "The men who visit there know what fulfillment *they* desire and have well-lined pockets to fulfill *your* desires in return."

She laughed at this, but not the way I had wanted her to. "I have no experience in the matter, sir. Tell me, please: would my desire for intelligent conversation somehow be fulfilled by forfeiting my virginity? And if so, how, exactly?"

What an ass I was. "You're not a prostitute," I said, mortified.

Now she laughed the charmed laugh that I'd hoped to hear. "That is *by far* the most original line anyone has used to woo me," she said, with delight in her voice. "That *almost* makes me want to dance with you."

I had not seen the woman's face, and truly I did not know who she was beyond her name, but I was smitten with Emilia.

Chapter 9

I COULD NOT STOP thinking about Emilia all the next day. Our encounter had ended abruptly when Roderigo, to my fathomless annoyance, came over to introduce himself. In his presence, she almost physically retreated. Shortly after his intrusion, Emilia had excused herself indoors. After that, I could not find her.

Given the mix of people at that fete, my guess was that Emilia was from a comfortable family but not a wealthy one, that she was likely destined to be the wife of a middling merchant; who owned a house but not one that fronted on a canal; who owned a business but was not known for being especially clever at it; who had a social presence but not one that made him any kind of wit. She, of course, wanted more than that for her future, and so she was fiercely scaring off all potential suitors of that ilk. This was the biography that I invented for her over the course of the following day. I conveniently forgot how entirely mistaken I'd been with the previous biography I'd invented for her, in which she was a whore.

* * *

LATE IN THE DAY I was informed by my brother that we were going to another masked ball that evening. This one was really prime, he explained; there would be senators and patricians, and only a few of the richest merchants in the city were invited. It was hugely significant, an enormous honor, that our family was welcome. (My mother had arranged the invitation, possibly by seduction.) I did not want to go, because I doubted Emilia would be there. But with gritted teeth, I agreed to attend, and again put on my military jerkin.

With the usual finery and elegance and personalized gondola and obsequious servants waiting for us, the usual broad marble staircases and ornately painted murals and alabaster handrails, with the usual smell of candles and the sounds of sackbuts and cornets and lutes, the usual delighted greeting from Roderigo, I found myself in yet another ballroom, this one at least as large and fine as the one to which Father had taken me the day he informed me I was to join the infantry.

In fact, for all I know, it was the same ballroom and the same senator. After five years of living in army barracks I could not make myself care about any of this frippery. Shortly before our arrival there had been fireworks in the adjoining campo, followed by a human pyramid; the guests had only just been ushered back into the hall, and now everyone was eagerly awaiting a Ruzante comedy about peasants performing improper acts with livestock. Actual livestock—although nothing larger than a goat—was being herded into one corner of the marble-floored room, and to cover the moment, the sackbut player was doing a solo rendition of a Willaert piece, the effect being that of an amorous weasel.

I looked around, hoping to see her, but Roderigo was the only figure I could recognize. He and my brother were among the few nonpatrician merchants who "deserved" to be at this masque, which meant excellent business opportunities for them.

THE NEXT HOUR was excruciating. Emilia wasn't there; I could feel her absence in my lungs. Despite my mask, my identity was no secret; I was identified by scores of people I had never met. I was treated as if I were an exotic feathered bird, and Roderigo was being subtly congratulated for having tethered me. On top of which, I had to watch some very bad actors pretend to do questionable things to goats while speaking trippingly in verse. The goats smelled almost as bad as the actors did but were more authentic in their performance. This was followed (to cover the cleaning up of goat scat) by a Luzzaschi tune, which did nothing to improve my mood.

At about the time I felt I needed a vat of wine to regain my humor, Roderigo eagerly steered me toward a dining table that had just been set up near one wall. More notably, he was steering me toward a large gentleman in an extravagant half-mask and expensive velvet costume. The fellow was already tucking into the gilded oysters making up the first course of the feast. "You will never believe who this is," Roderigo whispered delightedly in my ear, "or how he treats me now." And then raising his voice, he held out an arm and declared, "Tasso! Such a joy to find you here tonight!"

It was the nasty fellow from the neighborhood militia who had mocked him, five years earlier, and then falsely claimed that he could get him gunpowder. Tasso looked up from the oyster he'd been contemplating, recognized the speaker's voice, and smiled. With a small salute, he returned, "My darling Roderigo, the evening would not be complete without you."

"Look whom I have brought." Roderigo preened and presented me before himself as if I were a shy child. This gesture caught the notice of those just taking their seats around the table and—again—I found myself the center of attention among strangers.

"Tasso," I said quietly, with a bow of my head. Grudgingly, sensing it was what Roderigo wanted, I sat beside the fellow, and Roderigo sat to my other side. That Tasso now seemed friendly toward Roderigo did not impress me. In fact, given my mood, and my conditioned impulse to protect hapless Roderigo, I found Tasso's behavior highly suspect.

The expression revealed in the lower half of Tasso's face suggested I was exactly the man he'd been waiting five years to greet. "Iago!" he cried and held out his thick arms wide in greeting. "Welcome back to society!"

"Good evening, Tasso," I said coldly, without leaning toward his intended embrace. "Are you still lying to my friend Roderigo here? I am a master swordsman now, you know. I'll run you through if you ever try again to cheat this man."

The crowd of masked, cloaked figures had taken their seats. They tittered, and several even politely applauded. That was odd.

Tasso immediately laughed the hollow Venetian laugh I dislike. "What a loyal friend you are, Iago, to bear a grudge over a little jest five years dead! Keep this fellow close to your heart, Roderigo, do you hear?"

"It has nothing to do with Roderigo's heart; I am making a comment on your character," I retorted in a somber voice.

Tasso paused unsurely, aware that a score of masked faces were staring at the unmasked half of his face. How, I wondered, were they going to eat their oysters while wearing masks and gloves?

Finally, Tasso shrugged and declared, "My business is in ships, dear Iago. There is no way I could possibly cheat my good friend Roderigo even if I wished to, which I do not." He brought the gilded oyster to his mouth and triumphantly devoured it.

"Are you in shipping?" I asked. "Could you not easily overcharge him?"

"I *build* the ships, sir," Tasso said, with an affected gallant air, as if he had just bested me in a battle of wits but was too polite to rub my nose in it.

"Really?" I said, thinking of the sweating, burly men who had awed me, *building ships*, my first day within the Arsenal walls. "What tools do you use to build a ship?"

He chuckled indulgently. "By that I mean, of course, I hire men to build ships for my company. I do not build the ships *myself.*"

"Then why did you say you did?" I demanded. "Why do you Venetian gentlemen never say a damned thing that you mean? Has it been bred out of you? Your workers—who are men, as much as you are—*they* build ships. *You* do not build ships. You enable ships to be built, which is not the same thing."

The audience of *Bauta* masks tittered, and gloved hands applauded me—which again I found odd, and somewhat unnerving.

I pulled my mask off. Sun-baked as I was, I must have looked very ugly, but I did not care. The audience of diners applauded again, this time heartily, their gilded oysters still sitting on their plates like golden jelly. I stared at them with frustrated bewilderment. A hoarse male voice called out, from the head of the table, "That's quite a compliment, Tasso, to be treated to the attentions of a known truth-teller."

I turned in the direction of the voice. "I'm not complimenting him," I said.

"It is a compliment to him to receive your noncompliment," the speaker explained indulgently. He stood up and I saw him now, a monstrously fat old man, wearing colors too bright for his size. "He is worthy to receive your attention, and your attention, Iago, is exotic here," he said.

"What does that mean, *worthy* to receive my attention?" I was almost spitting now. "I do not want to talk to him, isn't that clear from *how* I'm talking to him?"

"You are talking to him more than to the rest of us," the elder pointed out, sounding pleased that now *he* was the one in the bear pit.

"I do not especially want to talk to the rest of you either," I said, with an emphatic gesture that tumbled my mask out of my hand to the floor. Roderigo immediately stooped in his chair to pick it up. "There. Does that make you feel special, sir?"

"I am already special, Iago," the older man said with unnerving complacency. "I am the man who made you famous."

I suddenly recognized the voice. This was Pietro Galinarion, the

owner of the famous hen. Seeing my startled expression, he continued, gravely and smug: "I have bragging rights to being the earliest
victim of your precociousness. The more popular you and your precociousness are, the better that serves me."

The table denizens tittered yet again and applauded. Tasso was
beaming beneath his mask. It seemed that Bait the Curmudgeon was
the new pastime for bored patricians. I did not want to play.

THE NEXT QUARTER HOUR I spent in a fog of irritation. I insulted
Galinarion; I was applauded. I threw my mask into the punch bowl;
I was applauded. I reprimanded the entire table for how mindlessly
they were applauding everything; I was applauded. I stormed out of
the hall, to applause, and left the grand house through the back steps
and the servants' entrance, imagining Emilia was there to see my
righteous indignation, and desperate to find her in the carousing city.

Roderigo had wanted to follow me, but I gave him a warning
glance, and he—alone of all the people there—understood how
upset I was. He relented. I appreciated that so much, I almost told
him to come after all.

I STORMED AROUND the streets of Venice aimlessly, trying to walk
off my ill humor in the crowded, noisy walkways. People crossed ex-
citedly from one ball to another, singing or shouting out things they
would never dared say in sunlight while unmasked. Some stumbled
happily down avenues and alleys, staggeringly drunk. There were
scores of parties tonight in the city; somewhere, in one of them,
Emilia must be dismissing all her suitors. How might I guess at
which one to find her?

Having nothing to go on, deduction was my only hope. We had
at least some acquaintances in common, or we would not have been
invited to the same party the night before. I presumed that hers was
not the wealthiest of families, so I made a calculation: which of our
family friends was well off enough to host a Carnival masque, but

only one of modest means? Once this would have been Roderigo's family, but his intrigues now put them in much finer circumstances. So I guessed another family, the Molins. I oriented myself: I was north of Campo San Polo. So I crossed cobbled streets and over bridges with purpose now, heading generally south, to see if there was a party at the Molins', just west of the campo.

To my joy, there was. I had no invitation, but it was late enough in the evening that the servants at the entrance were drunk, and they were startled by my military garb. They stood there, staring, as I brushed past them and up the stone staircase, where a pantomime had just concluded in the broad, tapestry-lined, underlit and over-heated hall.

I saw her instantly, through a mass of young partygoers, although she was in the opposite corner of the room. It was the same gown, the same *Moretta* mask, the same coiffure. All of these things pointed to a modesty of means, which was promising; a wealthy family would never allow a soldier, even a petty officer, near their daughter.

My entrance was so abrupt, my jerkin so stern-looking, and my appearance taken as disheveled, that the population of the party— less powdered and poofy than the earlier ball—gave me their full attention, assuming I was there to raise an alarm. "Good evening," I boomed. "Joyous Carnival to all of you!"

Jollity returned. Cries of "Welcome, Iago!" were interrupted by the drunken demand: "What's happened to your *mask*?" from the middle of the hall.

"I outgrew it," I retorted. The partygoers tittered slightly, and turned away to resume their own conversations. How refreshing: here, I would not stand out freakishly. These folk were the model of another Venetian tendency I normally disliked but now was grateful for: perfect self-absorption. A few eyes stayed on me out of curiosity, but otherwise I was just another reveler.

A reveler making straight for a particular woman.

Emilia seemed startled by the intensity of my approach and

glanced to either side, aware that she was literally cornered. I felt my palms sweat and could feel my pulse quicken inside my ears.

"Good evening, disdainful lady," I said, with an ironic bow. Behind me I heard servants pulling out trestle tables; supper would be served soon.

I saw her eyelids blink a few times rapidly through the eyeholes of her mask. "You assume I am disdainful before we've even spoken? You must have been chatting with a fellow I met last night."

"I have no idea what you're talking about."

"Really? A fellow about your height and build, hanging about with libertines and slanderers and dullwits?"

"If I ever meet the fellow, I'll tell him what you think of him."

"Oh, do not, it would break his heart. Although I suppose that way at least he'd lose his appetite, and that would save our hosts a partridge wing or two. I can't say they've overstocked the dining table."

"You owe me a dance," I said abruptly, and felt myself redden.

She smiled behind her mask; I could see it in the shape of her face. "Are you not at all surprised I knew who you were? You were masked last night."

"I am, like yourself, dressed the same as I was last night. You saw the same man walking toward you. Masks never really hide much."

"That has always been my opinion too," she said.

"Then you may as well take yours off," I suggested.

"On the contrary," she answered, "if it's not hiding much, there's not much to reveal, so why bother? The ribbon is all caught up in my hair."

I glanced involuntarily at her hair, just behind her ear, at the nape of her neck, and imagined helping her untangle the ribbon from the hair. It was a romantic—in fact, erotic—moment of imagining. Her laughter interrupted it.

"Have you any idea how transparent you are?" she teased. "I know exactly what you're thinking at this moment."

"And do you approve of what I'm thinking?" I asked, knowing she could see me blush.

"More than my parents would, if they saw me talking to an unmasked wild man who does not fit their merchants' notion of whom I should be talking to."

I felt victorious: my imagined biography of her was accurate. "They want to marry you off to someone boring."

"Not a particular someone," she clarified. "There is an array of someones to choose from."

"Then what is the deciding criterion?"

She shrugged, and looked away into the room. Without my noticing, the pantomime had finished, and now some acrobatic clowns were working their way across the hall. "My parents lack imagination and humor, so they do not value those qualities in me. They would like to find somebody to whom I may be useful, but they can't quite figure out what I'd be useful for."

I was brazen: I eyed her slender, curving body up and down with undisguised desire. "I can think of something you'd be very useful for."

To my great relief, she merely chuckled and crossed her arms over her chest, as she had the night before. "So it's true what they say about you: you really do just blurt out whatever comes into your mind to say."

"How . . . do you know who I am?"

She gestured around the room. "A dozen people called your name when you walked in here, and you wear a soldier's garb. Of course I know who you are." She sobered. "I'm sorry for your father's recent passing."

"Thank you," I said awkwardly, suddenly feeling—ironically— exposed.

"My father is a wheat merchant," she said. "His cousin is a very successful designer of Carnival costumes, it is the only reason my family is included in any of these festivities. I don't belong in this world any more than you do." She gave me a look that, even through the mask's expressionless eyeholes, pierced right into my soul.

"Do you wish you *did* belong here?" I asked, holding the gaze.

"Absolutely not," she said immediately.

"Then marry me," I said.

Chapter 10

THERE WAS A PAUSE. It was a long one. Emilia looked away. I felt myself first blush, and then turn pale. I could read nothing of her expression from around the edges of the mask, nor from her body language.

"I'm sorry," I stammered. "That was a ridiculous proposition. I would try to pass it off as a jest, but that would be insulting to you, and we both know I meant it honestly."

"My parents will be looking for me," she said softly. "They are expecting me to meet them by the door. I hope"—now she looked back at me—"in all sincerity, sir, I hope our paths cross again soon, and perhaps at greater leisure."

"Please forgive my—"

"There's nothing to forgive," she said. "You have given me something to think about. Unlike you, I do *not* blurt out whatever comes into my mind. Women are not allowed such behavior."

"So you are not rejecting my proposal?" I pressed, wishing I was not saying the words even as I heard myself say them.

"For your own sake, I am going to forget you made it," she said. "If, having overcome your impulse to be somebody's paladin, and if having gotten to know me with any kind of depth—having a passing acquaintance with my face, for example—you still feel compelled to make such a suggestion . . . proposition me then."

* * *

IT TOOK ME until noon the next day to get dressed. I lay in bed, disgusted with myself for behaving precisely the way a spoiled young Venetian gentleman would behave if he were mooning over a lady he desired. But I could not stop thinking of her. I did not know her well enough to obsess about anything in particular; I did not even have a face to dwell moodily upon—and yet I could not stop thinking of her. Her voice, her hair, the shape of her body, and her words. Her words, her words, her words. I could not get them from my mind. I lay on my feather mattress beneath silk drapes and stared out at the transom window of my rose-painted room. The sky mocked me with its brilliance. I parsed and reparsed each sentence I could remember with all the skills I'd ever learned as a battlefield tactician. I could not decide what she thought of me.

I must have looked so hideously ugly, compared to all the others in the room. My face is nothing handsome to begin with, plus between soldiering and neglecting my cosmetic toilette, I am weathered and darkened beyond my age, and I stand out even on the streets in daytime for having not the slightest styled coiffure to my battle-ready hair. Dust-colored curls surround my face, hardly darker than the face itself. I must have looked horrendously unkempt. How ridiculous to imagine that she fancied me. She did not. So there was absolutely no reason to get out of bed.

On the other hand, she spoke with me more willingly than she had with anyone at the first evening's party. So perhaps she fancied me a little. But that had been before my mask came off. The night I did not wear the mask, *that* night she rejected my proposal and did not even allow me the dance I felt I was owed. Given her class, she had far more men to choose from than patrician daughters, who were limited to marrying among those families with the right pedigrees. She could have anyone. Just because two nights in a row there was no man she fancied more than me did not mean she fancied me at all. Nor did it mean she wouldn't find, before the end of Carnival, some handsome man to fancy. So there was absolutely no reason to get out of bed.

And even if she fancied me, what then? I could not deserve to keep her interest. When I thought she was a prostitute, it had been easy to banter with her; even when I realized she wasn't, that breezy beginning to our discourse had allowed me to continue the playful chatter. But the moment I realized my heart was thudding for her, I'd become irritable and clumsy with words, and remained so all the next day until I saw her again—at which point, despite a few rounds of decent repartee (which I recounted to myself ad nauseam to reassure myself that yes, I had been charming for a moment), I was so unbalanced that I demanded that she marry me without my having even seen her face. Extended time in her company would render me ridiculous and speechless, and she would grow disappointed with me, and I would lose her love. So there was absolutely no reason to get out of bed.

I WAS FINALLY roused for dinner by a servant. We ate with Mother and my silent sister-in-law as Rizardo informed me there was another masque to attend that evening.

"Really?" I said. "*Another* one? I cannot believe the accursed superciliousness of this city!"

"You don't need to believe it, but you do need to attend," my brother said curtly. "Especially this one, as it is at the Confraternity. I would appreciate it if you could keep your mask on, or at least not throw it in the punch bowl when you decide to take it off."

"I need to get out of this city," I said. "I need to get back to a posting and play cards with people who get dirt under their fingernails."

"I do not disagree," Rizardo said humorlessly, "but you won't be doing that before nightfall, so please cooperate with the servants this time and allow them to find you something decent to wear."

I did so, but on principle I kept my dagger, sheathed, at my belt.

THIS MASQUE WAS at the Confraternity of San Rocco, of which my brother and Roderigo were both members. The wealthiest of all Venetian confraternities (or poorest, depending on who was describing it), San Rocco featured two halls large enough for balls; tonight we were to entertain ourselves in the upper hall, which was hung with decorative tapestries that hid, among other things, a wooden altar and several recent painting by Tintoretto (although his better work was in another room—*Flight into Egypt*, the title of which struck me as an excellent undertaking). The gala was attended by more youths and maidens than I'd ever seen assembled outside a Grecian fresco. I fretted about this because the flirtation levels promised to be astronomical.

She was there, of course.

THIS TIME SHE was surrounded by a conspiracy of young men. And she seemed to be engaging, willingly, in conversation with them. That was disastrous. She was the only female in their troop, which was not true of most other troops of young people scattered around the room. I suddenly could not breathe well. My aging mother had an aging lapdog, who when asleep sometimes would yap helplessly from a dream it could not escape. I felt like that lapdog now. The most I would possibly be able to manage, if I could even get near Emilia, was a yap.

This was jealousy, and it was new to me. Resentment I was used to, having been weaned on it within the family, but not jealousy. While I had often been unhappy with my lot, I had never actually coveted what somebody else had—until right now, when I was jealous of every man in that group for having her attention. It was the most atrocious sensation I had ever felt, as if some tiny monster were crawling around within my guts while somehow sending spasms of shock through my limbs, my throat, making everything inside me tighten, tight as a drum, twisting everything inside me into a knot.

Ignoring the screeching actors in an offensive comedy about a Nubian and his albino bride, I forced myself to walk calmly in her direction. The other men sensed but pointedly ignored the presence of a new rival; Emilia herself, though, did look up at me, and stopped in the middle of whatever she was saying.

"Good evening, Iago," she said neutrally. "Do you have the pleasure of these other gentlemen's acquaintances?"

"If their presence interferes with my having a dance with you, my lady, I can't say it would be a pleasure to be acquainted with any of them," I said, the words sounding echoing and far away from my own ears. *Stop being an ass*, I ordered myself. *You sound petulant.*

The men in their slashed and puffed velvet all exchanged glances behind their masks. They knew who I was; I had a reputation now, inflated or otherwise; they had not known I fancied Emilia, but they must know that I was a wild and unpredictable rascal, based on my behavior at the senator's ball the night before. Or so I assumed.

But to my surprise, each nodded, as if sharing an unspoken thought, and each took a step back from Emilia, giving me space to approach closer to her.

"If the lady is spoken for by a gentleman of your standing, we yield the floor, of course," one of them said, speaking for all. With delicate bows and gentle kissing of her hand, the men all quickly excused themselves, leaving Emilia and myself alone. I was astonished.

She looked up at me, her eyes glittering sharply behind the mask. "That is an efficient way of getting rid of your competition."

"Are they my competition?" I demanded.

"They had all hoped to dance with me, if that is what you mean."

That's not what I mean, I wanted to say, but I bit my tongue, not wanting to add petulance upon petulance. I heard my own breath inside my skull, quick and shallow; I felt unwell, and if it were not for fear of losing her company, I'd have sought an empty room somewhere to lie down. I managed to pull my wits about me and said, holding out my hand, "Allow me to make it up to you by dancing with you now."

She thought about it for a moment. Then she held out her gloved hand and laid it gently on my ungloved one. The pressure of her fingers touching me was the most remarkable sensation of my entire life. She rose from the bench at which she had been seated. We walked together past several Persian tapestries onto the polished dance floor, where a *chiaranzana* was just beginning. We did not speak; it was as if we had tumbled forward through time and were already a married couple in a pother at each other.

Two dozen other couples joined us, all masked and gloved, which created the eerie effect of phantoms congregating. All I could remember of this dance was that the first verse was exclusively with one's partner, but then it became an ensemble affair, in which each refrain briefly separated the partners to dance with others. "You may need to remind me of the steps," I said grudgingly under my breath. "While all your other wooers have been practicing this vanity, I have been defending our borders in the wilds of Terraferma where we have no such niceties as ballrooms."

She turned her head to look at me directly, and I could see her gaze soften. "That's very brave of you, Iago," she said. "To step out on the dance floor knowing you might blunder. That takes courage."

"Do you think after five years of military duty, a blundered dance step will really try my courage?"

She drew her chin back, chastened. "I suppose not," she said. Then, in a slightly archer tone, "In that case, I suppose you shall not need my assistance after all, for what's a few fumbled dance steps among friends?"

"For the sake of the other dancers, who will be inconvenienced by my blundering, I beseech you to assist me," I said.

"Of course I will," she said, in a tone of casual affection. I melted for her all over again.

We began the dance; the steps returned to me more readily than I'd expected from my awkward adolescent years, despite the sackbut being piercingly too sharp.

"You're doing very well," she said after a while. My pulse quickened.

"As well as your other suitors?"

"Absolutely. No difference."

"Am I like them in other ways as well?" I pressed. "Am I just another possibility who has not yet retreated or been turned away by you?"

"That is a conversation for after the dance, I think," she said.

"Oh, no, lady," I said. "I will not survive this dance if I must worry both about my footing on the dance floor and also my footing with you."

"Fair enough," she said. She took a slow breath in. "You want to feel special," she began. "You want to know that I like you above all others."

"I know what *I* want," I said churlishly as we pressed our raised palms together and pivoted around them. "I want to know what *you* want."

"The others are attractive," she said thoughtfully. We turned away from each other and then back again, to the music. "Some of them have handsomer features than you do, and most of them have better fortunes."

"I know that too," I huffed. "That is not what I asked you."

At that moment in the dance, we had to turn away from each other to dance with someone else. It was torment.

"And?" I said, as soon as we were back together.

"And none of them have disappointed me."

I felt a sick feeling in my stomach. "How have I disappointed you?" I asked; it came out as a strangled whisper.

"I expect nothing from these other men," she said as we once again pivoted around kissing palms. "But I thought I could rely on you to always show me your true face, and here you are tonight wearing a mask."

"I will remove it as soon as I find a punch bowl in which to deposit it."

I could see her smile behind her mask again. "I heard about that," she said. "You certainly do know how to get your name around." We turned away and then back toward each other, hands still touching.

"I do nothing in order to *get my name around*," I said, on the return.

"I know," she said consolingly, which made me feel again that I'd been petulant. "I'll see you in a moment."

Again we turned away from each other, again I somehow survived the turns and footfalls of the dance with some woman I did not know and could barely manage to exchange pleasantries with. And then I was back with my raised palm pressing Emilia's.

"I do like you, Iago," she said quietly. "I like the way I feel in your company. I can imagine sitting down to dinner every day with you for the rest of my life and never wishing I were somewhere else. I have never felt that about another human being, including my own parents."

I was so thrilled, it frightened me. I could not speak.

"Have I answered your question, sir?" she asked at last.

"It is a sufficient answer for now," I was able to say. I heard her chuckle affectionately behind her mask. Oh, my Lord, if only I could see what was behind that mask.

SOMEHOW WE GOT through the rest of the *chiaranzana*. I did not trust myself to speak again; she seemed content with silence when we danced together. I noticed a few times that in her turnabouts with other partners, they would say something to her, and she'd tilt her head back with laughter. That monstrous feeling of jealousy snapped my guts each time she did so.

The dance finally completed, she invited me with a glance to step through some heavy woolen tapestries out to the balcony with her, to avoid another pantomime. We overlooked a moonlit alleyway, and nobody else was out here. It was brisk, but the cold was a welcome change. The tapestries hushed the noise of the crowd within; we were thrillingly alone. In the moonlight. Alone. On a balcony. Alone. "Your servant ever," I said, and untied my mask, letting it hang loose from its lanyard around my neck.

"I should return the favor, so you know whom you serve," she said. "But my hair and the ribbon are all entwined. If you have any steel on you, perhaps you can simply cut the ribbon for me."

Is it some perversion in me to have found this request erotic? I pulled my dagger from its sheath, which was tucked into my belt. I saw her eyes study the metal as I held it up before her.

"Do you trust me with it?" I asked.

Her eyes moved toward mine. "Entirely," she said.

Trembling, I reached toward her temple and took hold of the ribbon near the mask. I pulled it away from her temple, which pressed the mask closer against her face. Very carefully, trying not to be distracted by feeling her breath on my neck, I placed the point of the dagger against the ribbon, and snapped the ribbon with my blade. Her hand flew up to the mask to hold it steady in place, and she turned her head to expose the other side to me. I cut this side as well, then sheathed my dagger. With the ribbon still entangled in her hair, she lowered the mask and looked at me.

Hers was the loveliest face I had ever seen in my life. It was quietly perfect—nothing unusual, nothing startling, simply right, everywhere, every angle, every pore, every eyelash. Her eyes were hazel, placed just right, just the right size and just the right distance apart. It was so thrilling to see her face, the effect on me was as if she'd just disrobed.

"My God you're beautiful," I said breathily.

She smiled and looked down. "Thank you," she said. "I believe I am quite average."

"Nothing about you is average, it is all superlative," I said.

She looked back up at me. "I think I have to say the same of you."

"Have you ever considered the life of a soldier's wife?" I asked.

She laughed. "Only since I met you."

"And what are your considerations?"

"It would have to be the right soldier."

"I just made officer last month."

"I didn't say the right rank, I said the right soldier."

I wanted her so badly that I could not bear it. Abruptly, suddenly, in a rush, it seemed to be much easier to scare her off than to pursue this and risk my entire well-being. "It is a hard life," I warned, "Nothing like living in Venice. Everything is very rough and primitive. I am very rough and primitive."

"If you, in your person, reflect the life you offer, I find it attractive."

"No, no, that's not what I meant," I said, blushing, stumbling over my words. "I meant . . . I don't know what I meant. My lady, you have robbed me of my wit. I can't *speak* in your presence."

She smiled, looking genuinely puzzled by this. "Why?" she asked.

I had never had fewer coherent thoughts available to me. "I am used to wanting something and not having it. My career has been negotiated entirely by my father, for example, regardless of my wishes. But I have never in my life wanted anything so deeply, as what I crave right now, which is your company, forever, every day for the rest of my life. I believe that you are on the edge of offering it to me, that it *might* happen. That *might* undoes me. Denied this, I would feel so deeply robbed, the pain would warp my character and turn my regard for you to violent fury."

She considered this a moment, as if she found it droll. "Are you saying you'd want to kill me if I did not cleave to you?"

"Of course not," I stammered. "I mean . . . if you are merely being playful with me, tell me now. I cannot keep this light between us."

"That's good, for I am not a light woman, regardless of what you first thought of me." She smiled.

"If there is any part of you that thinks you might find a lover elsewhere, leave this balcony right now and go to find him," I ordered in a choked voice. "In fact, do me a favor and do that anyhow. Spare me from the dizziness your presence causes. You should marry somebody who does not have such monstrous capacity for passion." I closed my eyes and made myself continue speaking, feeling as if I might retch. "My friend Roderigo is looking for a wife, you know, and he is very wealthy."

"The only thing your friend Roderigo has going for him is that he is your friend," Emilia said pertly.

"There are others I could introduce you to," I managed to choke out. "Even some of my fellow soldiers are Venetian, if you are inclined that way."

She gave me a troubled, confused look. "I thought you wanted me," she said. "You just *said* you wanted me."

"But I can't stand the thought you might not want me too," I said, and wished I could have died on the spot.

"Have I said anything to imply that?" she demanded. "Have I not rather said just the opposite? While we were dancing? Was I not clear?"

"Did you *mean* it?" I demanded, grabbing her slender arms. A callus on my thumb caught on her silk sleeve; I noticed it more than she did.

"Why would I *say* it if I didn't *mean* it?" she demanded in exasperation.

"Because since you said it, you have surely changed your mind, as I am proving to be such an awkward jealous blunderer," I said.

She smiled at once and laughed gently. "I would not trust any man who could stand before me now and speak his feelings honestly, as you have, without blundering at least a little. I would not trust you if you did not blunder. Thank you, Iago, for blundering. It reassures me of your sincerity, and I find you all the more attractive for it."

So there was nothing that I had to prove to her. She knew me already better than I could have described myself—better than I *would* have described myself. I was imperfect, and it did not trouble her. Had anyone, ever, in the history of my life, been so indulgent?

"You are a perfect human being," I gushed.

Her eyes widened in alarm. "No, I'm not, Iago, do not saddle me with such an impossible responsibility!"

"May I enjoy the illusion of your perfection at least for this evening?"

"Only if you promise not to punish me when you realize I'm not."

"Do you think I would do that?" I protested.

She gave me a long, appraising look. I felt as if I'd known this woman all my life, and more than that: I felt as if she knew me. Better than any other person ever had.

"Yes, I think it is a possibility in you," she said frankly. "Just as you were punishing yourself for not being my perfect wooer, and just as you punish others with harsh words when they displease you—I think you have the capacity to be harsh to me when I fall off the pedestal you're trying very hard to put me on."

I grabbed her hands—her mask clattered to the balcony floor—and held them in both of mine. "I promise not to put you on a pedestal," I said.

"Iago, you already have," she said patiently.

"Then let's tear down that pedestal together," I urged, having no idea what practical application could be had from that. A woman who truly did not want to be placed on a pedestal! All the more reason to adore her!

I WAS A man of action, a man of study, a man of purpose and ambition. I needed to have things to *do* all day—lying about and sighing for a woman was utterly unlike me, utterly unlike the image I had of myself. But there I was the next day and the next, lying about and sighing. Books were unread, blades unsheathed, chess pieces unmoved. I did not like who I was becoming, how my time in Venice was softening me, making me prone—literally—with ridiculous preoccupations. That was not the kind of man I had grown to become.

AND THEN AN invitation arrived. It was delivered by a boy in livery, addressed to me care of my brother. It was from Emilia's father.

He was inviting me to dine with the family the following evening, at their home in Cannaregio. This meant I had to live through an entire day, an evening, and then a second day before I could see her again. *What can I really offer her?* I whined to myself, staring out the window like the clichéd Venetian youth in love. Although I was a petty officer, I had no posting, I was not currently employed, so my rank was abstract, conceptual. But it was also all I had for social equity. I went to my brother, who sat working in what I still thought of as Father's office. I told him about Emilia, and my intentions.

To my surprise, Rizardo was pleased for me. I think all he wanted for his truculent younger brother was that I prosper. Career satisfaction and a wife both seemed un-Iago-like attainments, so surely (he must have thought) I was evolving into somebody better than myself—somebody more like him. So it was easy for him to be pleased.

THE DAY PASSED somehow, the evening too, and even the next day. When finally the shadows lengthened, I dressed in my red-and-white-striped jerkin and combed my short hair. I walked, carrying a lamp, the half mile of the journey. I kept my boots clean, and the exercise of it was good for me. Up through San Rocco and San Croce, crossing the westernmost bridge of the Grand Canal, then doubling back east and north, to Calle Riello, through alleyways and across campi, on the coldest evening we had had all year. Everyone in the streets was heading in the opposite direction, toward the Rialto or San Marco square, for more Carnival spectacles. As I walked on, every conceivable thought went through my head, and every conceivable emotion clutched my stomach.

EMILIA'S PARENTS WERE almost aggressively bland. Both of them were ginger-haired and hazel-eyed, which explained her coloring; her slenderness came from her father and her curves from her mother. Our introductions in the antechamber of the modest great-room were unremarkable. Emilia, dressed in dark blue wool, watched with smiling eyes and a very composed face as I bowed to her father and kissed her mother's hand. They welcomed me to their humble home (it's true, it was quite humble—and made of wood), and invited me upstairs to hall for dinner. I had never been invited to a home in Venice to have a private dinner with another family.

The staircase was polished inlaid wood—attractive, but still wood. In our house, nothing but furniture and occasionally wall panels was made of wood. The hall here lacked the lofty ceilings I was used to; the tapestries were mostly flax, attractive but unoriginal. I smiled politely, aware that Emilia was waiting to see if I would judge her for her family's modest means. I had always known myself to be an intellectual snob; this was the first time I'd ever faced the possibility I was perhaps a social snob as well. I was too ashamed to admit to myself that I might be.

The table was set and waiting for us. From the aromas rising from the kitchen, I could tell the main course would be fish. The room was lit entirely with candles—that was an expense for them, surely, but the effect was beautiful and softly romantic.

Her parents' attitude toward me, from the moment we sat down, bespoke a pragmatism tinged with either curiosity or impatience—as if the unspoken message of the evening was: "Are you *sure* you want to marry her? If so, let's get on with it." I sensed they wanted to know by the end of the evening if I would be The One, because if not, they wanted to get a jump on making other plans. Whether I was well suited for her, or would make a loving husband, or even if she cared enough for me—these details were never probed.

This distressed me, for it reminded me of my father trying to arrange my life without regard for what would make me happy; my life was a business transaction and was to be handled efficiently. These people treated Emilia in the same manner, and so I felt protective toward her. She radiated pleasure and contentment during dinner, however; if that is indeed how her parents managed her life, she either did not mind it as I did, or hid her resentment much better than I could. I doubted it was the latter. She was simply more at peace in the world than I was. Inspired, I smiled at her often rather than growling at her father, as I wanted to.

After dinner, we gentlemen retired to her father's study, which adjoined the great room. It was unremarkable and dominated by a wooden desk. He encourage me to sit, and then with a preparatory intake of breath, he began:

"Emilia is a decent cook, and I think she'd make any man a good wife, although she is better at cleaning than at tidying. From what we can tell she would be an excellent hostess of parties and events, which is why, although we have a decent enough dowry to offer, we are not adverse to her being taken on as a mistress, for in many ways she'd make a better mistress than a wife, given that she can throw a party better than she can clean it up. So if you're already promised to somebody, or your brother has a profitable match in store for you, but you are interested in Emilia, she may still be available, provided you can offer assurance that you would not return her to us if your wife insisted on it. But I'd need to know your intentions quickly, because there are a number of gentlemen, including a patrician's son, who have expressed an interest in her as a mistress if you don't want her. She's rejected all of them so far, but that just makes their friends and associates more intrigued, so I expect they will be presenting themselves to me soon. It's a relief to have her actually interested in somebody, and my strong preference is for you to have her, but again, sir, it would be very inconvenient for us if you cannot make your mind up quickly."

He finally paused.

I blinked. My head was spinning like a whirligig. I had only re-entered into Venetian society four days ago, and already I was exposed to outright madness. On the one hand, it was certainly as blunt and honest as anything I'd ever said, but it absolutely lacked humanity. Were all discussions of marriage like this? I suddenly wished I'd asked my brother for advice. "Don't you want to know what kind of life I'd offer her?" I said.

He shrugged. "She knows you're a soldier, does she not? If she's not bothered by it, I am not either."

I blinked, incredulous at his offhandedness. "She is a young woman, caught up in her emotions, and perhaps misjudges what is best for her. Is it not your business as her father to look at what I offer with objective, weighty measuring?"

Again he shrugged. "I'm responsible to get her married, she's responsible for what she makes of it," he said agreeably.

I felt hugely indignant on Emilia's behalf. "You know I have received my officer's commission," I announced. "That greatly improves my living conditions wherever I am posted, so she need not be discomfited by her surroundings."

"That's good," he said indulgently. "Then you've just proved I don't need to worry about her making the wrong choice. She's yours if she'll have you, sir, and I'd be very pleased about it. Truly her mother and I thought we would never get her to agree to anyone."

"Thank you, sir," I said uncertainly.

"Oh, no, thank *you*, sir," he replied heartily, and shook my hand.

Unsettled by this encounter, I left him in the study and went back to Emilia and her mother in the great-room. "May I have the honor of a word alone with your daughter?" I asked my future mother. The lady said of course, and happily humming to herself, she scurried back toward the kitchen.

I stood by the open window and pushed the tapestry away, needing air. I gestured Emilia to come near to me. Smiling, she rose from the table and did so. She looked so lovely in the candlelight.

"I have had a very strange conversation with your father," I began. She laughed.

"I'm sure you did," she said. "He seldom has any other kind."

"Among other things I was not expecting to hear, he offered you up as my mistress. In case I wanted to marry somebody richer later on. He is fine with that, so long as I'd still keep you as my mistress."

"How very considerate of him," she said with her sweet small laugh. "I'd rather be your mistress, Iago, than anybody else's wife."

After taking a moment to steady myself from that declaration, I said, "I cannot afford to keep a mistress."

She leaned in toward me so that our faces were nearly touching. "Well, in that case, you'd better marry me, do not you think?" she whispered.

I finally dared to kiss her. It was delicious. She kissed me back, and when I wrapped my arms around her she pressed into me so hard she nearly backed me against the wall. A week ago, I had not known of her existence; now I could not imagine life without it.

THE WORST THING about being married is that one must have a wedding first. We were all in agreement that we wanted to keep it small and simple, but small and simple in Venetian terms is still Venetian. Both houses obligingly hung tapestries in all the windows. At the church overlooking Emilia's campo, I went to meet her, with her gorgeous auburn mane hanging loose over a white dress; she was surrounded by female friends and relatives I'd never met and hardly ever saw again, none of them anything close to her in beauty or wit. Roderigo and my family were all the witnesses I brought. After we exchanged vows, we repaired to her parents' home for a reception, which consisted mostly of everyone getting drunk on Lagryme di Christo (a Venetian specialty). This was on the second day of February, Candlemas, the day on which—it is said, at least in Venice—you can begin to tell the days are growing longer in anticipating spring. She chose this day specifically, she told me, "Because you have brought the sunlight to my life."

IF THE LORD gave me the chance to freeze time, I would freeze it there, the moment after she made that declaration. Even if it meant there never was a wedding and I never had the chance to know her as a wife, even if it meant I never had a chance to prove myself as a commissioned officer. She was the best soul I had ever known, and it was I who brought the sunlight to her life. What higher peak is there to ascend to?

Chapter 11

WITHIN A WEEK of our wedding I signed a contract with the army—an officer's contract—and immediately after that I received my new posting, which would send me to Stato da Màr, the seaward face of the Venetian empire. Emilia and I spent the next two years on Corfu.

An army posting on Corfu, even for an officer, hardly differs from an army posting out in the far western reaches of Terraferma. My lodgings were better, and of course I shared my bed and my meals and my free hours with a woman I continued to consider the greatest prize any man could ever win.

My days were duties (more interesting than they'd been before, and fewer hours on guard duty), continuing my fencing studies, and teaching others how to shoot. I still read a lot, and played chess, with officers and with Emilia, who had no knack for it but was always happy to try. She befriended the wives of the higher-ranking officers, no matter their background—most officers were not Venetians but mercenaries from all different backgrounds. She would patiently practice the Venetian dialect with them, teach them dance steps and table manners, and in all ways prepare them to blend into "society" should their husbands ever find themselves in Venice. The aging patrician commissioners who were here fulfilling their civic obligations were happy to have dance partners less than half their age. I commented, more than once, on the irony that Emilia herself had never been all that concerned with blending into "society," and here she was, herself *creating* it.

I was a jealous husband, I admit that. Some of the higher-ranking officers, seeing their wives mincing merrily about the mess hall in the evenings, asked Emilia to show them how they themselves should dance. At least once every week I had to watch her in the arms of some other man—usually of a higher rank than I was—moving about in harmony to a tune that she would hum aloud from memory. They did nothing improper, but I still felt a thrill of nervousness course through me every time she had a dance partner. She teased me for my jealousy and said she liked how, later at night, in bed, I possessed her so intensely.

"Perhaps I should flirt with some of them," she'd whisper as I lay spent and breathing hard on top of her, in the cold dark bedroom on a hard bed with weathered sheets, still inside her, feeling I'd reclaimed her from the world. "Then you would *really* have a go at me.

I'd be walking awkwardly for days, and everyone would know it was because Iago was such a master over his mistress, and they would so envy both of us." The darkness would sparkle with that soft, sweet laugh of hers, and I'd be hard again.

We spoke of children. We knew we wanted, someday, to have a family, but also knew it was not the time. We were too immersed in each other's presence; there was no room yet for a third. "We will get used to each other soon enough," she'd say. "That happens in every marriage I have ever seen. We will bore each other someday, and then it will be time for offspring. That's just how the world works."

TWO YEARS INTO IT, we were not used to each other, and we were not bored, and we were no more inclined to share each other with a child than we'd been on our wedding night. Emilia learned ways to prevent conception; there were concoctions from the older wives of officers, who had in their turn learned it from older wives before them. Once her flux was late and very heavy, and she seemed melancholy for a day or two. "That might have been a babe, but it's good it was not, it's not time yet," was all she said, and smiled and caressed my face. That was the only moment of our time on Corfu that was not perfect domestic bliss.

Professionally, however, it was a time of political upheavals. I will attempt to summarize in a manner that does not seem as if I am inventing or exaggerating. Two officers, let us call them Sforza and Orsini, each wanted to be the highest of the high in the armed forces. Sforza had the higher rank, but Orsini (for reasons too Byzantine to explain here) was in a position to be promoted to a rank above Sforza's, and Sforza didn't like that. As a result, each of them had a secret pact with a different branch of the government that they would never have to be subordinate to the other one. It all got quite out of hand and resulted in Orsini finding some other form of employment, and Sforza leading the cavalry on Terraferma. This created an absence of leadership for the infantry.

Neither man was Venetian, but they were both Italian. The commissioners leaked a rumor that the Senate was looking farther afield for military leaders. If a Greek or Pole or Russian could be hired to lead our troops, then there was no risk they would get caught up in complicated family ties or local political pressures. There was a rumor that the Senate's first choice was a mainlander who believed Venice should seize Rhodes from the Turks. This was a thrilling proposal, but it was in complete opposition to the doge's edict that the last thing the army should attempt was further conquest of any sort.

I was glad these were not my headaches to sort out. As a young ensign, I would not be working directly with the new general anyhow, but I had ambition and intended someday to rank high enough that I might serve near him. I had fought beside Greeks and Poles and Russians, and I would be content with any of them as my commander in chief. I would be equally well-disposed to obey the orders of a Croat, a Spaniard, or even a Christian Turk!

Not that the Senate would ever consider an apostate heathen to govern our armed forces.

Chapter 12

EMILIA AND I RETURNED to Venice near the end of Carnival. I was two years into a three-year contract, and so, until I was posted again, we were quartered at the Dolphin, an inn in the campo just outside the Arsenal gate. The view out our window was almost identical to my first sight of the famously guarded entrance, that hot August afternoon some seven years ago. I marveled almost every morning at what the years had wrought.

* * *

IT WAS PLEASING to live in Venice without living under my family's roof. I liked the city much better when I had only a room, a small closet, and Emilia. Our first week home, we paid dutiful visits to our families. We then burrowed into our lodgings, having brought back the finer outfits from our respective boudoirs.

"We should go out to celebrate Carnival," Emilia said, running her fingers fondly over the red wool skirt I'd first seen her in, the one dear thing her parents had given her.

"I'm sure the styles have changed insufferably in our two years away," I said, looking for an excuse. "If you make an appearance wearing that you will be noted as terribly unfashionable."

"I will be noted as someone who has been abroad long enough for the fashions to change," she countered, now holding up the skirt with nostalgic admiration. "That, I think, shall make me exotic." She glanced over toward me and grinned bewitchingly. "Would you not like to parade your exotic wife around at a few balls?"

This was unlike Emilia. Perhaps, as with my time on Terraferma, absence made her appreciate what she'd left behind. My nostalgia had proven temporary. I hoped that hers would too. "The only thing I ever liked about those balls is that I met you there," I said.

She moved over to the table where I sat with my Aldine octavo of the *Divine Comedy*. She grinned down at me.

"Indulge me. Let us invent our own divine comedy tonight. If you are hating every moment, I promise to flirt with some masked stranger and make you so mad with jealousy that you will drag me home and ride me ferociously for all night, and I'll yield to you completely and beg and beg and beg for more."

"Then why are you not dressed yet, hussy?" I grinned, closing Dante.

WE WORE OUR MASKS, which had each survived Venice in our absence. We had no invitation anywhere. But as an army officer, wearing my ensign's insignia and jerkin, I was welcomed into almost any party. We decided we would wander through the streets of the Rialto at whim and drop into whatever house emanated pleasing music, delicious aroma, or (if we knew them) the hosts.

The first fete we decided to infiltrate was at the home of a patrician named Gratiano, who lived in the best neighborhood of San Polo. Although not a senator, he had a high-ranking post within the government. His event was enormous, spilling out into the campo in front of his palace. Both indoor and out it was brightly lit with chandeliers and braziers and torches and huge, heavy-scented beeswax candles that must have each been equal to Emilia's dowry. There was an impressive acrobatic act on the campo as we arrived—not only the traditional human pyramid but also stilt walking and a contortionist. As the acrobats finished, a hundred sets of gloved hands applauded, and a cornet summoned people back indoors. We simply went along with them.

The house resembled the setting of any other ball, except for a trio of young men passed out in a corner, which seemed graceless in such a setting.

"Have you seen him?" a masked woman with a gravelly, elderly voice asked Emilia as we came in. "I just caught a glimpse of him over by the wine. It's true, what they say."

"What do they say?" Emilia asked, imitating the gossip's eager tone so perfectly I almost started laughing.

"They say it's not a mask at all! They say that is his real face! Can you imagine? So ugly and so dark?"

Emilia and I exchanged glances, and I saw permission glitter in her eye. I reached up to untie my mask.

"I am ugly and dark," I informed the woman, revealing my face to her.

She looked vaguely affronted, but then said impatiently, "You're just sunburned. This man is a different *color*. As if his face was *painted*."

"How shocking," I said, "Nobody ever paints their face in Venice. What could he be thinking?"

"No, it's *not* paint," she explained with exasperation. "That's what is so incredible. Several young men took bets with each other and tried to wipe the paint off, it will not come off!"

I tried to imagine the humiliation of some poor stranger having his face swiped at by a group of drunken youths. "What did he do?" Emilia asked, reading my thoughts.

"Oh, he would not have it!" said the gossip. She pointed to the unconscious trio near the stairway, whom I'd assumed were passed out from drink. "He smashed each one across the pate and knocked them out!"

"Good for him," I said at once. I said it aloud in hopes of inflaming the gossip.

"Absolutely!" she agreed. "Just because he isn't quite human does not mean he should be treated as an animal!"

I felt Emilia stiffen beside me. "What do you mean, he isn't quite human?" she demanded.

"Well, it isn't *human skin*," the masked lady pointed out. "Human skin is not that *color*."

Emilia immediately took my hand and pulled me gently toward the middle of the room. "Iago, I'm very thirsty, please come with me to get some wine."

"Of course," I said, and with a small nod to the woman, I stepped after my wife. Safely away from the gossip, immersed in gowns and masks and fragrances and chitchat, I whispered to her in a tone of mischief, "Were you afraid I was going to torment her, or were you simply so sickened you needed to get away from her?"

"Both," she answered, not amused.

We walked perhaps two dozen paces, down the length of the semicrowded hall; we heard three inane and mystifying conversations about the man whose face was a living mask. I assumed they were commenting on a circus performer.

"They've been having trouble with Italians," an older gentleman was saying to two others and a grey-wigged lady. "Surely you've heard about the manipulations and double-crossings. Shamefully, there are no Italians equal to the task."

"But where did they find him?" the lady asked. "Who gave him the appointment? How do we know he's not a Turk?"

"He's much too dark to be a Turk," one of the gentlemen said.

Emilia and I exchanged glances and slowed our pace.

"Excuse me," I said as we reached them. "May I ask whom you are discussing? I am just arrived from Corfu and I fear I missed some news while I was at sea."

"The Senate has approved a new general," the first speaker said. "He is attending tonight, his first public appearance since he was invested, and he is causing heads to turn."

"Except for those three drunken louts, I must say he is being very good-natured about the scrutiny he is receiving," said one of the others.

"We hear he is not wearing a mask," Emilia said slyly. "Is that why everyone is staring at him?" And with a marvelously wifely glance at me, she added, "Iago, put your mask back on at once. I *told* you not to take it off."

The men chuckled, and I, pretending for Emilia's amusement to be henpecked, hurriedly retied my *Bauta* mask. "It's true he is not wearing a mask," said the second gentleman, "but that is not the cause of the consternation. He is of a different race, and his complexion and his dress make him . . . stand out."

"We've just arrived this moment, so we have not seen him," I said. "Will we recognize him?"

"Oh yes," all four said at once. The first speaker added, with a gesture toward my soldier's jerkin, "You should introduce yourself to him, he is now your commander in chief."

Emilia pretended to find this terribly exciting. "Oh, my goodness, Iago! Behave yourself and you might find yourself promoted to lieutenant before the evening's over!"

"Why is he in Venice now?" I asked the man.

"He's just been officially invested," he explained. "He'd been fighting in the Levant, for different armies, but always against the Turks, at least a decade now. Last year, he was hired as captain of a

Venetian unit out there. He rose in the ranks quite spectacularly, and after this last embarrassment with Orsini and Sforza, the Senate agreed with the Great Council that he would make an ideal candidate for governor-general. He heads to Rhodes next month—"

"Really? I'd heard rumors about trying to take Rhodes from the south," I said.

"Well then," said the third gentleman. "If you know about military matters, you should strike up a conversation with him! Poor fellow is being besieged by repetitively meaningless chatter all evening."

"Does he speak our language?" the lady asked.

"It's accented, but it's understandable," the first gentleman said. He turned to me. "The general might enjoy some conversation of things martial, being so entirely out of place at a gathering of this sort."

To my side, I heard Emilia take a quick breath in, and her hand tightened around my elbow. "Iago, there he is," she whispered. "Look at him. How remarkable!"

I glanced at her—her lower lip was hanging slightly slack behind her mask—then turned to look where she was staring.

A dozen paces away from us, taller than the handful of people in the way, stood a tall, broad-shouldered man whose skin was nearly the same color as his tightly curled black hair. The dimensions of his features were bizarre by Venetian standards—still he struck me as decent to look upon, although his color startled me. As if to emphasize his darkness, he wore an unusual outfit of brilliant white—a long loose tunic, over loose wide trousers. Heavy, simple gold chains of different lengths hung around his neck, and incongruously, a white kerchief with lace and embroidery was tied around his throat. There was no other decoration to his costume, save the ceremonial red-and-white banner of a Venetian general, which draped from his left shoulder to his right hip.

"His name?" I asked.

"Othello," said the older man, respectfully.

The General

Chapter 13

was captivated by the expression on Othello's face: he was entirely out of his element and yet entirely comfortable to be so. He knew everyone was staring at him, but rather than resenting it or squirming with self-consciousness—as I had done when Roderigo was presenting me to strangers—Othello seemed to welcome it as a benign dare: *I am the man charged with keeping your empire intact, so I know you must be decent to me.* He was the living embodiment of confidence—genuine confidence, that rare quality that needs no arrogance to bolster it.

Emilia and I forgot about the people we'd been speaking to and moved together slowly toward him, as if drawn by a magnet, not even realizing we were doing it.

The party's host, Signior Gratiano, approached Othello and greeted him warmly. With Gratiano was his famous cousin, Senator Brabantio, whom he introduced. I did not know Brabantio personally, but he (via his personal tailor) was one of my family's wealthiest customers. I'd heard stories of him from both my brother and Roderigo, and my instinct upon seeing him greet Othello was that he wanted something from the man. Most likely, to shine in his reflected glory.

". . . must come to my house," Brabantio was saying as we reached hearing distance. "My wife has passed, alas, and my only child is shy as a kitten, so will likely not come out of her rooms, but that will give us a chance to speak more freely. I wish to hear your stories—your life has apparently been quite remarkable."

"Tomorrow Othello will not remember Brabantio's name," I predicted quietly as we watched.

"Especially since he cannot even see his face," Emilia commented. Then, glancing around at all the masks: "Or anyone else's."

Inspiration struck. "Guess what I am going to do."

"Shall I untie it for you?" she asked, and reached up for the ribbon to my mask.

"I love how well you know me," I whispered to her.

"And I love knowing you," she whispered back. "You go on. I'll watch. Call me over if you think it's proper, otherwise I shall wait to meet him."

The perfect wife. I had the perfect wife.

Glowing with the pleasure of having the perfect wife, and cocky (or trying to feel cocky) about being the only other unmasked person in the room, as well as the only other military officer, I strode toward the general.

Othello, seeing my military jerkin, grinned—yes, a grin; an innocent, open, trusting, childlike grin, revealing intensely white teeth. Even his lips and gums were dark, which only made his teeth the whiter. The kerchief tied around his neck, I saw now, was emblazoned with embroidered strawberries, and looked out of place. Ignoring Brabantio, he held out both arms toward me; when I offered my right hand to shake, he clasped my entire arm up to the elbow.

"A fellow officer!" he declared. "And you even have your own face!" He laughed. It was a warm, deep laugh, like friendly grunting. His accent was unfamiliar, although I was used to many accents from spending most of the past decade living with foreign mercenaries. "I do not recognize you, friend, from my investiture ceremony."

"I was not present for it, General," I said. "I was en route back to Venice from being stationed at Corfu."

"Corfu!" he said, his eyes lighting up—the whites looking almost opalescent against his skin and irises. "I was at the Siege of

Corfu. I was barely a child. That shows you how old I am, eh? What is your name, my friend?"

"Ensign Iago Soranzo, General," I said, and bowed.

"Iago," he said, almost eagerly. "I do not mind being in a strange place where I am stared at, this I am used to. But I do not like having no other military men about me, it makes me feel almost naked, as if I did not have my sword. You will accompany me for the remainder of the evening."

I tried not to look dazzled by his order. I had never been addressed by any officer above a captain in the whole of my military career. "General, of course, it would be my honor," I replied.

"I am sure you know these gentlemen?" Othello said, referring casually to Gratiano and Senator Brabantio.

"I have the honor of knowing who they are," I said carefully, extremely aware that I had just usurped them both.

"Gentlemen, this is Ensign Iago Soranzo. Iago, introduce yourself."

He was using me to be reminded of who they were, which he had no doubt forgotten in the blur of names.

"Signior Gratiano, it is an honor to meet you," I said, bowing my head. "And likewise, Senator Brabantio." I said both names slowly and distinctly, then looked up at Othello and almost winked.

He gave me an openly conspiratorial grin. "Excellent, well done, Iago," he said. "Very polite man. I like that in an officer. And now, Signior Gratiano and Senator Brabantio, it has been an honor to meet you, and Senator Brabantio, I would be honored to be a guest in your house, and Signior Gratiano, I thank you for this marvelous party you are having for me, where nobody has any faces, and now I need a moment with my ensign to discuss military matters."

He called me his ensign. *His* ensign. It was said lightly, in the moment, to excuse himself from yet two more aging patricians he was tired of being ogled by, but still . . . my heart raced. "Come, Iago," he said, as if we had been friends for years. "Let us get some fresh air on the balcony and talk about the fortifications on Corfu." He took my arm and plucked me along with him. I glanced over my shoulder and gave Emilia an amazed look.

She mimed applause, gave me a quick wave, and swiftly moved toward a group of women about her age, excitement in her step. I loved that woman.

I followed Othello out through heavy tapestries onto the broad, chill, well-lit balcony. "Thank you, Ensign, for freeing me," he said and released a long sigh. "My goodness, there is no air in that room at all."

"I am honored to be of service to you, General," I said. "I hope you do not find them rude."

"Not rude, no, just a little . . . uninspiring, eh?" He glanced at me, grinned, nudged me with his elbow, and laughed that amazing bass laugh. "Do you not find it is hard to return from a battleground and spend all day around such men?"

"I've never—" I stopped myself. I was about to say "I've never been in battle," but that seemed an unwise thing to tell one's commander in chief, when one's commander in chief had just taken such an interest in one, and one was ambitious. "I have never enjoyed these kinds of gatherings, even before I was in arms," I said instead.

He looked surprised. "So you are from here?" he said. "A Venetian? A Venetian who is actually in the Venetian army!" He chuckled. "I would not have guessed that. You do not seem like any of the others."

"Why not?" I asked, a shade eagerly.

"Well, first, you have a *face*," he joked. "This makes you much more trustworthy than anyone else in here."

"Well, more trustworthy than the other *men*, let's say." I wanted him to meet Emilia. I wanted to show them off to each other. "There is a woman in here even more trustworthy than I am."

He grinned again. "Ah, so there is a Lady Iago?"

"There is," I said.

"She has a good husband?"

"I hope so," I replied.

"Good." He took a deep breath and turned back to look into the room. "They will be expecting me in there. I mean this, Ensign Iago: stay beside me for the evening. I require it for my sanity. I apologize now if you must hear the same comments and stories seven hundred times in one night, but you will be doing your general a service. Are you up to it?"

"Absolutely, General."

"They will be staring at us, Iago," he warned, as if he found it amusing.

"They have stared at me plenty over the years," I said, cockily.

He gave me a delighted grin. "Ah. Later, I must hear why this is true. But I think this means we will get along just fine, you and I. Come, let us begin."

We walked back into the ballroom. A ballet had just begun, entirely deserving of our neglect.

OVER THE COURSE of the evening I learned many things about the general. Some of my knowledge came from listening to his politely repeating and repeating and repeating certain details of his life to everyone who asked, so that they could the next day make a casual comment to their friends about how well they knew the great Othello. As we watched acrobats, jugglers, clowns, and another ballet; as we ate (he asked me to sit beside him) a supper of fifteen courses, including peacock, pheasant, crab, and rabbit.

From these talks, I heard mostly about the battles he had been in; but he spoke too about his rambling as a solo mercenary offering his sword. These travels had taken him from empty deserts to floodplains to sprawling mountains, where he'd crawled through enormous caves in search of rumored treasure. He claimed he had battled cannibals in eastern Scythia—men who, wearing the scalps of their conquered enemies on necklaces, gave the appearance of having heads protruding from their chests. That story was usually enough to make the other guests smile wanly and excuse themselves.

But some of what I learned was for my ears alone, muttered quietly to me between partridges, pigeons, and pine nut cakes. These moments made the evening heady to me, heady almost as the night I first danced with Emilia. Othello trusted me with intimacies he had not even shared with the senators who promoted him. One example: for all his martial victories, there was one pivotal battle he had lost. He had been vanquished, taken captive, and sold into slavery. He'd earned his freedom after years of toil, and after being forced to swear an oath that he would never again fight against the tribe who had enslaved him. That was far to the east of here, east even of the Levant. It was in honor of that oath that he had come west, seeking to be a soldier in these far-off Mediterranean climes.

More remarkable to me than any of the remarkable things about his life, the great man asked me to talk about my own life. He must have been bored with talking ceaselessly of himself; still, as he heard my relatively tepid history, he seemed to take a genuine interest. When we were between gaggles of attempted sycophants, he coaxed from me details of my military background.

"So you are well trained in gunnery and also swordplay?" he said, looking thoughtful, and ignoring a new ballet—the third of the evening, this one depicting the birth of Venus—as the trestle tables were cleared from supper. "It's rare to find these two skills, advanced, in a single man."

"I would leave it to the general to decide if I am indeed skilled, but yes, I have had expert tutelage in both arenas. I suppose my father's tyranny is to thank for that, however accidentally."

Othello looked at me from the corner of his eye, and smiled. After two hours in his presence I'd seen him smile more than anyone I knew in Venice, with the possible exception of my wife. "I learned something when I was captive," he said. "It is under the thumb of the worst tyrant that we can achieve our best potential. Never were my arms so strong as when I was enslaved. Never did I learn to work harder on an empty stomach than when they tried to starve me. When we are pushed against our will, Iago, it not only sharpens our will but also teaches us new strengths. I welcome hardships for this very reason. I sense we are alike that way."

Every injustice, inconvenience, and misfortune that ever befell me paled in contrast to what this man had lived through. Yet he considered us alike. It left me speechless.

"I would see you with the sword and with the matchlock," he announced. "Tomorrow in front of the Sagittarius building."

"The Sagittari—" I began in confusion; then I realized he meant a particular building just inside the Arsenal gate. The lintel there, unlike the usual unadorned Arsenal gateways and doors, was carved with a fanciful depiction of the zodiac sign Sagittarius: a centaur armed with bow and arrow. This building had once been the crossbow magazine. It had recently been converted to quarters for high-ranking officers, and no doubt included Othello's temporary lodgings.

"I would be honored," I said, bowing my head. "Name the time, and I will be there."

"I do not attend the churches here, but let us wait until the bells toll after mass so we do not offend anybody's sensibilities." He had been watching my face more intently than I realized, because after a pause—and another grin—he added, "I do not go to church here, so you are wondering if I'm an *infidel*."

"I am curious," I admitted. "I'm sure the entire city is."

"I think the answer depends on whom you ask," he said with amused archness.

"Where are you from, then?" I tried.

"I was a child in Egypt, but that is not my race," he said. "Still I learned many things from that great people, although the Turks have subjugated them. I have especially much fondness for their women," he added with a laugh.

"What is most worth the fondness? Or the fondling?" I asked.

He closed his eyes a moment and smiled. "The land that gave us Cleopatra teems with infinite variety."

"I think you'll find the same in Venice," I offered. "Or so I recall from my bachelor days."

"What, no recent expeditions? Your wife keeps you happy, then?"

I began to reply half a dozen different ways. None of them did justice to Emilia, and several of my answers would have been, although titillating to Othello, disrespectful to her. So finally I just said, "Yes," emphatically.

He threw back his head and laughed. "Spoken like a man in love!" he announced. "I have never felt this thing, but I recognize it when I see it. May I meet the lady whom you orbit?"

He had asked to meet my wife. This was going very well, without a moment of deliberate strategy all evening. The stars must be aligned, I thought, for this to happen. I glanced around the room and saw Emilia talking to . . . oh, dear—Roderigo had found her. He was speaking to her with great excitement, no doubt about his mercantile successes in the two years we'd been gone to Corfu.

I turned to the general. "If you will excuse me from your side a moment, I will fetch her."

"By all means," he said. "But do it quickly or I shall once *again* be asked to tell that story about what happened in Aleppo."

The hall was growing crowded—so crowded that the dancing acrobats had to be replaced by more static entertainment. Perhaps word had spread around the city that the new general was available for ogling. I pushed my way through to Emilia, wondering how quickly I could excuse myself from Roderigo.

"Iago, my brother!" Roderigo cried out as I approached. He gave me the usual earnest hug and double kiss as an Agostini tune began in the background. "Your lovely wife has grown even more beautiful in your time away, and I see you have already made friends with our fearsome new general. What a time this is for you! It is also such a time for me! I must tell you—"

"Have you already told Emilia?" I interrupted.

"Several times," Emilia muttered pleasantly.

"Then, Roderigo, I am afraid I must excuse myself, the general has asked to meet my wife."

Roderigo's face lit up. "Would he not perhaps also like to meet your oldest friend?"

I made myself take a breath before responding, as gently as I could. "I am sorry, Roderigo, this is not the time."

"Ah," Roderigo replied. Then, after an awkward pause, "Well, better that way, I'm sure I would make a fool of myself, the fellow scares me. He looks like a barbarian. Of course, he *is* a barbarian, but to *see* one, in a *dance* hall, here in *Venice*—I don't need to meet him." A shorter pause, then: "Not likely he'd be buying spices from me anyhow, he probably eats raw meat."

"I seriously doubt that is the case," I assured him. "I have just spent an hour in his company and he seems civilized. Emilia, love, come with me. Good night, Roderigo."

"I may speak with you later!" he said, suddenly cheerful again.

As we worked our way back through the crowd, I gave Emilia a playfully questioning expression.

"He's wealthier than ever now, he's bought several farms on Terraferma, and there is a new young lady he's in love with, who will not give him a moment of her time," she neatly summarized. "But there are also a least a dozen ladies fawning over him, whom he rejects."

"How long did he take, telling you?"

"Approximately half an hour. And what should I know about your new bosom friend?"

I was not sure how to answer that. "I believe I prefer his company to any man's I've ever met," I said.

"Is that ambition speaking?" Emilia asked knowingly.

"No, it's really not. But I am pleased ambition could be satisfied here. He wants to see a show of my skills tomorrow morning in the Armory."

I heard her gasp behind her mask. "Iago, that's remarkable! Now aren't you glad you listened to your wife and came out to socialize tonight?"

"This must be the lady. But how sad I cannot see your face." Othello's bass voice startled me; he had been moving slowly toward us as we had moved toward him. He was probably trying to avoid another mossy-brained patrician.

"It is an honor to meet you, sir," Emilia said at once, dropping into a curtsy. "If you wish to see my face, it shall be available tomorrow morning when my husband demonstrates his martial prowess to you."

Othello blinked in surprise. "You will be there? Despite the violence and gunpowder?"

"To watch my husband's excellence? Nothing would deter me."

He considered her for a moment, then a smile slowly spread across his broad, dark face. He glanced at me. "This is a superior wife you have selected. May I ask her name?"

"Emilia, sir," we both said at once.

THAT NIGHT WE lay together in bed, our warm naked limbs sliding across each other, sleepless with anticipation for the next day's demonstration. "This could make you entirely," Emilia whispered.

"Could. Might. Might not," I said tersely in reply. "I hope you will not be disappointed in me if he is not impressed by what I do."

"I could not be disappointed by you if your very arms fell off," she said, almost chastisingly. "I am not your father, Iago. And if he were here, I think he would be bursting with pride that you have such an extraordinary opportunity awaiting you."

I sat up in bed. "Let's not talk about it any more. I cannot stand the tension of anticipation. Let me take my mind off it now."

"Of course," she said. Reaching for me, she offered, "Let me put your mind somewhere else."

Chapter 14

"YES, MY FRIEND, that was *remarkable*," Othello repeated with his broad smile as he reached down a hand to help me rise.

We were in the da Cremona shooting yard, the very yard I'd learned to shoot in, and it was a bright, cloudless day. The third swordsman he had set against me had bested me, landing a smarting blow to my sallet that sent me hard to the paving stones. I deserved it—his attack was straight from Agrippa, and I had tried to counter with a move from Marozzo, just to preen. In my exhausted state, it hadn't worked.

All the same, I'd disarmed the first two opponents he had set against me (although one was a Florentine, and therefore hardly counts), and this third man was the best under Othello's command. Plus, I had begun the dueling after half an hour of presenting my artillery skills: I had had to demonstrate how fast I could reload an arquebus and a light musket; how far I could shoot both, with relative accuracy; how swiftly I could load a cannon and how close on Othello's mark I could time it to go off. Othello had looked delighted throughout the demonstration. He continued to look delighted as I bested the first two swordsmen. And he looked equally delighted now as I lay wincing, cramped with pain, breathless, on the ground.

I reached up my left hand to grasp his, and allowed the heft of his large arm to haul me to standing. Nearly retching, my lungs about to burst, I pulled my sallet off my head.

"You are an excellent soldier, my friend!" Othello declared. "The one adjustment I would make to your style is to keep your dagger in your boot, as I do, and not in your belt. As you have just seen yourself, there are times it is better for your opponent not to know you have the extra blade. Otherwise, well done. Now we will try your wrestling skills."

I thought I might vomit. "General, sir, I—"

He laughed. "I am jesting with you. You have done enough for today. This is the best work I have ever seen in an ensign. Ensigns are usually no better than desk clerks. Captain," he went on, turning to one of the many officers who had been watching, and no doubt placing wagers on, my morning's exertions. "See to it this young man is put into my unit, under my direct command. He will ship to Rhodes when we go next month."

Just like that, I was a made man. I flushed, lungs still heaving for air, and bowed deeply before Othello. I arrested my impulse to smile, as I suspected I had just made several enemies among these men, who had no doubt worked for years with Othello and would not like to see a newcomer effortlessly end up at his elbow. But Emilia, standing with the other spectators, could not hide her pleasure: she gasped, "Oh, Iago!" and clapped her hands together, her face beaming.

"You honor me, General," I said.

"You honor the art of war," Othello said breezily. He turned to Emilia. "But, lady, I thought you were fonder of him, and would wail about his going."

I realized what he meant by this and felt my heart sink a little even in its celebration. For a moment, Emilia looked confused. Then she held up a finger almost pedantically and announced, "I shall be going *with* him, General."

"A fortress is no place for ladies," Othello retorted.

"I and many other ladies just spent two years with our men in a fortress on Corfu," she retorted.

Othello made a dismissive gesture. "That is Corfu. This is Rhodes. The fortress is in the hands of the enemy—we go to *seize* it, not *caretake* it."

"But, General—" Emilia began to argue, without rancor or whininess. Othello held up a hand, suddenly sterner.

"I have said no," he announced. "And so, it is no. I brook no argument."

The officers surrounding him looked uncomfortable: Emilia's face suggested she had no intention of backing down.

"Emilia," I said warningly, loving her spirit. "Enough. We will discuss this later."

"I have one specific thing to say to the general that I believe will change his mind," Emilia said, directing the statement to me so she could not be accused to talking back to Othello.

"I will let him know that later, wife, at a more proper time," I said in the most scolding voice I could muster. "A courtyard in the Arsenal is no time for wives to be passing messages to generals."

"Oh, come, then, out with it," Othello said, suddenly cheerful again. "The poor man has been exercised nearly to death, let his wife have her one specific say."

Emilia curtseyed in his direction. "If you please, General, it is not for public hearing, I must whisper it directly in your ear."

Othello's eyes popped wide open. The men around him exchanged disbelieving looks. Even I was taken aback. I had no idea what she would say to him.

As I watched, Othello returned his face to a neutral expression and gestured Emilia toward him. The two officers in her way quickly stepped aside. Emilia was fairly tall for a woman, but still she had to stand on tiptoes, and Othello had to lean his head down, for her to whisper in his ear. Every gaze in the courtyard was fastened to his face, and he knew it. So despite his initial amazement at whatever he was hearing, he was very careful to keep his face expressionless.

But he allowed himself to comment.

"Really? . . . Are you so certain of that? . . . Are you telling me the truth?" He pulled away and looked at her for a moment with this last query, absently fingering the kerchief tied around his neck. She nodded, and then gestured him to lean his head down again, and added something else.

"But can you prove it?" Othello pressed her. She whispered more. He grinned a little, and then began to laugh. "You are quite the woman, Emilia, wife of Iago," he declared and stood up straight again. Emilia curtsied hurriedly and then backed away. "All right," the general said cheerfully, turning toward me. "She will come with us."

I was too startled to say anything. Half a dozen voices said, "My lord?" in exactly the same tone of surprise.

"That is my final word," Othello declared, waving one hand dismissively. Turning his attention to the man beside him, he said,

"Make sure that Iago is given a wider berth on the ship, and enough housing for his wife when we reach Rhodes."

"Thank you, milord," Emilia said adorably.

WE WERE BACK in our room at the Dolphin. It was the first fight we had ever had. She did not want to tell me what she'd said to him, and I could not imagine why she'd keep a secret from me unless there was something very wrong about it.

"Is it not enough that I can go with you?" she demanded.

"What did you offer him?" I demanded back, through clenched teeth. "Did you say you'd make yourself available to him as well? Do you plan to whore yourself to the higher ranks? Don't think I haven't heard about what officers expect of lower-ranking wives."

"Iago, you are being silly now!" She laughed, which only further upset me.

"Don't mock me!" I shouted, slamming my fist against the bedpost so hard the farther bedpost hit the wall and made the whole room shudder. "Tell me that's not what you said."

"Of course that is not what I said, you petulant, jealous man!" she snapped, suddenly losing her humor.

"Tell me that your going with us has nothing to do with your sex," I demanded.

"Iago, it has *everything* to do with my sex! It has to! My *not* going had everything to do with my sex, so what else did I have to argue with?"

I closed my eyes and shook my head in confusion. "What does that mean?" I asked.

"I told him," Emilia announced, lowering her voice and glancing randomly about the room, as if afraid there would be eavesdroppers, "I told him that our lovemaking is what makes you such a capable soldier, and that if you are deprived of your bed-mate, your skills with sword and gun will deteriorate quickly." She grinned, thinking she had ended the argument with this confession.

I gaped at her. "Emilia, that is ridiculous," I said. "You did not say such a thing."

"I did!" she assured me, like a proud child.

"You did not say such a thing to the leader of the Venetian army, one day after meeting him."

"Yes, I did!"

"You did not say such a thing, and he would never have relented because of it, and you are lying to me," I said angrily. I walked across the room, pointlessly, but needing a physical release of my irritated energy. I wished I were outside so I could kick something without being billed for damages.

"Ask him yourself, Iago!" Emilia said. "There are so many beliefs about sex and war that go back before the dawn of time—"

"They almost always have to do with *abstinence*," I said, in a disapproving tone that horrified me by sounding like my father.

"But not always," Emilia countered cheerfully. "I do not know his background, but I'm sure there are some superstitions in it, and something inside me knew that he might believe me, and I was right."

"Emilia, he did not believe you," I snapped. "He thought whatever you said was *amusing*. You *amused* him into saying yes."

"So what?" she retorted, arms held out before her. "He still said yes, and isn't that what matters?"

"You engaged in filthy discourse with the man, having just met him," I roared. "He thinks you're loose. When a woman talks to a man like that, a man *knows* what it means. And if she is brazen enough to do it right in front of her husband and a dozen military captains—heaven alone knows what she's capable of. You may as well have whored yourself already."

Emilia started laughing again, which threw oil on my fire. "Iago, talk to Othello directly, and it will put your mind to rest at once. Perhaps you are right, perhaps he did not believe me, and yielded to me only in amusement—"

"Not perhaps. Of course!"

"If so, it is an innocent amusement—"

"There is nothing innocent about your talking about your extraordinary sexual powers to my commander in chief!"

"He thought it was charming of me to want so badly to be with you," she insisted. "That's all it was, love."

"You're a stupid fool if you think that!" I snarled.

She looked as if I'd struck her. She took a moment to compose herself, shocked, and then finally, in a meek voice, she said, "I'm very sorry if I am a stupid fool. My affection for you perhaps affects my reason. Please tell me what I can do to win back your regard."

I stood there awkwardly, openmouthed, angry but now impotent to act on it. "Emilia," I said in an imploring tone. "You should not come to Rhodes with me."

She put her hands over her face to hide it, but I could see the tearful grimace form around the edges of her palms. "You would rather separate us than trust me?" she asked from behind her lovely fingers, choking on the words. "You suspect my promiscuity more than you value my company? That easily?"

"It sounds terrible when you put it like that."

"There is no other way to put it, and it *is* terrible," she shot back.

She started weeping. I had never seen a woman weep—not sincerely, I mean—and I could not bear it. Immediately, every part of me could focus on nothing but how to stop her weeping. If she was weeping, it must mean I'd done something terrible to her, and I could not abide that evidence.

"Perhaps I have misconstrued the situation," I offered grumpily. "I will talk to the general to clarify the situation."

I heard her take in a shaky breath that suggested she was trying to control the tears. I sighed with relief.

"Yes, please speak to him," she begged. "Perhaps I am ignorant and offered him something without realizing it. Perhaps it is better all the way around if you excuse your stupid fool of a wife to him."

"You are not a stupid fool, and I'm sorry that I said it," I said hurriedly, and finally let myself go to her and hold her. She collapsed against me and pushed her head against my cheek.

"Do you know what?" she whispered.

"What?" I said into her hair.

"This is our first fight."

"Yes, it is."

"After two years, we've only had one fight."

"That's true," I said.

"That's pretty good," she said, and kissed my collarbone. I squeezed her, as if I would engulf her, swallow her with my whole body. My God, I loved that woman. No man ever had a better wife.

Chapter 15

EMILIA, OF COURSE, did not come with us; Othello had relented publicly for sport but called me to his quarters the next day to tell me the hard truth of the matter. I, with a confusing mix of emotions I was not proud of, informed Emilia that she would stay behind.

THE TURKS HAD taken Rhodes from the Knights Hospitaller back in 1522. Venice had briefly laid claim to some of its neighboring islands over the years, but Rhodes itself had never been a stronghold for us. Othello had convinced the whole of the government that the Venetian Empire was well defended from the Turks *except* for the threat of Turkish Rhodes, and thus by taking Rhodes we would become indefinitely secure. My own five years of idleness on Terraferma was an excellent example of why we did not need so much of our manpower to the west of Venice, despite the simmering resentment and envy of the rest of Europe. So the mass of the army was to be redirected toward protecting Stato da Màr, the maritime half of Venice's great empire.

Besides which, ridding Rhodes of Turks was good for the whole of Christendom. Upon this argument, Othello and the Senate had already convinced the papal army, the French, and even the Holy Roman Emperor to send their forces too. By the time Othello had claimed me as his ensign, his plan was already in place, and we were waiting for the seasonal winds that would allow the plan to work.

His plan called for the Venetian navy to transport the Venetian army to the southern tip of Rhodes, the farthest point from the capital city and its impenetrable fortress on the barbed northern coast. The Turks, knowing we were coming, would send men both overland toward us and also in ships around either side of the island, to get us in a pincer either while we were still at sea, or just as we reached shore. At this point, most of the combined forces of the rest of Christendom would appear on the western horizon as our backup, with the exception of the Holy Roman Emperor's fleet. This had already set sail and was traveling innocuously far to the south of Rhodes, under rumor they had Levantine scores to settle. Othello's plan called for them to pass Rhodes entirely, then abruptly circle back and besiege the capital city up north, while it was conveniently underprotected because its garrison was mostly in the south fighting us.

WE HAD REACHED the southern tip of arid, rocky Rhodes and sent half the army to settle on a pedunculated islet attached by a land bridge to Rhodes proper. Othello took command of these forces, leaving the admiral of the navy to strategize the naval component of the fighting. From our camp we could be attacked from nearly every side, but in turn, we could attack easily with artillery through a full 360 degrees.

As Othello's ablest gunman and his new right hand, it was my duty to establish where among the sun-bleached crags the guns should be set up, the gunners and cannons both, and then to see to it that appropriate powder, shot, and match went where it was meant to go. I did all this efficiently; Othello was pleased, and I delighted, that I seemed to have a preternatural ability to anticipate his next requirement or tactic. We worked together so well that he often entirely ignored his aging lieutenant, Zuane da Porto.

Zuane was the tallest soldier I had ever known. Long, lanky limbs, a mop of grey hair, and a nose as fierce as an eagle's beak, he struck me as an aging wild feline who would sooner sleep than fight; but he had in his day been capable of impressive feats. I do not mean to question his honor or integrity, but I think he must have "fallen upward" into his position through family connections. He was competent but lacked all drive or ambition. Da Porto, from what I could tell, was looking forward to retirement more than he was looking forward to engaging with the Turks, and so he was just as grateful as I was that Othello and I seemed almost to share one mind.

BOTH TURKISH ATTACKS—naval and overland—came nearly within the very hour Othello had anticipated, in precisely the formations he'd predicted. The first thing you learn in the heat of battle is that nothing you learn outside the heat of battle, about the heat of battle, is worth a damn. In training you learn strategy and tactics; in real life, it is more about improvisation than anyone will ever admit. The improvisation may be informed by years of training, but it is improvisation all the same.

Our first round of artillery did astounding damage to the enemy, and for the first time in my life I saw what gunpowder and shot could do to human beings. Hardly one man in twelve of the Turkish infantry got as far as the land bridge, where our own infantry was waiting with bows and swords to prevent them coming closer.

In the sea we were not as effective: we wounded many vessels but did not destroy any; our navy set upon theirs but was rebuked in turn by their fire. This was not a great concern to us, for we knew France and the papal army were imminently coming to our aid. So focused was Othello on the ground warfare that it was not until nearly sunset that he realized how very tardy our backup was. The Venetian navy was nearing exhaustion for it.

* * *

AS THE HEAVENS darkened that first night of the siege, the Turkish ships backed away and headed slightly north. It was clear they would make anchor and then disgorge their manpower to meet ours on land; they had done enough damage to our navy. To my ears this was very bad news, but Othello fairly beamed with confidence when it was reported to him.

"The delay of the French and the papal forces will prove to our advantage," he informed his captains (and myself and his lieutenant, the two officers who never left his side). We huddled together in the cool night, around a fire pit outside the command tent, where most of us would sleep. Evening insects of springtime sang and echoed all around us, indifferent to the havoc of war-crazed humanity. I found their presence oddly reassuring. "The Turk has now been conned into believing it is only us. They think there is nobody but us to vanquish. And so, when our allies surprise them—as I am sure they will at sunup—they will all be exposed and unready all along the shore, with no time even to set up their own defensive artillery. Our allies will annihilate what is left of their navy, which is now mostly unmanned ships. This is a *fortuitous* development."

HE LIKELY WOULD have been right about that, if the French and papal ships had arrived. But they did not. Ever. In the ferocious fighting that followed all that day, I bitterly imagined them cheerfully snug at port in Marseilles or Genoa, their men all drunkenly toasting the demise of Venice's navy. Perhaps some of them toasted also to the health of the Holy Roman Emperor's army, should it indeed take Rhodes City. But in my enraged imagination, few of them cared much about that part of the plan: the important thing was that the armed forces of their powerful neighbor Venice would end up in tatters, having been gulled into a battle we could not win alone.

IT WAS LATE afternoon on the second day of engagement, and we were in trouble. We were nearly out of powder and completely out of arrows; what was left of our navy managed to protect the army from seaward attacks, but there were few such attacks anyhow, as now most of their fire and steel was attacking us on land. We had cornered ourselves on our rocky hillock, barely keeping the Turks from reaching the land bridge. The smell of blood and pus and oozing bone marrow, the mud that's made of human innards being ground into grass and clay . . . there is no training to prepare anyone for this. The roar that never ends, that is both fear and ferocity, that is fire and steel and humanity and horses (the Turks had horses) and livestock—Othello was startlingly unmoved by these horrors, being used to them for many years. I was horrified for hours, then numb, and then enraged.

The general and I were in the command tent, on the highest crag of the islet. We were both covered in grime and dirt and dust and other men's blood. The maps and charts were forgotten now; this was not the battle he had planned. "All those lives are on my conscience," he said softly, without guilt, staring out the tent flap at the front. "Somewhere, if not here, we must have a victory that justifies all the tears that mothers and the wives will shed for this."

"We must have a victory against our damned *allies!*" I hissed furiously, collecting the diagrams from the tactics table. Othello looked at me, the black eyes calm in their remarkably white orbs.

"Iago, we do not *know* that they are foresworn. You must not hurl accusations without proof. We have no proof. They may appear on the horizon any moment, although we shan't assume it now. We must retreat while doing the greatest damage to the enemy on the way and preserving ourselves as well as possible." He saw the color rise in my face. "Are you thinking, my young ensign, that you are shamed not to see victory in your first engagement as an officer?"

"I'm thinking many things," I said tersely and placed the collected diagrams into a chest. "That is one of them."

"I think rather you have learned more than most men do in a whole lifetime of soldiering," he said, in an almost paternal tone. "When there is time for reflection, when we are safely aboard ship and bound west back to Venice, you and I will sit in my cabin and drink excellent wine, and you will tell me at least seven things you know now that you did not know three days ago." He held out his hand. "Are we agreed?"

His calm and confidence were contagious. I took his hand. I would follow this man anywhere. "Provided we are both alive and there is a boat to carry us," I said.

"Well now there must needs be, we have just shaken on it!" the general said, with something like a chuckle. He released my hand and patted my arm. "Come along, I will show you how to make a proper retreat."

Chapter 16

"I LIED TO YOU about the wine," Othello said. "It is not excellent. In fact, it's swill."

"It is the swill of the gods," I said heartily, and downed the contents of the wooden cup in one huge swallow that burned the back of my throat. The whole cabin reeked nauseatingly of valerian, used as a disinfectant on my arm. "And is this indeed your cabin, General?"

We were not on his ship; his ship had gone down at Rhodes. We were in the captain's cabin of another galleass—the largest surviving ship in the fleet, with the largest captain's quarters, which Othello and the captain were sharing. All officers were crammed together into cabins and all enlisted men into the berths. There were enough surviving soldiers that the surviving ships—packed tight to start with—could hardly carry them home. The Turks were not pursuing us; word had reached them that we were merely a decoy, that the city fortress was under attack from the ships of the Holy Roman Emperor.

On our nightmare retreat down to the ships, I had learned

what it feels like to rip apart a man's body with my sword, to have a man's entire life in blood spurt at my face and seep into my clothes; I learned that such horror does not dampen the thrill of victorious survival, that the rush of winning the battle to live comes by forcing someone else to lose. I learned the pain of an unbated blade tearing into my own flesh, although the wound was on my left arm and not deep. I had more than seven things to report to Othello; I easily had seventy, and each one was known to him already.

"This is the soldiers' life," he said, almost dismissively, pressing his favorite scented kerchief under his nostrils. "The mercenaries know this. Few Venetians really understand. Now that you do, son of a merchant, will you continue in the service?"

"Yes," I said without hesitation. What we had lived through was a nightmare, but such a vivid one as made any other kind of life a pallid daydream.

"Do you see why your lovely wife could not come with us?"

"Yes."

"And do you think you can go home to your lovely wife and remain a gentle husband to her, knowing what you now know of the real nature of a soldier?"

This time I hesitated. Othello gave me a compassionate but knowing look.

"Yes," I said.

Othello considered me a moment in the swaying lamplight, and then he smiled. "I believe you, Iago. I do not mean I believe you're right, but I believe you mean it. You will never view a masked ball the same way again."

"I never liked those balls, I told you that," I said, adjusting the pungent bandage over my wound.

"Yes, you sneer at all the Venetian gentility. But now, Iago, besides sneering, you will be jealous of them."

"Are you jesting, General? I'll scorn them more than ever."

"No," Othello said, philosophically smiling. "Most men in your position would, my friend. But, Iago, you are made of different stuff.

You and I have the same ore. We earn our lives, we earn our dignity, and we are very proud of that—but sometimes it is tiring. We know," he said, sitting up now and looking more animated, "we know that we *deserve* the feather beds and eager mistresses and fine puddings and private chamber music and beautiful clothes and furniture and palaces. We know we deserve it better than any of those who actually possess those things. But we will never have those things, Iago, because it is not in our nature to pursue them. We do not *really* want them. We *want* to want them. We know, you and I, we *know* that if we really wanted those things, they would be ours. Somehow. We would get them. We know that we are men of such integrity and strength and drive, if we wanted something enough, we would find a way to get it. This I know about myself, and I sense it about you too, as I have sensed it about no other Venetian I have met. If only I wanted feather beds, they would be mine. And life would be so easy. But I do not want them, I cannot want them, I cannot"—here he made a contracting gesture—"I cannot make my soul small enough to be content with them. The soldier who pines for a feather bed, he will just be scornful and resentful. But the soldier who cannot pine for the feather bed, he will be jealous of the *ability to pine*."

I sat up, startled. "You're right," I said. I had never thought that about myself until he had said it, but the moment that he said it, I realized I'd known it all my life.

"Of course I am right." He grinned. "I told you, the same ore, you and I."

I shook my head, hardly comprehending that. "Until this battle, my life has been very sheltered compared to yours."

"I am not talking about experience, I am talking about the *ore*," Othello said, shaking a clenched hand to emphasize the last word. "The very elemental essence of your soul. Now we will go back to Venice, and of everybody in this army, you and I, the two of us alone, will never be at peace."

I dearly hoped that wasn't true. "I intend to be at peace as soon as I am in Emilia's arms again," I told him.

He made an impatient gesture. "I do not mean that."

"I am not bloodthirsty, General. I may not crave the feather bed, but neither do I crave another battlefield."

"But if you had to pick between the two, Iago—which would it be? If you say the feather bed I know you are lying."

"That does not mean I crave a *war*," I argued.

"Then what do you crave?" he challenged.

"I crave my wife," I said, feeling my cheeks grow hot. "And not just the way you think I mean."

Othello gave me a thoughtful smile. "In that case," he decided, "*I* am jealous of *you*. And, Iago, let me assure you, I am not a jealous man."

Chapter 17

"THE WHOLE OF Christendom hates you," explained the papal legate phlegmatically, to the bilious Venetian Great Council. The acoustics of the enormous, crowded room made him sound loud but bored. "No nation on earth has any reason to see you prosper, and many are the nations that would celebrate your ruin. Pope Pius himself says this. You have for centuries run roughshod over the entire Mediterranean and never taken any interest other than mercantile in any combined Christian endeavor."

"That is nonsense," huffed Senator Brabantio, his aquiline nose raised so that I, standing on the floor near his dais, could nearly look up his nostrils.

Othello, Zuane da Porto, and I were attending this extremely tense parley between the entire Patriciate of Venice and representatives of all the states and cities who had not shown up as promised, at the would-be Battle of Southern Rhodes. Although Othello was the primary witness, the huge hall was so overstuffed with patricians that once he finished his official report, he had been herded with da Porto and myself literally into a corner. This at least placed us near a door, and it opened outward into a stairwell, from which some air filtered in.

"We provided the entire fleet for the Crusade of 1202," Brabantio was expounding. "We have outfitted and supplied untold pilgrims on their way to protect the Holy Land. We have opened trade routes and secured treaties when nobody else in Europe was able to—"

"—and thus created a virtual monopoly," the legate from Rome declared, "of nearly everything. Whatever in the known world travels east to west or west to east, nearly all of it must go through Venetian middlemen."

"And so you *betrayed* us?" Othello demanded, more bemused than angry. I could not believe his calm. In his place, I would have been shrieking with righteous anger.

"We changed our minds," the legate said delicately, to which the entire chamber of 2,500 patricians broke out into furious and ill-mannered comments. If this man did not represent the Lord's Anointed, I suspected someone would have hurled a dagger at him. But interdiction was not in the interest of the Serene Republic, and so order, although challenged and stretched, was not quite broken.

Othello took one step forward out of our crowded corner perch, in his unusual white dress, the banner of his rank across his body, arms crossed, legs wide, staring furiously at the legate. "This was an action of revolting dishonor, sir, and you may tell His Holiness so. Because we can no longer trust you, you who are our *own allies*, we must now put our forces back along the Terraferma border in greater numbers than have been there in years, and this means fewer forces left to guard da Màr, and that is bad for all of Christendom, not just Venice. Has Venice not always behaved honorably in military matters? Did Venice not provide ships for His Holiness in '37 although the battle was not ours? Suleiman offered a pact with Venice against the rest of Europe, and Venice turned it down, on principle, because we were honor bound to protect our fellow Christians no matter how bad they were at defending themselves. We created the Holy League as a favor to you, and look how you have used it against us! Tell me, did the emperor's army succeed in taking Rhodes City?"

The legate looked taken aback. "It did not," he acknowledged, almost sheepish.

"Then Rhodes is still with the Turk," the general scolded, his voice rising. "And mark my word but Cyprus will soon be too, when the Turks realize that Venice will have taken men *away* from Cyprus, to put them on our *western* borders, to guard *those* borders against the nations that ought to be our *Christian allies!*" He was shouting now, and his bass voice shook the inset paintings that decorated the ceiling. Quite literally, the angels looking down above us trembled at his voice. "If we fall, you will suffer too! Are you all so short-sighted that you do not realize that? Do you not understand that Venice in her grandeur safeguards *all* of Christendom?" His arms were flailing and his face was that of a man possessed; this was not a side of him I had ever seen before. "Tell your Roman pope and tell your French king and tell your emperor too—if Venice falls, *they all fall with us!*" He was gesticulating so wildly he seemed not to have control of himself.

And then I realized he did not, in fact, have control of himself.

I had seen this before; it had sometimes happened to my uncle, and my priestly brother when he was a boy. I knew what was coming, and I was determined to keep it from happening in the Council chamber.

"Distract them," I muttered to Lieutenant da Porto. A distraction was hardly needed at this point, for the assembly of visitors was on their feet and screaming back at Othello as loudly as he was screaming at them.

"Gentlemen!" da Porto began, stepping forward with his long stride; he was echoed by the doge and half the Council, and I took the opportunity to grab Othello by the arm and drag him back, stumbling, out the door behind us. Fortunately it opened outward and I kicked it closed behind; a sound that, no matter how it may have echoed, was lost in the din of voices within.

Othello's massive body shuddered and collapsed, nearly on top of me; he was almost too large a figure for the landing, and I think it was pure luck we were not both propelled down the stairway by his seizure.

I had nothing to put into his mouth to keep him from swallowing his tongue, nor could I do anything but hold his arms, so much stronger than mine, and let them flail wildly, as if he lay on ice. He broke into a sweat, so that his white cotton tunic appeared a shade of fawn, pressed against his shivering dark body.

FOR A MOMENT there was silence in the darkened stairwell. A slice of lamplight cut between the door panels back into the Council chamber. I prayed Othello had not harmed himself. This was mostly genuine concern for my friend and leader. But a selfish voice within me also wailed that I could lose my chances of promotion; Othello was the man who made me, and I was more dependent on his power than I admitted to myself.

He regained his senses almost instantly. "Where am I?" he whispered, his eyes darting around nervously in the dark, turning anxiously toward the slit of wan light.

"You're with me, General," I whispered. "Iago, your ensign. Do you know me?"

"Iago, yes, where are we?" Impatiently he pulled his arms out of my grip, and shakily sat up.

"We are in the stairway outside the Council chamber," I said quietly. "Nobody in there realizes what just happened to you."

He gave me a long, exhausted look, as memory returned. "Oh heaven," he said quietly, and then swore—I assume—in his native tongue. "Iago, you have just saved me."

"No, General," I said. I stood and offered him a hand to raise himself.

"Not the weakness itself, but to let it show itself at such a moment, in such a heat," Othello said. He sounded shocked. "Yes, that would make the Council pause. This has not happened to me in so many years." He gave me a worried look, the first time I had ever seen such an expression on his face. "But never under strain in battle, Iago, do you understand me? This has never happened to me on the field, no matter how—"

"I believe you, General," I said solemnly. "Not one ounce of my faith in you is shaken." I lowered my gaze. "I have family given to these seizures, and I know that strong emotion brings it on." I looked back up at him. "And I have seen for myself that even in the worst of battle, you are calm and confident. You remain my general. You remain *their* general. Go back within and show them that."

He stood slowly, leaning on me for balance. With a sigh, he adjusted his sweat-soaked clothes.

"Am I presentable?" he asked. I nodded. "Iago." He sighed again, and clapped both hands around my shoulders. "You are the truest friend I have." He suddenly pulled me to him and embraced me in so strong a hug I wondered if my ribs would crack. I embraced him back and realized that I was shaking more than he was.

He released me and gestured to the door back into the Council hall. "And now we go," he said, with his perennial grin, "so I may finish insulting the rest of Europe."

"They deserve the insult," I said. "They deserve far worse than that."

Chapter 18

OTHELLO'S WORDS WERE applauded by the Venetian Council and dismissed as heathen provocation by the representatives of all the other states. Venice was still hated, and was still seen as the bully of the seas, rather than as the best final protector Christendom had from Ottoman infidels.

And therefore, indeed, it was required that we take men from Cyprus and other outposts of da Màr to fortify our Terraferma borders. Just when we should have been refortifying Famagusta in the east, we were instead putting garrisons along our western bounds. Othello oversaw all of this and then stationed himself at the most dangerous part of the border, Rovigo, where neighborly transgression was likeliest.

This was due to the bombastic disposition of the Este family in Ferrara, who had once had Rovigo in their grasp and, allied status notwithstanding, thought they might like it back. Technically, Ferrara was a papal state and, therefore, the Estes should have considered themselves part of the Holy League. But their private army had a way of forgetting such political niceties and would occasionally cross over the border to see if Venice was still in residence. I found it appalling and infuriating that allies would behave this way—neither the pontiff nor the Holy Roman Emperor (the ruling Este's father-in-law) ever tried to curtail them. I was all for razing Ferrara to stop their dishonorable behavior; Othello, grinning at my "righteous pugilistic enthusiasm," would not do so.

And so Ferrara, with its imported Flemish painters and excellently constructed lutes, remained smug and intact.

And so I found myself again in Terraferma, in another garrison posting. This time, happily, Emilia came with me. The army garrisoned in a drafty tenth-century castle, and made the best of it.

WE SPENT TWO long years here. They were more eventful than my years on Corfu, but nothing near as awful as what had happened at Rhodes. There were border raids from Ferrara, but no fatalities on our side, and only enough casualties on their side to make them behave themselves . . . until some new commander took control, on their side, who wanted to impress the Este family . . . and then we had to show them all over again that our border was not to be tested. Their raids were infantile and disorganized—combatting them resembled smacking mosquitoes more than fending off warriors—but they were capable of murder, rape, and pillage, and approximately once a month we had to remind them not to do those things.

"I do not like fighting allies," Othello would say at the end of each of these engagements.

"Venice has no allies anymore," I would reply. "And I think our government prefers it that way. Fewer compromises that way."

"But more of these ridiculous *squabbles*," Othello would reply.

The duties here were similar to my earlier garrison postings, but the civilized aspect of life was strangely . . . civilized. The fortress was large enough that officers' wives would usually dress for dinner, as if we lived in civilization, as if we were not soldiers, as if at any moment we would not be called away to shatter another human being's spinal column. Othello was even petitioned to install chandeliers imported from Murano, to create a semblance of Society.

We protected our women, some thirty-five in all, as diligently as we protected our borders. We protected them from their own anxious imaginations, with Murano glass chandeliers and well-dressed dinners and sometimes dances, and in daylight with courtyard demonstrations of swordplay and archery (not artillery, though—the powder was too dear).

Emilia charmingly transformed the officers' wives into a little mock Venetian clan, much to the delight (as on Corfu) of the elder patrician commissioners. So once again I had to smile with tight politeness watching Emilia dance with other gentlemen. I was getting better about it. Compared to Corfu. Really I was. Even the evening, two years on, when I found myself in the mess hall, the trestles removed or pushed against the walls, the room well lit by the Murano chandeliers, and half a dozen amateur musicians playing dance tunes . . . and there I was, standing beside one Venetian commissioner, who was smiling at the dancers with nostalgia.

"They make a handsome couple," he said to me approvingly, as if we were longtime confidants. "Truly, a happy, handsome couple."

I followed his gaze—to see that he was referring to Emilia and Othello. Emilia was teaching the general a dance step he was slow to learn, and the two of them were laughing together as comfortably as either of them had ever laughed with me.

"They are *not* a handsome couple," I said to the gentleman.

He looked confused.

"That lady is my wife," I announced.

I saw the color rise in his cheeks. "You must excuse me, Ensign, I assumed they . . ." I stared at him. He reddened more and said, "That was presumptuous of me. There is no reason for me to assume that."

The moment was made either better or worse (both, in a sense) by another older Venetian gentleman, who had been eavesdropping; this fellow broke into the tense silence with a lunging laugh and the announcement: "Did you think the lady was married to the Moorish general? I thought she was married to Lieutenant da Porto! And Niccolo had a wager with me that she was actually the mistress of the payroll commissioner! How droll!"

"How very droll indeed," I said, forcing myself to smile.

A week later, a pact was signed between Ferrara and the Serene Republic. We all hastened back to Venice, where I intended never to watch Emilia dance in another man's arms again.

OTHELLO WAS AGAIN quartered in the Sagittarius building. It was just inside the main gate of the Arsenal; Emilia and I were in the Dolphin, across the campo.

Othello spent hours and days debating with the Senate and the Great Council about how to reassign the bulk of infantry and resources across the great Venetian empire. He was concerned about what he was hearing of the defenses on Cyprus, and particularly its port of Famagusta, the easternmost point of the Stato da Màr. Every day, he came to the Dolphin in the late afternoon. Here, sitting outside on the campo with a bottle of wine to share with me, he would regurgitate that day's discussions, because he found relief in my sardonic commentary about circumstances he could not control. The Senate had the right to overrule the commander in chief, and often did.

"Today they interviewed an engineer," he began one day, perhaps a fortnight after our return. The days were shortening, the heat abating, and that year autumn in Venice seemed designed by loving angels. "This man wants to construct glacis around the Citadel of Famagusta, rigged with explosives that can be remotely detonated. That way, when the Turks come running up to the fortress—"

"—assuming the Turks agree to run up to the fortress," I said. "Assuming they do not, for instance, do something inconvenient like use artillery—"

"Exactly," Othello said, with a broad sweeping gesture toward me. "I should bring you to these meetings, Iago; da Porto is with me as lieutenant, but that man, I swear, he never says a word. I speak, but I am just one voice. And I do not belittle them as you would. And you would," he added with emphasis, seeing me about to object. "I know you, brother—you are not two-faced, nor are you a coward. There is nothing you say about someone that you would not say to their face. You would shame them into listening to reason. They are so excited about this remote-explosion idea, it sounds so modern and technical to them, they are completely unable to consider all the reasons why it will not work."

"By what means do the munitions explode?" I asked.

Othello almost choked on his wine, with what turned out to be a laugh of disgust. "Ropes!" he said. "We tie ropes to explosive devises, that are buried in the dirt of the glacis, just outside the citadel walls— the ropes and the devices both are buried, and the other end of the rope goes through a hole that will be drilled through the twenty-foot-thick walls, so somebody inside the citadel can pull the rope at just the right moment that the Turks are walking over the explosive device—"

"A moment which they themselves cannot see, because they are on the other side of the wall!" I almost hit my forehead on the table from laughing so hard.

"Stop laughing, man!" Othello cackled. "I had to listen to this with a sober face! At least make an attempt to do the same now!" He raised his glass. "To whimsical inventors."

"May their ideas never make it to Cyprus," I concluded, joining him in the toast.

"It is frustrating that the senators agree to meet with these fools. I wish that I could always be here to keep an eye on them, even as I am at a posting. There needs to be two of me."

"I'll tell you how to do that," I said, reaching for the bottle to pour us both another glass. "Buy, or perhaps rent, a home here in the city—a large house, a palazzo if you can afford it. Have some designated agent, someone not in the army but whom you trust, live in the house when we are stationed elsewhere, and that person's work will be to argue on your behalf before the government in your absence. Then when you are in town, you reside in the house and invite lots of patricians to dinner so you can woo them to your ideas." I grinned at him over my wineglass. "You could even throw a masked ball."

"You are a devil," he returned cheerfully. "But I'm glad you are *my* devil."

"I am only trying to educate you on the ways of my people."

"I am always happy to be educated," Othello said. He gestured expansively in my direction again. "Please you, another lesson."

"What does the general feel he lacks an understanding of?"

"Well," he said, exaggerating a thoughtful look. "It seems to take three thousand times as long to say something on the Senate floor as in any other setting. There seem to be formulas for speech that do not accomplish anything but take up time. It is like a coded language."

"You are exactly right, General," I said. "It is a kind of code. If you know all the right phrases, it means you are a member of their special circle." He laughed; I shook my head at him. "I am serious, Othello. That shadowy exclusiveness is part of what I despise about this society."

He nodded. "But every culture has this. However in Venice it seems so . . . precious, sometimes." He sat up straighter. "Come, Iago, teach me some of these phrases so that I may be one of them."

I made a skeptical face. "I think it is a waste of time—"

"Just one phrase," Othello insisted, smiling. "A phrase I may actually need to use sometime."

"If the general insists, so be it," I said. "Let us say we are not in Venice, but posted someplace far from here, which I would very much like. The Senate sends you a message. How do you greet the messenger?"

He shrugged. "This happened while we were on Terraferma. You saw what I did: I said, *You are welcome, kindly give me your message.*"

"And then what?" I prompted.

"I held out my hand, and whoever it was, a courier, a patrician, whoever it was, they would hand it to me."

"And then?"

He gave me a bemused look. "And then I broke the seal and read the message. What else should I do when I am given a message?"

"I'll tell you," I said. I sat up and glanced around the table for a prop. There was nothing but the wine bottle and the glasses. I gestured to Othello's favorite kerchief, tied around his neck. "May I borrow that?"

He untied it and handed it to me. I stood up and held it at arm's length. "Say this is the message. The actual letter that the senators, or the doge, or whoever else, has sent you. Are you watching?"

Othello smiled and gestured me to continue.

I brought the kerchief to my lips, bowed, and kissed the kerchief gently. "I kiss the instrument of their pleasures," I recited.

Othello threw his head back and roared a great bass laugh. "Come, Iago! You are inventing that!"

Grinning, I sat beside him and gave him back the kerchief. "I swear I'm not."

"I *kiss* the instrument of their *pleasures*? Are you serious? The *instrument* of their pleasures? And I *kiss* it? Truly? That is the most lecherous formality I have ever heard. If I ever said that to them, they would be horrified."

"They would be pleased," I assured him.

"They would think me a barbarian!"

"They would think you a Venetian."

He shook his head and chuckled. "This is the strangest culture I have ever fought for," he said. "Thank Heaven for you, Iago, and also for Emilia. Otherwise this people would make no sense to me at all."

THE NEXT DAY, at about the same time, I was in our rooms, about to head down to the outside table in anticipation of Othello's company. Emilia was repairing a tear in one of my shirts and thought she would come outside with me where the light was better. We were startled by the sound of heavy boots, which approached our door and nearly kicked it in, before heavy hands began to pound upon it.

"Iago!" came Othello's ringing bass voice. "Iago, are you in there? I need your help immediately!"

I had the door open as soon as I heard his voice. "Come in, General," I said. Emilia had leapt up and was already moving toward the wine jug to offer him a drink.

Othello stepped into our small apartment, and then pulled up short. He had never been inside the Dolphin. "You live in *here*?" he asked, in an appalled voice. Before I could answer, he was speaking again. "Iago, you must come with me tonight to dinner."

"All right," I said in an expectant tone, and then waited to hear what emergency was brewing.

". . . and Emilia too, perhaps," Othello added, considering her.

She and I exchanged mystified glances. "Certainly, General," she said, with a curtsy. "May I ask where precisely we shall be dining, so I will know how to dress?"

"These senators, they peck at my soul!" Othello said with sudden vehemence. "Do you know, every single night since we have been back from Terraferma, every *single* evening, I am summoned to be a guest in some senator's home. How many senators can one city have?"

"That . . . is considered quite an honor, General," I said tentatively, adding quietly, "although to me it sounds like a Venetian form of hell."

"I am a *curiosity* to all of them!" he groused. "Do you think that in the history of this entire Republic, the senators usually vie to have the general of the army—who has almost always been some uncouth barbarian like myself—do you think the other uncouth barbarians were asked to supper with this frequency? No," he answered in a clipped tone. "I am not Othello to them, I am not even the general of their forces, I am rather something to show off to their neighbors and their servants and themselves. I help them feel pleased with themselves, they are so cosmopolitan and perhaps even *brave* that they chat with somebody who hardly looks human to them. I am so sick of it, Iago, I am so damned tired of it all. I cannot wait until we quit this damned city again."

"I understand, General," I said gently.

"So tonight, tonight, I was leaving the Senate chamber. I had just told them not to hire an engineer who wants to tear down the Citadel towers in Famagusta and rebuild them to be round. I thought I had escaped, I thought finally I will have one night at leisure, to wander around the city and finally see its famous beauty—and at the very last moment, that Senator Brabantio—"

"The one with the large nostrils," I said.

He paused, and grinned. "Yes. This is why I require you to come with me, Iago, you will help me keep my humor. He tugged my sleeve as I was almost out the door and insisted I come to his house. "It is one senator too many. I could not say no without causing offense, but this time, I need my own people with me. You will come. And you come too," he added to Emilia. "For just as I need Iago to retain my humor, I believe that Iago might need you."

"I agree," I said at once.

Othello laughed. "Very well, then! Meet me at the Arsenal gate at seven. And thank you, both." He bowed with a courtier's flourish to my wife, clapped his hand over his heart in my direction, and strode out of the little room with as much energy as he had entered.

Emilia and I exchanged glances, and she laughed. "So I am to dine with a *senator* tonight," she said, and rolled her eyes theatrically. "Good heavens, I have *nothing* to wear."

Chapter 19

BRABANTIO RADIATED SENATORIALITY. To meet the man was to meet the very archetype of Venetian senator; it was a role he played, one he excelled at, one he loved. I do not know what he had done when he was younger to make money, or to preserve the money made by the Brabantios before him. I could not imagine him a younger man—he seemed to have been born exactly this age, and a senator. He wore—this day and every day I had ever seen him—black doublet and hose with a long-sleeved crimson robe loose over it. A black sash over his left shoulder indicated that he was not only a senator but also a member of the Council of Ten. I suspected he wore his full regalia even in his sleep. He had been my father's wealthiest customer for as far back as I could remember, and he continued to heap business upon my brother. But I had hardly ever met the man.

CA'BRABANTIO, SOUTH OF the Rialto Bridge on the west side of the Grand Canal, was sumptuous without being at all original. Having seen the dining rooms and great halls of other senators in my time, I could not have distinguished this one. There were murals on the walls and ceilings, inlaid marble floors with complex designs, expensive rugs on all the windows, paintings everywhere. I disliked the ostentation, but I appreciated the power and wealth behind it. It was not unpleasant to dine with fine linen napkins under elegant chandeliers while eating sumptuous foods. Emilia—the only woman at the table—shot me little looks throughout dinner that seemed to say: "Is this not precious? We must opine about it all in private later!"

Brabantio, like every man, wanted to hear Othello's history. The general had developed abridged versions of his adventures, the variants of which he could recite by rote. At this point in our friendship, I could nearly recite them by rote myself, having heard them repeated ad nauseam to every officer and commissioner in Rovigo. His recitations occasionally included the cannibals, but always left out his stint as a war-slave. The cannibals had not come up yet tonight, but I anticipated they soon might, as Othello looked a little tired; he tended to use the cannibal story as a way of jolting his hosts into a quick, polite, but shocked good night.

DURING THE FIFTH course there was a movement from the ornamented door to the kitchen. All evening, such doorway movements had preceded the arrival of a new culinary invention. I hoped there would not be a sixth course; my stomach was already distended. I expected to see the majordomo of the household, or perhaps a servant, step through the door.

Instead, a slender blonde in a pale silk gown, the neckline and sleeves decorated with lace and gold thread, backed gracefully into the room. She pulled a cart on which rattled a variety of wine jugs. She turned to face us, and even Emilia drew in a breath of admiration: this may have been the prettiest young lady in Venice. Hers was the classic Venetian beauty—pale skin, hair so pale it was almost white, a high broad forehead, softly sculptured features. She gave us all a wide-open stare, and her eyes were so blue we could see the sapphire from halfway across the dining hall.

"Father," she said quietly, "may I join you for the dessert wine?"

There was something in the tone of her voice, the pause before his answer, the way he glanced at her, that made it clear: they had earlier agreed she would not dine with us, and her request now took him by surprise.

"Of course you may," Brabantio said, laying down his napkin and turning full to face her for a moment. "If you would like to do that, I would be very pleased."

Emilia and I exchanged glances, wondering.

"Gentlemen, madam," Senator Brabantio said, gesturing to the pale Venus by the wine cart, "this is my daughter, Desdemona."

Chapter 20

SHE SMILED AT US POLITELY, a smile as beautiful for its restraint as for its sincerity. "Good evening." Turning her eyes directly to Othello, she said, "It is an honor to meet you, General." Her voice—strangely, for one so young and sheltered and privileged—was warm with compassion, as if she knew how tiresome such a dinner was for him, and was impressed that he had the grace to show up anyhow.

Othello, his usual broad smile looking somehow foolish in her presence, nodded his head. "Lady," he said, hand to his heart and bowing his head. "The honor is mine." Then relaxing somewhat: "And here is my ensign and bosom friend, Iago, and his lady wife Emilia."

"Oh, is she your wife?" Brabantio said to me, with passing interest. Without looking at Emilia he said casually to Othello, "I assumed she was with you."

Emilia immediately laughed and took my hand reassuringly; I reddened and said nothing. Othello gracefully responded, "You honor me to think I would be deserving of the lady's favor, but I assure she is extremely married to my ensign. And *he* is even *more* married to *her*."

Having stumbled over that obstacle, all the pleasant, proper courtesies were exchanged. Othello was at the senator's right, and I to his left with Emilia beside me; the chair beside Othello was empty, and he gestured to it. His was not the graceful, mannered gesture of a nobleman; it was the casual, familiar gesture a soldier makes to a colleague. Desdemona stood up a little straighter, like a startled whippet, as if she had never seen such behavior before. A fleeting smile animated her face as she finally took his meaning, then she composed herself, and crossed to sit beside him primly. "Pray continue your discussion, gentlemen," she said demurely. "I did not mean to interrupt; I will offer the wine when there is a lull in conversation."

"*WHEN THERE IS a lull in conversation,*'" Emilia repeated hours later in an arch tone as we were undressing for bed. "That girl is a filly straining at her halter. She does not want to be the mistress of that house, but by the brightest heaven, she is determined to play the role well, simply because she has nothing else to *do*. Tonight's dinner was surely the most interesting thing that has happened to her in months."

"Dining with General Othello is always the most interesting thing to happen to *anyone* in months," I said dismissively, slipping my nightshirt over my head. "*Years*, perhaps." I got into bed.

"She was fascinated by him," Emilia said, combing her hair.

"Everyone is fascinated by him," I said, laying my head back on the pillow. "As he himself often complains, he is a most fantastic conversation piece."

"I think he likes Brabantio better than most," Emilia said.

"Do you speak from your extensive experience of joining him in his senatorial dinner gauntlets?" I said. "Since you are so obviously his mistress?"

She ignored that, and I was grateful. "I kept expecting him to tell the story about the cannibals, but he never did." A pause. "Do you think that really happened? About the cannibals, I mean?"

It had never occurred to me that Othello would embellish any story. The man was an open book, guileless, almost simple in a way. "Why would he do that?" I demanded.

She shrugged and lay her comb on the table. "To shock people into leaving him alone."

"Oh, he definitely does that," I agreed. "But that doesn't mean he made it up."

"WELL," OTHELLO ANNOUNCED, the following afternoon, "Brabantio has invited me to return immediately for another meal. You are both invited, and I insist on it."

"Whatever will you talk about on a second assignation?" I teased. "You covered your entire history quite efficiently on your first one."

"There is always the cannibal story, to make an early end of it." Othello sighed. "Meet me at the Arsenal gate at seven bells."

THIS SECOND EVENING was a little different. Having heard most of Othello's tales the night before, Brabantio now pressed for details: in which mountains did he seek the treasure? What battle tactics worked best against the Turks in the Levant?

Brabantio himself held forth, somewhat pompously, about Venice's glorious history, of its remarkable history of democratic (well, oligarchic) rule, of our supremacy for centuries of the waters. If brevity is indeed the soul of wit, his holding-forth was somewhat witless. He informed Othello that Venice had been founded by refugees, survivors from Troy; not ten minutes later, with no apparent awareness that he was contradicting himself, he announced that the city had been founded at midday on the vernal equinox in the year of our Lord 421, by a group of Paduans who were fleeing Attila the Hun. (I refrained from pointing out that Attila was, at that time, about fifteen years old.) These were tales Emilia and I had grown up on, as stimulating to us now as tired nursery rhymes. Othello listened patiently, with a pleasant expression on his face. Given his own life, I suspect the entire history of the Serene Republic did not make much of an impression on him.

The daughter, Desdemona, supped with us this time. She remained very quiet through the meal, and often excused herself to check things in the kitchen. Given how many servants there were, this struck me as an excuse to occasionally relieve herself of our company.

Each time she began to rise from her chair, she would hesitate for the briefest moment, with a questioning look in Othello's direction. He never noticed. After the hesitation, she would push back her chair, stand gracefully, and excuse herself. On her return, there was an inverse: the same hesitation on her part and obliviousness on his, before she sat herself beside him again.

FINALLY, THE DESSERT dishes were being cleared away, by servants wearing a silk print my family had been selling Brabantio since I was weaned. Brabantio settled farther back into his chair at the head of the table, clearly wanting to engage in further discourse with his chief guest, or perhaps soliloquize some more. Emilia barely squelched a yawn. Othello noticed this and shot a quick grinning glance at me.

"Senator," he said, "allow me to share with you a story I do not often tell, because it is so remarkable. It is of my encounter with cannibals."

Emilia and I exchanged knowing, grateful looks. In rapid but deftly vivid detail, the general described his encounters in Scythia with the men who tore their enemies' heads from their bodies and wore the scalps on ropes as gruesome necklaces. As he had all evening, Othello split his attention between Brabantio at the head of the table, to his right, and Desdemona, to his immediate left. As Othello spoke, Desdemona's pale face grew paler; as he described the killing ritual the cannibals engaged in, a fine sweat broke out on the girl's upper lip, and I feared she might be ill.

"General," the senator interrupted urgently. "While I find these tales fascinating, I think they are not appropriate to be told in the hearing of ladies, and most especially my daughter."

"My deepest apologies," Othello said at once, to both of them. "I did not mean to cause such a lovely young lady any distress, and

I apologize if I have given offense. I see it is time for us to bid you a grateful and fond good night."

"Oh, on the contrary, the evening is young yet, let us merely change the subject," Brabantio said with his senatorial authority. "I think a bit of air and a constitutional should evaporate the brimstone of these tales. Under other circumstances I would be delighted to exchange such tales of sorcery and witchcraft; Venetian history is full of sorcerers. But we should do it of an evening without ladies present, I think. Desdemona, will you show our guests the collection of Levantine tiles we have in the sitting room? They are not so exotic as your cannibals, sir, but they are more attractive for mixed company."

Desdemona looked chagrined. I assumed she was hoping to be rid of us as much as we were eager to be gotten rid of. But she smiled politely and said, "Certainly, Father. General, if you and your party would care to step into the sitting room . . ." As she had all evening, she pushed her chair out and gave Othello a look he did not notice; nonplussed, she moved her chair out farther and stood up.

Sensing my wife's exasperated impatience, I leapt up and held Emilia's chair for her, looking pointedly at Othello, hoping he would understand what he had failed to do all evening. He did not.

"The general is not accustomed to the niceties of Venetian table manners," I said quietly, directing this at both father and daughter.

"No reason he should be," Brabantio said.

"What have I done wrong?" Othello asked, curious but not concerned.

"Not *wrong*, exactly, sir." Brabantio laughed. "But it is considered good form, when dining beside a lady, to pull her chair back for her if she is about to rise. My daughter is courted by half the city's youths, and the very few who ever make it to the chair you sit in now would have been hovering over her all night, pulling out her chair every time she had to leave the table, holding it for her every time she rejoined us."

Othello's warm smile bypassed Brabantio and was all for Desdemona. "Pardon me, my lady, I meant no disrespect."

Desdemona shook her head in a forgiving gesture, but did not speak. Obviously Othello had overshot the mark by embellishing the cannibal story; she looked distressed now, the slightest crease between the brows on that alabaster face.

"Please follow me, sir," she managed to say, nearly in a whisper, and gestured toward one of the smaller doors on the side of the room.

"I will be along in a moment," Brabantio said from his chair, not looking at all as if he intended to get up from it.

WE PASSED INTO the next room, where a servant had gone ahead to light three oil lamps. The entire room—walls, floors, and ceilings— was inlaid with highly decorated tiles, white with dazzling blue designs and dabs of red on them. It created a stunning effect, as if we had just entered into a celestial cave.

"I have seen such tiled rooms in their homelands," Othello said. "They are common in mosques and wealthy homes. Are they not beautiful?"

As Emilia and I murmured assent, Desdemona reached out shyly and rested one pale finger on Othello's dark forearm. He turned sharply toward her, as if he had received a shock. "Please forgive my father's presumptions," she whispered. "I would very much like to hear the rest of the cannibal story."

Othello blinked in surprise. "Does the lady feel she must indulge me?" he asked.

"Not at all," she said. "I found it riveting, and full of matter for questions. My father is overly cautious. He thinks I am as fragile as my face."

Othello blinked again. Emilia took my hand and squeezed it.

"I am delighted to know you are not offended by my tale, mistress," Othello said carefully. He smiled.

"Might I hear the rest of the story?" she pressed.

Othello, Emilia, and I exchanged surprised expressions. "What, now?" he said. "I think if your father entered and heard me talking to you on the subject, he would find me objectionable."

Desdemona dropped her eyes, as if suddenly fascinated with a particular tile in the wall. I saw one of her hands curl into a tight fist, so tight her arm shook. "Perhaps another time," she said vaguely. "Come, there are some particularly lovely tiles on this other wall," and with a surprisingly long-legged stride, she led us toward the far side of the room.

Chapter 21

THREE NIGHTS LATER, Othello—and Emilia and myself—were summoned to the senator's again. This time it was a dinner party for about twenty, at which Othello was the guest of honor for his defensive leadership against Ferrara. We were the only nonpatricians at the affair, and Emilia looked as if she'd spent her life around these people. I found it almost poignant that we had been drawn together in part by our dislike of Venetian superficiality, and yet we found ourselves increasingly willing to float within that sea. Not only willing, but in Emilia's case, extremely capable. We were accepted by all these people as if we shared their birthright. I confess we were both fired up by it. I was physically stronger and at least as educated as any of these gentlemen. I need not scorn them, but I need not be sycophantic either. I deserved the company and was determined to continue in it. Especially to watch Emilia glow.

Emilia attached herself to Desdemona, and I hardly saw her all evening; Othello was of course besieged by curious sycophants and did a fine job maintaining his cheerful composure, although I hardly saw him, either. I spent most of the evening being chattered at by minor gentility, who wanted to know what it was like to be a confidant of a Moor. I failed to give them any useful information, as

I had nothing to compare it to, and no report at all of bizarre or un-Christian ways.

Over the next several weeks, Othello was constantly feted everywhere, and brought Emilia and myself along. On more than one occasion, I had to listen to the passing comment that the general had a beautiful wife or mistress or concubine, and each time, I took a deep breath before explaining that no, he did not. There was nothing improper in Othello's and Emilia's behavior toward each other—I knew that, I realized it was pure presumption on the speakers' parts. I did not begrudge my wife and my friend a public ease with each other. But I was concerned that Emilia might innocently establish a light reputation for herself. And I disliked the humiliation of setting things straight with strangers. A bigger man than I, I am sure, would have found amusement in the misapprehension; I wished I were that bigger man.

BRABANTIO'S PALACE WAS the one to which Othello was most often summoned. Othello stopped complaining about these invitations; to that house alone he seemed content to go, even eager. It became common for the summons to reach him in his office at the Saggitary, while I was with him. The custom had developed that he would hand me the embossed card and say, "Meet me at the Arsenal gate at seven bells. With Emilia, if she is so inclined."

"He likes the girl," Emilia said conspiratorially at about half-six one evening as we were dressing. "And she likes him."

"That," I announced, "is ridiculous in both directions."

"Do you think he is so fond of the senator's pomposity that he looks forward to a new dose of it several times a week?" Emilia demanded, brushing some lint off the back of my jerkin.

"Certainly, the girl is food for the eyes," I said. "Prettier than any of the other unavailable female flesh he might have occasion to ogle."

"She likes him too." Emilia grinned, moving around to my front to make sure my laces were neat. "I was with her at that first large dinner party. She never took her eyes off him."

There was a single sharp rap on the door. I crossed, and opened it. An officious young man who clerked at the Saggitary saluted and then informed me that Othello did not require our presence that evening.

"Why did he not come to tell us himself?" I asked in surprise.

The youth looked at me as if I were an idiot. "The general does not run such errands," he said.

I dismissed him.

"Do not even say it," Emilia said at once, reading my expression. "This has nothing to do with you, Iago. The lad's quite right, it would be odd for Othello to come in person."

"He came in person to summon us, the first three times!" I protested. "He came as a friend, asking our assistance! Why can he not, as a friend, now come and at least thank us for our service to him, or explain the rudeness of dis-inviting us?"

"It is hardly our service to him," Emilia countered. "We have been the ones dining far above our place for weeks now. It was if anything an indulgence on *his* part, to take us along."

"That may be how it looked to outsiders, but that is not the real matter, and you know it," I argued. "He *ordered* me to go with him, his need of my company was so great."

"Go meet him at the gate and ask him why he didn't come in person himself, then," Emilia suggested with a comfortable shrug. She turned her back on me. "Here, loosen my corset for me if we're not going out tonight."

"There will be people at the gate; I would look like a fool," I snapped, not offering to help her.

"Since when do you, Iago, care what other people think of you?" she asked, amused.

That brought me up short. "I do not care what others think of me, just what *he* thinks of me," I said brusquely, and grabbed her laces to untie them. "He would think it foolish of me to upbraid him at the gate."

"That's because it *would* be," she said in a tone of exasperation, amplified by a sigh as the laces loosed. "I think it is wonderful that he has gained his equilibrium enough to navigate the artificial sea of Venetian manners. Good for you for teaching him to steer it; good for him for being an apt pupil."

"I never thought of it as student and pupil. I thought of it as two friends appreciating each other's company," I growled through closed teeth, tugging at the lower laces. "I do not see why I should suddenly be deprived of his company because I have been a good enough friend to help him feel comfortable on his own."

She glanced over her shoulder at me with a look of confusion, and then laughed. "Iago, my dear, are you jealous? Are you jealous of the whole of Venice, just because Othello, heaven forbid, might make another friend from among its many inhabitants?" When I did not answer, she added in a knowing tone, "Or are you jealous there is one in particular who might borrow your friend's heart and not return it?"

A spasm of anxiety gripped me. "What do you mean?" I demanded.

Emilia turned to face me, stretching, sinuously arching her torso beneath the loosened corset. If I were not distracted, I would have found this irresistibly seductive. "No man ever likes to see his friends give up their bachelorhood, even if they themselves are married," she said comfortably. "My father had three widowed friends, and each of them, remarrying, distressed him more than he had words to say it. He never liked their new wives."

"Are you mad? The man's not getting married. He's never even spoken a word in private with that girl. And good Lord, she must have the most desirable dowry in the city—do you think her father would dispose of her to a man who is not a patrician? Who is not even a Venetian? Who would forever change the family's *race*?"

Emilia blinked in shock. "Do you really think that way?"

"Of course not, but Brabantio does. I know these men, Emilia, I grew up in their shadows. That girl will be married off to—"

"Her name is Desdemona, you know," Emilia interrupted

sharply. "You've never once to my ear called her that. You call her 'that girl,' as if she were an object, not a person."

"That's because she essentially *is* an object," I said heatedly. "No fault of hers, and certainly I pity her for it, but she will be married off according to her father's will. It has not even entered my mind that Othello would cease to be a bachelor. So stop preaching at me for being afraid that it could happen. It cannot, and it will not. She will be married, yes, and probably soon, but by her father's choosing." A new thought came to me, and I felt strangely comforted by it: "I am sure Othello does not realize that. Perhaps you're right that he fancies her. But just as he did not know he should pull her chair out, perhaps he doesn't know the rules here. I am probably the only man in Venice qualified to tell him so, without his losing face."

Emilia grinned and pushed the corset off elegantly. "Excellent, a way to make yourself more important than the girl," she said. "I am *so* glad you're not the jealous type."

Chapter 22

LATE THAT EVENING, when I was sure Othello would be home but not yet abed, I crossed the campo and was admitted to the Arsenal, and then the Saggitary. A servant let me in, and I found the general staring intensely out his bedroom window at the moon.

"Good evening, Ensign," he said without looking at me. "I hope you did not take it amiss that I did not ask you to come with me tonight."

"Truly, General, I was put out by it, but Emilia lectured me and I realized that I was being childish."

Othello turned back into the room and slowly smiled at me. "No other officer would answer me so honestly. I do love that about you, Iago."

"Others do not find it lovable, General," I replied. "Others find it churlish."

"Fie on others, then," Othello said. "Anyway, I dearly wish I'd brought you along, if that helps your wounded pride. It was a horrible affair this evening."

I was ashamed that I felt mollified at hearing this. "Why, General?" I asked.

Othello took a deep breath and then began a monologue delivered in the most peevish voice I'd ever heard him utter. "There was a gallant present, the spoiled son of some patrician. He was in the full-on silly Venetian paraphernalia, with tresses and pale complexion. He was the only other guest but me, and he was there to court Desdemona through her father, right in front of me. It took me nearly an hour to realize that is what was going on. He flattered her, but only to her father." He paused a moment, his fingers fidgeting with the kerchief tied around his neck. "At the end of the evening, he took her father aside to speak to him in low tones, and a servant woman came out and stood by the table so that Desdemona and I would not be left alone. If you or Emilia had been there, there'd have been no need of the servant woman, and I could have conversed with Desdemona freely, but the damned hag looked as if she'd pinch me if I so much as glanced directly at the lady. Desdemona kept trying to send her away with excuses, but the woman would not move. Then the senator returned to the table alone and announced the young man had left the house. To which Desdemona said, *Thank you, Father,* and Brabantio replied, *He really would have been fine, you know.* Do you know what they were talking about, Iago?" His tone was rhetorical, but I decided to answer anyhow.

"The man was Desdemona's suitor," I said. "He asked her father for her hand and her father said no, at Desdemona's request."

"Yes! And they did this *directly in front of me!* Is that not shocking?

What if the answer had been yes, and there I was, sitting right at the table, clearly courting Desdemona for myself?"

I could not speak for what felt like one quarter hour, but the silence must have lasted no longer than a heartbeat. "You . . . you are courting Desdemona?"

He looked equally startled. "It is not obvious?"

I smiled almost sheepishly, with a passing sense of relief. "No, General," I said. "Except to Emilia, of course, who seems to notice everything."

"You have a marvelous wife there, Ensign," Othello said, offhandedly, before pressing on. "I consider it extremely obvious. My constant dining at their table—surely far more often than any other suitor has ever spent there—I thought this made me nearly family. Tonight was my attempt to play the role without you there to lean on, for honestly, Iago, I cannot imagine myself in any of these houses without knowing you are in it somewhere too."

"Thank you, General," I said quietly, but he hardly heard and kept going.

"And then I was treated as if I were a piece of furniture! Or a pet! They allowed—no, *invited*, somebody else to come in and press his suit in front of me! Desdemona said no, of course, but Brabantio chided her for it—*in front of me*. I have never been insulted so— and, Iago, you know I am not the sort to take offense. I was going to chastise him for it, but then I thought perhaps there is some strange Venetian custom I am not aware of, and since you were not there to warn me of it, I decided to hold my tongue until I could speak to you about it in the morning. I am very glad you've come tonight—forgive me, in my annoyance I have not even asked you why you've come."

"Our minds are much alike, General," I said. I felt protective indignation on his behalf. But also, I felt almost as if I stood outside myself, watching some other Iago experience a flood of childishly pleasurable emotions that were not manly but still very real. "Emilia was quite adamant that you had a growing fondness for the girl, and—although, as I admit, I was too blind to see it myself—I wanted to alert you to the ... as you said, the strange Venetian customs. If you care to hear about them. Perhaps I should come back in the morning, when you are calmer."

"No! Speak to me now or I shall never sleep tonight," Othello declared. "Wine!" he called to a servant waiting by the door. He pointed to a stuffed chair by the unlit hearth. "Sit," he said. "Explain what I need to know so that I may court Desdemona in the Venetian manner."

"Are you sure you want to court her, General?" I asked despite myself. "She is extremely beautiful, I grant you, but she has barely exchanged words with you. You do not know the lady."

Othello grinned. It was one of his hearty, playful grins, which had seldom lit his face since ... well, come to think of it, since we first dined at Brabantio's. "Your wife is craftier than you know, Iago," he said. "Sometimes at parties and fetes she has been the chaperone for Desdemona and I to speak together. We have had more of a chance to come to know each other than—"

"Emilia?"

"Yes, Emilia." Othello smiled. "It is not a regular courtship, there is certainly nothing untoward. But, for instance, there was a dance at the senator's dinner party, do you recall? And we three stood together away from the dancers. She stood between us, but then deliberately turned her attention to some painting on the wall. She gave us a chance to have more conversation than we could at Brabantio's table. And she has done similarly at other gatherings."

"Why would she not tell me this?" I demanded.

He laughed. "Iago, it is hardly a conspiracy. She performed a little kindness below the notice of others, that is all. I have not tried to make love to Desdemona. I have been a gentleman. I have never even expressed my interest in her, but the interest, by its very nature, is obvious."

"Meanwhile, Emilia has been deceitful," I muttered, appalled. "To *me*."

"She was being *discreet*," Othello corrected. "I am indebted to her for it—and by extension to you, Iago, so there is nothing amiss here."

My panicked feeling made no sense, but still the panic was there. "Why did you not take *me* into your confidence?" I demanded. "Why was *I* not a part of this great secret romancing? Why is Emilia deeper in your confidence than I am?"

"You silly man," Othello said, sounding slightly impatient now. "There was no secret about which to take you in. I did not solicit your wife's assistance, nor did she ever overtly offer it; she simply made sure to find herself in conversation with Desdemona on occasion—a natural thing—and then with Desdemona beside her, she would find her way toward me—also a natural thing, as I know Emilia well and her husband, as you may have heard, is my ensign and close friend. She would stand there for a bit while Desdemona and I exchanged pleasantries and stories. Then Emilia would move on, and Desdemona with her. For all I know she took Desdemona to converse with every would-be suitor in Venice, but I do not think so. I prefer to think I was the only one whom she assisted."

"Neither of you ever *told* me!" I said hotly.

Othello began to answer, then stopped, looked at me a moment, and began again. "Iago. What have I just described to you? If you heard an account of that, would you not dismiss it impatiently as women's talk, as party chatter? You would think it trifling and berate Emilia or complain to me that we were wasting precious moments of your life with such trivial nonsense."

"There was a secret among those close to me, and I was kept from the secret," I said stonily, feeling my pulse all the way into my stomach. "Even tonight when Emilia spoke to me, she did not tell me this."

"What should she have said?" Othello said, increasingly impatient. "*I know they are taken with each other because sometimes I stand about at a party with the two of them, and they talk to each other?* Is she deceiving you because she did not share such a specific little comment with you? Do not be childish, Iago, childishness becomes you no better than does jealousy. Anyhow, this is not about Emilia. You came here to explain to me Venetian courting customs, and I am eager to hear them—precisely *so that* Emilia no longer has to be our self-appointed chaperone. So." He settled into the chair across from me and accepted the wine the servant offered. He gestured for me to take the other cup from the tray and said, "Begin."

I made myself tuck away the seething anxiety I felt about Emilia. I had come here with a real purpose, and not an easy one.

I accepted the wine. "You see, General, Senator Brabantio is a patrician."

"Of course he is. That is tautological, Iago, that is like saying, 'the father is a man.' He would not be a senator were he not a patrician."

"Correct. And the patrician class only marries within itself."

"I have heard this," Othello said, unruffled. "And who made them patricians? Their forefathers, or they themselves, by achievement, Iago. It is well known throughout the world that Venice, alone of all civilized states that ever were, has a ruling class into which one may ascend *by merit.*"

Ah, the myth of Venice. Now even more, I did not want to have this conversation. It would crush him and enrage him, and I did not want to be the man to hurt him so.

"That was true at one point in time," I said carefully. "And it was true for centuries. But a long time ago, those who were patricians decided there were enough patricians and literally closed the ranks. Today the only way to be a member of the patriciate is to be born into it." As his eyes opened in their startlingly white orbs, I added apologetically, "Once, yes, a man might have won his way into those upper ranks, but that—like so many other things that made Venice splendid—that is in the past. It does not happen now."

"The Duke of Urbino was granted hereditary patrician status," Othello recited promptly. Oh, heaven, he was in deep then: he had been *investigating.*

"By the pope," I corrected him. "Not by Venice. In fact, the pope gave it to him while he was fighting *against* Venice."

"An exception could be made today," Othello argued.

"Perhaps if the exception were Venetian by birth," I said, hating that I had to be so unpleasantly precise.

Othello sat upright and put a hand to his own cheek, gently, as if in ginger discovery. "Here, in this great republic, where my race has not prevented me from ascending to the heights of—"

"You may ascend," I said, "but not your offspring. You may become a citizen, in time, if you settle here and pay your taxes. But never a patrician. Forgive me, General, for speaking bluntly, but you wanted to know. It has never once crossed Brabantio's mind to think of you as a suitor to his daughter. You could give her roses and jewels and serenade her in front of him, and he would not consider you a suitor. He was not being rude tonight, when he allowed a suitor to make one last plea right in front of you. If you had chastised him as you felt the urge to, he would have had no idea what caused your upset."

Othello put down his wine cup and sprang to his feet, smacking one hand into the other fist with terrible agitation. "If this is true, then why does Desdemona give me her courtesy? Am I just some . . . *curiosity* to her, as to all the others? I cannot believe that. I have seen an expression on her face that I have never seen from another human being in my life. She loves me, sure."

"I'm not saying that she does not," I said quickly. "The heart does not care what the mind knows. She may be yours entirely, in her imagination. But she knows, even better than I do, how impossible it is to pursue." I could not tell if he was heeding me; he was agitated as he strode across the room, slamming one fist into the other hand. "And so, General," I said, taking a deep breath, "the most honest answer to your query is that you *cannot* court her in the Venetian style, because you are not Venetian. She is patrician, and you are not. She is Brabantio's only child. His heir. Unless some foreign royalty presses a suit for her, she will be married within the Venetian patriciate."

"That damned obstinate man!" he bellowed.

"If I may say so, Othello," I said gently, "the fact that he allows her to reject her suitors makes him quite an indulgent father." Pause. "But not so indulgent that he will reduce his house by marrying her outside the herd, so to speak."

He stopped moving. He stopped slamming his fist into his palm. He seemed suddenly deflated. He stood by the window, and the moonlight made him nearly blue. "I did not come to Venice seeking a wife," he said. "I never thought to have one. And I know I will survive if this young lady is never mine. But by heaven it galls me that something so ridiculous would prevent it, when it is for this very same patriciate that I risk my life and well-being."

I wished I were somewhere else. "They pay you in money," I said. "They pay their own kind in favors. Desdemona is destined to be such a favor, to somebody—but not to you, General. It grieves me to be the one to tell you that, but I must remind you, you did ask—"

"Yes, Iago, I do not begrudge you the news, I thank you as always for your honesty," Othello said. "Now leave me, please, I require some time alone to muse upon this. I am very grateful to have been properly informed of my status. I had allowed myself to think I was in all ways appreciated as a man here."

"I feel sickened that my nation treats you thus. I wish I had the power to change it."

He gave me a weak smile. "I believe you, Iago. Go, now, and give Emilia my regards. The next time I am summoned to eat at Brabantio's or anywhere, I will be sure to bring you with me. To help me remember my place."

I'd never heard such bitterness in that warm, ringing voice.

"WHAT AN EXCELLENT project for you, encouraging a romance you know may never happen," I snapped at Emilia a quarter hour later.

"Never mind that you kept it a secret from me. What other secret meddling do you keep from me?"

Her face reddened against the pale flax of the bedsheets. "I did not think of it as a secret. It was so benign, it was so innocent. You'd have done the same if you were aware of their attraction. Or," she added cockily, propping her head on one bare arm, staring up at me from the bed, "perhaps you would not have. You might be too jealous for his affections."

"He may not marry her," I repeated clearly. "You gave him false hope. And I had to tell him that, because of your feminine meddling."

She took a breath and looked down. "I'm sorry," she said. She pushed herself to sit up straighter, looking now more eager than cocky. "Really, I am, Iago. I meant it as a favor to them both, but you're right, it showed no forethought."

"So do not do it anymore," I said, satisfied. I began to unlace my doublet. "With them, with anyone. Do not meddle, Emilia, you are not the meddling sort, and I love you for that, but you're not *good* at meddling, so for the love of God, do not interfere, do not scheme. And above all, wife, do not *hide* things from me! I could have told you weeks ago the danger of your abetting them. Then Othello would not have fallen into such a reverie of false hopes, and he would not be as miserable as he is right now. Do you understand?"

She fell back against the pillow. "I'm so sorry," she said in a softer voice, eyes closed. "I understand."

"I did not hear you," I snapped.

"I understand," she said louder, opening her eyes to stare at the ceiling.

"Look at me," I said. "Say it straight to my face, meet my eye and promise me that you will never scheme or interfere in other people's lives."

She sat up again and turned to face me, her lovely neck bare and pale in the lamplight.

"I promise," she said. "Now I feel ashamed."

"I don't want you to feel ashamed," I said uncomfortably. I turned away from the bed as I pulled off my shirt. "But I want us to trust each other, and I cannot trust you if I think you are likely to do something like this again." I glanced at her and saw her eyes filling with tears; in a moment she would be crying, and then I would not be able to think clearly. "Emilia, I love you very much. I believe we have a marriage of true minds, a marriage to be envied by all others. In large part it's because I trust you to be as smart and honest and industrious as I am. You have a clever mind, and I adore your clever mind, but for the love of God, do not use it to make mischief, even if you think the mischief's innocent."

"Shall I apologize to the general?"

I shook my head. "That will just humiliate him." I hung my shirt on a wall peg. "Let it go. Brabantio himself has no idea of any of this and will surely call Othello to supper again. He will likely ask us to go with him. We will all go on as before, sans secret romance. I'll wager we all dine there tomorrow night."

AND INDEED, NEXT DAY, an invitation arrived. We all took a gondola to Ca'Brabantio for supper. That night we met a handsome young Florentine soldier newly graduated from Castelvecchio in Verona. His name was Michele Cassio.

The Florentine

Chapter 23

t dinner, I learned three things about Michele Cassio. First: he was good at math, something he wanted all of us to know. Second: he did not partake of wine, something he did not want us to notice—but his glass remained untouched all evening. Third, he embodied every stereotype I'd ever heard about the men of Florence: he was an attractive, charming fop.

His face was handsome, in a classic, even rugged, Roman-soldier way. He had excellent teeth and beautiful long lashes. He was tall, broad-shouldered and slim-waisted; his carriage was immaculate; his dress was amended with niceties far more expensive than a soldier's purse could probably afford. He was exceptionally charming to Emilia and Desdemona, holding Desdemona's chair for her and offering a discreet comment on the sweetness of her perfume. He greeted both ladies by pressing three fingers to his lips and then opening his hand toward them; he then kissed both ladies' hands in an extravagant, Florentine manner and smiled at them both within an inch of decency's limit. I did not know Desdemona well enough to read her, but Emilia—Emilia, of all women, who was never charmed by any gallant of Venice—seemed charmed by him. He uttered Florentine small talk with a Florentine accent and it made my wife—*my wife*—giggle. Perhaps her giggle was politely veiled mockery, but perhaps it wasn't. And anyhow, when had I last elicited a giggle from her? What could I do to make her giggle that way later, more intensely than her passing giggle now? For a moment I was distracted, worriedly inventing an answer.

Michele was not a soldier masquerading as a fop, but quite the other way around: the man, at twenty-three years, had never seen battle. He had only served in a sleepy garrison along the borders of Terraferma. Yet I cannot deny it: when he entered the room, his whole bearing suggested grandeur; his jerkin looked sculpted onto his body, and his sword hung at his side with some inexplicable extra gallantry (until Brabantio's majordomo requested he remove it).

Othello had heard from me, for years now, of the rivalry between Venice and Florence. Even as political allies, we enjoy hating each other: Florence is the only city-state in Europe that comes close (but not very close) to the cultural richness of Venice, and naturally feels the need to demean La Serenissima, as if that could somehow make them superior. We return the favor by demeaning them. Over decades this has calcified into absurdity. In Venice we have "fool Florentine" jokes, and I am sure the Florentines have "fool Venetian" jokes, although no doubt those are not as funny. Lest you think my nativity gives me bias, consider this: Florentines from Machiavelli right up to Giannotti have been preoccupied with the study of Venice, while no Venetian writers of note have expressed the slightest interest in examining Things Florentine (except for Marco Foscari back in '27, who didn't like them anyhow). The men of Florence all were prissy, overdressed, effeminate, lacking manly valor despite their pretty looks, and valuing their tailors above their armorers. Even more than the Venetians, I mean. The extra feather in Michele's hat—a long, curling ostrich feather dyed bright blue—was to me the embodiment of his native frivolity. On the other hand, he was proper, almost stiff, within his gallantry, as if he were playing an overwrought part at which he was very familiar and well rehearsed.

IT WAS INTERESTING that he did not touch the wine. More precisely, he put his glass to his lips at just the right moments—toasting our host's health, and so on—and even wet them, but took in so little that the serving boy never once refilled his glass.

"Michele has come to us to assist in strategy against the Turks, in our Cyprus defense," Brabantio explained. He said this directly to me. I realized, with a shock of displeasure, that he was explaining it only to me because Othello already knew it. How, and why, did the general know something I did not? I was his constant aide, far more than was Lieutenant da Porto; he made no decision without at least thinking aloud in my presence. And now Venice had imported some *Florentine* to work beside the general, and I knew nothing about it?

I smiled tightly. "The general did not mention it," I said.

"Surely I did, Iago!" Othello said, about to ladle some soup into his mouth. He set the spoon back down in the bowl. "Do you not remember we were talking about needing new defenses in Famagusta? And moving men back there, now that our Terraferma border is more secure again?"

"Of course I remember those discussions, General," I said, trying to sound casual, and trying not to obviously pitch my volume in Michele's direction. "I was your chief adviser in these matters. But I do not recall your wanting to bring in a specialist for anything. What are you, sir, an engineer?" I asked the Florentine.

"A strategist," Michele corrected me with a complacent smile. "I studied under Marco Sapegno and wrote a text that has been quite highly regarded, on the matter of transporting men and materiels most efficiently over land, as compared to over water."

I almost laughed out loud; Othello, recognizing the expression on my face, gave me a warning scowl in which I sensed some shared amusement. "How remarkably useful to our particular scenario," I said. "May I assume you wrote this text specifically in the hopes of gaining General Othello's attentions?"

Michele sat even more upright than he already was, and his face registered surprise. "Not particularly; what makes you ask?"

"There are few armies but Venice's that need such a particular accounting of resources," I said. "It is not as if you were, say, writing a manual on the use of cannons, which could be of use to nearly every army in the world."

"I was aware that Venice might find my talents useful," the young man said, with that same smile. "But Genoa would too, as well as Spain. I did not write the article *for* Venice, but I am very happy to present it *to* Venice."

"So. You are a *theoretician*," Othello said congenially. It's a good thing he said it then, or else I would have done so in a less congenial tone. "You study and comment on what you have learned by studying, and then you pass the information on to men of action like myself and Iago here, to act on it."

Michele's face reddened, hearing in the words a slight that Othello did not mean (but which I would certainly have meant, were I the speaker). "That is one way to look at it," he acknowledged. "Although I pride myself on being a disciplined soldier as well. I am in fact finishing my training here in Venice."

"So I have heard," Othello said. Another thing I myself had not heard. "Well, Iago and I will look over your text tomorrow, and I am sure when you are ready for actual soldiering, I would be happy to have you in my unit. Although you will not be able to dress like . . . that." There was a gesture toward the ostrich feather. As an outsider, Othello said it without malice, as a simple statement of fact; as Venetians, the rest of us around the table exchanged barely suppressed snickers. Even Brabantio, bless him.

"I want to read this article as well," declared Brabantio. "Then I can report to the Senate. Tomorrow we shall all four convene to review it. I work from home tomorrow, so come at ten, and we will examine it then."

MICHELE WENT WITH US back toward the Arsenal; like myself and Emilia, he was staying at the Dolphin. His departure from our hosts was elaborate and full of complicated gestures involving both of his wrists, most of his fingers, and at one point an elbow; he showered so many compliments on Desdemona's beauty that she looked embarrassed by the time the gondola finally pulled us away from the beautifully sculpted water gate.

"You know she will wed a member of the Venetian aristocracy," Othello informed Michele as soon as we were out of earshot of Ca'Brabantio.

"Who?" Michele said absently, then immediately smiled and bowed his head. "Ah, the lady Desdemona. Yes. I am from a titled family myself and I know how these things work."

"She cannot marry you," Othello insisted conversationally, with satisfaction. "Even if you are good stock. You are not good *Venetian* stock."

Michele gave the general a quizzical, polite smile. "But I have no interest in the lady," he said. "I hope I did not appear to be paying court to her."

"No more than you were courting my wife," I said archly.

"Your wife?" Cassio's eyebrows shot up.

"Iago!" Emilia laughed and batted me with her fingers. Emilia was not the finger-batting type. "Pay no mind to him, sir. He is jealous of me."

"I would be too, if I had such an exquisite lady to call my own," Cassio said gallantly. "But please know, Ensign Iago, I have no designs on the lovely Emilia, and I admit I did not realize she was your wife."

In the gondola's shimmery lamplight, Othello, Emilia, and I all tried to read one another's expressions without being read ourselves.

"You thought she was the general's mistress," I said, with a rueful smile. "Did you not?"

"I apologize if I have offended somehow," Cassio deflected and turned his attention solely to Emilia, kissing his fingers and then gesturing toward her with them. "In Florence we take enjoyment in the presence of attractive women."

To my immense gratitude, in the wavering torchlight from the bow of the gondola, Emilia gave me a knowing look, and kissed me on the cheek.

Our lovemaking that night was exquisite.

Chapter 24

MICHELE CASSIO WAS, INDEED, excellent at math. He had calculated things precisely that it was my duty to know in general. His attention to detail was almost cowing—albeit it was abstract detail, idealized detail, theoretical armies and numbers and ships and harvests and bags of burlap. But given the Platonic ideal of people and objects he was working with, he had thought through a great deal. There was some kind of working brain behind that handsome face and bobbing blue ostrich feather.

Over the course of two dull hours, in Senator Brabantio's study, Michele read aloud his own text, in which he listed the exact amount of weight each soldier's provisions should weigh (assuming no man cheated and brought extra—such an assumption did not enter into his figuring), and how that would affect the speed of a boat when freighted, compared to the speed of a wagon train over various terrains, adjusting for the extra but varying weight and mass of, for example, horse feed or ballast for the ships. His algebra was quietly elegant. While he said nothing revolutionary, he reaffirmed what Othello, Othello's civilian superintendent Marco Salamon, myself, and the Senate had suspected: that we should keep all our cavalry on Terraferma and move only men to Cyprus.

But his calculations also showed us that we should move them with more supplies than we would have anticipated. The extra tonnage, freighted, would in the end cost us less resources and manpower than sending an extra ship later with additional supplies.

At the risk of sounding ungracious, that was the only thing of value we gained in two hours of narcotic verbiage.

FAR MORE INTERESTING than listening and responding to Cassio's figures, to me at least, was our one interruption. Brabantio's majordomo knocked and, upon invitation, opened the door, carrying on a tray a large silver box, like a casket or a Byzantine reliquary. "This arrived for your daughter, sir," the majordomo said dryly. "Will you accept it on her behalf? The gentleman awaits personally in his gondola for an answer."

Brabantio rolled his eyes and made a grunting sound. His manner suggested this sort of thing happened nearly every day. I noticed Othello tense and crane his head to get a better look at the thing.

"Let me see it." Brabantio sighed. "I need a respite from all these calculations."

The majordomo set it on the desk before the senator. I barely suppressed a gasp. The casket had gold chase-work on it, and the gold outlined a stylized pepper tree, which had become the emblem of a certain childhood friend of mine.

That casket was from Roderigo.

"Aha," Brabantio said dryly, holding up the gift and examining it from all sides, as if he were a farmer checking the health of a piglet. "That spice merchant again, I see." He handed the casket back to the majordomo. "Of course we won't accept this. The man is not even a patrician, for the love of angels, why does he think I would let him near my daughter?"

I felt Othello's bright black eyes swivel in their sockets toward me; I met them with my own and as compassionate a look as I could muster. Inside, though, I was strangling sad bemusement: poor Roderigo, now the richest citizen-merchant in all Venice, still pined for women he would never have.

I also felt a shamed kind of relief: nobody here knew the wooer was a friend of mine. Brabantio had just made it plain that in these rarefied circles I had stumbled upward into, Roderigo's efforts were fit for mockery, not sympathy. How should I interact with him when our paths next crossed, as they unavoidably would, at some social event? I found him increasingly tiresome as the years went by, but the ties of childhood instilled a very deep loyalty.

A FEW NIGHTS LATER, Othello and I were invited once again to Senator Brabantio's for supper. Emilia was not invited, and Desdemona did not join us—but several other senators did, as well as Zuane da Porto, Othello's lieutenant, and Marco Salamon, Othello's civilian counterpart.

Military and civilian have always been rigorously intermeshed in Venice. The commander in chief must answer to a committee of twenty civilians, all patricians in various government committees. The army is lousy with senior senators and retired military men, all functioning as "commissioners," who constantly watch over all things military. To prevent disgruntled officers from surreptitiously forming private militias capable of threatening the state, patrician superintendents are designated to shadow every officer, from captain general to paymaster. Remarkably, this baroque arrangement has always worked well for Venice, and over the course of nearly a millennia nobody has ever managed, or even seriously attempted, a coup. When the army, Senate, nobles, and richest merchants are all in bed with one another, it creates a marvelous unanimity of purpose. However, it also creates a stupefaction of endless meetings.

The subject today was the refortification of Zara against a Turkish incursion. Zara, just across the northern Adriatic from Venice, was the linchpin of the Dalmatian coast. If the Turks were to seize it, they would be in an alarmingly secure position to attack Venice, the Italian peninsula, and Hungary. It was a very small city, but its famed defenses and location gave it enormous strategic significance. Giulio Savorgnan, who governed there, had sent a long list of what the city required to withstand a Turkish siege. So we would be taking with us lots of explosive devices, artillery, munitions and other arms, baskets and buckets and bricks and carbon and iron, masons, physicians, and of course plenty of hangman's rope to deter deserters.

"Where is our young Florentine?" I asked, pleased by his absence. "Is not this sort of reckoning his specialty?"

"Cassio's servant sent word that he was indisposed tonight," Brabantio said.

"We have no real need of him," Othello said. "This is not an abstract conversation but the making of specific plans, involving real men and real oceans and real stones."

Cassio's servant? I wondered. Michele Cassio had a servant, staying with him in the enlisted men's barracks? Even if he were from a wealthy family, I found this arrangement odd, but nobody else around the table noticed. So I said nothing and joined the conversation with full attention, as we established the size of the force Othello would be taking with him to Zara, and which officers—in addition to da Porto and myself, of course. We pulled out charts and maps and diagrams, and discussed what specific part of the fortress wall required amendment; we established from where the rock would come; what best route to take to get there; whom to hire for carving and whom for smithing. We attended to details that went unnoticed in Michele Cassio's meticulous arithmetic: the political leanings of the local masons and their guilds, the religious tensions between Catholics and the Orthodoxy, which families with direct kinship ties to Venice lived on the landward side of the walled city....

THE MEETING ENDED LATE. It had been too long since I had been entirely in male company attending to military matters, and even if the senators were not military men themselves, they understood and appreciated the three of us who were.

Othello, da Porto, and I went by gondola through the close canals of Castello, debarking near the Salizada dei Pignater Bridge. We had then only a short walk along a street that was (thanks to its proximity to the Arsenal) almost as redolent with brothels as was the

Rialto. Othello was preoccupied with the results of the meeting, and wore silence like a cloak.

I walked to Othello's left, da Porto to his right; as we passed beneath one open balcony full of laughing half-dressed women and drunken half-dressed men, something caught my eye, and I glanced up over my left shoulder. One of the brunette whores, her nipples plum-colored in the lamplight, was wearing a soldier's cap with a bright blue ostrich feather stuck into it.

I looked away shocked, and then looked back again.

The tall, broad-chested young Adonis who was fingering the plummy nipples was none other than Michele Cassio.

He was far too drunk to have recognized me—or so I thought, until our eyes met. My own eyes widened in amazement, and I stopped abruptly. Othello took another preoccupied step or two before realizing he had lost his ensign. He stopped, turned to face me, da Porto behind him.

"Iago?"

I snapped my eyes away from Michele and down onto the cobbled street. "I'm sorry, General, I thought I lost a buckle. I heard something clatter on the pavement. It must have been a noise from within." Before he could look up and notice Cassio, I began to stride purposefully in the direction of the Arsenal gate. "That was a very useful evening," I said.

"Indeed," Othello said. (Da Porto almost never spoke.) "Now we need only establish a departure date, and debate whether or not you will bring your charming wife with you." He grinned and in the dark, nudged me playfully. "I am sure you do not want to leave her here with the likes of that Cassio around."

"Oh, General," I said pleasantly, unruffled. "I may be a jealous husband, but I am confident Emilia is not Michele Cassio's kind of woman."

THE NEXT MORNING, I entered Othello's office in the Sagittary unannounced, a privilege I'd earned. I surprised young Michele Cassio in earnest whispered conversation with him. Their conversation ended abruptly, almost guiltily, upon my entrance. I felt a twinge of unease as I realized something was being hushed, but I assumed Cassio's embarrassment was due to my seeing him on the whorehouse balcony.

"Good morning, General," I said. And nodding to the other, "Sir."

"Iago," Othello said, welcoming. "Cassio and I have been adjusting some figures for the packing of supplies on the ships to Zara. Your arrival is fortuitous."

"My arrival is predictable," I said, trying to sound offhand. "This is when I appear every morning except Sundays. It is my duty to oversee the provisions of the ships, so I am very glad you did not go too far into your discussions without my presence."

Othello looked bemused. "You are peevish this morning, Ensign. Did you not sleep well?"

"What new information have you got for me, General?" I said. "If there are extra supplies to be ordered, I must delegate my staff to obtain them at once." I made no attempt to smile at Cassio. "Are you coming with us, sir?"

"No, no," Othello said. "Michele is staying here, he has some bit of his training to finish yet—funnily enough, Iago, it is his artillery he must improve upon. I would leave you here to train him if you were not so indispensable to me, but as it is, of course, you are coming with me."

The pleasure and relief I felt at this declaration almost embarrassed me. "Thank you, General," I said at once; sensing something more was needed, I turned to Cassio and added, "Artillery practice requires precision, which seems to be your strength in many ways, so I am sure you will excel at it quickly enough. And by the time we return, I believe you shall be an officer. But what has happened to your feather, sir?"

Cassio automatically reached up toward his cap for the blue feather. The quill was broken two-thirds of the way up, and the end of it flopped over like a wounded limb. "It was a dancing accident," he said smoothly. With his Florentine elegance he managed to say this without sounding ridiculous.

"How does one break a feather in a dancing accident?" asked Othello, amused.

After a blink, Cassio explained, "I doffed it to a lady I was partnered with, and it was crushed by the gentleman beside me losing his balance and falling against me suddenly. The feather gave way under his weight but was pinned at such an angle that there was some damage done. I have replacements, of course." He said this with a reassuring smile, as if we might be concerned he didn't.

"Why haven't you replaced it, then?" I asked. "You are *point-device* in your accoutrement, it seems unlike you to let a broken feather linger in your cap."

This time the hesitation was longer. "To be honest, I have not been back to my quarters since the accident occurred," he said.

"Oh, ho!" Othello said with a hearty chuckle. "I thought I smelled stale wine upon your breath when you came in. You have a secret life as a carouser, do you not, Michele?"

Cassio reddened. "Nothing interferes with my duty or my commitment here, General," he insisted.

"Your clothes are very neat for having been out all night," Othello commented, with a gesture.

"Perhaps they were not on him for much of the evening," I postulated dryly.

Realizing he was going to be merely teased, not punished, Cassio reddened further and allowed himself a small sheepish smile. "The gentlemen are astute in their observations," he said.

Othello turned to me with a grin, his gesture still pointing toward Cassio. "This Michele is a strange fellow," he said in a conspiratorial tone. "He is so careful to appear proper but then he has nude dancing accidents when none of us are looking. Ha!"

"I would attribute it to his bachelor life," I said. And with a meaningful look at Michele, I added, "I am sure his blue feather has survived plenty of dancing accidents before this one."

"*I* am a bachelor and *I* don't have that life," Othello said.

"Or that feather," I pointed out.

"That must be it." Othello chuckled. "Michele, get rid of the feather and do not replace it. It encourages uncouth behavior for an officer, and you will be an officer very soon."

Cassio instantly snatched the feather from his cap, pulling the cap off his head along with it. "Of course, sir," he said awkwardly and fumbled to pull the feather loose. It was the first time I had ever seen a Florentine fumble. Venetian despite myself, I enjoyed bearing witness to it. He replaced the cap.

"Give it to me," Othello said sternly, of the feather. Cassio did so.

With a sudden grin, Othello reached up and poked the damaged quill into his own curly hair. "Let's see if it brings me your luck with ladies." He laughed.

I smirked; Cassio managed a nervous little chuckle. Othello pulled out the quill and tossed it on his desk. "Enough of this silliness," he said. "Michele, you will observe and honor every detail of what we discussed?"

"Of course, General," Cassio said, immediately the smooth and polished Florentine again.

Again I winced with a twinge of unease. I longed to know what they were referring to, but I was too proud to ask.

Chapter 25

EMILIA, BY OTHELLO'S DECREE, was to remain in Venice. He announced it would be a brief but tedious posting, and surely a lady as lovely and lively as my wife had better ways to spend her time. I cannot say I appreciated this sentiment.

We had an unremarkable sea crossing to Zara. Once encamped there, the enlisted men did nearly all the work. It was hard labor, without glamour: doubling the thickness of one segment of the city wall surrounding the city. Zara is a virtual islet lying snug against the Dalmatian coastline; it is connected to the mainland by a narrow land bridge. The wall of the land gate too was to be fortified.

I could not tell what purpose there was to Othello's presence. This undertaking seemed unworthy of his attention. There was nothing for him or us, his staff, to do. The other officers liked the calm; the general and I both chaffed at it. At least I had access to the library, in the mayoral palace where the officers were housed. I prac-ticed reading Greek. My weekly letters to Emilia must have been a bore; each week I simply told her what I had been reading.

But Othello was distracted and spent hours a day alone in his office. My duties required me to keep record of what supplies were used; he went through a remarkable amount of paper, quills, and ink. I waited for him to tell me what he was using them on, but he shared nothing with me.

I was not used to that from him.

THERE WAS A regular sea-courier service between Venice and Zara. About once every ten days, a vessel would arrive in port, dis-charge cargo and messages, take on new forms of each, and sail out the next day.

One day I saw Othello's domestic page carrying a small packet out of the palace, heading in the direction of the nearest harbor gate. I was curious; Othello had mentioned nothing that required report-ing back to Venice—nor had he given me a hint about his newly forged writing habits.

I followed the lad; he went down to the ship bound for Venice and handed the packet to a red-bearded mariner. The mariner gave him a similar packet in return. I tailed the boy back up the slope, toward the palace, and saw him head to Othello's office. A moment later, he came back out, now empty-handed.

I wondered what was in both packets, of course. But more than that, I wondered why the general never mentioned either to me.

Several weeks in a row went by this way: the boy, with the packet; the red-bearded mariner, the other packet. Never a word from Othello.

And so one day when I followed this page boy from the palace toward the harbor, I overtook him in a narrow street, in such a manner that I most unfortunately tripped him; in tumbling, he dropped the packet.

"How very clumsy of me," I apologized effusively and reached at once for it, to hand it back to him; my sole purpose was to read the label on it.

For Michele Cassio, it read, *The Dolphin Inn, Castello District. Confidential.*

THE BOY, NOT noticing my distress, accepted the package and hurried down toward the harbor gate.

I stood a moment in the alleyway, willing the sun to continue warming me, for I was suddenly cold all over. There was some collusion between my general and that intruder, some secret I was being excluded from, some intensely significant secret that was operational *right now*. The thought dismayed me on several levels, but mostly it was personal. Whatever it was, I was excluded from it—and far worse than that, a womanizing Florentine who could not hold his drink, but could keep his hair immaculately coiffed—*he* somehow deserved Othello's confidence. About *what*, for the love of all saints? In what arena of life that Othello valued could Cassio possibly provide a service I could not better provide?

My distress was so severe I felt dizzy. I wished Emilia were with me now, to gently tease away my uneasiness, give it some practical interpretation, or at least distract me with a loosened bodice.

I WENT BACK to the mayoral palace. Fencing practice was still on, and Othello was in the yard. I kept my displeasure to myself, geared up, and for only the second time since I had known him, bested Othello at the sword. He was very pleased for me.

We dined in private that evening, and it was as it had ever been between us, our conversation familiar, lively, far ranging, and comfortable.

And as was always true of our discourse, army matters intermingled with the personal.

"The captain of the refectory," Othello said—his preferred way of referring to the head cook—"he tells me we must requisition more wheat, the laborers are going through it as if . . . as if they were laboring."

"I will add it to the list of supplies," I said. "I must requisition more paper as well; your office is going through an enormous amount of leaves."

"Really? The calamari is very good tonight, no?"

"Excellent. It reminds me of a recipe Michele Cassio described once."

"Perhaps he has been to Zara himself."

"We're also using a lot of ink," I said.

"Is ink expensive?" Othello asked disinterestedly.

"Not the kind we use."

"That's good," he said, looking up from his dinner with a smile. "Then it should not be hard to get it, eh?"

"It's strange that we are going through so much ink and paper."

He shrugged. "You know the Senate is obsessed with forms and inventories—"

"Yes, of course, but for some reason, during this posting, that proclivity of the Senate's is suddenly using more paper and ink than before."

Othello sat back in his chair and smiled at me admiringly. "'Proclivity,'" he echoed. "You are very good with words, Iago."

"Michele Cassio thinks I use too many of them." I gave him a very direct stare.

He met my gaze unflinchingly, looking warm and open as ever.

"That's because he is Florentine, and they are always jealous of how superior Venetians are. Eh? You taught me that, brother," he said with a grin. "You are teaching me to be an excellent Venetian."

"Not if you're modeling yourself on me, General. I am a terrible Venetian."

"Why do you say that?" he asked, reaching for the wine.

"Venetians lie. They lack candor. They keep secrets from their closest friends."

Othello grimaced thoughtfully. "Then I would have to say, you are much better than most Venetians. Would you like some wine?"

Not even the tensing of an eye muscle.

"Is this wine from Florence?" I asked, holding up my glass.

"No, in fact, it is the last of the stock from Rhodes," he said. "The excellent wine I promised you as we prepared to retreat? I could not give it to you on the ship. This is it. This is the last bottle. You are the only person I know who deserves to share it with me."

How could he be so openhearted, and yet so full of guile?

"I thank you," I said. When he had poured me a glass, I held it up for a toast. "To bad Venetians. May neither of us ever be one."

"I will drink to that, brother!" The general laughed, and drained his glass.

Somehow this open, trusting, and trustworthy man was suddenly so skilled at keeping secrets that he could lie by omission to me, all day, every day, without a shred of guilt. I was almost sickened thinking of it. And yet, before supper was over, he had taught me the Egyptian lullaby his mother used to sing to him; I reduced him to gasping fits of laughter, describing the incident with Galinarion's hen; we arm wrestled, and although his arms are twice as broad as mine, I won, because I knew a trick—which I showed him, to his delight.

By the time I went to bed that night, my alarm at the secret correspondence with Michele Cassio had almost abated.

ALMOST. BUT NOT QUITE. I was unnerved by how unlike myself I managed the situation: for some reason I did not dare to ask Othello about it directly. I was frightened of what the answer might be. But I was burning with anxious curiosity to understand. So—very much unlike myself—I took a route indirect.

THE FOLLOWING WEEK, the day before the next courier ship was due in port, I let myself into Othello's office while he was at fencing practice. Zuane da Porto was napping somewhere. Zuane spent more and more of his time napping; I was eager for him to retire so I might officially take his place, as I was already performing most of his duties (in addition to my own).

I went to the desk, determined if necessary to search every drawer—even the hidden drawers, which I knew about and had access to—to discover what Othello was writing to Cassio.

But I did not have to search at all. Lying plainly on the leather desktop was a letter filling three sheets of paper with Othello's square, inelegantly clear handwriting. I was startled by frightened elation as I realized the secret correspondence was *right here*, I could read it *now* and know *now* what conspiracy with Cassio was being kept from me . . . but as I regained my wits and prepared to read, I heard the door open. I had time to glance at only the first line before looking up to see who'd entered.

That first line read: *My beloved Desdemona.*

"*Iago,*" said the general from the doorway.

Chapter 26

WE WERE BOTH acutely ill at ease, and silent for a moment.

"General," I said at last, and pointedly turned away from the desk.

"Iago," Othello said again, with a tone almost of pleading in his voice now. "I see you have discovered my Achilles heel."

"Do you refer to your epistolary romance with Senator Braban-tio's daughter?" I said, still turned away from him.

He laughed, but there was discomfort in the laughter. "I am in love with the lady, Iago, and she with me."

"But you cannot have her, and so you are torturing both yourself and her with an exchange of letters," I said coldly. "Torture yourself if you must, but you are being unfair to the lady."

"Iago, when you met Emilia, could you help but express your feelings to her?"

I turned to meet his gaze. "General, forgive me, but it is not a fair comparison. I courted her because I knew she would be a suitable *and obtainable* wife."

Othello stared at me levelly. "Iago, remember for a moment how it was when your heart first fell for Emilia." He paused.

"Yes?" I said.

"Take a moment—this is an order from your general—take a moment and tell your logical, practical mind to shut the hell up. Ask your heart what it knows— remember exactly how it *felt*."

I did, because I respected him and wanted to continue to respect him. I did not want a beautiful patrician whelp to spell the ruin of a friendship that meant so much. And yes, remembering that first moment with Emilia was a pleasant memory, a very pleasant memory, and I enjoyed the flood of emotion that came with it. Othello, seeing the shift of mood on my face, nodded with satisfaction.

"If she had suddenly said to you, I am the daughter of a senator, and you can never have me, would you have turned and walked away from her?"

I tried to answer sharply, but could not. "My heart goes out to you, that you have these feelings," I said. "I do understand, completely, the impulse to indulge them. But there can be no happy ending to this romance."

"If it must end in heartbreak, let the heartbreak come later," he said evenly.

"How do you communicate with her?"

"I send the letters, sealed, to a friend."

So he was not going to tell me of Cassio's involvement.

"Ah," I said.

"A friend who dines quite regularly at the senator's home. He always finds a way to give my letters to Desdemona and to receive letters from her, which he then sends to me."

My confused, baleful emotions got the better of me. "What you are doing will be considered an outrage if you are ever found out. You are too useful to the state to be demoted, but everybody else will suffer for it. Desdemona will be shamed, Brabantio labeled a laughingstock, and Ca— your *friend* whipped or even jailed for his conspiring with you both."

Othello froze for a moment, then took a deep breath and slowly let it out. "As always, Iago, I appreciate your bluntness and your honesty. Your advice, almost without exception, is unerring and useful to me, from military concerns to Venetian table manners. But in this case, I must make my own judgment." I stared at him in disbelief, and he added, with an attempt at levity, "*You* are not going to reveal me, are you?"

"Of course not," I said impatiently. "I am not upbraiding your actions in themselves; I am warning you that they will come to an unhappy end."

He smiled the familiar, soothing Othello smile that said we were brothers under the skin. "I appreciate that, Iago." He took another deep breath and sighed. "I do know, of course I must know, that this is folly. It cannot end in marriage, and I would never besmirch her by taking her as mistress. But indulge me in simple enjoyment of a few hours' secret forgetfulness each week, will you not? You have Emilia's letters to distract you. Allow me my own distractions."

"What happens when we return to Venice?" I asked. "Have you thought that far ahead, great strategist that you are?"

"When we return to Venice, it shall be just as it is now," he assured me, relaxing as he sensed my anger abating. "I shall send her letters from a chaste distance, and she shall return letters chastely to me. And we shall do that until it grows old and ceases to entertain us, regardless of whom her father marries her off to. If it is an arranged marriage, surely her arranged groom cannot begrudge her having an admirer who never even *touches* her. Consider my conduct toward her in person, Iago. The Florentine Michele Cassio has touched more of her person than I have, by kissing her along the hand and wrist. And that spice merchant Brabantio dislikes, he has pressed his suit in ways I would never dream of."

"So this is a harmless flirtation? You will not shame the lady, nor bring trouble on your own head?"

He smiled. "You are a good man to care about these matters, Iago. Yes, I promise you, happily I promise it, I will not shame the lady. And now please come outside with me and let us exorcise, with exercise, the tension we have built up in this room just now."

I followed him out into the bright Zaran sunlight, knowing he was lying to me. To me only. Not to Cassio or to Desdemona. He was, in fact, lying to me *with* Cassio and Desdemona. Two people we had never heard of six months ago were now in collusion with my general and closest friend. The duplicity with Desdemona I could understand—that was sex. But Cassio? Why Cassio? What was Cassio to him, or he to Cassio, that he should lie to me?

Chapter 27

WE RETURNED TO VENICE within three months. As I disembarked I took an appreciative deep breath of mild Venetian springtime air, which did not smell like vinegar and filthy men, but instead like all the scents I'd missed without ever thinking of them. I was very glad to be home.

As soon as I was off the boat, before I had even gotten my land-legs, I stationed myself at the trestle table set up on the tar-smudged dock, to oversee the tedious task of releasing each soldier from service. All I could think about, as the paymaster and I worked through the rolls, was the scent of Emilia's skin. Three months without her had been so difficult. I could hardly focus on the ritual of paperwork and leave-taking required of me. Two hours later, finished with the clerical drudgery, I went directly to Othello's office at the Saggitary for official leave.

Here I found Othello, frowning in disbelief at Lieutenant da Porto.

"Tuscany?" he was saying as I stuck my head in. "Come in, Iago, come in." And back to the lieutenant: "What on earth is there to interest anyone in *Tuscany*?"

"I have a daughter there, and I have missed her growth and the birth of my grandchildren," the man said peaceably. "I will sit under olive trees and drink wine and watch children play, and then I will die. It will have been a good life."

It was the longest statement I had ever heard the laconic fellow utter.

I knew the Moor's face so well, I intuited what he was thinking: such a man had been a mercenary? Had risen to first lieutenant? Othello had not so promoted him and never would have. Da Porto had been assigned to him in the midst of a political crisis; he had accepted da Porto without appraising him. Indeed, Othello had hardly *noticed* him. Da Porto had made himself so entirely replaceable that in function if not title, he had consistently been replaced—by me. I did not dislike da Porto but still my heart leapt as I understood his meaning. He was retiring. This meant my advancement. That I should be first lieutenant to the general of the entire army! If only my father could have known.

THE GENERAL DISMISSED da Porto and was about to begin a final review of the Zara project with me, but a rap on the door interrupted us. The boy minding the door stepped inside and solemnly announced the arrival of Michele Cassio. Before he could control the instinct, Othello glanced at me. I looked away. If he would not admit to having a secret with Cassio, then I would not admit to knowing about it.

With Othello's permission, Cassio stepped into the room and saluted us both with his right hand. In his left, he held a now-familiar parcel. I felt my stomach tighten.

"Greetings, Michele," Othello said with his usual warmth. "It is good to see you in person after so long an absence."

"As it is to see you, General, Ensign," Cassio said, now bowing like a courtier. The gesture brought his right hand down toward his bent knee and his left hand up behind him. I could not contain myself: I reached, as if playfully, for the packet of letters and plucked it from his hand. "And what is this?" I asked.

Fast as a whip, Cassio straightened, looking at me and then at Othello in alarm.

Othello was absolutely calm. For a long moment, he examined me, making no move to get the parcel from me. In fact, he clasped his hands behind him. "I appreciate your attentiveness to my well-being, Ensign," he said. "I also appreciate how much you trust my judgment in certain matters." Smiling, he released his hands from behind his back and held out one of them toward me.

Unhappily, I handed him the letters. There was nothing else I could have done with them but show them to Brabantio, which I would never do. I did not want to reveal Othello's weakness; I wanted it to go away. I particularly wanted it to go away if it gave Cassio a special tether to Othello that I did not have.

"Thank you, Michele," Othello said. "Please return tomorrow for instructions in this matter. And congratulations upon becoming an officer. We will celebrate at the great feast of San Marco."

Cassio's Florentine cheeks flushed as mine paled. Yes, he had finished his training; yes, he was now an officer, albeit of nothing in particular. This untested gallant was now technically my equal in the army. I found this annoying, but allayed the annoyance with the cheering thought that a lieutenancy loomed before me.

CASSIO DISMISSED, OTHELLO and I finished our work, and I left at last well after dark had fallen. I hoped Emilia would be waiting for me with a loosened corset and clean sheets. Losing myself in her arms, her thighs, her smile . . . my limbs shivered with anticipation.

And there she was, even more wonderfully prepared for a home-coming than I'd fantasized, in nothing but her shift, her long auburn hair tumbling over her shoulders and down her back. I slammed the door behind me and lifted her so high in my arms, her breasts pressed against my chin. Without a word, I carried her to our bed, and it was hours before our mouths said more than our bodies. *We could have children now*, I thought as I entered her the first time. With a lieutenant's salary, with a lieutenant's quarters, we could manage it. Little Emilias and little Iagos running around as visible proof of our love for each other—I almost fainted with pleasure and passion at the thought. I kissed my wife ferociously. This beautiful, clear-eyed, charming woman—my wife. How could a man be so lucky?

THE NEXT MORNING, as we prepared to go to breakfast, I was not feeling so enamored of her. She told me, with a sparkle in her eye, that she knew about the letters being passed between Othello and Desdemona—who now considered her a bosom friend, because she was the only woman to whom Desdemona could safely share her de-light about the secret correspondence. As wife of Othello's closest confidant, Emilia was trustworthy, sympathetic, safe.

"So everyone except Othello's closest confidant had been taken into confidence on this matter," I growled.

"That is a silly way to look at it," Emilia said. "You sound jealous, Iago. Are you jealous of *me*? I am sure Desdemona would be happy to gush about her faraway paramour to you as well."

"I do not much want to hear about it," I said. "And may I point out, Emilia, that he is no longer far away. They are in the same city now. They will frequently be at the same house, dining at the same table. How do you expect that will go?"

"I think that will depend on how discreet everyone chooses to be," Emilia retorted, and added pointedly, "including you."

I sat up straighter, nearly huffing. "Are you implying I would give them away?"

"Not deliberately," Emilia said in a placating voice. "But subtlety and nuance are not your strengths, Iago. I know how you feel about secrets and lies, and I understand if this situation discomfits you."

"You were never an admirer of secrets and lies, either, yet you seem quite taken with the whole thing."

She paused, and then nodded. "I admit that over the past few months, I have grown to appreciate that society may be not only *mocked* but *undercut.* I know both Othello and Desdemona. A good man, and a good lady. They are very fond of each other. They are not allowed, by the conventions of our society, to even *attempt* an open courtship."

"I agree with you that is most unfortunate for both of them," I said impatiently. "And I agree it is the fault of our ridiculous culture that they are suffering for that."

"But you see, Iago, they need not simply rail against the injustice of it," Emilia said, moving to stand before me, and then kneeling down so she could look up into my face. "They may at least *express* their regard. They relieve their hearts in words, if not actions. Thank heaven there is another outsider who is willing to defy the conventions of Venetian society."

My stomach clenched. "What do you mean, another outsider?" I demanded, sitting up straighter.

"Michele Cassio, of course," Emilia said. "He and Othello are both foreigners here. It is only natural one of them should have a sympathy for the other's plight."

I shook my head and stood up; she rose with me. "Emilia, Michele Cassio is a Florentine. He is every bit as attached to class distinctions and noble exclusivity as any Venetian, perhaps more so. He and Othello have *nothing* in common." I pushed her away gently and went to stand by the window, looking down onto the campo outside the Arsenal gate. "If Cassio is passing notes for them, it is not out of *sympathy* for Othello's *plight*. The man goes whoring almost every night. He does not appreciate what Othello feels for Brabantio's daughter."

"Iago!" Emilia laughed. "What makes you say something so appalling about one of your fellow officers?"

"Please do not refer to him that way," I said through clenched teeth. "The man is a fop. He is an intemperate, womanizing, Florentine fop. Oh, yes, he puts on a very elegant show of being proper and gallant, I know, I remember, I have seen it," I said. "I have also seen him on the balcony of a bawdy house, half-undressed, with a naked whore in his arms, and I've seen him the next morning with wine on his breath—"

"He does not even drink, Iago!" Emilia said with a sharp laugh. "Are you so threatened by this gentleman that you feel the need to *fantasize* about him?"

"He does not drink in good society, because he cannot handle it," I corrected her sharply. "He is a sot, I'm telling you. He refrains from drink at dinner parties because he knows he would make a fool of himself once he started."

"Has he *confessed* this to you?" Emilia demanded, amused, and took my seat.

"I deduced it within a week of meeting him," I said. "Allow me some credit for observation, Emilia."

"Iago," Emilia said. She took a breath and then spoke in the lower tones of her mellifluous voice. "Be reasonable for just a moment. I too am a native of this place that is so full of artifice. I recognize insincerity a canal's length away. And Michele—"

"You recognize *Venetian* insincerity," I interrupted. I could not bear hearing my wife speak sweetly of that man. "He is not Venetian. He has his own language of duplicity, at which you are not fluent."

She sighed again, stood up, and made a gesture of frustration. "There is no talking to you, then. I do not know what has caused you to have such a terrible feeling toward the gentleman. He is unfailingly pleasant every time I have encountered him. He has been a constant breath of fresh air here in your absence, and he is the only agreeable male to sit at Brabantio's table these past three months. He is doing a favor to your friend and to my friend, and we should be *grateful* to him for that, we should not *defame* him."

I crossed my arms.

"Iago, my darling husband, listen to me," she pressed on. "Brabantio likes him. The other senators like him. The upper echelons of our own class like him. He has made an excellent name for himself in Venice in a very short time."

"Why are you telling me this?" I demanded. "Why do I need to know this? When did I ever care about someone's reputation?"

"It is *pleasant* to see them embrace somebody who is unlike them," Emilia said. "It causes me to realize that we need not be just like them, and yet we may still be respected by them. By all these patricians who currently only let you near them because you're with Othello. If you would make the effort to be, *occasionally*, charming, you would find yourself admired by the entire patriciate of Venice— for *your own merits*, not because you are Othello's man. I know you, Iago, I know that is important to you."

I stared at her, resenting her accuracy. "Emilia, it was our mutual dislike of such people that brought us together. How can you now be encouraging me to become their sycophant?"

"Not a sycophant! Just civil!" she countered. "To be given as much as you deserve." She gestured around our small apartment. "You are the right-hand man to the leader of the army, and they stable us in here."

"Cassio's rooms are surely worse than these," I said.

She shook her head once. "Not anymore. He charmed the quartermaster of the Arsenal at a dinner party six weeks back, and now he has a suite of rooms in the Sagittarius."

Now I resented Cassio even further. But worse, now I questioned my wife's judgment. "You want me to become a fawning would-be courtier in order to give you a nicer bed to lie in? Is that what you, Emilia, are telling me?"

"I did not mean to anger you, Iago. I'm sorry. I find it peculiar that you take such offense to what I am saying when I know you have ambitions."

"You," I repeated, "you, Emilia, my wife, you of all people I have ever known, *you* are admiring a guileful fop for his ability to gull people into giving him things he has done nothing to deserve. Do I have that right?" I could feel the tendons in my neck standing out. Emilia looked amazed at my wrath.

"I am saying," she said carefully, "that there is no virtue in refusing to be pleasant to people who can help you to your just deserts."

"I do not need their help," I snapped. "I have my own merit. I do not have to *charm* to have merit. I already *have* merit. With my merit, I earn what I deserve. There is an integrity to that, which nobody I know—except, I thought, you and perhaps Othello—has any understanding of."

"I know and love that about you, Iago. I admire it about you enormously. I am only saying—"

"I know well enough what you're saying." I stormed toward the door, grabbing my cloak from the peg. "I am going out now, I need to clear my head."

Chapter 28

I HAD NO IDEA where I was headed. Native custom and the need for a long walk took me toward my old neighborhood, even toward my old house. Not wanting to arrive there, I diverted down a back alley with no particular intention except to avoid paying a visit to my brother. Rizardo was not somebody I could turn to for advice, encouragement, or soothing.

I realized I was at the back gate of Pietro Galinarion's home, the man whose egg Roderigo and I had stolen all those years ago. The richest patrician in our neighborhood—although not, from what I'd heard, as rich as Roderigo himself was these days.

I wondered how Roderigo was doing. Was he still leery of his professional rival from Florence? (How ironic, we had something in common.) The last I had heard of him was Brabantio's demeaning refusal of his proffered gift to Desdemona, before we'd left for Zara. Hopefully he was on to some new unconquerable lady by now. He must have had plenty of admirers—he was handsome and rich, and this was Venice.

I heard men's voices laughing within Galinarion's courtyard. There was a sound, and a small leather ball landed on the other side of the iron gate, near my feet.

"Well now you've done it, uncle!" I heard a man's cheery voice cry out. Feet moved nearer to the gate, until I could see them, and the runner: he was wearing very fine clothing and presumably the latest style of collar—I'd never seen such a protruding ruff before. He was looking for, then reaching for, the ball. He noticed me. He looked familiar, but I could not place him. Until I could: It was Zanino, one of my fellow cadets from the Arsenal. He saw me through the grating of the gate, and his eyes widened.

"Iago Soranzo!" he cried out with gusto. Immediately he reached up to unlatch the tall gate. It was really not so tall, now that I was no longer ten years old. "Iago, my old friend, what a tremendous surprise! I knew your brother lived in this campo but I did not expect to see *you* here! What a pleasure! Come in and meet my uncle Pietro!" He already had the gate open, had grabbed my arm, and was nearly hauling me into the yard. "He's heard about your exploits at the Academy for years! And of course everybody knows you are an aide-de-camp to General Othello."

I had last seen Galinarion when I'd stormed out of a masquerade ball during Carnival, the night after I'd met Emilia. Now I thought of Emilia's words from an hour earlier. Galinarion was precisely the sort of man she wanted me to be able to charm. I was nauseated by the thought of it.

On the other hand, I wanted to please her if I could. That is the plague and weakness of a devoted husband. Here was a safely private opportunity to experiment.

So when I was introduced to the senator this time, as his bulk lolled in a couch whose wooden legs were brushed with late-morning dew, I bowed deeply and expressed my heartfelt pleasure at being in the presence of so grand a gentleman. Likewise I showed pleased surprise that my beloved colleague Zanino was his blood-kin. "I did not realize patricians trained for the artillery," I said.

"Oh, we had no intention of sending him into the service." Galinarion coughed from his velvet couch. "His parents simply wanted to get him out of the house for the worst of his pubescence." Zanino laughed agreeably. "But come, young Iago, would you care for a drink?"

The enormous man and his gangly nephew were both tipsy, hours before noon. I tried to imagine a life in which I could possibly allow myself to get drunk before noon. What did such lives consist of? The memory of Emilia's angling for larger rooms by ingratiating myself to such as these made me briefly clench my teeth. "I follow a soldier's schedule, Senator, and never drink before sundown, but thank you for the kind offer."

"I hear Lieutenant da Porto is retiring," Zanino said, playing with the ball. He tried to interest a very old, tired-looking black dog into chasing the ball, but the dog was not interested. Zanino threw the ball anyhow, and then went after it himself.

We had returned but the day before; how quickly word spread! "Yes," I said, pleased. "Da Porto is retiring."

"You'll be taking over his position, I suppose?" Zanino said, eyes blazing with admiration.

"I suppose," I said, with what I hoped seemed a casual smile. "There is no guarantee, of course; it is up to the general."

"But the general adores you, everyone knows that!" Zanino said, throwing the ball again; this time it hit a piece of statuary, a nymph trying to flee a satyr.

It delighted me to hear that this was part of the general gossip of the city, at least among those who, like Zanino, fancied themselves military insiders. "I have my hopes," I confessed. "I am married to a beautiful woman, and I would certainly like to give her more than just an ensign's quarters."

"Why only *hopes*? Are you at all concerned he will not pick you?" Galinarion said, making a feeble attempt to sit up a little higher.

I bowed my head with more humility than I really felt on this matter. "There is no way to know what the general will choose to do. I believe I am the best man for the post, but should Othello find another more skilled or more experienced, I shall accept his decision."

"I will talk to him about it," Galinarion declared, oozing lordliness.

Few things would appeal to Othello less than a drunken senator telling him what to do. "Thank you, Senator," I said, forcing myself to smile.

"I will ask some of my friends to speak to him as well."

"I am even deeper in your debt, Senator," I said, forcing the smile to broaden.

"Aha! I have it!" Galinarion said, extremely pleased. "My friend Facio is not only a senator but also deeply involved with the military, and I believe he knows the general well. I will instruct him to speak to Othello on your behalf. Perhaps you know him? Senator Brabantio?"

Despite myself, I laughed at the poetic irony of this, managing to pass the laughter off as gleeful gratitude. "That, I do believe," I said, "would clinch it for me."

* * *

OTHELLO'S CIVIC SUPERINTENDENT, Marco Salamon, possessed a rare shrewdness regarding the use of civic celebrations. No city or nation on earth loves a festival as well as Venice does. The Serene Republic creates festivals, spectacles, masquerades, and feasts for any occasion her denizens can think of. To observe the confluence of San Marco and Othello's return from Zara, the city planned a celebration with spectacles, fireworks, and lots of feasting.

Salamon proposed that the supper feast in the Doge's Palace be transformed into a "Ceremony of Merit," at which Othello would announce promotions and medals before an array of patricians, citizens, and carefully chosen commoners, thereby demonstrating to the Venetian population that the army was an exciting and rewarding enterprise. Othello agreed, mildly amused by Venetian culture once again.

"This will not seduce anyone into joining the ranks," he said to me in a conspiratorial tone after Salamon had left us.

"I doubt Salamon cares about that," I replied, equally conspiratorial. "He wants to make an impression on the patricians of the city. He wants to coax them to take an interest in the civil posts they are supposed to be volunteering for."

Having Othello's leave, that same day Salamon approached the admiral of the navy, the captain of the cavalry, and the captain of the artillery, who all agreed to invent some promotions or awards of merit within their own branches. And so the feast plans rapidly expanded into a sprawling fete, so enormous its planned location was moved from the doge's public dining room to the cavernous Great Council chamber.

EVERY NIGHT OF the week that spanned from our return to the Ceremony of Merit, Othello dined with Brabantio, and Desdemona sat at table with them. Usually Emilia and I were invited along; sometimes we were not. I preferred the nights we were not. When we were present, it was unnerving to watch Othello and Desdemona, knowing—as Brabantio could not know—all that was unsaid. Every moment between them was in code; I did not know the code but I knew that it existed, and I knew that Brabantio did not know even that much.

Emilia beamed, watching the two of them pretend to be casual with each other. Her joy disturbed me. The thoughtlessness of the two people I most admired and loved, one rendered foolish by his infatuation, the other rendered foolish by her delight of that infatuation—these were the silly dramas and romances of the Venetian patriciates, and we, the ones upon whose backs and shoulders the Serene Republic leaned, should not stoop to such absurdity. I was never the praying sort, but I prayed daily that the two chaste lovers would cease their obsession with each other, so that Othello would return to his soldier's life. But their mutual regard grew every day until I was amazed Brabantio could not see it in the glowing of their faces.

THE AFTERNOON OF the feast day, Othello and I were in his office, reviewing the latest plans for refortifying Famagusta. As always, these were fairly risible.

"I suspect we shall have to go ourselves to see it," Othello said.

"I wonder if anything about the fortress will actually resemble what we have been told," I mused.

"I have seen—" Othello began, but stopped abruptly as his office door jerked open.

Michele Cassio nearly entered—then, seeing me, he pulled up short.

"Michele," said Othello in a low and suddenly urgent tone as he rose from his chair. As if I were not present, he crossed to Cassio in the doorway, leaned in to him, and muttered something softly in his ear. Cassio whispered back. Othello whispered once more. Cassio nodded with Florentine precision, bowed, and then strode away with purpose and a bit of smugness.

"I have seen the fortress of Famagusta myself," Othello said to me, returning to his seat—as if there had been no interruption, as if he had risen merely to open a shutter for ventilation. "The depictions we have seen are not so very far off. It is only the engineers' intentions that are too fanciful. Look, here is another example of their proposals," he continued, pulling a large piece of vellum from the collection on his desk.

I opened my mouth to ask "What was that about?" but found I could not speak.

OUR MEETING ADJOURNED, Othello excused himself with strange abruptness. Out of habit, I considered seeking Emilia's company, but then realized, feeling sad, that I did not really want to. She was grown so enamoured of the secret love affair that she had begun to crave a patina of romance in me that wasn't there, and never had been. In her company, I would feel ashamed for not having done more to please her.

As I stood outside the Saggitary door, deliberating where to spend the next few hours, I was approached by tall, gangly Zanino. "My uncle has summoned you with news of his advocating your lieutenancy," Zanino announced. His eyes were bright, and his cheeks flushed, so excited was he to be inside the Arsenal gates again.

The ceremony was that evening and I was confident of my position; still, my pulse quickened when I heard this.

By gondola and then on foot we traveled, and despite Zanino's attempts to chatter with me, I could not but focus on my private, unspoken, ruminative monologue. I did not know if Brabantio had actually been solicited on my behalf; he had never referenced it at table all week, and I had been on tenterhooks each visit there, wondering if he would. I could think of no other officer worthy of the post—although I suddenly worried that Othello might give the position to Cassio to reward him for playing pimp. I quickly dismissed this as mad. Even besotted Othello would never let his romantic needs supplant his military duty. Cassio would no doubt receive a bonus or promotion he did not deserve, but nothing that might have direct bearing upon the governance of the army.

When we arrived at Galinarion's, we were ushered into his salon, where he was enjoying an afternoon engorgement. "I want you to know, my dearest Iago, that I went to Brabantio's the other night, and we together, with our friend Dominic Zen, met with your general. We raised a glass with him in celebration of the ever improving standards of the army, and we observed that you would make an excellent and obvious first lieutenant." He paused, and shifted his large frame within the chair as he reached for a sausage on a heated serving dish.

"And . . . what did the general reply?" I asked. I was surprised that I felt nervous. It was some twisted fear in me, the residue of childhood insults from my father, that could make me doubt Othello even for a moment.

"He was not very gracious to us," Galinarion said and closed his enormous mouth around the sausage. I then had to wait for what felt like a fortnight as he chewed and swallowed to his satisfaction. "He made a face of incredulity and told us he did not need the advice of aging gallants to be told who should be his lieutenant. He told us that we were being presumptuous! We! The men who raise his salary!"

I relaxed at that, and even repressed a laugh. Of course Othello would say that to a triad of stuffy patricians. On principle, he would refuse to listen to them. I understood that stance; indeed, I *applauded* that stance.

All the same—why could he not have upbraided them and then added that *of course* he was naming me as his lieutenant?

For the love of the saints, I chastised myself. *The man is your dearest friend. Go and talk to him directly.* I should have done that days ago.

I excused myself from Galinarion's great house and took a gondola all the way along the lower Grand Canal, past the Doge's Palace, and eastward back to the Arsenal.

* * *

A GUARD I did not know was standing at the door to the Sagittary.

"Please wait outside, sir," he said as I was reaching for the latch.

I was thrown by this—it was the first time I had not had immediate access to Othello.

"Why?" I asked.

"I am only following orders, sir." No vocal inflection, and he would not look me in the eye. I stood on the pavement by the entry and watched cadets practice marching in formation. They were awful.

AFTER WHAT SEEMED like half an hour, the Sagittary door opened, and Michele Cassio came out. He wore a face of such smug satisfaction I wanted to slap him, without even knowing the cause of his expression. He gave me a greeting that was less Florentine than usual, and more military. He headed toward the gate.

"You may go in now, sir," said the guard.

I ENTERED THE OFFICE and saw Othello, alone, in a state of mild agitation. What had Cassio said that would unnerve the general? And why would Cassio look so pleased about it? Perhaps it was the beginning of some wonderful intrigue that would unravel their clandestine fraternity.

I saluted Othello. His face brightened with relief, and he grabbed me by the arm to pull me into an embrace. "Iago!" he cried. "Iago, thank heaven it is you, there is nobody else in the world whose company I could bear right now."

I returned the embrace weakly, both reassured and startled. "You look distressed," I said.

He rubbed his broad dark hands together briskly. "Anxious," he corrected. His hands curled into fists and he beat the air with them, then laughed, relaxed the fists, massaged his temple for a moment, began to rub his hands together, paced around the office quickly. "Just a little anxious, my friend." He glanced at me and chuckled nervously. I must have looked concerned, because he stopped chuckling, stopped pacing, and now adopted an attitude of forced nonchalance, arms folded over his chest.

"What is going on?" I asked, slowly and deliberately.

"There is a banquet and ceremony tonight in the Doge's Palace," Othello began.

"I know that, General, I am actually here to talk to you about that very—"

"And after the banquet, Iago, after the banquet . . ." He rubbed his hands together again despite himself, looking away. Then he raised his head and looked straight at me, his black eyes brighter than I had ever seen them before. "After the banquet, I am eloping with Desdemona."

Chapter 29

A MOMENT OF total silence as I tried to find my voice. "*What?*" was all I could manage.

"There is no other way for us to be together, and I can no longer bear this secrecy and furtiveness. Her father will be at the banquet with us, so she will be able to slip away from his house. When he returns home, he will assume she is already in bed. She will come here to my rooms in the Saggitary and wait for me, and then a priest will marry us. Tomorrow morning, we will go to her father and reveal ourselves, and he will have no choice but to accept us. Iago, why do you look so shocked? You were the first to know of my feelings for the lady."

"You . . . you said you would not shame her," I said. I chose these words because they were the only ones I could string together; there was so much more I wanted to say, to protest, but such words failed me.

"And I won't," Othello said. "A priest—one of your own Catholic priests—shall marry us before I lay a hand on her."

"Her father will disown her," I said.

"Then she will have to make do, being the wife of Venice's chief general. She is content with that."

I was dizzy trying to think straight. "I . . . why are you telling me this?" I finally demanded, a fury rising within me.

He laughed nervously. "Because you are my closest friend and I wanted to take you into my confidence."

"Really?" I demanded sharply. "You *might* have done that *months* ago."

He sighed. "I knew you were concerned about this. And I knew how inexorable it was. I wanted to spare you from the distress of anticipation, of watching it bud. I decided to wait to tell you until it was in bloom. It happens tonight. It is now in full bloom." Seeing my expression—still dazed and wary—he said soothingly, "Iago, you are free from any blame here, but I would have your blessing on it."

I had to stop this from happening. For his sake—for hers too, but I hardly knew her. But Othello . . . good heaven, he had made me what I was. I was honor bound to protect him, even from himself. Perhaps they were drawn to each other by the exotic allure of their differences, or perhaps they had some relatively innocent flirtation that the licentious Florentine had encouraged and nurtured, to give himself a way to insinuate himself into Othello's confidence . . . whatever it was, it was a madness, it was a promise of catastrophe, and I had to stop it.

But then he said: "I love her with my life, Iago." He spoke with innocence and hopefulness and tenderness, and a little nervousness too. His eyes shone. I realized he meant it deeply, as I had meant it for Emilia, and I knew I would not stop him. Jealousy aside, it is hard to begrudge one's best friend a joyful heart.

"I will happily give you my blessing once you have accomplished it," I said tentatively. "In front of her father, even, if you wish it."

His smile brimmed with fondness and amusement. "There's my gentle Iago," he said. With an abrupt change of pace, he crossed toward the door. "Come, travel with me, we will be late for the ceremony."

"I have a matter I wish to discuss with you, General, before we go—"

"Let it wait until tomorrow, there is no time now," Othello said. He reached for his cloak on a peg.

"It has to do with the feast tonight," I said.

"The feast tonight! Ha! I think I will hardly be able to concentrate on the feast tonight!" Othello laughed. He opened the door and gestured me out of it. The guard at the door saluted. "We require transport to the Doge's Palace," Othello said to the man, who turned and yelled this request up to a guard on the Arsenal Bridge, who in turn yelled it to somebody outside in the canal.

The porter turned back to us, awaiting new orders.

"Come with us," Othello said to him, for no reason I could discern. It was irritating, as it meant I had no privacy to speak to Othello about the lieutenancy. "Yes, it will be most challenging to focus at the feast tonight, I am sure my voice will quaver and my hands shake as I announce who are my good men and true." He was walking quickly now toward the gate; I was almost breathless trying to keep up with him, and our one-man honor guard was almost running. Othello gave me a sideways grin. "Of course you *know* you shall be called up."

Yes. Good. A tension I had grown too accustomed to released. *Thank heaven*, I thought, *thank heaven*. That would satisfy Emilia and also show her the irrelevance of the strategy she had tried to foist upon me; she would get over her recent superciliousness, and I would have harmony at home again.

"I assume there will be others singled out for service," I said, attempting to sound casual.

"Oh, of course," Othello said, with a brief and almost bitter laugh as we were let out of the gate. "Da Porto is to receive a pension that he has hardly earned, and I will present it tonight. There are others to be puffed up too. And not always for their military merit. Michele, for example, requires a bit of back scratching—greetings!" he called out to da Porto, who was approaching us at the wharf. The wave of disgust that almost choked me—literally almost choked me—had to be hidden as we each saluted da Porto.

Here we were, the original three, who had been through so much together over the years. We were now to be sundered. And then with a shocked sinking feeling, I realized what Othello meant: I would replace da Porto as lieutenant, but Michele Cassio would—undeservedly—replace me. I would get what I wanted, but I would be saddled with the presence of the Florentine fop for the rest of my soldiering days. I swallowed a groan of protest.

Surely after the delirium of his romance had subsided, whether he remained married to Desdemona or not, *surely* in time Othello would realize the rashness of this action and judge Michele Cassio on his own worth as a soldier, which was: *nil*. If I could be patient, justice would be served. Ultimately—in time—I would have the life I merited: happy in career, happy in marriage, happy in friendships. I held my heart out and offered it that happy future day, to calm its clamoring within my rib cage.

A gondolier offered a hand to Othello. When we were all in the boat, the gondola moved down the short Arsenal Canal, swept out into the lagoon and then, turning right, stopped at the Piazzetta before the Doge's Palace. It was a short trip. We pulled up and debarked. General Othello and I strode beside each other into the magnificent stone building. Before I left this place tonight, I would be Othello's first lieutenant. I gave the gods of Rome a thousand thanks and forgave them for every headache and heartache they had put me through these past few months.

THE FEAST BEGAN with an oddly unsatisfying air, though it had all the pomp of a traditional Venetian festival: there were acrobats and jugglers and magicians as we assembled; there were pretty women dancing along the narrow pathways between the rows of trestle tables. The Great Council chamber is enormous, larger than the largest ballroom in the city many times over. It was very crowded, accommodating at table all the senators and other patricians, all the military and civil leaders of all the branches of the military, and all the officers and enlisted men who would tonight be in some way acknowledged, thanked, promoted, or rewarded for their service to the Republic.

I was seated so that I faced across my own board to the next one, at which sat Othello and Senator Brabantio, side by side and facing me. Brabantio was carrying on to Othello about the irritating persistence of one of Desdemona's suitors: a spice merchant named Roderigo. Othello was chuckling sympathy.

The tenderness I'd felt for Othello's predicament when we were alone together, when I saw his vulnerability—it vanished watching him speak to Desdemona's father. That camaraderie was fake: Othello was chatting with the man as if he were not about to rob him of his only child. Brabantio suspected nothing. I was furious at Othello's duplicity and almost as furious at Brabantio's obliviousness. And I was furious at myself for my impotence to act on my fury.

AFTER WHAT SEEMED to be months, supper was over. The trestle tables were cleared away, and most of us collected along one long side of the Great Council chamber. I found a place to stand near the corner doorway to a stairway landing. This was the same landing to which I'd dragged Othello several years ago, to conceal his epilepsy from the Great Council.

A dais was set up opposite the crowd, along the other long wall. The aging, long-bearded doge, Girolamo Priuli himself, serving as a master of ceremonies, introduced in turn the leaders of the artillery, the navy, the cavalry, and finally the infantry. Each leader rattled off a brief yet still tedious speech about the glory of their particular branch of the military and their appreciation for their men, both Venetian and *condottieri*. Then each in turn called up to the dais a stream of men who served under them, presenting ribbons, gold, sealed parchments—all manner of recognition and acknowledgment.

Othello was the last leader to present. The ceremony itself thus far had taken close to three hours, and the meal before that, two. By now, there was no doubt, Desdemona was securely in the Sagittary. Othello must have had the same thought, for his face was beaming with an excitement I had never seen before, not even in the throes of battle. "It is late," he began, "so I shall be brief."

"BRIEF" IN THIS CASE did not feel brief. Othello began among the enlisted men and worked his way up through the ranks, thanking various infantry and offering certain soldiers rewards for valorous or long-standing contributions to the army. When he reached the officers, I was acknowledged for my general excellence, honesty, and steadfastness. Michele Cassio received an even more vaguely worded citation for strategic assistance, which he accepted with a fresh blue ostrich ribbon bobbing from his cap.

By this point the temperature in the Council chamber was unbearably hot, and the polite applause that accompanied each name was fading nearly to silence. Finally Othello called Lieutenant Zuane da Porto up to the podium. He explained that da Porto was the longest-serving soldier in the Venetian army, and dutifully began a summary of his life service, which I had written for him after interviewing Zuane. Zuane stood beside him, looking extremely grateful to be done with military life.

I suppressed a yawn, but yet my stomach began to flutter in anticipation of what would follow this. I deliberately turned my thoughts in other directions. I thought of Emilia, with conflicted emotion. Even with a lieutenancy, I would not—could not—become the sycophant she seemed to suddenly want me to be. I anticipated rows ahead, if she ceased to be the woman I had married.

The thought of marriage led me to thoughts of what Othello was doing after this event, and that soured me. From now on, my general would be a married man; that would change everything. He would have a new confidante; I knew that, because I knew marriage. Emilia, not Othello, had always provided the most sympathetic ear for me; I had played that role for Othello but I was now to be supplanted, by a deceiving young woman whose deceit delighted my wife. Everything about that was severely disagreeable to me. And besides these unfortunate inevitabilities, Michele Cassio was about to become a fixture in my daily life.

But I would be Othello's lieutenant.

It was an immense accomplishment, and rightly earned. In time, the rest would sort itself out. Emilia was not really the creature she seemed to be right now; it was a passing silliness that would fade as the honeymoon giddiness of the new marriage faded. I did not know what to make yet of Desdemona, but I knew Othello's character well enough, and despite the recent upset of his love affair, I *knew* him. We were closer than family. Everything would somehow come out all right.

HIS VOICE CHANGED TENOR, and I turned my attention back to the dais. Exhausted, limp applause began around the chamber. Othello saluted da Porto and then bowed deeply to him; da Porto did likewise, accepted a sealed scroll from the general, and descended from the dais, to fade into the fading crowd. I saw him being congratulated and embraced by those around him, but most everyone else's attention turned back to the dais, wanting Othello to finish so the evening could be over.

"And *finally*," Othello said, with a quick grin to acknowledge how desperate we all were for the end, "finally there is the matter for the army of replacing da Porto as my first lieutenant, and without further trying everyone's energy with flowery introduction, I will immediately announce the deserving man." He gestured to a place in the crowd nowhere near where I stood and declared, "Michele Cassio!"

Chapter 30

SHOCK, HUMILIATION, AND RAGE blinded me and muted me. I needed to get out of that room before I harmed somebody or made a fool of myself; being near the doorway, I slipped out to the stairs unnoticed and closed the door behind myself. I stood in the darkness of the stairway, onto the very same platform where I'd dragged Othello earlier to save his career. I retched. Had I actually managed to eat anything during supper, I would have covered the landing with vomit.

Unable to put coherent thoughts together, slapping myself in a bootless attempt to wake up from the nightmare, I managed to get down the stairs to the ground floor. The anteroom I staggered into had servants in it; they assumed I was sloppy drunk from the feast upstairs. They had no idea who I was but politely helped me to get out of doors. I wished to heaven I were as drunk as they thought I was. Drunker, really. I wanted to be permanently too inebriated to understand what was going on around me—I could not understand it sober, and sobriety has fangs when life is chaos.

SOMEHOW, STILL LITERALLY REELING and still unable to form a clear thought, I found myself walking toward the Grand Canal near the Rialto. It was very late now, so late it was early, and the streets and canals were unusually empty and quiet. Out of habit, I had wandered to the area near Senator Brabantio's house, just on the other side of the Grand Canal. I stood there, staring at Ca'Brabantio, fascinated, knowing Desdemona wasn't there because Othello was about to claim her as his bride. Or perhaps he already had. Suddenly I felt empathy for Brabantio with a clarity I had not had before, even at the banquet. Othello the Moor was a man of guile. I did not want to face that, but still it was true. He was rewarding a boozing womanizer for helping him to deceive one of the most powerful men in all of Venice—and to do that, he was robbing me of something I had taken years to earn. There was no justice in the world. There was no justice for me, certainly—and so there should, there *must*, be no justice for Othello either.

I heard a heavy sigh some dozen paces to my left. Startled, I pulled out my dagger and turned to see who was there. I recognized the forlorn figure instantly, and sheathed my blade.

Roderigo stood on the embankment, staring sadly across the Grand Canal at what had been, until tonight, Desdemona's bed-room window. That poor besotted fool. For a moment, I was dis-gusted with him.

Then I changed my mind.

"Roderigo, my old friend," I called out, as jovially as I could muster. "It has been far too long since you and I have enjoyed each other's company. Come, walk with me and tell me why you're sigh-ing so."

After

Roderigo

Chapter 31

top talking!" Roderigo demanded. Accusation suddenly lit his face. "Why did you not tell me this *before* it happened, when we might have *prevented* it? I trust you as a brother—how could you have *failed* me in this?"

"Listen to what I am saying," I repeated. "I. Knew. Nothing. Do you understand? Nothing. I knew he wanted her. But I never dreamed *this* could happen."

Roderigo considered me for a moment, finally calming.

"And now you say you hate the fellow?" he demanded. "The man who made you, the man you have worshipped for years?"

"I know my worth," I said. "I deserve to be lieutenant, and Michele Cassio, that . . . *Florentine arithmetician*, does not deserve it." I knew Roderigo was too preoccupied with his own upset to care about mine, but the bile spewed out: "He has never been in the field, he's never seen battle, everything he knows is theoretical, from books! I served with Othello at Rhodes and Rovigo, and what is my reward? To be kept exactly where I am!"

"I wouldn't follow him, then," Roderigo said. Momentarily distracted, he smiled. "Shall I employ you instead?"

I ignored this well-intentioned but preposterous offer. "Believe me, Roderigo, if I stay with him now, it is not out of love. I will *not* be one of those dutiful fools who spend their life doing as they're told out of love." I spat out the words as I felt my craw tighten; until this night, I would gladly have been such a dutiful fool in Othello's service. "I'd sooner throw in my lot with the Cassios of the world," I declared contemptuously. "The ones who *seem* to serve dutifully only as a feint to gain their own advantage. This is the time for unjust men to thrive."

I glanced at Roderigo, wishing him to ask about my stratagem, like when we were children. But the poor fool was still staring across the canal at the darkened house.

"As heaven is my judge, Roderigo, he'll be sorry for treating me like this."

Still nothing from Roderigo. I sighed and tried to calm my spleen. I had no idea what to do; I did not even know what I *wanted* to do. An hour after the appalling surprise, I was aware of nothing but a desire to punch Othello in the gut. But of course I would never do that, and in truth, I wanted something else: I wanted my lieutenancy, for heaven's sake.

I swore to myself that I would have it. Somehow. Even if I did have to follow the model of Michele Cassio, who had brokered for himself such undeserved success. "I will be dutiful, but not for duty's sake," I carried on to Roderigo, who was still not listening. "Not anymore. Now it will be a means to an end: my end, not Othello's, not the army's, not the Serene Republic's. No more the honest, blunt fellow too stupid to see he was going to be passed over!"

Even as I said the words, I knew I was not capable of such a seachange. But it felt good to make a pretense of it.

"If thick-lips gets away with this—" Roderigo said, staring across at the darkened house. Nothing was going to penetrate his skull unless it had to do with Desdemona.

"Call up to her father," I urged. "Rouse him from sleep. Don't let Othello succeed with this—tell Brabantio to hunt him down."

"He's probably already had her by now," Roderigo said.

"So you're going to sulk and let him enjoy his win?" I demanded. "He may have plucked the flower, but even if it cannot be put back in the bush, it can still be taken from him."

Roderigo's face brightened. "That's true," he said and began to run toward the bridge. "Come! Let's set Brabantio on him!"

I followed him, hoping my impulsiveness wasn't starting something that I would grow to regret. I had no sense of duty to Brabantio; I only wanted, childishly, to spoil Othello's joy, as he had spoiled mine.

We crossed the wooden Rialto Bridge, its shops shuttered for the night, and moments later I was directly under the portico of Ca'Brabantio. Brabantio knew me as Othello's man, so I could not let him see my face. Roderigo stood a little to the side so that he could look up at the balcony.

"He's asleep, and likely drunk from the festivities," I said. "Be *loud.*"

"Senator Brabantio!" Roderigo called up. Rather absurdly, he knocked upon the nearest stone column, as if it were a door. "Senator Brabantio! Wake up."

That would never do. I opened my lungs and hollered, so loud I could not be recognized, my voice was so distorted: "*Wake up, Brabantio!*" I grabbed my nose between thumb and forefinger to further disguise my voice. "There are thieves in your house, they've stolen your daughter! Thieves! *Thieves, I tell you!*"

Immediately, with a screeching of wood, the shutters were shoved out. Roderigo suddenly looked frightened. He glanced at me unsurely; I gestured him to speak.

"What is all the racket about?" I heard the senator demand, directly above me.

Again, Roderigo stared at me. Again, I gestured him to speak. "Er . . . Senator, is your family home?"

"Are your doors locked?" I shouted up, nostrils still clamped shut.

"Who wants to know?"

Roderigo tensed and appeared to be trying to make himself physically smaller. He opened his mouth to speak, but no sound came out.

"You're robbed, Senator!" I shouted. "Go check your daughter's chamber!" I paused but heard nothing from above. "This very moment, even now, an old black ram is tupping your white ewe!"

Roderigo gave me a chastising, disgusted look for that; from above, I heard Brabantio huff again with aggravation.

"You're mad," the senator declared disparagingly.

Roderigo looked at me; for a third time, I gestured him to speak. "Er, Senator," he called up, again tentatively. "Do you know my voice?"

"No," Brabantio said with such disinterest I thought he might dismiss this as a prank and return to bed. "Who are you?"

Roderigo glanced at me for confirmation; I nodded.

"It's Roderigo Rosso, Senator."

Brabantio groaned. "You must be drunk. I told you to leave my house alone and my daughter in peace. I'll set the watch on you."

"Oh, no, sir, I beg you, Senator—"

"I'm warning you, Roderigo," Brabantio said. From the subtle change in how his voice echoed—and from the wide-eyed stare Roderigo was suddenly frozen into—I guessed the senator had finally seen the merchant, in person. "I can put you in a lot of trouble for harassment. Remove yourself immediately and never show your face here again."

"I beg you, Senator, listen to me just a moment—"

"You're telling me my house is robbed, while I'm in it!" Brabantio huffed. "This is Venice, man, such things do not happen here. Go home and leave me in peace."

"Senator Brabantio, I swear I've come to you in total goodness—" Roderigo implored; I intervened.

"You obstinate fool!" I shouted. "We have come to help you and you're treating us like ruffians—you *deserve* the bad fortune we're trying to protect you from, you ass!"

"How dare you speak to me that way?" Brabantio demanded irritably. "Who is that—where are you, whoreson?"

I could not risk his recognizing me. I squeezed my thorax with my free hand, to further disguise my voice. "I am one, sire, who comes to tell you that your daughter and Othello are at this very moment making the beast with two backs!" Silently, I thanked the whores of my Arsenal days for expanding my licentious vocabulary.

Finally I had his full attention: "You *villain*!" he hollered into the darkness. "Roderigo, you shall answer for this assault upon my daughter's dignity!"

Roderigo took a deep breath and found himself a little courage. "I'll answer anything you like, Senator. I'll answer your questions about how your daughter snuck away from here in a gondola while you were at the feast, and went to the Arsenal, and is at this moment in bed with Othello in his apartments at the Saggitarius building there. But don't take my word for it, Senator. Go to her room and check for yourself. If I am lying, arrest me. Whip me, even. *Kill* me."

He looked to me for approval. I clasped my hands together in a gesture of valor.

I heard a scuffle above and then Brabantio's voice, more distantly and echoing, clearly back in the house: "Lights! Wake Desdemona! Light, I say—why is there nobody here to light a lamp?" . . . and by then his voice had faded into the house.

Roderigo joined me under the portico. "Well, then," he said, eyes shining. "No turning back now, eh?"

No. There wasn't. I felt my own face ablaze with energy. "Good man." I clapped him on the shoulder. "I'll leave you now."

His excitement immediately withered. "What?" he demanded. "No, we're doing this together!"

"I'm Othello's man," I reminded him. "And I am happy to help you, but I cannot release myself from his service, no matter my anger. If I'm found in conspiracy against him, it will not only ruin me, but it will also demoralize the army command, and for the good of Venice I cannot indulge in that. We head to Cyprus soon. He needs me, and I need him to need me. So I cannot remain in this now. Take Brabantio to the Arsenal. But if you see me there with Othello, you must pretend I've had nothing to do with this business tonight. Do you understand?"

Roderigo nodded solemnly. "You want to destroy from within," he declared.

I had not considered that. "Perhaps," I said.

Chapter 32

RUNNING THROUGH DARK and twisting alleyways took as long as a leisurely walk in daylight. And raising Othello from his wedding bed would be a challenge, as I would sooner have cut off my own foot than set it in the marriage chamber. Once I reached the Arsenal, I convinced a red-faced page to inform the general I had arrived in crisis.

A few moments later, pulling on his loose-cut breeches, bare-chested and smelling of sex, Othello trod heavily down the stairs and outside to meet me on the terrace between the gate and the Sagittary.

"And what is the crisis, Ensign?" he asked, a coddling parent.

"Brabantio knows," I said. "He's sending men in this direction."

Othello did not look the least alarmed.

"He spoke so abusively of you, I wanted to *hurt* him," I tried.

"Thank God you didn't," Othello responded, almost jovially.

"He's out for you. Are you married indeed? Because he is set on annulling it—by divorce if possible, by widowing his daughter if he must. And the law is on his side in this, for he is a patrician and you are not. *You are in danger,* sir."

Othello shrugged, refusing to rise to the alarm. He leaned his bare back against the stone wall of the building and crossed his arms. "I've done enough service for the state that the complaints of one senator will not spell my demise," he assured me, almost condescendingly. "You know that, Iago. I understand his anger, but we would have courted openly if his people allowed it." He stood straighter and pointed, without concern, to something behind me. "What are those lights?"

I glanced over my shoulder. The porter had allowed a small party through the gates. One man holding a torch rushed toward us across the small paved area, followed by two others.

"It's Brabantio and his men. For heaven's sake, go inside."

Othello shook his head. "No," he said. "I have nothing to hide now, so better just to meet directly and discuss it." He frowned a little, staring. "Are you certain that's Brabantio?"

"Who else could it be?"

It could be—indeed, it was—Lieutenant Michele Cassio, making his first appearance *wearing my sash*.

"Good evening, friend," Othello said warmly as Cassio's torchlight blended with the wall sconce outside the Sagittary door. "What's the news?"

"The doge requires you back at the palace instantly, sir," Cassio said, his face flushed from running, his voice coming out in gasps.

How remarkable: Brabantio had gone, not to Othello's home, but to the doge's, and the doge was taking immediate action against a heathen upstart! What an efficient and swift end to the affair.

So there's an end to it, I wanted to say, *that is what you get for your duplicity.*

This consequence never entered Othello's mind. "What's the matter?" he asked Cassio.

Cassio took a gulp of air, and then, collecting his Florentine self, said, "It's got to do with Cyprus, General. Just before the ceremony tonight, a galley came in from Cyprus with an alarm that the Turk was planning an attack, and an hour later they were followed by another galley that had set out a day after them but made up the difference— and that one said the Turks were just refortifying Rhodes, but by the end of the festivities, they had been overtaken by yet *another* galley with the message that no, it was for Cyprus after all. I had stayed late because everyone was congratulating me, and as I was about to depart, the doge's secretary asked me to stay until they knew more. The Council of Ten has been called into emergency session, and the doge sent three different messengers to find you and call you in at once." A discreet pause. "I volunteered to be the one to check your lodgings," he said in a lower voice.

The two of them exchanged a knowing glance that sickened me. "A good thing it was you," Othello said softly. I wanted to spit. "I need just a moment inside, and then I'll come with you." He leapt up the steps and entered the building.

Cassio and I found ourselves standing in the torchlight with a brace of the doge's guards. We both knew Othello was going up to tell Desdemona why he had to leave her bed.

"Good thing you knew to look for him here, eh, Michele?" I said heartily.

Cassio glanced uncomfortably at the doge's men. "Well, it is the middle of the night, and this is where he sleeps," he pointed out.

"And tonight, of course, he's not sleeping alone," I said, grinning. "If he can keep it all lawful, he's a made man, no?"

Cassio turned his back to the guards. "I do not understand," he said in a deliberate tone.

"He's married," I announced loudly. The two guards blinked in amazement and turned to each other with questioning faces.

Cassio anxiously cleared his throat in a feeble pretext of off-handedness. "Is he really?" he said. "To whom?"

I heard Othello's quick but heavy tread descending the stairs. *You cowardly whoreson,* I wanted to say to Cassio. *Even now, when it is done, and you suspect I know you know—even now* . . . instead of saying what I wanted to, I met his false innocence with my own. "Why, surely you've guessed it, he's married to—" But then Othello stepped between us down the stairs. "Come, Captain, will you go?" I asked, turning my attention to the general.

Cassio almost sagged with relief. *Oh, you but wait,* I thought, *you won't escape this unscathed. You'll be called to account yet.*

"Let's go," Othello said, and as a pack we moved the twenty paces or so to the gate. The porter, saluting, let us out.

The moment we crossed down the steps, a fast-moving cluster of men erupted from the alley that connected to the Calle Largo, their skittish movement illuminated by a drove of torches held aloft.

"That'll be more of the doge's men looking for you," Cassio said and raised his hand in greeting.

With a thrill, I recognized the stout form of Senator Brabantio and the lanky one of my childhood friend. Every man among them brandished both torch and drawn sword. "No, it's Brabantio!" I said. "General, be careful, I warned you he is out for blood."

Othello's eyebrows raised slightly when he saw all the blades. "You there!" he called out. "Stop where you are. Do not approach with weapons drawn, I am your general."

"It's him, Senator! It's the Moor!" Roderigo's voice rang. He grabbed Brabantio's arm, and Brabantio clapped a hand over it. Apparently on their way here, the senator had changed his opinion of the Pepper King.

"Take him down!" Brabantio cried. Roderigo and the men with them leapt toward us. Instinctively, Othello, the doge's men, and I all drew our own swords; a heartbeat late, Cassio did too.

None of our accosters wore uniform garb. That meant they were militia, not constables; Brabantio had called upon his neighbors to form a *posse comitatus*. Militia men are famously uneven in their skills, and I had no intention of shedding blood tonight. So I chose the safest target: "Hey, you, Roderigo! Come, sir, I'm for you!" I waved my blade in front of his face in a series of brief arcs, which seemed to bedazzle him.

Othello's voice was both parental and commanding. "Put up your swords—all of you, both sides."

Nobody sheathed, but I ceased my flourishing, and rested my tip on Roderigo's chest. His face was even more flush with excitement now, and I worried he might burst into a giggling fit at my pretense of violence.

"My dear Senator Brabantio," Othello continued, bowing his head respectfully. "You shall command me with the wisdom of your years, not with the swords of your henchmen."

"Thief!" Brabantio shouted in Othello's face. "Where are you keeping my daughter?" Without waiting for an answer, he demanded, "Have you used your heathen magic to enslave her with lust?"

Othello blinked, once, slowly. "Do you mean that?" he asked.

"That girl does not have a marrying hair on her head!" her father railed. "She has shunned every Venetian gentleman who's asked for her, no matter how wealthy or handsome—there is *nothing* in her being that would prefer your ugly black face to any of them. You've drugged her, or taken her by force, and I'm arresting you for rape. Gentlemen!" he shouted to his companions. "Grab him! If he resists you, *kill him.*" His face was purple in the yellow torchlight.

Almost abashed, two men handed off their torches to a third and stepped toward us. Othello, calm throughout the tirade, simply held up one hand. "Cease this nonsense," he said gently, but with such authority the men froze. "All of you, put up your swords, put down your fists. I assure you, Senator, if I felt any need to fight, I'd have done so by now and you would all be lying senseless on the ground. Your charge is unfounded, but I shall do you a courtesy and answer to it, to your satisfaction. Where shall I go for that?"

"To prison," Brabantio snapped. Othello's effortless intimidation of his militia made him less cocksure. "Rot there until the courts hear my case against you."

"I can do that," Othello said reasonably. "But then you shall have to explain to the doge why I am not answering his very urgent request that I come to him immediately."

Brabantio started, and looked at those of us surrounding the general.

"It's true, Senator," Cassio said. "The doge has convened an emergency council. No doubt but a messenger is at your house right now to call you to join them, too."

Brabantio blinked, then pressed thumb and forefinger against either eyebrow, as if in pain. "What?" he whispered. "The doge has called a session in the middle of the night?" He stared at Othello as if the Moor had staged this diversion. "Bring him with us," he ordered the militiamen.

"I am going there anyhow," Othello said pleasantly. "In fact, I will travel with you, if you like."

"Do not think this means I'm rescinding my accusations," Brabantio warned. "This is not nothing, my charge against you. Every member of the Council will share my outrage, and then it will be the worse for you, you . . . you . . . Moor. Not one man in the state of Venice will abide a foreign black heathen siring the next generation of our senators."

"I am sure we may discuss that once the doge's business is resolved," Othello said. "Shall we go, Senator?"

THE ASSEMBLY OF men began to move into the darkness. I saw Roderigo hesitate, then resolutely follow after.

Chapter 33

BRABANTIO SHARED A GONDOLA with Othello and glared at him the entire hurried ride to the Doge's Palace, but he did not speak again. Othello could surely feel the glare but seemed indifferent to it. He was now the general, answering his prince's summons on a military crisis; even the blushing Desdemona was a dull glimmer in the back recesses of his mind.

We were led by the doge's guards straight up to the Council of Ten. Every seat but one around the table was occupied. The Doge, Girolamo Priuli, sat at the head, wearing his ceremonial finery from earlier in the evening—every article from cap to boots in gleaming white and gold, but looking wilted now. Even his thick beard, a hint of chestnut still showing through the grey, looked wilted. His dark eyes had bags under them. He was exhausted. I'd never seen him close before, and I'd certainly never seen him look so human.

Othello strode to the doge's right side and bowed deeply, hand on heart. Without preamble, Priuli announced, "Othello, the Turks are planning to invade Cyprus with at least one hundred galleys. We are sending you there at once." Only then did he look up and notice anyone else in the room. "Ah," he said. "There you are, Brabantio. We sent for you earlier. We could have used your counsel."

"Just as I could use yours now," Brabantio said, striding to Priuli's left side and bowing as Othello had. "Pardon me, but I am consumed by a personal crisis, Your Grace. It can be dealt with swiftly, but I cannot turn my attention to other matters until you have helped resolve it for me."

Priuli frowned at him. "What's the matter?"

"My daughter—" Brabantio began. He took in a deep breath and made a choking sound. "My daughter . . ." He could hardly speak. "She's been stolen and corrupted and raped and bewitched."

At the reference to witchcraft, Othello's face twitched. He met my eye and gave me a look I was long familiar with: our look of private merriment. This was the sort of comment we ought to laugh about later over a shared bottle.

But it was a patrician daughter's virginity at stake, and such hymens, hard to come by, were increasingly rare and therefore very valuable. "We will punish him, Brabantio." Priulu grimaced. "We shall get her back and you may do whatever you desire to the transgressor, whoever he is. But now—"

Staring triumphant daggers at the general, Brabantio bowed deeply. "I thank Your Grace most humbly," he interrupted, then stood again and pointed across the doge's face to indicate Othello. "Here is the man!"

Priuli looked up between them, following the velvet sleeve of Brabantio's accusing arm. Othello gently raised his eyebrows.

The doge sighed heavily. "Well," he said to heaven, "*that's* unfortunate." He pushed aside Brabantio's arm and turned in his seat to look more directly up at Othello. "What have you to say, General?"

"There's nothing he can say but confess to it!" Brabantio shouted.

Othello bowed his head to Priuli, then looked up to acknowledge the senators around the table. "My lords," he began, glancing at me as if for reassurance. "Excuse my roughness, I am a soldier, and you know I am not good at giving speeches. It is true that I have married this man's daughter." Ignoring the shocked responses around the tables, he continued levelly, "I have done this with her willingness and without the aid of any witchcraft. I am amazed the good senator thinks me capable of such powers."

"If it wasn't witchcraft, it was potions!" Brabantio shouted across the doge at him. "She is the shyest, quietest virgin in all of Venice. I remember her response to you the first night she saw you—she was terrified of you. If you haven't taken her by force or magic, at the very least you've tricked her somehow."

As the rest of the Council sat staring in amazement, Priuli looked up again at Othello. "The senator sounds quite certain in his accusations, General. Did you force her? Did you—" His own hesitation revealed he shared Othello's opinion of what he spoke next, "Did you employ witchcraft to seduce her? Or is this a love match?"

Brabantio opened his mouth to shout some more, but the doge, without looking back, held up a commanding hand to silence him.

Othello smiled with absolute confidence at the doge. "Send for the lady herself from my apartment, and hear what she has to say. If she speaks against me in any way, take away my office. Take away my *life*."

"Someone fetch Desdemona," Priuli said.

Othello gestured to me. "Ensign, take them, you know which building."

Surprised to be addressed, I bowed. I was not pleased about the assignment but followed after the guards at once. Roderigo, still in Brabantio's entourage but forgotten by him now, lurked near Cassio in the shadows. He was staring at me pleadingly. I held up one finger in a subtle gesture of reassurance, then went down the stairs with the doge's men. As soon as I was outside I regretted doing that. *I should have signaled him to go home,* I thought. The poor fellow had had enough upset for one evening.

WE TOOK A gondola back along the southern shore of the city to the Arsenal. At the gate, I hesitated. I was not eager to break in on a new bride awaiting her husband's return. Especially this bride.

"Men should not go in to her just now," I said to those who had escorted me. I pointed to the southern end of the terrace. "Let me get my wife; we lodge just there at the Dolphin."

EMILIA, OF COURSE, would be asleep. I had not seen her since hours before the feast. I wondered if she'd waited up for me—it was so late now, nearly dawn. I wondered if she'd heard the news about Cassio and the lieutenancy. I wondered, most of all, if she knew about the elopement.

If she did know, and had not told me . . . then I could never trust her again. This mawkish drama was imprudent—including my share in it. It was usurping the far more urgent matter of the Turks at Cyprus. I wished I'd never told Roderigo anything.

With a lamp provided from the gatehouse, I sprinted across the campo to the inn, up the steps to our rooms, and opened the door quietly, my heart beating strangely hard in my ribs. I wanted her to be ignorant of everything. I wanted her to care nothing for it. I wanted her all to myself.

For a moment, I had that. She had fallen asleep in her best gown, a blanket wrapped loosely around her, seated on her wooden stool with her head and back against the wall. On the table before her was a small bouquet of flowers, which she must have bought at some expense. She had covered the table with the brightest cloth she owned. She had set up a celebration for me to come home to . . . and I had not come home.

All the rest could wait for a moment. I placed the lamp by the door and crossed to Emilia as softly as my boots allowed it. I knelt beside her, resting my head on her lap. Gently I reached up and felt for the curve of her cheek, cupped my palm against it.

She awoke with a start. "Oh!" she said, then realizing it was me, I felt the cheek pull back into a smile, and she rested a hand on my head. "Hello, my conquering hero. What time is it? I waited hours, I'm sorry I fell asleep."

At least I still had this, this lovely woman, the gem who had been there before anything else, even before Othello. I looked up at her, smiling, and then rose to my feet, her hands clasped in mine. "Emilia," I said, "I need you to do something right away. Are you fully awake? I require your attention."

"Of course," Emilia said, standing. "What is it?"

"Tell Desdemona to come with us to the doge's palace."

She gave me a confused frown, which made me happier than I had been in hours. "Why me? Why not one of her women? Or her father?"

"She's nowhere near them at the moment," I said. Lest she was being disingenuous, I studied her face for a trace of excitement. There was none.

"What do you mean? Where is she?" She shrugged the blanket off of her; it slid to the floor around her feet.

"At the Sagittary," I said.

She understood at once: her eyes and mouth opened wide. "Oh, Iago!" she said, shaking her head. "Oh heaven, are you serious?"

"They eloped tonight." Pause. "With Cassio's assistance." Her eyes widened even more with that declaration. "Emilia, do not stand here gaping. Her father and Othello are with the doge at this moment; the doge has summoned her at once to clear Othello of rape charges, and I do not—"

She threw open the door and was already running down the stairs.

I grabbed the lamp and caught up with her. The porter let us into the Arsenal, and together we ran into the Sagittary.

But I stopped outside Othello's bedroom. "Explain to her, and I'll wait here," I said, and offered her the light.

Emilia nodded and went inside.

I WAITED IN DARKNESS. I heard the sound of female voices within, delicately running up and down a trilling scale. I tried to think what I should do now. Any hope I'd had of Othello being punished for eloping was about to be squashed: not only would Desdemona avouch that it was a mutual affection, but the Turks had just rendered Othello absolutely necessary to the Republic. If Othello were removed from office, young Cassio would suddenly be in charge of most of the army as it was preparing to go off to meet our mortal enemy. Not even Brabantio would want to see that happen.

What, then? How could I, without endangering the army, demand satisfaction from Othello for his duplicity? From Cassio, for usurping my place?

The door opened and Emilia came out, motheringly embracing Desdemona in one arm. The senator's daughter looked so pale and fragile, I felt pity for her—this privileged, bewitching young liar. She looked at me, shy and sheepish.

"Good Ensign," she said quietly. She clutched something against her: Othello's prized kerchief, with the strawberries embroidered into it.

I smiled reassuringly and took the lamp from my wife. "Emilia has explained the situation?" I said.

She nodded.

"Are you able to travel to the palace?"

She blushed slightly and looked down. "Yes, Ensign, thank you for your solicitude. I suppose I should be grateful this is happening now. It would have been even more awkward tomorrow morning."

"I think it already is tomorrow morning," I said. I wondered if she had ever seen her father enraged, if she had any idea what she was about to have to face.

WHEN WE REACHED the palace we were ushered up the steps to the Council chamber. On the stairs, Desdemona—looking much smaller than Emilia— nervously reached up and grabbed my hand, pressing her lips together between her teeth. I smiled, squeezed her hand gently, nodded, trying to calm her. "It will be fine," I promised her. "Just speak the truth." Again I regretted telling Roderigo anything.

We entered.

I ASSUMED THAT while waiting for us for nearly an hour, they had moved on to the far more urgent matter at hand: the Turks. But Brabantio was raging again when we entered. Othello had not moved, remaining at the doge's right side; Brabantio had propelled himself to the other side of the table, near the door, so that his back was to us as we came in. He stopped at the sound of our entrance and swirled around. He looked as though he might vomit when he saw his daughter, hurriedly dressed, her mussed hair falling down her back.

The entire table murmured greeting—

"Be quiet!" Brabantio brayed at them, turning back around. "Let her speak! If she admits she was in any way voluntary in this, I'll cut my own heart out in front of you."

Desdemona looked alarmed at this declaration; Emilia, still holding her hand, squeezed it. Again Brabantio turned to her.

"Come here, my girl," he said, trying to contain his voice, to sound parental and affectionate. "Where in this room does your allegiance lie?"

Desdemona took a moment. I saw her exchange looks with Othello, but nothing was revealed in either face. They were veterans of hiding their feelings before others.

"Father," Desdemona said, taking a step toward him. His face lit up with triumph. But after that one step, she stopped, and moved no closer to him. "You know I have a duty to you: you gave me life and raised me, gave me education and taught me to respect you, and I do. But, Father—" And here she walked right past him, holding out her hand toward the Moor on the far side of the table. Brabantio followed her movement with his head. "Here's my husband," she said, reaching Othello.

Finally Othello smiled and held out his hand to embrace hers. She kissed him briefly on the lips, to the voiced shock of the entire room; then she turned back toward Brabantio.

"Just as my mother parted from her father to marry you, so I do likewise in my marriage now. My duty lies with my husband."

Everyone was staring at Brabantio. I sidestepped from behind him and slipped farther into the room so I might better see. He looked as if he would be sick. His breathing was harsh. Othello calmly placed an arm across the front of Desdemona's shoulders.

"God be with you," Brabantio finally said, in a voice of tortured resignation. He cleared his throat and said, "Please, Your Grace, move on to the state affairs."

There was a respectful pause, and then the doge reached for a paper that lay before him on the table. The other councilors likewise reached for papers near to them. "Regarding the number of galleys," Priuli began, "these numbers do not agree—"

"It's a good thing you're an only child!" Brabantio let cry again, his face relit with choking fury. "If you had any siblings, I'd whip them skinless just to punish you by proxy!" His voice was choked. He turned away. "I'm done, my lord," he promised Priuli miserably.

The doge lowered the papers. The senators did likewise. "Brabantio, I understand your grief. I would be heartbroken too, if it were my daughter deceiving me so. But there is no wisdom in mourning a mischief that's been done. If you are wronged and do nothing but sulk about it, you wrong yourself even further."

If you are wronged and do nothing but sulk about it, you wrong yourself even further. I must take that to heart, I thought.

Brabantio waved this away as if the doge's words were an annoying insect. "I beseech you, sir," he mumbled, "on to the affairs of
state."

This time, the doge did so with purpose. He picked up the paper
again and began to speak even as the councilors were reaching again
for theirs. "Our intelligence is unreliable. We have three differing
reports of Turkish warships anticipated, but we know the Turks plan
to attack Cyprus, and Othello, you know the place best. We have a
unit stationed there and a rector I have full faith in, Montano, but he
is no general. I must deprive you of a honeymoon and send you there
immediately."

Othello released Desdemona and bowed to the doge. "I would
expect no other orders. I am the general of the army before I am anything else, even a new-made husband." Desdemona beamed at him.
At least you know your place, I thought. "But since I *am* a new-made
husband, I humbly ask the state to house my wife well in my absence.
The Sagittary is not fit for a woman, especially one of her breeding."

The doge shrugged. "Let her stay at her father's while you are
away," said Priuli.

Brabantio swung back around to face them. "Oh, no," he said bitterly. "I won't have it."

"Nor I," Othello said.

"Nor *I*," said Desdemona. "It would be unbearable for Father, and
I would not hurt him further. But more than that, Your Grace, please
hear me," and here she turned to the doge and broke from Othello's
side to kneel at the princely chair.

The doge looked down at her and made a gesture for her to rise.
"What would you, Desdemona?"

Desdemona stayed kneeling, face and eyes averted. "I married
Othello to be with him all the time. That means in war as well as
peace. Let me go with him to Cyprus."

Tonight was a night these sleep-deprived senators would be talking about for years to come—for decades, if their age allowed them.

I glanced at Emilia; she was watching with the fascination I had found so disagreeable since she'd become moonish about the secret love affair. I looked next at Othello, in the wan hope that he might not want Desdemona with him.

But his feelings were obvious. "Please, my lord, let her have your approval. You have heard it yourself: the request comes from her, not from me. Her presence will not affect my work, just as my ensign's wife's presence has never distracted him."

The doge glanced around the room, then shrugged again. "It's all one to me whether she stays or goes; your choice. But make the choice immediately, Othello, because you are sailing before sunup."

Othello put his hand on his heart and bowed to the doge and then the table. "Of course, milords," he said.

"We'll reconvene here at nine tomorrow to determine further steps," the doge announced wearily. "Othello, leave an officer behind to follow in a day or two with orders and supplies."

Othello smiled. "Please, Your Grace, let that be Ensign Iago, the best man in my service." He gestured grandly toward me; again taken by surprise, I almost smashed my hand against my chest before bowing my head. I wanted to sneak a look at Michele Cassio but stopped myself. "He's the most trustworthy man I've ever worked with," Othello continued. "In fact, Iago—let Desdemona come with you to Cyprus. You may bring Emilia to keep her company."

"Let it be so," the doge said. Looking exhausted, he said, "And good night to all of you."

The other senators—all in robes hanging over their nightdresses—began to push back their chairs, collect their papers, and make toward the door.

"Brabantio," Priuli, standing, called out over the tired hubbub. Unwillingly, Brabantio moved toward him. "Good Brabantio, I hope in time you can appreciate what you have in your son-in-law."

Brabantio looked appalled by the use of this term. He turned away from Priuli without speaking. The doge wished good night to the general and his bride, and then exited with his attendants through a private door that led back toward his own quarters.

* * *

THERE WAS AN AWKWARD, quiet moment in the chamber now. Roderigo was still there in the shadows, unnoticed by everyone, perhaps mistaken for a guard; Emilia had moved from the doorway to let the senators exit, and waited now near it, eyes shining. I stood near her, watching the three other people left in the room: Othello, Desdemona, and Brabantio.

Chapter 34

DESDEMONA LOOKED IMPLORINGLY at her father. I could not see Brabantio's face from where I stood as he drew near them.

"I have one thing to say to you, Moor," Brabantio said, his voice dripping contempt. "She deceived me. She may deceive you just as easily."

Desdemona's face fell.

"I trust her with my life," Othello answered evenly.

Brabantio turned and walked heavily out of the room. When he had disappeared into the darkness of the stairwell, Othello and Desdemona both heaved sighs, and turning to each other, kissed. I looked away.

"Iago, my friend," Othello said. I made myself look back. "I'm leaving this beautiful woman in your care, and Emilia's. Bring her with you as soon as you can."

"Of course I will," I said evenly. Emilia made a joyful noise from the corner.

Othello took Desdemona's hands. "I have one hour of freedom to spend with you, chuck." He smiled suggestively. "Let's use it well." Allowing himself an almost gleeful bass rumble of a laugh, he picked her up and threw her over his shoulder, her long pale hair cascading nearly to his ankles. She laughed, a sound I'd never heard before. She had a lovely laugh, almost as lovely as Emilia's.

But hearing Emilia's laughter near the door did not endear her to me at that moment. "Iago!" she gushed, "isn't this remarkable! And best of all is that I will come with you to Cyprus!"

I did like that, and I managed a smile to show her so. "It's very late, Emilia. Take a gondola home, and I'll be there as soon as I can. I have one bit of unfinished business here."

She beamed at me and put her hand over her heart like a soldier. "Yes, sir, Lieutenant Iago." She grinned.

My stomach sank into my legs. She did not know yet. I would have to tell her. Later. That would happen later. Right now I had a mission of compassion.

"Good night, love," I said, returning the salute halfheartedly. "Don't wait up for me this time. But I'll be along as soon as possible."

When she was gone, I turned to face the shadows.

"Well," I said, "that did not go as planned. I apologize, Roderigo."

Roderigo stepped out of the shadows. I'd rarely seen that handsome face look so despondent. "Iago." He sighed.

He was going to want succoring, and I did not have the energy for it. "What is it, my friend?" I said, forcing a sympathetic smile.

"Iago, what should I *do*?"

I looked at the poor man. I did not regret trying to undo Othello's marriage, but I did regret, a little, that I'd brought Roderigo into my scheme. The mooning fool would have heard the news eventually, but he would have heard about it far from me. "Go home, Roderigo," I said, as kindly as I could. "Go home and get some sleep."

He responded with an insulted expression, and then suddenly, most unexpectedly, he drew himself up tall and erect, almost cocky. "I," he announced, suddenly a tragic hero, "am going to drown myself."

With an unexpected intensity of purpose, he marched out the door and started down the stairs.

I followed after him, barely suppressing a snort of laughter in the dark. "*What*? If you do that, Roderigo, I will remember you without an ounce of affection, as the *silliest* man who ever lived."

Without looking back at me, he challenged me, his voice resonant and echoing in the stone stairwell: "Do you think it's *silly* to stay alive when life hurts so much and I can oppose the hurt by ending it?"

"Oh, please, stop your poetic nonsense," I scolded.

At the bottom of the stairs, a boy opened the outer door for us, and Roderigo exited into the Piazzetta. I followed on his heels.

Roderigo began sprinting.

Toward the lagoon.

"Roderigo!" I hollered and broke into a run, overtaking him in three quick strides beneath the column of the winged lion. I grabbed his wrist and jerked him to a standstill. He glared at me, his face red and tear streaked. "Good God, don't drown yourself! In all our shared twenty-eight years upon this world, I have never heard of one sensible man dying for love. Men die, and worms eat them, but not for love, Roderigo, never really for *love*."

"Then what do I *do*?" he demanded furiously, pulling his wrist free. "I know it's a weakness to be so obsessively fond of someone, but I haven't the virtue or the character to rise above it."

"Must we delve into moral analysis at three in the morning?" I asked. He gave me a look of superior disgust and began heading again—at a brisk walk this time—toward the dark water.

I walked alongside him. His legs were longer than mine and I had to take five strides for every four of his. "Listen to me. You can recover from her, it's just a matter of willpower, Roderigo. Set your will to achieve something, stick with it, and you will achieve it." He huffed dismissively and sped up. "There's nothing fated or mysterious about it," I insisted. "Life works like that, all the time, every day. Your career is splendid proof that you can do that."

He kept walking.

I was tempted to just turn away. I hadn't the energy to console myself tonight, let alone another. But his sudden firmness of purpose unnerved me, and I would never forgive myself if he did himself harm. There were no gondoliers here—there was a night watch, but they would do nothing until someone was actually drowning. If then. So I continued jabbering: "We'd all of us spend all our time eating and drinking and chasing women if we hadn't the will to resist those impulses. If you can will yourself not to spend the whole day in debauchery, surely you can will yourself to forget about one pretty little virgin."

"There's more to it than that," Roderigo lamented at the waterside. "You don't understand the depths of my passion."

He pushed me away as he crouched, preparing to leap into the greasy water; I lost my balance and grabbed his arm, pulling him back onto me as I fell. We collapsed in a scuffling heap on the paving stones.

"Roderigo, what are you doing?" I snarled as he scrambled to his feet. "Be a man, for the love of God! *Drown* yourself? Over a girl? Don't be ridiculous!"

He was red-faced. To distract him from turning back to the water, I held up my arm; he took it and helped me to my feet, abashed.

For the first time in our lives, I admired him. He was as upset as I was, for different reasons and in different ways, but by the brightest heaven, he had the courage of his convictions! He had become a man of action: he really would have killed himself. I loved him for that simple, if misguided, courage. In his timorous way, he had more integrity than General Othello; Othello would never have drowned himself if *he'd* been robbed of Desdemona. Suddenly between the two of them—the two-faced warrior or the wealthy sap— the wealthy sap seemed the more honorable companion.

And the perfect means for undermining Othello's dishonorable intentions.

I took Roderigo's hand. "Listen to me. I am your oldest friend, yes?" He nodded. "And no tie binds closer than the ties of childhood friendship, yes?" He nodded but gave me a questioning look. "Then trust me, Roderigo. Perhaps I can get you Desdemona after all." The questioning look shifted to something between desperation and disbelief. "She won't stay with him. He won't stay with her. They hardly know each other. They are each fascinated with the other because they are so *different.* But familiarity breeds contempt, and before long he will cease to treat her as if she were a princess, and she'll regret her choice. The trick is to make sure that *you,* Roderigo, are right there under her nose when she renounces him, and that you appear to be the perfect suitor to replace him."

I could almost hear gears working in his head as he contemplated this. "How do I do that?" he asked.

"Come with the army to Cyprus."

"*What?*"

"Disguise yourself as a soldier—I can easily get you on the rolls of the enlisted men."

Roderigo thought. Then: "How can I impress her if she thinks I am a common soldier?"

I knew Roderigo so well; I was merely telling him to do something he would have done on his own, if only he'd had the imagination to think of it. "Is winning Desdemona truly the most important thing in your life?" I asked.

He met my eye, put his hand over his heart, and nodded. He was so earnestly sincere, how could I not exert him to see it through?

"Then sell everything you have—your business, your farms on Terraferma, your summer homes, all of it—put money and jewels in your purse and bring it all to Cyprus. Woo her with it there. Let her know you're really a brilliant, wealthy gentleman in disguise."

He blinked. "How? As a soldier I'll never have access to her."

I smiled. "But I will," I said. "She has a proven weakness for intrigue. If I see to it that she receives mysterious packages of jewels and love letters from you, I'll wager she'll fall for you. That is how Othello won her over—and he did not even use jewels. Imagine what some fine pearls and rubies will accomplish. I know this much for a fact: she loves intrigue."

The color rose in his cheeks; I could see it in the lamplight. His breathing grew quick and shallow as his imagination sketched out for him how this could really happen. Suddenly I understood Emilia's fascination with the secret romance—there is something powerfully seductive in the prospect of helping to make a friend's fantasy come true.

"Do you really think that this could happen?" he whispered, eyes beaming.

"Attempt it and find out. That is certainly better than *drowning* yourself, no?" I said.

"And if I do all this, Iago—if I sell everything and come to Cyprus with the army—I can count on you to help me?"

"Roderigo. Have I ever in our lives disappointed you or let you down? I stood up for you against that bully Tasso, I protected you whenever we got into trouble as children. I will look out for you now."

"But this is much bigger than any of that. You would be in collusion with me against Othello's interests—you're his ensign and his confidant—"

"But *not* his lieutenant, as I should be," I amended. "Didn't you hear me ranting against him before? I bear a grudge, Roderigo. I want to see him get his just deserts. If it happens by your cuckolding him, frankly I'd enjoy that almost as much as you would. If we work together, we can accomplish it. Are you with me?"

He nodded, mouth slightly slack.

"Good man. I must get home to Emilia. We'll talk more tomorrow. Come to the Arsenal. No, my inn, the southern end of the terrace before the gate. Good night."

"I'll be there," Roderigo said, with an awkward attempt at a salute.

"Excellent. Good night." Suddenly exhausted by the events of this past day and night, I patted him on the arm and began to cross the Piazzetta back toward the Doge's Palace. I stopped myself and looked back at him. "And Roderigo?"

"Yes?"

"No more talk of drowning, do you hear?"

He grinned. "I swear it," he said. "I am a changed man." He turned his back on the murky waters and ran toward the grand Piazza of San Marco. I watched him disappear into the darkness, hugely relieved he would not hurt himself.

My conscience was uneasy, though. Even if Desdemona forsook Othello, she would never take up with Roderigo. I knew that. But it gave him such joy to believe it, and the romance of secretly wooing her gave him more pleasure than his estates or money ever had. He did not need the expensive trinkets he was about to entrust to me. And Desdemona would not want them. I would be doing him a service, in fact affording him great pleasure, by taking them from him. Better his wealth rest in my brotherly custody than wasted recklessly.

Chapter 35

OTHELLO AND CASSIO DEPARTED, on separate galleasses, within hours of the Council meeting. The ladies and I were to set sail two days later in one of five light galleys that convoyed east through the Mediterranean. Altogether there would be five hundred Venetian infantry en route to Cyprus.

In the hurricane of preparation and packing before we rowed out of the lagoon, I told Emilia I had not been made lieutenant. Her response was more confusion than disappointment: it was so enormously, obviously unfair, yet she was incapable of believing the worst of Othello, or even Cassio. She thought it must be a misunderstanding, which could be cleared up once we reached our destination. When I tried to impress upon her that *no*, I had been *cheated*, I had been *wronged*, by somebody I'd *loved* and *trusted*, she dismissed my claim impatiently and turned her attentions to helping Brabantio's wayward daughter pack her trunk. This did not improve my attitude.

* * *

ONE COULD EASILY FILL a book with complaints about the exquisite and particular miseries of sea travel. I was accustomed to it now. Even Emilia knew what hardships to expect. But because I was responsible for Desdemona, and knew her to be ignorant of hardship, I was suddenly acutely aware of everything disagreeable about the journey. There is plenty to offend each of the senses:

Nothing but water, in constant motion; no hint of solid land or any other stable object for days or weeks. The light off the water, when above, glaring bright; below, too dark; swinging lamplight causes strange shadows to disfigure otherwise familiar faces.

The creaking of the lines, the wind buffeting the sails, the endless throbbing of the drum to give the rowers their time, until it becomes a constant thrum inside one's head.

The odor of unwashed men, permeating everything; the acrid cleansing smell of vinegar that smarts the eyes; the mysterious smell of tar.

The dried biscuits and dried fish that make up almost the entire diet; the bitterness of herbal laxatives, which everyone has need of.

Everything sticky to the touch, from salt air; clothes and hair and face and arms, all. The world in constant movement, ever rocking, never resting; almost settling into a rhythm, but never one that can be relied upon for constancy.

Desdemona was wide-eyed but silent the first few days, which I took as signs of shock. Emilia never left her side, even to sleep. Emilia shared her cabin on the afterdeck—while I, a mere ensign, shared my small cabin below decks with five other petty officers.

EVERY DAY OF our voyage east I mused on all the ways there were to extract satisfaction from the men who'd wronged me. I did not dwell overmuch on Roderigo's hopes, or on his having altered his life at my suggestion, so that he was now crowded in, like almonds in a sack, to one of the infantry galleys. He was in better stakes than if he'd drowned himself.

There was one shortcoming in my plan to use Roderigo against Othello—besides the fact that it would never work. I did not *expect* it to work, I did not even *need* it to work. The fantasy of it—Othello, betrayed by the woman for whom he'd betrayed his own better nature—scratched an itch in me that needed scratching. That was enough. I had encouraged Roderigo to pursue Desdemona, not because I believed he would end up with her, but for the charity of giving him a distraction from his despondency. And also, yes, to indulge my righteously vengeful imagination.

But my righteously vengeful imagination was not fully indulged, because Michele Cassio went unpunished in this scheme. My rage at Othello was greater, of course—only a great love can turn to a great hate—but Cassio disgusted me, and *he had my place*. If I was going to fantasize and seethe, I wanted my fantasies to skewer the Florentine as well as the Moor. So I required a better fantasy.

Cassio was on another ship (in a private cabin, of course, because he was *lieutenant*), so at least I did not have to see him. He and Othello both took on hideous magnificence in my imagination. Their unrepentant selfishness and duplicity, their disrespect and disregard, Othello's lack of gratitude and Cassio's sycophancy—I gnawed these bones as daily diet. Anger was my meat and I supped upon myself. I so enjoyed my wrath that I did not want to ever reach Cyprus; on Cyprus, the dreary daily grind of reality would require me to face the actual men I had (I knew) mythologized to suit my appetite. I preferred to engorge my bitterness on mental obsessions. I was not proud of that, but before you judge me, please do not pretend you have never done such a thing yourself.

OUR THIRD DAY OUT, I went on deck for some air, standing amidships, where the rocking was the least and the drumming not entirely deafening. There was a brief lull as one set of oarsmen relieved another. One of the many shirtless, sweaty men saluted as he walked past me toward the hatchway ladder. "Ensign Iago, sir, an honor to have you on our vessel!" He grinned, looking at once sly and stupid.

I returned the salute on instinct but had no idea what to say in response. "Sailor," I said, to acknowledge him, doubting this was correct, since he was not, in fact, a sailor, but an oarsman.

I could tell from his expression that I had erred, and that he was delighted by the feeling of superiority this gave him. "Only an oar, sir, only an oar," he said. "But we are honored to have General Othello's right arm on board."

"And how do you know that I am his right arm?" I asked.

He grinned and winked. "All the men know how close you are, sir," he said, with another salute—but this one had audacity in it, as if he knew he could get away with impudence as long as he saluted. "You're so close you occasionally let him borrow your wife, do you not, sir?"

The expression on my face would have stopped an ox. It would have silenced any gentleman of Venice and probably any army man who knew me. But this fellow, whose life was already so miserable he hardly had a thing to lose, was delighted he had gotten a reaction and pressed on: "Do not worry yourself, sir, none of us would dream of asking to borrow her in like manner, she's safe as glass with all of us. We understand it's a special arrangement between the general and his officer, sir. We think it's very big of you, sir." He grinned again and by then he had passed by me, an equally stupid, grinning oarsman before him and another behind him.

I was so horrified I could not even challenge the fellow, or any of his stupidly grinning cohorts. I just turned away.

I had to find Emilia. I would not tell her of this, but I needed to feel her in my arms. She was in the cramped passageway just outside Desdemona's primitive cabin. Her scent, the color of her hair, the remarkable shape of her body: these qualities relaxed my soul. She smiled at me and I spent a minute or more running my hands over her lovely curves and covering her face and neck with kisses. She smiled at me and kissed me back. But then, as always: "I must go in to Desdemona, darling; it is not fit for the general's wife to be left alone on a ship full of lecherous sailors."

"It's not only the sailors who are lecherous," I growled into her ear, my hands squeezing her buttocks and pulling her against me. She made a purring noise, nibbled my earlobe—but then pulled away.

"I must go," she said softly, and opening the narrow door, she pushed herself through it and out of my view.

FOR SOME FEW HOURS every day, I managed to be sociable with the ladies. Indeed, I came to know Desdemona well enough to understand why Othello might fall in love with her. She lacked Emilia's wit and humor; when we, the married couple, indulged ourselves in teasing banter, she simply smiled benignly and watched. But in more serious conversation, she was intelligent and thoughtful. And she was calm. Her current circumstances were extraordinary, yet she took them in stride. Her only excitement was the anticipation of being reunited with the man she loved. All the rest of it—being cast out by her father, knowing every tongue in Venice was wagging about her, enduring the hardships of life on a galley en route to a battle far from home against heathens—did not spook her one bit. I was impressed.

WHEN I WAS not with the ladies, I would usually lie in my tight berth, staring at the berth above mine, in search of a fantasy to watch the waning of my enemies, the bugs and goblins in my life; a fantasy that would strike just the right satisfying note of vengeance in my soul.

The requirements for this fantasy were: it must disquiet Othello; it must humiliate Cassio; it must give me my lieutenancy.

But how to accomplish all of this? And without putting Emilia in harm's way, or casting any further aspersions on her? She deserved defilement of character no more than Desdemona did. In fact, Emilia was more innocent than Desdemona yet currently suffered a worse reputation.

Desdemona. The beautiful little creature who was, at the core of it, responsible for all the intrigue, all the mischief—all my troubles. I felt no particular grudge toward her, but neither did I feel protective—and if my wife was to be slighted, then why not *his* wife too, who was so much more guileful?

So, although I was a gentleman, I permitted myself the liberty to include Desdemona in my furious deliberations.

That turned the key.

Suddenly, it was obvious and easy: I would make Othello fear that he'd been cuckolded by Cassio.

They had all set their own traps: Cassio, the charming ladies' man, was known by Othello to be capable of intrigue. Othello likewise knew that Desdemona was capable of deceit—their wedding had depended on it. There was nothing far-fetched to the notion that the familiarity between Cassio and Desdemona was more familiar than either had let on. If she was going to carry on with foreigners, of course she'd *marry* the army general—but wasn't the Florentine fop abler at pitching woo?

The plan was clear as a cloudless sky: if I could put into Othello's mind even the vaguest fear that Cassio had seduced Desdemona—or merely had designs on her—he would want to distance Cassio. He would decommission the Florentine and finally give me the lieutenancy. With, no doubt, a heartily embarrassed apology for his misguided ways. If my anger was abated, I might embrace him back as friend, although never with the guileless trust of early days. Cassio would be sent away, which meant (among other things) my wife would stop admiring him. Desdemona would risk a reputation like Emilia's, but nothing worse; Emilia would face no risk at all.

It was a marvelous scheme. Desdemona was beautiful, sweet, and rich: why wouldn't Cassio fall in love with her? He was handsome and gallant: why wouldn't she respond to him? There was plenty of opportunity for them to have been lovers. There was no proof it had *not* happened. Even virginal blood on wedding sheets could be faked, if Desdemona did not want Othello to know she'd already caroused with Cassio.

Othello was so trusting, he could easily be led to believe that all this had happened right under his nose without his suspecting it until his loyal ensign, honest Iago, warned him of it.

This plan was much more comprehensive, and much more plausible, than the fantasy I had prescribed for Roderigo.

In fact, it was so plausible as to be realistically attainable.

I would do it. Not just sit and seethe and fantasize. This was a plan that I could reasonably *act on*. And get results.

Suddenly I couldn't wait to get to Cyprus.

Chapter 36

WE SKIRTED A SQUALL as we neared Cyprus. If you have had this experience of the wind and the rain, you know how miserable it was; if you haven't, find someone else to describe it to you; I do not care to dwell on it. Desdemona was sick for a few hours, with Emilia nursing her tenderly. When she recovered, she was robust as ever. That young lady had a spine to her.

FAMAGUSTA IS A panoply of man-made defenses, which begin before one even reaches the city: an enormous rock jetty delineates the harbor, beginning at the southern edge of the walled town and arching out into the water until it bends back toward the seawall at the Citadel, near the northern end of the city. The Citadel looms above everything; on the seaward side it thrusts out a wall that almost meets the jetty, the narrow harbor opening between them defended by a chain. On the landward side, the Citadel is the castle-keep from which extend the thick walls and towers surrounding the city. An enormous moat hugs the three city walls that are not seaward, a moat so deep that spring tides can reach it and turn the moat floor into brackish mud.

Incongruous with this martial aspect, the port lies *outside* the harbor, undefended, on the north side of the Citadel tower. It is nothing more than a paved beach, to which visitors and cargo are rowed in longboats from outlying ships. From there they ascend a broad paved slope, to a small terrace between the Citadel gate on the left, and a passageway to the city on the right.

There were soldiers mounting cannon along the seawall, and the harbor chain was raised, but we were given leave to moor and row to shore in longboats. Waiting beside the ladies for a longboat, I saw one galleass and several galleys already in the harbor.

Only one galleass.

Othello and Cassio had left on separate galleases. One of them had not arrived yet. A fearful thought shot through me; from the corner of my eye I saw Desdemona press her lips together fretfully.

Desdemona, Emilia, and myself, with several soldiers guarding, took the second longboat to the shore. The ladies were each carried like cargo by enormous dockworkers to dry land; the soldiers and I took off our boots and splashed the last few yards to shore with drenched stockings.

Desdemona immediately fell prey to land-legs: she had grown so used to shifting her weight with the movement of the boat, that now she could not balance and fell against me; I grasped her elbow and held her up. "That's normal," I murmured reassuringly, with a smile; Emilia and I were wobbly ourselves, but we had known to expect it. "You will be steady again in moments." She gave me a grateful smile; a wave of regret washed over me for bearing hostility toward her innocent sweet self.

The air was dry and warm, the southern sun baking us as it never did in Venice. The smells of bread and livestock wafted down from the city walls—civilized smells, far preferable to the stench of vinegar that was used to clean the innards of the galleys. Looking up, we saw the entire Citadel population, including maids and stable-boys, staring down at us in worried curiosity. Some of the army had already arrived . . . but why would Venice send fragile ladies to a land of war?

More longboats deposited three dozen soldiers and some trunks. We made our way up the slanting roadway under the beating sun, toward the gateway of the Citadel. Emilia put a steadying, soothing arm around Desdemona. Cassio or Othello—one of them had not arrived. None of the port workers said anything to us, but all of them looked grim. I wanted to ask for information but dared not in Desdemona's hearing.

It must be Cassio who was lost; Othello had about him an aura of invincibility that not even Neptune could destroy.

We arrived at the gate, in the shadow of a large square tower. The lintel of the gate bore a huge winged lion, for this was Venetian territory. From the tower above, soldiers and servants stared down at us in glum silence, as if they believed we were bringing them the plague.

The gate opened; a cornet sounded, and a dozen men in military dress marched grimly out of the gate. Leading them was a tall, leathery-faced man in white; this must be Montano, the rector of the city.

Then, with a sick feeling, I saw bobbing behind the soldiers a bright blue ostrich feather. Cassio was here. Which meant Othello wasn't.

An airy, almost soundless cry escaped Desdemona when she saw Cassio; Emilia clutched her tighter, and I moved closer to them both to catch her if she fainted.

Cassio, wearing the lieutenant's sash across his body, approached as if it were a day of celebration. I felt ill seeing him dressed that way—seeing him at all, given Othello's unexplained absence.

As if rehearsed, the honor guard parted and allowed him to stride ahead until he was standing beside Montano. With his usual Florentine flourish he bowed deeply over one bent leg and spoke to the Cypriots and army men around him rather than to the lady herself. "The greatest riches of the ship have come ashore! All kneel now and greet the lady Desdemona." He went down on one knee, and everyone behind him awkwardly did likewise.

Desdemona forced a polite smile. "Thank you, Cassio."

Cassio stood quickly, unobtrusively wiping off his stockings at the knee as the men behind him also rose. "And here is Montano, who governs in Venice's name," he added. Desdemona and Montano exchanged formal greetings.

An awkward pause.

"Where is my lord?" Desdemona said at last.

Montano pointedly took a step back, leaving Cassio responsible to give the news: "His ship has not arrived yet, my lady. But I'm sure he's well and will be here presently."

Desdemona stiffened slightly. "But . . . your ships were traveling together."

Cassio gave her a patently fake smile. "A tempest surprised us, and we were separated in the storm. He had the more experienced pilot, so I am sure he is well, just blown off course and—"

A row of guns blasted from above, and a host of guards on the walls began to halloo and point toward the harbor. The curving slope had led us up behind the Citadel; we couldn't see the water from here, but voices began calling down to us that a Venetian galleass was in view. A cannon sounded from the vessel in response to the Citadel's greeting.

Desdemona clutched Emilia's hands. Cassio smiled with relief. "You see, my lady," he said, "that's surely his ship now." He turned to one of the guards. "Run down to the port and get the news." As the man raced past me, Cassio's eyes followed him, and only then did he notice me. He smiled benignly. "Good ensign! Welcome!"

Desdemona stepped aside as Cassio approached; I saluted him as I must, and he returned it. I disliked being on display like this. His face lit up when he turned to Emilia.

"And the lovely mistress Emilia." He took her hand and bowed over it to kiss it. I glared. He looked up and winked at me. "Oh, come now, Iago, I'm a Florentine, do you really expect me to greet your beautiful wife in any other manner?"

He was growing cocky now he had his lieutenancy. *My* lieutenancy. I stood there without speaking, and having straightened, Cassio—as if mocking me—pecked my wife briefly on the lips. Emilia blinked in shock. I trembled from the effort of not instantly punching him.

"Well, sir," I managed to chuckle. "If she gives you as much of her lip as she gives me of her tongue—"

Desdemona laughed nervously. "Iago, be kind. Her tongue is always very good to you." She was innocent of how filthy her words sounded.

I heard tittering behind us, and turned around. The passageway leading from the city was crowded with amber-skinned locals. We now had an audience. I had to keep my humor.

"Her *words* may be good in your presence, my lady," I said, "but trust me, her *thoughts* chide me enough that I can *hear* them."

"You know that's not true," Emilia scolded affectionately, and used the moment to step away from Cassio.

"Oh, come, Emilia," I scolded back. "Speaking as a man renowned for his honesty, I am pained to inform you that you—and all ladies, if her ladyship will excuse me—you are three kinds of dishonest. In public you're the very pictures of innocence, but at home you nag and complain, and then in bed, of course, as *every* married man knows—"

"Iago," Emilia said warningly, smiling despite herself.

"You slanderer!" Desdemona said over her laughing.

"I am but speaking plain and honest," I insisted.

Emilia put her hands on her hips with a saucy affectation, as she had the first evening I ever met her. "Heaven *forbid* you ever praise me in public," she said.

"I don't need to praise you anymore, you've already married me," I retorted cheerfully. "Now I may take you for granted."

Desdemona smiled and charmingly took one of my bare hands

in both of her gloved ones. "You cannot take *me* for granted," she said. "So tell me, what would you say in praise of *me*?"

I gently broke her grip, holding my hands up in surrender. "Do not ask me that, lady, everyone knows how barbed my tongue is."

"Oh, but give it a try," she insisted, grabbing my hands again. Her face grew serious a moment and she whispered, "Someone's gone down to the port, yes?"

"Yes, lady," I assured her.

Her smile returned, but her voice stayed low. "Everyone is watching us, Iago, and I would not have them see me distressed. Help me seem merry until my husband joins us." She raised her voice to a normal speaking level. "Come, tell me how you'd praise me."

Emilia nudged me in encouragement. With a heavy, put-upon sigh, I nodded—not displeased that Cassio was being left out of the banter his unseemly action had set off. "I will attempt it, lady, but praise does not come easily to me. My inner muse must labor hard to think of anything fair and witty to say." Emilia stepped on my toe with her heel, and shifted her weight there. "But in this case, of course, it is no labor, since the creature I am to praise is already so fair and witty herself."

Emilia smiled and removed her heel from my toe.

"Very nice," Desdemona replied archly. "But do you mean, then, it would be harder labor to praise a lady who is witty but dark?" Her eyes floated toward Emilia's deep auburn hair, then returned to meet my gaze, pointedly.

"The dark and witty lady has a dark wit all her own," I said, and took my wife's hand to kiss it.

Desdemona smiled, as Emilia immediately challenged me: "Well then, how would you praise a woman who was fair but lacked wit?"

"Oh, no need to praise her," I said. "If she's fair enough, trust me, *somebody* will want to sleep with her."

The townsfolk behind us cackled. The Citadel men looked horrified that I was speaking with their general's wife this way.

Desdemona, however, was delighted. "You are quite abominable," she said approvingly. "What do you make of his wit, Lieutenant Cassio? Is he not a scoundrel?"

Cassio, the elegant Florentine, was pink-faced. He said, apologetically, "He is a soldier, my lady, not a gentleman. He doesn't always know the proper way to address a lady. As I do. If I may speak in private with the lady?" He held out a hand and led her some half dozen paces away from the group. He began to whisper to her, smiling politely and kissing her hand.

I watched, as a fencing master watches his pupils to see if their form is correct. He may have been imparting some confidential information to her, but he was also, by my lights, flirting with her. The three-fingered Florentine kiss was a gesture I was now used to; but I'd seen him use it on prostitutes as well as ladies. *Go ahead*, I thought, *kiss her and kiss her and kiss her again. Later if Othello hears from me how you've been kissing her, I won't even be lying, you fool.*

Cassio was going to make this very easy for me. He was going to hand me my lieutenancy on a platter.

Chapter 37

A TRUMPET SOUNDED down the slope—three short notes then two longer ones: Othello's signal.

"The general's here!" I called out sharply; Cassio instantly released Desdemona's hand and moved back to the collection of officers.

"You're right," he declared unnecessarily, and gestured them to stand at attention—which they were already doing on their own. "How could he be here so quickly? We've just seen his ship on the horizon."

"He must have lowered a longboat," I offered. Bowing to Desdemona: "He was that eager to be reunited with his bride."

"Let's go down to the water and meet him," she said.

Cassio gestured down the slope and saluted sharply; we all turned in the same direction and did likewise.

Othello, his pale clothes splashed with seawater and his hems soaked with it, was striding briskly, if wobbly-kneed, up the incline, four attendants scrambling after him, and a small clutch of fascinated port workers trailing after them. My heart jumped at seeing him: here was the human face of the friend I had been demonizing. The two Othellos, colliding, confused me.

His face brightened when he saw Desdemona, who gave a shout of joy and ran down the slope toward him; he broke into a jog to reach her, grabbed her, and pulled her against him as if he would use her body for a breastplate. No couple in Venice would have greeted each other so in public; no military leader I could think of in all history would greet his wife this way before his officers.

It was the first time most anyone present had seen the two of them together; a few had not even heard the general was married, and there was startlement among the soldiers. The quiet woman and the rough-spoken general were fairly dripping in poetry, virtually making love in front of us, before finally Othello turned his attention to the rest of us and gave us the extraordinary news that should have been the first words from his mouth:

"There will be no battle," he shouted out. "The great tempest that separated my ship from the rest has destroyed the entire Turkish fleet! Cyprus is safe."

Stunned silence. Then we were all shouting, shouting loudly with relief and joy. The townsfolk began dancing together; the cheekier ones sashayed toward the guards with arms outstretched in greetings, and the guards whooped and danced with them. Emilia and I, clutching each other tightly, laughed and jumped around like children. No enemy! No danger! Safety and serenity! All is well and all shall be well, and all manner of things shall be well . . .

* * *

OTHELLO HALLOOED to get our attention back.

"This is my bride," he informed both the Citadel guard and the citizens of Famagusta, with a flourishing gesture toward Desdemona. "Treat her well. Desdemona, these good people love me, and I think they will love you too." He glanced about, caught my eye, and suddenly looked almost sheepish. "Enough of my prattle. To work. Cassio, you'll command the first watch on the walls tonight. Iago, go down to the dock and bring my trunks ashore, and bring the captain of the ship with you up to the Citadel. He deserves special thanks for saving us from the Turks' fate. Well met in Cyprus!"

With that there was further huzzahing and cheering. Othello took Desdemona's hand. He gestured Cassio to walk beside him—a simple gesture that jarred me back to the wearying challenges of my own life. They began to head up the slope together, through the great open gates of iron, toward the fortress, with soldiers and the more brazen citizens behind them. Emilia kissed my cheek, and then rushed to join the happy throng.

I WAITED UNTIL every one of them was gone around the curve up through the Citadel gates, until the shyer townsfolk had made their way back through the passageway and their workaday lives. It was a relief to be alone, alone in an absolute way as I had not been in months, perhaps years, perhaps ever. I could hear the beating of my heart, the air was so silent and so still. In the azure sky above, some bird of prey was circling, interested in all the activity. I took a moment to feel my emotions churn. Seeing Othello and Cassio before me as living men had not abated my fury at either of them, had not dampened my determination to set in plan the scheme I'd developed on the ship coming over here.

Without the danger of imminent warfare, Othello would no doubt lock himself up with his bride and not show his face in public for several days; somehow, I would have to meet with him before nightfall. Just to insinuate, to plant the seed of doubt. Just enough to make him feel discomfitted, and consider sending Cassio away. There was no shame in such an act; it was righteous vengeance. They each deserved whatever unhappiness it brought them, and I deserved to gain my rightful lieutenancy. It would be a neat, almost chirurgic undertaking. It did not require heated emotion on anybody's part.

"Iago!" cried a voice full of heated emotion, from behind the open gate that flanked the passageway into the city proper.

"Ah, Roderigo," I answered, trying not to wince.

Roderigo had disguised himself by shaving off his lovely mop of ringlets to the skull, and having grown some scraggly facial hair, mostly a mustache, on the sea voyage over. What, pray heaven, was I to do with him now?

"Come with me down to the harbor," I said. He glanced around nervously from his hiding place between the stone wall and the opened gate. "Come along," I urged, trying not to sound impatient. He stepped out of his spot and joined me on the broad paved walkway. "You are not recognizable," I reassured him. "If I did not know your voice, and weren't expecting you, I'd have no idea it was you. I must go down to the harbor and fetch the general's belongings, while Cassio goes with him on his triumphal entrance to the Citadel."

"What is the plan?" Roderigo demanded, deaf to my grousing. "Is she tired of him yet? How do we begin the wooing? I've got a walletful of pearls to give you for her. Heaven but it was an awful stink in the belly of that ship! How do those men *survive*?" He pulled out a scented handkerchief and touched his upper lip with it.

"Cassio has the first watch," I said as we descended. How best to meet with Othello?

"What has that got to do with anything?" Roderigo asked, sounding almost petulant.

I checked an impulse to embrace Roderigo. He was going to make this very simple. I would not have to lie to Othello; I would not even have to *speak* to him, and I would still get my lieutenancy. "I don't want to say this," I said—which was true, as overt fabrication always made me uncomfortable. "Yes, as I predicted, she has tired of the Moor already. All the honey you just saw at the gate was entirely for show."

"A strange show for a general to indulge in."

"What I did *not* predict," I pushed on, "is that she has already given her heart to someone else, and that is Michele Cassio."

Roderigo stopped short. "Michele Cassio, that Florentine? That's not possible! How is that possible? With a *Florentine*? Those accursed Florentines are trying to steal my trading route!"

I put a finger to his lips until he nodded a promise to stay quiet. For a flash I thought we were children again, preparing our next prank. "Listen to me. Just as she fell hard and suddenly for Othello, she fell hard and suddenly for Cassio. There's something in her nature that requires her to be swept off her feet by some intense quality she senses in a man. With Othello it was his fierce difference from anyone she'd ever known, but she quickly grew sick of that and looked for its very opposite, a man so effete he is barely a man." I gestured, and we resumed walking. "Also, Cassio knows how to play people and make them love him, and he has done so with her. Just as with Othello, it isn't real love she feels, just a bedazzlement. Cassio is admittedly handsome and young and oozes the kind of energy an unseasoned young woman would fall for, especially a woman with too much passion."

Roderigo shook his head as we continued down the roadway toward the port. "I just can't believe that of her. She's so *pure.*"

"You don't even know her, Roderigo," I said. "The wine she drinks is made of grapes, same's the rest of us. If she were really so *pure*, she would not have fallen for Othello." He sighed and shook his head, taking in a breath, as if he would contradict me. "Roderigo, were you there when Cassio came out to greet us? Did you see that?"

"Yes," he said.

"Well then," I said, "did you see him take her aside and whisper to her and kiss her palm?"

"He was just being courteous," Roderigo said glumly.

"Lecherous," I corrected. "He was signaling to her what he intends to do to her later on tonight. They were so close together, their lips were so nearly touching. Their very breath entwined."

Roderigo slowed his pace. I slapped his arm and gestured him to hurry with me. "If he's a Florentine, then I suppose he's capable of anything," he allowed. "For all I know, his family is the one trying to buy the loyalty of my Egyptian middlemen. It is a suspect coincidence that he happens to have come to Venice, of all place—"

"I assure you, there's nothing to that," I interrupted him briskly. "He came to Venice with ambitions that undo *me*, not you."

"But knowing this, what shall I do now?" he asked.

"Trust me," I said. "I brought you here all the way from Venice, so you and your intentions are my responsibility. I will put you on tonight's roster for guard duty on the wall. Cassio is leading the watch, and he doesn't know you anyhow, especially in your disguise. I'll be near you and I'll coach you through everything I'm about to describe. Find some excuse to upset Cassio—he angers very easily," I assured him, trying to remember if I'd ever seen Cassio the least bit angry ever, at all. "Shout at him, or argue with him if he gives you orders, or whatever opportunity comes along."

Roderigo looked queasy. "Well . . . ," he began, and then said nothing else. I knew him well enough: the idea of anything that could result in violence was terrifying to the poor fellow.

"Roderigo, he angers very easily. It really won't take much to stir him up—one sentence and he may very well strike out at you."

"Strike out at me!" He came up short again, and again I tugged his sleeve to make him move along. We could hear, around the bend, the sounds of men unloading cargo from the longboats, calling out to one another in Greek, while Venetian soldiers tried to tell them what to do. If the Cypriots understood the orders, they were pretending not to.

"He won't hurt you," I said. "I promise you that. I'll get him drunk, and his arm will not be steady. And even if he hits you, what then? You'll have a black eye, but you'll also have your ladylove."

"How do you figure?" he asked suspiciously.

"The people of Cyprus are all on edge—they've spent the last months believing they were about to be murdered by Turks. One misstep on the part of somebody in a position of authority, and they'll make such a fuss, Othello will have to get rid of him. And there you are: your rival for Desdemona's hand is out of the way."

"But she won't pine after him when he's gone?"

I shrugged. "I cannot see why. Her opinion of him will change for the worse when she hears how he's conducted himself." I nudged him as we walked. "So make sure he conducts himself very poorly."

Roderigo nodded thoughtfully, to himself and not to me, as we rounded the final bend. Now we were on level ground, portside, and only a stone's throw from where the longboats to the general's ships were being unloaded.

"I'm not promising anything," Roderigo said at last, "But I'll go on guard duty, and if the opportunity arises, I'll do it."

"Excellent!" I said, with sincere heartiness. "Go back on up to the Citadel. I'll meet you by the enlisted men's barracks after I've collected his things. I'll make sure you're in the roll for guard duty tonight."

"Thank you, Iago," he said, "and adieu."

Ah, no, I thought to myself, *it's I should thank you, Roderigo. You are going to do my dirty work for me.*

Chapter 38

OF COURSE I put myself on guard duty as well. Our watch was to begin at ten bells and it had just tolled nine. The crew before us—all of them Cypriots or Venetians already here—had had a dull watch, as we new arrivals unpacked, settled in, and made ourselves familiar with the layout of the Citadel.

The fortress was a rectangle around a courtyard, with a tower in each corner. The largest tower—housing armor, arms, and munitions—bore the antiquated title "castle-keep" and faced seaward. The wing south of this had a ground floor of rooms for armoring, repairing equipment, and magazines; the second floor were offices, and the largest of these, Othello's. To the other side of the keep, on the north wing, was the closest thing to domestic comfort the fortress offered: a string of rooms equipped with beds and tapestries to house the commander and his officers. Othello took the room closest to the keep; Cassio was assigned the room next over; a few rooms were left empty, for Desdemona and Emilia to have at their disposal in the heat of the day; and then, the smallest chamber, farthest from the keep, was to be mine and Emilia's. We were just beside the gateway out of the fortress. The other two wings of the rectangle contained barracks housing, a kitchen, refectory, hospital, and chapel. A passageway lead out to a huge walled yard. This was four times larger than the Citadel itself; here were gunnery ranges and a makeshift gymnasium, and room for fencing practice. And trees and shrubs, where soldiers could take the whores who had long ago figured out how to gain easy access to the fortress.

LUXURIATING IN THE exquisite taste of foreshadow, I found it suddenly easy to be in Cassio's company as he gave me a tour of the grounds. I decided I would even prod him a few times, as one prods raw beef, to tenderize it for the seasoning to come. Cassio had a genius for presenting me with such opportunities.

First he insisted we start the watch early—that is to say, when Othello excused himself to his bedroom with his radiant, eager young bride. Before sundown, the ten o'clock guards were brewing a party inside the tower keep.

"Oh, come now, Michele," I argued with Cassio, when he told his assistant to read out the specific posts for each soldier in the armoring room at half-nine. "We're not on duty yet. Othello just sent us out here so he could take his wife to bed." I winked at him. "Which is certainly understandable. She's succulent, isn't she?"

Cassio reddened slightly.

Was he enamored of Desdemona? That would make this even easier, not only practically but morally. "The lady is exquisite," he said, with that damned Florentine gallantry.

"And no doubt horny," I added heartily, strapping on my sword-belt.

He blinked and appeared to be forcing himself to smile. "She . . . I really would not know," he said. Now he was bright red.

"Oh come now, Michele!" I said, slapping his middle with the back of my hand. "That expression on her face? For him, of course, but let's be honest—she looks at everyone like that. Wasn't she flirting with you a bit, while we were waiting for Othello to arrive? Just a bit?"

He looked disoriented. "Er . . . well, she wasn't *not* flirting," he said. "But don't take that the wrong way—she is actually extremely modest."

"And that little laugh of hers?" I added.

Cassio looked almost panicked. How remarkable—perhaps he really was in love with her.

"Our general's wife is a wonderful woman," he said decisively, not looking directly at me.

"Indeed," I said, deciding to let it be. For now. "Happiness to their sheets!" I gestured the still-blushing Florentine to the far side of the readying room, toward a large stone basin, intended for washing up. It was filled with local wine, procured by two helpful soldiers in my unit. "Look, Lieutenant! A gift for us from the natives. Brought by a couple of Cyprus lads on duty here at the keep with us tonight— they want us to drink the bride's health." I reached toward a shelf above the basin for some cups.

Cassio grimaced and shook his head. "Not tonight, Iago. It would not be good for me to drink before I go on guard duty."

"Oh, *Lieutenant*," I said cajoling as I buckled a greave onto my shin. "Just one cup. It's how they cement friendship here, they'll be insulted if you don't join in. Let's just each have the one cup, and after the initial toast, I'll drink yours with you if you want."

He shook his head. In a lowered voice he explained, "I already had a cup at dinner, in one of the, mmm . . ."

"Bawdy houses?" I prompted. Oh, excellent Florentine! He kept making this easier for me with each passing breath. I finished fastening the second greave, then contemplated my armored shins.

Cassio made an equivocating sound. "Well, I wouldn't quite call it . . . it's a private home, just the one woman, Bianca, and we were introduced by—"

"Say no more," I interrupted understandingly. "I don't really need greaves, do I? We're just on watch, it's not as if we were going into battle."

"Anyway, I had a drink there—"

"So to speak." I winked and began to unbuckle the greaves I'd just put on.

He frowned at me. "I had a cup of wine. I never have more than one cup a night or the demon gets the better of me."

"You seem fine to me," I said lightly.

"I won't risk it," he said.

"What could possibly happen?" I asked. If he had not already had that first glass, my tone alone would likely have alerted him: I never spoke like that. "Come now, Michele, everyone's celebrating tonight—the entire watch will probably end up drunk! And I do think these lads will take it amiss if we don't at least toast with them." I put the greaves back on the shelf they'd come from and reached up to a higher shelf for my sallet. "What do you say?"

He grimaced again. "Where are they?"

"Just in the next room, gearing up. Go on and invite them in—they've already got their cups, they're waiting for their lieutenant to invite them, eh?" I grinned at him.

He sighed. "All right, I'll do it, but I want it on record, I don't think it's a good idea."

"Pfft! It's a night of revelry, Lieutenant! These young men will grow old in your service—start your time with them on a happy note, eh?"

Cassio glumly began to walk toward the door. We were in the larger armoring room, with ancient arrow slits that looked out into the harbor; it was nearly dark now, but a chandler had lit it well with torches, and the light bounced dully off all the metal armor. Cassio plastered a smile upon his lips, threw open the door into the smaller gearing room—and gasped. Then bowed.

Montano, the governor of Famagusta, stepped into our gearing chamber, with at least five Cypriot guards behind him. I had not planned that. The stars were aligning fortuitously in the heaven of my invention. Cassio would not only get drunk—he'd get drunk in front of Cyprus's highest civilian authority.

"Sir!" I called out to Montano, bowing deeply. Cassio scrambled to imitate me (which was ironic, since I was using his flowery Florentine bow).

Regal, leathery-faced Montano was in high spirits: his island had just been spared battle, and his rule had just been lightened by the appearance of the military. If any man had reason to get pickled tonight, it was Montano. He was destined to be my ally, however accidentally: as Cassio rose from his bow, Montano gleefully grabbed him by the ear and half-poured, half-tossed the contents of his brass cup into Cassio's mouth. Sputtering from the shock of it, Cassio pulled away and turned into a corner to hack his lungs clear.

"Be a man, Lieutenant Cassio!" Montano laughed to his backside. "Take your liquor like a soldier!"

The group of fellows behind him laughed with him. So they were all drunk. That would make this so much easier. Every detail of this enterprise just kept getting easier.

"The wine!" I announced, gesturing grandly toward the stoup. "Bring your cups and let's toast to our general!"

* * *

SOMEHOW, IT WAS suddenly an hour later, and a score of us had all moved up onto the wall walk by the keep, in the breezy early-summer night . . . and Cassio was as drunk as any of them.

But he was not quite drunk enough.

I tried to remember the drinking songs of my Arsenal days; they were all immensely stupid, but the very simplicity of the tunes made them easy to recall. One of them went: *"A soldier's a man; a life's but a span; why, then, let a soldier drink. Some wine, boys!"*

"An essellent song," Cassio informed me, nearly falling against me. Hm. Perhaps he was drunker than I realized.

"I learned it from an Englishman; they're the biggest sots of all."

"Really?" Cassio asked as his buttocks slid down the stone parapet and found their way to the stone floor of the wall walk.

"Oh, absolutely," I assured him, as if we were discussing fencing techniques. "The Danes, the Germans, the Dutch—they're all heavy drinkers, of course, but not one of them could ever hold his own against an Englishman. Speaking of drink, your cup is empty, Lieutenant—hey, boy! Fill the lieutenant's cup here!" I called out to the only other person on the walls beside myself who was not soused: Montano's page boy. He was scurrying around with a large pitcher of wine, keeping all the cups full.

Cassio watched the wine go into his glass with the fascination of a dim-witted child. He was almost endearing in this state. "Why . . . how . . . so tell me . . . you said the English drink a lot?"

"Oh, yes," I assured him. "A Brit can drink a Dane under the table, and the Germans who try to keep up with him end up puking all over themselves. And the Dutch—*there's* a competition that gets *very* ugly . . ."

Cassio's attention had wandered already. He opened his mouth as if to say something, then closed it again, having immediately lost his thought. Then with a suddenly renewed vigor, he sat up straight, held his cup high, and cried out, "Give me some wine and let me speak a little! To the health of our general!"

"Here here!" Montano said from a stone's toss away down the

wall walk, where he had been singing an equally idiotic drinking song in Greek. "I'll drink a cup to him with you, and raise you another cup!" The page boy, halfway between the two men, hesitated, deciding whose cup to refill first. He chose Montano's.

To keep Cassio's attention distracted, I began another drinking song, this one filthy; it demanded a toast at the end of each verse, and with his first drink, Cassio announced this was the most exquisite song he had ever heard in the whole of his life.

Was he drunk enough? I considered signaling to Roderigo to move in for the end-game, but Cassio startled me by suddenly leaping to his feet—without falling over. "There are souls who *must* be saved!" he announced, out of nothing, to everyone in hearing distance. By now the party included guardsmen who were supposed to be dispersed along the whole of the Citadel's wall walk. "And there are souls who *not* be saved," he added, for clarity.

Since I was the closest man to him, a number of men looked to me, as if my response would tell them how to mark their own responses.

"True enough," I said.

"*I*," said Michele Cassio grandly, "hope to be *saved*."

You won't be, I thought; aloud, I said, in an agreeable tone, "And so do I, Lieutenant."

"Me too, me too!" shouted some dozen voices around us in the flickering torchlight. Cassio, ignoring them all, held up his hand to me. "Very sorry, Iago," he slurred, "but you'll not be saved before me, cuz I'm a lieutenant and you're jus' an ensign, and the lieutenant comes first."

I tried to keep a disinterested look on my face but I could not do it; I could feel my eyes blaze. So he wanted to talk about that, did he? I was more than ready. "Indeed?" I said softly. "And exactly how did you come to be lieutenant, my friend?"

Cassio was drunk, but not *quite* drunk enough to miss my tone. He waved his hand unsteadily before him, as if dismissing a very large insect. "No more o' that," he said, and hiccupped, and then giggled at his hiccupping. He looked up and noticed that men were staring at him. "D'not think, gentlemen, that I'm drunk," he slurred. About to lose his balance, he fell onto me, his long arm draping across my shoulders. I grimaced broadly; but, good soldier that I was, I held him up. Cassio giggled at me affectionately. "Thiss my ensign," he said, gesturing to me. "Thiss my right hand." And with a giggle, holding up his free arm: "And thiss my left hand! See, not drunk."

He pulled himself off me to show he did not need me for balance; immediately he slumped backward against the wall where he'd been sitting.

The guards with us, not quite as drunk as he, but pretty close, applauded him and went back to their cups.

"I tol' you," Cassio said, and gestured for the page boy to come to him. Cassio handed the boy his cup, then used the page's shoulder for balance to raise himself. "Nobody here is 'lowed to think I'm drunk, yes?" And he staggered off, reeling, through the open door into the keep.

Without looking at Roderigo, I signaled for him to follow after Cassio. Then I turned my attention away; I could not afford to be infected by Roderigo's fear, which I was sure was eating him alive right now.

Their lieutenant absent, the guards looked around at one another uncertainly. Montano, the Cypriot leader, had sobered up a bit over the past hour, perhaps from all the singing. He moved closer to the keep door. "All right everyone, come, let's set the watch! Disperse," he called out. He glanced at me and with one expressive eyebrow, summoned me to step closer. I did. With a second expressive eyebrow, he gestured at the door through which Cassio had just staggered away.

I nodded with rueful understanding. "Cassio is a soldier worthy of Caesar," I said quietly. The soldiers were all spreading out along the wall walk, but there were two stationed right here at the keep entrance, and I wanted to appear as if I didn't want them to hear me. "He has just the one vice, but it rules him often. Honestly, in confidence, I beg you: it worries me how much Othello trusts him."

"Is he like this a lot?" Montano asked.

I nodded and bit my lip regretfully. "Every night—he can't sleep if he hasn't soused himself up. I feel for him, but it is a serious problem."

Montano looked incredulous. "Othello knows this?"

I made a face. "I probably have not been as direct with him about it as I should be, as Michele is a friend of mine."

Montano—older, wiser, and tipsier than I—shook his head in gentle chastisement. "I have heard about you, Iago, how you are always blunt and honest, and do the right thing, and stand by your words. It is precisely somebody like you who *must* tell the Moor that his lieutenant is a sot."

"I cannot do that to Cassio. My intention is to cure him of the evil, before Othello even knows about—"

My pathetic attempt at sycophancy was cut short by a shrill cry within the keep:

"Help! Heeelllp!" squealed a painfully familiar voice.

A moment later, Roderigo came flying out the keep door onto the parapet, Michele Cassio close on his heels, sword drawn, tripping over his own heels. His drunken state was possibly the reason Roderigo was still alive.

The two men guarding the keep door stared as their superior stumbled past them hurling names at Roderigo, too slurred to even understand; Roderigo, wide-eyed, bald and bewhiskered, looked like a confused bat that had been cornered by a snake. He gave me a beseeching look as he scampered around this open spot on the wall walk. I was afraid he'd try to hide behind me.

"What's the matter, Lieutenant?" Montano demanded, stepping up to Cassio.

"This knave talked back to me!" I think is what Cassio said; it sounded more like: "Thisnaytawbatomeee." The two guards exchanged amazed looks and snickered. Montano gestured sharply, and they stopped.

"I didn't!" Roderigo cried, now trying to curl up into a perfect circle right there in the middle of the walk.

"Illbeatim!" Cassio declared.

"Beat me?" Roderigo nearly shrieked, straight at me, a cry for help. I could not risk his calling me by name.

"Shutupy'rogueyou!" Cassio demanded, and took one staggering step in Roderigo's direction with his sword raised.

I knew I should have stepped in to save Roderigo; I felt a shot of guilt for failing to. But it was hypnotic to watch my own machinations working out so exactly right, before my eyes, with so little effort on my part. It was seductive.

Montano took the step I should have: he reached out and grabbed the sword from Cassio's hand. Although certainly drunk himself, he was more sober than Cassio, and his wavering gaze wavered less than the lieutenant's. "Stop that now, Lieutenant," he ordered. He tossed the sword to the stone floor of the walk, and then reached again, this time constraining Cassio with a wrist-grip.

"Lemme go, sir," Cassio growled. "Lemme go or I'll knock you ri' off th's wall."

"Cassio," Montano said gently, paternally. "Cassio, you're very drunk."

It added fuel to the fire of his self-righteousness. "Dr'nk? D'you dare call meee dr'nk?" he sneered at Montano. With a sharpness and a quickness that belied his state, Cassio reached for the dagger in his belt and pulled it out flashing it in the torchlight; he turned on Montano and would have stabbed him with it, but Montano too was sharper than he seemed: he released Cassio's wrist, leapt out of the way, drew his sword, and pressed the point of it on Cassio's collarbone.

Cassio slapped it away on the flat side with his palm; Montano, not expecting this, let the sword fall from his grasp but then pulled out his own dagger. The two lunged stumbling toward each other. I took a cautious step forward, wanting to pull them apart without being myself struck. Roderigo, beyond them, was trying to get my attention. Urgently, I gestured him to leave; relieved, he tore down along the wall watch and disappeared into the darkness.

I turned my attention back to the duelers. "Lieutenant Cassio, put up!" I ordered. My plan did not require anyone to get killed, or even wounded. This was getting out of hand. "Montano, sir, you are not so drunk as he, contain yourself!"

They circled each other, looking for an opportunity to reach out with a blind and ill-considered stab. It was the kind of fight they'd have had as first-week recruits learning defense skills.

"Help!" I shouted at the two guards at the keep door. "The watch! Somebody call the watch!" That was ironic: here were the two *leaders* of the watch. But Roderigo must have set the alarm as he retreated; the bells on the chapel tower began to peal, and all the guards along the Citadel walls called out to one another, asking what passed. Far down below, doors swung open onto the streets of the town, and I could hear the mustering voices of anxious Cypriot civilians.

Montano, when the bells began, instinctively looked over at them. Cassio used that moment: he leapt forward and slashed at Montano's abdomen.

Montano shouted from the pain. He fell back onto the stone, curling around his bloody middle. The men along the wall walk began running toward us.

Cassio, crazed now, was about to step in for a direct downward stab at Montano's side; I jumped against him to send him sprawling against the parapet; he nearly rebounded off it, finally landing on his ass. "Hold, Lieutenant, for the love of heaven!" I shouted at him, grabbing his right arm when he tried to rise again.

I prayed Montano would be all right even as something inside of me exulted at the injury: Cassio had just attacked the governor of Cyprus! He would never live down the shame of this evening. My plan was working better than I ever dreamed, in front of two dozen witnesses, and none of it was traceable to me. I'd never felt such power in my life. It was hard not to laugh aloud with the thrill of it.

And then, the perfect coda to my fabulous concerto of revenge: at that moment, through the keep door, erupted Othello, wide-eyed and half undressed.

"*What is going on?*" he demanded, still tying on his sword-belt. Four attendants scurried after him with torches. "Are we under attack—"

"I'm bleeding," Montano shouted out in the haze of inebriation and pain. "Help! I'm bleeding to death!"

Oblivious to the outrage he was creating for himself, Cassio responded to this plea by struggling again to rise, as if he would have another go at the governor.

"Hold, Lieutenant!" I shouted; I yanked him back down and caught his wrist at such an angle he could not keep the grip on his dagger. After a furious moment of resistance, he let it go, and it clanged to the stone beneath us. "For God's sake man, what are you trying to do?" I demanded. When Cassio began to explain to me the hurt he intended for Montano, I overrode him: "The general is here, Lieutenant; for the love of heaven, shut up and listen to him!"

It took Othello a moment to recover from his rush of alarm. In the light, I watched his dawning realization that this was a drunken brawl. There was a flicker of relief, then much disgust . . . then fury.

"Are you mad?" he demanded in a low, dangerous voice. "So we do not need the Turks, we can all just kill ourselves off? Is that it? Put your blade away, Michele—and the rest of you. The next man who makes the slightest move toward violence will die by my hand." He glanced up, and suddenly his voice expanded to fill the whole night sky: "Stop that dreadful bell, for heaven's sake! You are scaring the population half to death! They'll think the Turks have landed after all." He turned his attention back to all of us on the wall walk. "Somebody tell me what's the matter here."

None of us spoke. His eyes strayed over all of us, and—of course—rested on me. The bells stopped.

"Iago, it is up to you. Speak. Tell me who began this."

I said nothing.

"Speak, Iago. If you are my friend, tell me honestly what happened here."

Oh, that was so like him—not to simply order his ensign, as was his right, but to call upon a bond of friendship to invoke loyalty. A quality I loved in him, more than I wanted to right now.

For a long moment I said nothing. I had created all of this, so easily—it had been no labor. In fact, except for Montano's wound, it was all good entertainment. And best of all, I was about to reap the benefits of it. All it required of me was the smallest lie of omission. Although even that caused a twinge of conscience.

"I do not know," I said, with an apologetic shrug. "They were friendly, everyone was getting along well, and then suddenly . . ." I shook my head. "Suddenly there were drawn swords and screams and insults. I'm sorry I've got nothing more to say to it. I have no idea what happened."

Othello turned unhappily toward Cassio. "Michele, explain yourself."

Cassio, almost shivering with embarrassment, and fighting off the fog of drunkenness, did the only intelligent thing possible: "Forgive me, General, but I can't speak," he managed to say, his face resting hard against the cold stone of the parapet. I was afraid he might throw up on me.

Othello frowned. Turning away from us, he tried Montano. "Governor," he said patiently, "I do not know you as well as I know these others, but I know you have a name for gravity and wisdom. Tell me what makes you throw off that reputation to become a night-brawler?"

Montano did not move from his curled-up position. "I'm badly hurt," he moaned. "I need physic. Iago can tell you everything. I was defending myself."

Othello looked around at the men. "Can no one tell me *any-thing*?" he demanded. "Who started this nonsense? This is a town of war! People's hearts have been brimful of fear for months now, and we, who are supposed to ensure their safety—we're now the ones who make them fearful! What fools among you do not understand how monstrous that is?" His voice grew quick and stern. "Iago, tell me *now*, who began it?"

Seeing me hesitate, Montano grunted in a pained voice, "Tell the truth, Iago, or you are no true soldier."

"Do not say that," I retorted, grateful he was giving me so many opportunities to play the role of regretful truth-teller. "I'd rather have my tongue cut from my mouth before I let it say anything against Michele Cassi . . . oh." I looked away from Othello with sheepish worry. I did it so well that I almost fooled myself.

"Go on, Iago," Othello said through clenched teeth.

"I will," I said, "but if you listen to the whole story you'll see that Cassio is not to blame. We were all out here talking, and suddenly, Cassio and some stranger came running out from the tower, and Cassio had his sword drawn on the stranger. I'd never seen him look like that before. Signior Montano here stepped in to try to stop Cassio from attacking the stranger, who was unarmed—that's all it was. Montano got in the way. I don't know why Cassio was so enraged at the stranger, but Cassio is a rational man, I'm sure the stranger had it coming and Cassio had every right to be after him."

There was a longish silence, during which Othello perused my expression as if I were a piece of art he was contemplating buying. Finally, with a sigh, he looked away and said, "Iago, your loyalty to a friend is forcing you to make light of the matter. Michele Cassio," he said, with a small cough of distaste, and then turned full on to Cassio. I helped Cassio in his attempt to scramble to his feet. Othello held out his hand, palm up, as if expecting something. "Cassio, I love you like a brother, but you will never be an officer of mine. Give me the lieutenant's sash."

Victory!

Fighting back Florentine tears, Cassio tried to pull the sash off over his head. It got caught on the ostrich feather. I was near enough to help him remove it, but that seemed a graceless gesture. I wondered how long it would be before Othello finally did the right thing and awarded me the sash. Perhaps he would do it this very moment . . .

. . . and he might have, but his wife showed up.

Blond hair mussed, in a white linen nightdress, with a red silk shawl wrapped about her shoulders, Desdemona stared in sleepy confusion at all of us.

"And on top of it all, you've woken my wife! You'll pay for that!" Othello snapped. *You are truly obsessed*, I thought, *if you make that as much a sin as terrifying an entire town.*

"What's the matter?" Her sweet, small voice sounded jarringly delicate after the masculine shouting and carryings-on. Her face was shadowed by the torchlight behind her.

"Nothing, sweetheart," Othello said, solicitously putting an arm around her. "This is just the soldier's life, being awoken in the middle of the night because fools are fighting with each other. Go back to bed. You there," he ordered a couple of the guards. "Take Governor Montano to the hospital, I will go after to see he is well. Iago—"

I nearly leapt toward him, so eager was I to be given the sash. "Iago, take some men and go about the town, make sure people know this was a false alarm, and all is well."

"Of course, General," I said, saluting smartly. I lowered my arm but stood at attention as the entire congregation filed into the keep, or out along the wall walk to their guard positions. Othello wrapped a large dark arm around his small pale wife, and ushered her back inside.

There was nobody left out here but Cassio and myself.

Chapter 39

HE SAT SLUMPED OVER, head resting in hands, so pathetic I was almost moved for him.

"What's wrong?" I asked. "Are you hurt, Lieutenant?" Ah, the delight of calling him lieutenant when he no longer was one.

"Past all surgery," Cassio mumbled in a miserable voice.

"God forbid," I said, and rushed to him, pushing him upright, as if to search for wounds on his torso. It reminded me of being a small child playing War with Roderigo.

Cassio pushed me away and intoned in a mournful voice, "I've lost my reputation!"

I laughed dismissively and smacked him on the shoulder. "Is that all? I swear to heaven, Michele, I thought you'd received some bodily wound!"

"I have lost the immortal part of myself. My *reputation,* Iago!"

Leave it to a Florentine to wax rhapsodic even at a time like this.

"Reputation is a meaningless nicety," I argued. "Half the time it's gotten unjustly"—here I refrained from referring to a certain previous lieutenancy—"and half the time it's lost unjustly too."

"Othello," Cassio mumbled, miserable.

"Calm down," I said. "There are ways to get back in his good graces. He was making an example of you in front of a crowd of new soldiers, that is all—he wanted to show them what he'd do to his most exalted, so they would all know better than to push him. But now he's made his point. Appeal to him and I'm sure he'll forgive you."

Cassio shook his head. "*I* would not forgive me, in his position. This all happened because I was drunk. Men behave like idiots when they're drunk. There's a reason drink is called the devil, it brings out the devil in all of us."

I ignored the moralizing. "Who was that fellow you were following? What did he do to you?"

Cassio shook his head despondently. "No idea."

"Really? None?"

He curled his hands around his head again. "I remember a mass of things, but nothing clearly. I remember a quarrel, but not what it was about. Oh God," he groaned, rubbing his face. "We put an enemy in our mouths and it steals our brains! Why do we *do* that? We transform ourselves into beasts and act as if it were something to *celebrate!*"

"You seem fine now," I observed.

"Yes, I am just sober enough to hate myself for being drunk," he lamented. "Another thing the devil does well."

I liked him more this way—not just that he was humbled, but also that he was sincere. "Michele, you're being too hard on yourself. It was a rough night for you, but since it has happened as it has, face it like a man. It should not take much to mend the situation."

He gave me a disbelieving stare and said tersely, "I'll ask for my place again; he'll say I am a drunkard. He'll be right! End of discussion!" He made a disgusted sound. "To go from sensible to foolish to beastly—only the devil can do that to a man—"

"Enough of that," I cut him off. "Will you stop obsessing on the evils of liquor and trust me with some advice?"

"Of course. Ach, I can't believe I got *drunk*," he moaned.

"Everyone gets drunk," I said, barely keeping my patience. "Let that go. Do you wish to get your office back?"

"Of course," he whined.

"Here's what you need to do, then. The general's wife is now the general—we've all seen that. Go to her. Ask for her help to put you in your place again. She is a generous soul, and she'd do anything for those she treasures. Ask her to splint this broken joint between you and her husband. Just as a bone mends stronger than it was, I wager Othello's regard for you will grow stronger too."

He thought this over for a moment, his hangdog expression leaning puppyward. "That's good advice."

"No more than you deserve," I said. Oh, how I meant that. I patted him on the arm. "Dear Lieutenant, I must carry out my orders, so I'll wish you good night now."

"Good night, Iago," Cassio said, with a weak smile in my direction.

I watched him walk unsteadily toward the door that led down into the keep. My heart smiled, but I kept my lips from showing it, even to the darkness.

Now: if I could put the slightest worry in Othello's mind that there might be something impure in Desdemona's regard for Cassio, then the more fervently she spoke on his behalf, the more she would be damning both of them, and tormenting Othello in the bargain. That suited me. I took satisfaction in the perverse irony that Desdemona's good intentions would turn on all three of them—just as my good intentions to all of them had turned on me. An eye for an eye, a turn for a turn, a measure for a measure.

I DECIDED TO follow the wall walk over to the next tower and descend from there to pick out a few guards and begin my rounds of calming all the townfolk. But as I took a step along the parapet, I saw a shaved head capping a familiar face, gasping for breath and glowering at me in the dark.

"Roderigo!" I said as cheerfully as I could. "Excellent work!"

He stood up; his face was close to the torchlight, and I could no longer pretend to not see his expression.

"Whatever's wrong, brother?"

He took a step closer to me. "I was exceedingly well cudgeled tonight," he said. "And while being chased as if I were a hare—not a fox, but a hare—the absurdity of what I'm doing here was suddenly extremely clear to me. I've thrown pearls at Desdemona and all I have to show for it are some bumps on my head and a little experience. I am going home to Venice."

I was so delighted with my own abilities, I wanted him to be delighted too; I could not brook the notion that he should be displeased with my advice. "Patience, Roderigo," I said with the confidence of my childhood. "We only arrived today; we cannot accomplish everything at once. Go to the barracks and get some sleep." He looked uncertain. "There is no easy transport to Venice anyhow, so you may as well give me a few days more to change your circumstances. Go to sleep. Just down that way." I pointed to the door of the keep. "The barracks are on the ground floor, across the courtyard. Trust me. Is it not better than having drowned yourself?"

Frowning, he left me alone on the parapet.

Desdemona

Chapter 40

 week went by. One little week. One entire, endless week, without rain, without an opportunity to speak alone with the general, as the grass in the courtyard grew daily browner. Magistrates held meetings with the general. Soldiers practiced their arms. The ladies did embroidery all day, shopped in the town, dressed well for dinner. Roderigo sent me, by boys well paid to remain discreet, a pocketful of jewelry every other day—strands of pearls, large rubies, emeralds, opalescent stones I did not recognize. These I stored in my wardrobe. If ever I envied Roderigo, it was that week. How could a man have so much moveable wealth that he could so heedlessly hand it over to another? My work in the world was as significant as his, my mind sharper, my determination steelier . . . but I could not yet afford to provide my wife a home, let alone *rubies*.

I chose not to dwell on this confounding outrage. More urgent matters required my full attention.

CASSIO, DESPITE HIS desperation to restore his reputation, did little but send meek notes to Othello asking for an audience. I intercepted several of these messages and made sure the general did not receive them—but even those he did receive, he did not answer.

This reassured me, but not enough, because the lieutentant's sash lay folded neatly on the corner of his desk. Othello had not yet offered it to me. There was no pressing military business to distract him.

"Why won't he just *present* it?" I fumed to Emilia one evening as we lay together in our small room. We were being housed in this suite not because of my standing with Othello, but because of Emilia's with Desdemona. The larger, nicer room that would have been Cassio's, had he lasted longer than a day—the room that should now have been mine—remained unoccupied.

"He is not thinking like a general, for a change," Emilia said, her head nesting on my shoulder and her hand stroking my chest. "He is completely preoccupied with love, and the world is not requiring him to do otherwise. When circumstances shift a bit, and he once again puts his mind to work, trust me, he will give you the sash. And deservedly so. It is a pity about Michele, though."

"I told you he had that weakness back in Venice, and you didn't believe me."

I felt her head move as she nodded. "Yes. Funny how an attractive face can warp a girl's judgment." She tipped her chin up just as I turned my head, and we were eye to eye. She grinned. "Your attractive face warped me right into a *marriage*."

"Flattery will get you . . . somewhere," I said, satisfied. I reached over to stroke her collarbone. And other things.

DESPITE MY NEARLY effortless success at decommissioning Cassio, I could not rest easily. Cassio was still around. I heard a rumor he had spent several days and nights in a whore's house in Famagusta, but then he returned to the Citadel, hoping to reenter Othello's graces. Until that lieutenant's sash hung over my left shoulder, Cassio was still a threat.

Having too much time on my hands during that brief, unending week, I ruminated on ways to prevent the Florentine's re-ascent. My scheme had worked so swiftly, I had not fully exploited it: the implied infidelity with Desdemona, for example, had not even been broached.

That, then, would be my emergency plan: if Cassio showed any signs of regaining favor, then I would worry Othello into suspicions about his wife's interests in the Florentine.

How to do this? Or more specifically: how to *prepare* to do this, if required, without drawing undo attention to my plans if they were not enacted? I needed a prop. I needed something small enough to plant on Cassio, if necessary; something that could have only come from Desdemona.

"You know the handkerchief of Othello's that he gave to Desdemona?" I asked Emilia the next night, in a falsely casual tone.

"The one with the strawberries?" she replied absently, combing her hair.

"Yes, that one. Do you fancy it? Would you like one like it?"

She smiled. "How very un-Iago-like, to want to ply me with gifts. It makes me wonder what you've been up to that you think you'll need to buy my favor." But then she grinned.

"Do you like it?" I repeated. "Do you think she'd let you borrow it, to get the pattern copied?"

She stopped combing, settled the comb in her lap, and looked at me appraisingly. "You mean that?" she said. "You want to give me such a gift? Why?"

Despite my recent forays into deception, I still was not an able liar, and I most certainly could not lie to this woman. "I cannot give you a reason," I said. "But I think you should, ahem, *borrow* it from Desdemona."

She smiled, in the mysterious way that women do when men are being dense about Things Female. "She never lets it out of her sight," she said and raised the comb to continue working on her hair. "I doubt she would part company with it for an hour, even. She sleeps with it tied around her wrist."

"That seems a bit extreme."

"Love does that to people." She laughed.

"Well, if she ever decides she can survive without it for a day or two, please alert me. I might have a wife who deserves a trifle of a gift."

She beamed at me, lowering the comb again. "You win points just for desiring to please me," she said, and gestured toward the bed. "Would you like to redeem them right away?"

TWO MORNINGS LATER, Cassio emerged from his shamed, bawd-laden hermitage and finally took my advice to approach Othello through Desdemona. So much for my lieutenant's sash, then; Desdemona really did hold enormous sway over her husband's sentiment, and if she argued on Cassio's behalf, Othello would give her whatever she asked for.

So I was not happy to see Cassio, in full red-and-white military regalia, blue ostrich feather bobbing, approach along the lawn from the gate. Two musicians, young men in native costume, followed him, playing a dirgelike tune on mandolin and lute. In this courtyard, protected from both the sea breeze and the town noises, their mediocre playing carried loudly. *Oh, heaven,* I thought, *he may as well be courting her.*

"Good morning, stranger," I said, making myself smile. I rose and crossed to meet him, giving him a hearty slap on the arm.

"Good morning, Ensign," he said, with a salute. He gestured to the two musicians, and they stopped playing. "I'm tardy in taking your advice, but now is my last hope for it."

"Never a last hope," I insisted. "Othello will surely hear you out."

He grimaced. "I was coming here to ask your wife if she would ask her lady to come out to speak to me."

Lo, how the mighty had fallen. Cassio, when useful to Othello, had had free access to Desdemona . . . now he was asking my permission to speak to Emilia, to whom he would then ask permission to speak to Desdemona. I found that delicious.

"I was just headed inside," I said, luxuriating in my ability to go where now he could not. "I'll send Emilia to you. However," I added, with a helpful smile, "I think the sad-eyed musicians are a bit much. Pay them for their troubles, and send them off."

"Do you think so? Thank you, Iago." He looked so touched by my offering advice, I almost felt bad for him. "Even among my fellow Florentines, I've never met a kinder fellow."

"That's high praise indeed," I said. "I'll send Emilia to you."

I let myself into the cool, shady rooms where the women were keeping themselves occupied, on the north wing of the fortress. Emilia and Desdemona were doing embroidery together, near an open door that faced out into the courtyard. I knew Emilia disliked embroidery (I suspected Desdemona did as well), and I felt sorry for it. They both looked up eagerly for a distraction. I gestured with a finger, and Emilia happily set her hoop aside and rushed over to me. Desdemona watched her, looking almost envious.

Emilia approached me, leaned in for a kiss; I gave her one on the cheek and whispered, "Michele Cassio is outside the door." In an even quieter voice, I added, "He wants the lady to help him get his commission back."

Her eyes widened, and she pulled back to meet my gaze. "Oh," she whispered, after a moment. "That's a bit awkward for us, isn't it?"

Thank God she understood. "He has asked me to ask you to go out to him, so he can ask you to ask Desdemona to go out."

"How Florentine," she said. "I do not suppose I can refuse to see him? Or refuse to carry the message to her?"

In that remarkable moment, I had to make a choice: either let her in on everything I thought and planned, or promise myself she never had an inkling of it. I chose the latter. I loved her too much to enmesh her in any unsavory scheme. And on a less noble note, I wasn't sure I trusted her not to give something away.

So despite my impulse to say *Do exactly as you please*, I said instead, with a paternal frown, "Emilia, I appreciate your impulse, but the man deserves to have his appeal."

"Why cannot he have it after you've been made lieutenant?" she shot back. I could see Desdemona out of the corner of my eye sit up a little straighter and cock her head with curiosity.

I kissed Emilia's cheek. "The best Cassio can hope for is a reinstatement as an officer. Othello will never consider him for lieutenant again."

"When will he consider *you* for lieutenant?" she asked.

I pulled away from her. "That is a different conversation," I said. "Attend to present business." I walked toward the interior door of the room. Here I paused and looked back. When I knew I had Desdemona's full attention, I concluded to Emilia, "Attend to this matter honorably and honestly, wife."

She saluted me. "You've a nobler heart than I have, husband," she called out, in a tone of admiring sincerity. I bowed my head to Desdemona and departed through a curtain to a corridor.

Chapter 41

AS I HAD ALL WEEK, I attended to Othello in his office. Daily he was briefed on the military and civic concerns of Cyprus, and particularly of Famagusta. Most of it was boring, dreary, officious paperwork and committee meetings, not at all what he was used to or cared for. Throughout the week, Marco Salamon, the paunchy Venetian patrician who was Othello's civic commissioner, was there, and by the end of the week, Montano was well enough recovered from his wound to sit in as well. The meetings were airless and pointless, and as soon as business was attended to, Othello would excuse himself, with me following him, and spend the rest of the morning with his officers training in arms in the courtyard of the fortress. We all shared mess together in the refectory, and the afternoon was variably spent each day.

* * *

THIS MORNING AFTER Cassio's appearance, the meeting and the boredom were no different. As always, Othello tried to rush through it, and as always, the gentlemen attending him seemed to want to slow the process down, perhaps because they had nothing more interesting to do with their day. And, as always, I eyed the lieutenant's sash and wondered when he would present it to me.

As it was the end of our first week, I scribed dictation on a summary of events thus far (nothing to report beyond Cassio's decommissioning, but taking seven pages to do so). Othello signed it; it was sealed; he gave it to me.

"Iago, give this to the pilot of the ship. Send him back to Venice, with our regards to the Senate as we await further orders from them. I believe the army's presence is useful here, but I do not know that mine is, now that the Turkish threat is past."

I saluted and took the packet from his hand. Why was he calling upon me to do these trivial tasks? Had he not, back in Zara, sent a *page boy* to deliver messages to the ship? But, of course, those had been secret missives; this was a matter of state. So perhaps it was an ennobling gesture, to show all the officials of the island that I was his right-arm man. *The best way to show them would be to give me that sash.*

"When you have done that, Iago, join me on the wall works," Othello was saying as he pushed his chair back. "Come, gentlemen, show me these famous fortifications." The perfumed gentlemen—among them, leathery-faced Montano and a famous engineer named Zuan Hieronomo—showed him out. I handed off the letters to a page boy.

I had no interest in tagging along with the officials as they showed Othello a fortress he had already thoroughly examined on his own time, with his own engineers. We already knew the main problem with Famagusta: these towers were at angles, not rounded, and (unlike Nicosia) they did not sufficiently project far enough out to allow room to cover flanking fire. Othello and I together had devised a solution to this, before we had been sent here: wooden curtains that could swing out with artillery attached. Othello now simply had to persuade Signior Hieronomo that this was Signior Hieronomo's own idea.

To avoid becoming entangled in that conversation, I wandered slowly through the armoring rooms, a level below the general and his sycophants, trying to sort out what to do about Cassio.

EMILIA WOULD HAVE greeted him and taken his message to Desdemona, because I'd told her to. Desdemona would surely have come outside to hear his plea. She would likely be sympathetic, because she knew and liked him, and of course felt beholden to him for helping carry out her elopement. If she agreed to petition Othello, she would win him over. Completely so: not only to reinstate him as an officer but as lieutenant.

I could do nothing to prevent these events from happening. I could only manipulate their meaning. That meant I'd have to call upon the second, uglier part of my revenge fantasy, and make Othello question Desdemona's motives. I felt my gut clench at the thought.

I need not convince him they are actually lovers, I told myself, *only that there is cause to be . . . a little wary.* A man so rapturously in love is naturally jealous and insecure—I had been so with Emilia. If I'd had a close friend back then, what words from a confidant would have caused me alarm? Such words, if I could summon them, I'd use with Othello, of Cassio.

Besides, I reassured that small part of me that quailed at my intentions, *Cassio does seem taken with her; this may well be an honest warning bell I'm ringing.*

I TIMED THINGS WELL and found Othello on the parapets having just bid good day to the magistrates.

"The artillery curtains?" I asked, catching my breath.

"Why, yes, my friend," Othello said with his winning grin. "Signior Hieronomo is a wondrously inspired engineer—he intended a notion of moveable artillery curtains. Wasn't that clever?

You and I, Iago, we should brush up on our engineering skills, then perhaps *we* would think of such clever things."

"Well done, General," I said. "You are learning how to navigate Venetian waters."

"Fencing?" Othello said.

With remarkable offhandedness I suggested, "Soon enough, but perhaps we might first repair to the ladies' wing and say good morning to our wives?"

He grinned. He always grinned in matters regarding Desdemona. I doubted we would catch Cassio still there, but it was worth the try.

We strolled the wall walk around the keep tower and turned onto the wing that housed the bedrooms. Just as we turned the corner, I saw, bobbing in the air below, a bright blue ostrich feather.

Chapter 42

THE OSTRICH FEATHER bobbed nervously in the opposite direction from us, and disappeared out of the fortress gate.

Oh, I liked the looks of that.

"Huh," I said, as if to myself. "I don't like the looks of that."

"What did you say?" Othello asked, taking a longer stride and craning his neck to see farther around the corner.

"It was nothing," I said dismissively. "I just ... no, it was nothing."

"Was that Michele Cassio down there? Talking to my wife?" Othello asked.

"Cassio?" I said, in a surprised tone. "I think not, the fellow down there darted off as if he were guilty of some crime."

"I think it was Cassio," Othello said thoughtfully.

Emilia looked up and waved to me at that moment; Desdemona, following her gaze, held both of her hands up to her husband. We were two floors up, but near the external stairs that could take us down to the courtyard level. We began the descent.

"Good morning, General!" Desdemona called out sweetly. "I've spent the morning being courted here by a suitor who is languishing in your displeasure."

Again, the heavens were surely working for me. Were I playing God myself, it would not have occurred to me to make Desdemona use the word *suitor*.

Othello stopped so abruptly I bumped into his shoulder. "Whom do you mean?" he asked.

She gave him an exaggerated look implying he should know better. "Your lieutenant Cassio, of course." She gestured to the scraggly lawn around her. "Join us, and bring your witty ensign there."

I avoided Emilia's eyes at the use of both these ranks, and followed Othello down the stairway to stand near the ladies. Desdemona, smiling like a mischievous kitten, moved toward Othello and held out her hands toward him, in a coquettish invitation to embrace her.

"My good lord," she purred as his hands came to rest on her shoulders. "If I have any power to move you, give Cassio his position back."

Othello's smile faded. He removed his hands from her shoulders and turned away. Desdemona, undeterred, immediately sidestepped to remain in front of him, and now she placed her hands on his broad shoulders.

"He worships you, Othello. He made a terrible mistake, and he's very sorry for it. Do not reprehend. I have absolute faith that he will never make that mistake again, and since he has no other weaknesses at all, I beg you to call him back."

Othello glanced at me. I shrugged, as if this matter had not the slightest thing to do with me. The general looked back at his wife. "Was that him, just now?"

"Yes," she said. Othello looked at me again, more abruptly, and this time I met his gaze, as if I were suspicious. "He was so upset about his situation that he's left part of his grief with me. Please, love, I beg you: call him back."

Othello frowned and brushed her hands from his shoulder; he turned away from her, toward me, looking stern. "Not now, sweeting, some other time."

Smiling angelically, she sashayed sideways once more to stay directly in front of her husband. "Will it be soon?" she asked adorably.

Othello sighed and smiled at her despite himself. "Only because it means so much to you, love."

"Perhaps tonight, over supper?" she suggested. "Shall we invite him to dine with us?"

"No," Othello said, a stern parent. "Not tonight."

"Tomorrow at dinner?"

"I'm taking mess with the captains at the citadel."

"Well, then," Desdemona said comfortably, unshakably confident of her power to soften him. She raised her arms to his neck, clasped her hands behind his head, and began to coo to him: "Tomorrow night, or Tuesday morning, or Tuesday noon, or Tuesday night, or Wednesday morning—"

"Desdemona!" Othello said, trying halfheartedly to disentangle himself. It was hard to tell if he was laughing or scolding. I moved a step closer to Emilia, and she held out her hand; I moved closer yet so that our shoulders brushed against each other. We clenched hands.

"That's it, then," she whispered. "Even if he does not like it, he'll say yes to her, because it's *her.*"

Desdemona was continuing to list all the possible times that Cassio might be received over the course of the next decade, and Othello continued to make a noise that was half laughter, half chastisement. Desdemona pushed him further: "I would never deny you anything, love, so how can you deny me something so easy to grant? This is Michele Cassio, after all—the man that helped you woo me! I would not now be standing with my arms around you being so annoying, were it not for his kindnesses! If my words will not convince you, believe me, I have other ways—" And she began, in front of us, to reach toward his groin. Othello pulled her arms off him and stepped back.

"Enough! Enough" he said sharply, and then, with impatient resignation: "Let him come when he will."

Emilia turned her head into my shoulder, muting a sigh.

"Stop that," I said fiercely into her ear. "That's your mistress and my master—do not embarrass me with personal pettiness in front of them." She glanced up at me, stung.

Othello had wrapped his arms around Desdemona and was squeezing her in a hug. "For God's sake, I cannot deny you anything."

Emilia and I exchanged brief, unhappy glances. "Contain yourself," I warned in a whisper. Chastened, she lowered her gaze.

Desdemona, enjoying her power, continued to ply her husband. I realized with mixed emotions that this suited me. "It's not as if you're doing me a favor," she insisted. "Any more than you'd be doing me a favor if you listened to me when I told you to wear your gloves or eat your dinner. It's a favor to yourself."

"Is it really?" he asked, releasing her, wearied from being henpecked in front of friends.

"Oh, yes," she assured him, smiling. "When I ask you a favor, for myself, you'll know it, because it will be impossibly difficult for you to grant it."

"I cannot wait. In the meantime, for now, leave me alone," he said, with a firm smile that made it clear he would brook no more flirting this morning.

"I shall disappear at once," she declared, victorious, and held her hand out to Emilia. "Come, we're leaving." Emilia gave my hand a final squeeze, then released it and followed her.

Othello, looking immediately regretful, called out as they headed toward the door, "I'll be in to see you in just a moment."

"Surely, surely, surely," Desdemona said gaily, knowing she took his heart with her in her palm. "Whatever pleases you."

I watched Othello watching her as she disappeared into the

building. He held his hand over his chest and murmured something to himself, his face radiant with love. He would give her whatever she asked for, even if she asked for something wrong or dreadful. I would never get that sash if I did not act immediately.

"General?" I said carefully. "Shall we to the fencing yard?"

He started from his reverie and turned to face me. "Did you say something, Iago?"

I gestured him toward the passageway in the far wall, and together we began to cross the courtyard.

This was the moment. Into the comfortable silence between us, I asked, "Othello, pardon, but your lady said that Michele helped you to woo her?"

"Yes, of course. Why?"

I shook my head. "I was just wondering."

"And why were you wondering?"

"I did not realize he knew her so well."

"Of course he did—he was our go-between."

I shot my eyebrows up. "Really?"

Othello frowned at me. "Iago, surely you knew that."

"I did not realize—" I looked away and brushed it off. "Never mind. I knew you were sending her letters. I did not realize they went through *him*, that he was so directly intimate with her."

Othello gave me an inquisitive look. "What does it matter? He's an honest man, is he not?"

I blinked twice, rapidly. "Honest?"

Othello stopped; I took one step more, then squinting into the glare of morning sunlight, pivoted to face him as he retorted, impatiently, "Yes, honest. It was a rhetorical question, Iago, it does not require a response."

I avoided his gaze for not quite one heartbeat, then met his glance and smiled comfortingly. "You're right, of course. I'm sure he is perfectly honest, as honest as any man who has any honesty in him. Come, there is a rapier with my name on it—" and I turned again in the direction we'd been traveling.

"Iago," Othello said from behind me, in a tone that stopped me again. "Why did you say it like that?"

Again a hesitation, then I looked over my shoulder at him. "Like what, sir?"

Othello shifted his weight back onto his heels. "Is there something you are not telling me, Iago?"

I glanced away quickly, then again looked at him, with an uncertain smile.

Othello frowned. "Tell me your thoughts, Iago."

"My *thoughts*?" I said with a nervous laugh, and my gaze darted away again from his face.

"Yes, your *thoughts*!" Othello huffed. "Why are you echoing me? Come, Iago, I know you too well. There is something going on behind those eyes that you are not telling me. That is unlike you. I want you to tell me."

I lowered my gaze and shifted my weight from one foot to the other. Othello sighed with impatience. His left hand resting on his sword hilt, he glanced back in the direction we'd just come. "Just a few moments ago you said you did not like the way Cassio was sneaking away from my wife when we approached. And then you said you did not realize how well they knew each other when I was wooing her. And now you are obviously avoiding telling me something you think about his character."

As he glanced toward me, I again glanced away. All of this felt genuine to me: I did loathe Cassio's character; there was no wrongness at all in letting Othello know it.

"Iago, if you love me, tell me what you're thinking."

I glanced at him and regarded the warm, commanding eyes. This man had been my best friend for years now. "You know I love you," I said simply.

"Yes, I think you do," Othello said with quiet satisfaction. He crossed his arms and settled back even farther on his heels. "And I know you well, Iago—you have a deserved reputation for extreme bluntness, but I also know how careful and weighty you are with your words. So your little hesitations, your glances away—like that!" he interjected as I looked down at my boots. With guilty speed, I raised my eyes to meet his again. "Just like that, Iago—when you, of all men, behave like that, I take it very seriously."

"My lor—"

"No, listen to me," Othello ordered, pointing a finger like a chastising father. I closed my mouth and put one finger to my lips. Othello crossed his arms again. "Usually when men cannot meet my gaze it is because they are up to something unsavory and they are afraid I'll be able to tell. But that is not you. There is something strange going on here with you, and I want you to tell me what it is."

I looked at him, and wished Michele Cassio did not exist. "I'm . . . I will swear that . . . I think Michele Cassio seems honest." How ironic: that was a lie, for I knew Michele Cassio was *not* honest.

"I think so too," Othello said quickly—but studying me. He also knew Cassio was not honest; he had *relied* on that to woo his bride.

"Good," I said, and clasped my hands together with finality. "Men should be what they seem."

"Mmm," Othello said, staring at me intensely, not moving. "Yes, men *should* be what they seem."

"Well, then," I said, glancing away from him. "I think Cassio's an honest man. Time for some swordplay." I took a step into the shadowed passageway that would lead out to the exercise yard.

Othello did not move. He kept staring at me, and I continued to avoid the gaze. "No, there is more to this. Iago, there is something you're not saying here. Do not deny it—" he ordered, seeing me open my mouth. "Tell me what you're thinking. Out with it. Give the worst of your thoughts the worst of words."

I pressed my lips together nervously. It was real nervousness. He was taking the bait, and I could not now dismiss the moment even if I wanted to. I was committed. "General, pardon me, but I won't do that."

Othello looked like he'd been slapped. "What?" he said. "Why not?"

"It is my duty to perform whatever *action* you command, but my *thoughts* are my own, and I prefer to keep them that way."

"Why?" he demanded. "It is *me*, Iago, not a stranger. I am not ordering you as your commander, but asking as your friend. What on earth would you not want me to hear?"

"They're just my thoughts," I said. "They are not reality. They could be wrong. They could be, they could be . . . evil."

Othello laughed stiffly. "Iago, that is ridiculous, you are not an evil man."

"But I can be a nasty one," I warned.

"Nasty is not evil," he retorted. "Yes, you can be nasty with your frankness, but that does not make you evil."

"Is there any man so saintly that he never has an evil thought?" I shot back. "Can you think of any soul alive—yourself included—who has *never* harbored thoughts they wished they did not have?"

Othello's stare intensified. "If you're having such thoughts now, Iago, and you do not tell me what they are, then you're doing me a great disservice. Both as your general and as your friend."

I leaned in closer to him. "Please," I said. "As you said, you know me well. You know I can be vicious. And jealous. And suspicious. Even when I am behaving well, it does not mean the vicious, jealous, suspicious thoughts are not plaguing me inside." How absolutely honest I was being. "As long as I have my thoughts under control, why should I have to tell you about them? It serves no purpose. It just humiliates me, to admit I have such unseemly thoughts. So, no, I am not going to tell you what my thoughts are." I meant it. Sincerely. Every word of it.

"Iago, what in hell are you talking about?"

I had no choice now; I had to go beyond the genuine. I turned away from him and leaned against the stone wall of the passageway. Again with a nervous pursing of the lips, and a small anxious shake of the head, I glanced at him and then away. "No man's good name should be trifled with. And no woman's, either."

Alarm flashed across his face. He had taken the meaning. "Whose good names? For the love of heaven, Iago, *tell me your thoughts.*"

I leaned back against the wall, my arms crossed over my chest. "Sorry, but no."

He looked at me. I looked back at him. The stare seemed to last forever. I watched the subtle workings of the skin around his brows and mouth, and wondered what was happening behind those bright-dark eyes. I kept my gaze as neutral as I could, a blank slate onto which he might draw whatever fears lurked within.

"I cannot believe you will not tell me," he said quietly. "It must be something very, very dark indeed, if you will not share it with your closest friend."

In a voice resonant with experience, I warned softly, "Beware of jealousy, my lord. It is the green-eyed monster that mocks the meat it feeds on."

"What are you *saying*?" he demanded sharply.

"You know the parable of the rich man who worries so much about losing his fortune that he is too miserable to enjoy it?" I smiled sympathetically. "Do not be that man. You have a treasure of a wife. Enjoy her, and do not worry about losing her."

He stared at me uncertainly. "What are you talking about, Iago? Why should I worry about losing her? Do you think . . . do you think I'm jealous over Desdemona?"

"I did not say that—" I began, straightening up.

"I assure you," he said with a chuckle. "I am not jealous. Why should I be jealous? Because others admire her? There's nothing suspicious about that—she is easy to admire! I love that about her, it does not make me jealous. How ridiculous. If all your anxiety is just about Cassio's *admiring* her, never mind, I am sorry to have wasted both our time. Come, let's to the yard."

He started to stroll again, with something close to a swagger; I walked beside him. For a moment there was silence. I contemplated what I should do next.

"After all," Othello said suddenly, in a boastful voice, "she had eyes, and she chose *me*." He glanced at me sideways. "No, Iago, I'm not jealous," he went on expansively. "I would never let myself hover in that awful unknowing place you speak of. I am too practical a man for that."

He was protesting too much against being jealous. Only jealous men do that.

"I'm glad to hear it," I said.

"But you know that of me already! I would need to *see* something, concrete, to even doubt her loyalty. If I doubted her, I'd demand proof immediately. If there was proof, I would stop loving her; if there was none, I would stop being jealous. Very simple." He looked cocky, but it was the kind of cockiness that strains to cover insecurity. Or so I guessed.

Perhaps I was not baiting him as I'd thought. It would perhaps take more brazenness than I'd anticipated. I sighed, cheeks puffing, as I considered my next move.

He looked at me again and slowed. "Iago?"

"I'm glad you said that, General," I said, turning my head away for a moment, and then looking back at him directly, blinking a few times. "The remembrance that you are not prey to jealousy . . . encourages me to speak more freely."

"Freely about what?" Othello demanded and came to a halt, grabbing my arm to make me stop too.

I took another deep breath and rubbed my hands together awkwardly. I almost spoke, then let the breath out, then drew another breath, then looked at Othello, then looked away again—

"Freely about *what*?" he demanded impatiently.

He would not make the leap on his own: I would have to push him. And now indeed I truly *must* push him, for if I did not, I left myself exposed. I felt a chill.

I put my free hand over his, where he gripped my arm. "Look to your wife, when Cassio's around," I said, apologetically.

His eyes widened, and the grip around my arm tightened.

"I am not telling you to be suspicious," I added quickly, "but do not be too cocky either. You are a trusting soul, and I would not have you abused for that. As I have often lamented, it is commonplace for Venetians to lie and keep secrets—and I am sure it may be so in Florence."

His face went slack as he released my arm. "What exactly are you saying?"

I shrugged, and averted my gaze. "Nothing. Only . . . remember, she deceived her father when she married you."

Othello blinked.

"So she did," he said. He looked confused.

"*Completely* deceived him," I emphasized. "With a skill that belies how young and innocent she seems. And she deceived him *even though* she loved him—" I cut myself off, seeing Othello's expression. He looked queasy. "I should not have said anything—forgive me, I should have kept my mouth shut, but I value your friendship and I worried—"

He made a brushing-away gesture. Then he took one of my hands in both of his. "For the insight you've offered, I am forever in your debt," he said, and attempted a wan smile.

"I have upset you," I said, frowning.

"Not a jot," he insisted. "Not one *jot*." He pulled away and walked past me into the shadow of the passageway.

"Yes I have, dammit," I said, moving toward him.

He kept walking, to avoid looking at me.

"I hope you know that I was only speaking from my love for you, but still—you're moved, to a degree I did not intend."

"I'm not," he said as he walked on.

"Remember, these are just my *thoughts*, nothing more. You demanded that I share my thoughts, and I warned you that they were degraded. You know I am not accusing her of anything—"

"I know," Othello said brusquely. He cleared his throat and kept walking.

"I hope you mean that," I said, following. "Because if you think

I'm actually accusing them of something, then I am the guilty one
here, for creating a false impression that neither of them deserves. I
would not lightly slander—"

He shuddered, and turned his face farther away from me as we
walked.

"Oh, General, you are moved," I said regretfully, reaching forward to put a solicitous hand on his shoulder. He shrugged away
from my touch.

"Of course I am not *moved*," he said gruffly. "Desdemona's honest,
I'm sure of that."

"May she remain so," I said heartily. "And may you always
think so." *Oh, God's balls*, I thought. *I am not going to accomplish anything with this, and now I've only further damaged my own standing
with him.*

Othello paused but did not turn back to me. He kept staring
toward the sunlit yard a few paces ahead. "And yet . . . anyone can
revolt against their own nature. She and I are both honest as honesty
itself, and yet, we deceived her father. Both of us. Both of us were
deceitful. I know how deceitful she can be."

Again I rested my hand on his shoulder. "But she has already
turned her back on so many men, I'm sure she will continue to do so,
if any tried to tempt her. Even Cassio."

Othello glanced over his shoulder at me. He suddenly looked
very tired. "Leave me, Iago. If you . . . happen to see anything odd,
or if Emilia does—you might want to mention to Emilia to keep her
eye out—yes, let me know. But for now, leave me, I want to work on
some . . . I have some fencing moves I want to work on alone."

"Of course, General," I said, my hand to my heart. I bowed my
head, then turned and began retreating back through the passageway toward the courtyard.

But a dozen paces down, I stopped and turned back to examine him.

Othello had sat down just where I'd left him. He sat cross-
legged, his sword resting behind him in its sheath. His hands were

at his temples, and he was leaning his head heavily into them. He looked miserable. I felt miserable. Playing with Cassio's career had been much easier, and far more satisfying.

This was different. I did not want him to care for her so much; I wanted to lead him by the nose to anger, or righteous paranoia, not heartbreak. And only for the lieutenancy. I had to keep that in mind; there was a distracting fascination in watching Othello mold himself at my direction, but that was not my goal. My goal was that lieutenant's sash. Had I troubled the waters enough? Could I stop now?

I cleared my throat and ran a few steps back toward him. He looked up from his miserable seated position. "General, I beg you," I said. "Do not think about this anymore. Let it go." He released an exasperated huff of breath. "The truth will out," I said, now in a fatherly tone. "Please dismiss our entire conversation as my worrying too much." My better nature urged me to add: "And especially, hold your wife free from *any* suspicion."

Othello grimaced and nodded, without looking at me. "Do not worry yourself over it," he said, staring at the ground. "Leave me now, Iago."

I had never seen him this dejected. He was nearly as dejected as I had been when I'd realized *he* was deceiving *me*. It had taken such little effort to achieve this parity.

Chapter 43

AGITATED BY MY own accomplishment, I took myself through the courtyard and back up to the wall walk. From there I gazed down upon the city, the sea, and the interior courtyard where officers were exercising. I considered joining them—I would have been welcome,

I always was; it was one of the few settings in which my lack of elevation made not a jot of difference to anyone. After Othello, I was still
the best swordsman among them, and they respected me for that, no
matter what my rank.

But I did not join them. I felt a tremor throughout my body, and
I worried it would reflect in my skill. Besides, the only path to get
there would take me past Othello brooding in the shadowed passageway. So instead I paced, and marveled.

WORDS. WORDS. WORDS. All it took were words. Othello claimed
he needed to see something concrete to be moved to doubt—but
I had shown him nothing, and still he doubted. I had moved him
more than the most ferocious battle ever had. I possessed a power
over him, far greater than any he possessed, or ever would possess,
over me.

The confused and troubling elation of that insight propelled me
along the ramparts into the bright, sunny morning. The sky was brilliant blue, and a crisp sea breeze pulled at my clothes; as I walked, I
could hear the grit under my boots with greater clarity than ever I
had heard it. I felt intensely alive, and in control—not only of my
own destiny but of another person's. It was a heady, thrilling sensation. *I win*, I thought.

I had never sought competition, and still did not believe I should
have been subjected to it: not with Cassio for a lieutenancy, not with
Desdemona for Othello's regard, not with Othello himself to grant
or banish happiness . . . but being forced into those competitions, I
was winning every one of them, and righteously so. It reminded me
of my early satisfaction in besting more seasoned fencing students;
in besting even fencing masters. My own skill delighted me, all the
more so because I had not known I had it.

I remembered the proverb: *It is excellent to have a giant's power, but
it is tyrannous to use it like a giant.* I would be a benevolent tyrant, I
promised myself. I trusted myself to exert my sudden puppeteering

power over Othello only insofar as I required him to be a puppet—there would be nothing gratuitous in my exercise of power, for I was not a villain. I had a task to accomplish, as a soldier in war has a task. A soldier does not continue to fire his musket once defeat or victory or truce is sounded. Neither would I.

HAVING SOOTHED MYSELF with this assertion, I descended to my bedroom. Emilia had a mirror, and I had a childlike desire to observe my face, to see if any of the excitement of the day was readable, or if I were as opaque as a Venetian mask. I strode into the room—and pulled up short to find my wife standing in the middle of it, her hands behind her back.

"What are you doing in here?" I demanded, more roughly than I meant to.

"Don't chide me," Emilia said with a superior smile. The attitude was unlike her. I mentally played over our last interaction: I had scolded her for revealing displeasure in front of Desdemona and Othello. "I have a thing for you," she continued, in a conspiratorial tone.

I took a step closer to her. "A *thing* for me?"

She nodded, meaningfully, but said no more. I took another step closer and reached around behind her; she backed away so that I could not reach whatever she was holding. Again I took a step in; again she backed away. Now a little smile teased her face.

"A thing for me," I repeatedly impatiently. "Well, it is a common enough thing to have a foolish wife."

She raised her head until her chin was pointing right at me. "Ha! Is that the best you can do? Your wit's a little slow this morning, husband. Luckily, mine is not. What is that handkerchief worth to you?"

I blinked in surprise. Had she really . . . "What handkerchief?" I asked.

"What handkerchief?" she echoed mockingly. "You know what handkerchief." A final backward step took her nearly to the far wall of the room, and she gave me a half-mocking, half-inviting smile. In the immediate thrill of the moment, I could not sort out in my mind if this was collusion or coincidence.

"Did you steal it from her?" I asked, stupidly.

She gave me a strange look. "No, of course not. She dropped it without noticing, so I scooped it up." The tone of her expression shifted to affectionate teasing. "Look . . . here it is." She released her hands from behind her back and, with a flourish, waved it at me: the little lacy kerchief with strawberries sewn into it, the one I'd seen a thousand times around Othello's neck, before it began to appear on Desdemona.

I was almost certain I would not need it now, but in case I did: *here it was*.

I took a steadying breath and reminded myself how this moment must look to Emilia. She thought I wanted the handkerchief so that I could get a copy made as a gift for her. I could not let her suspect otherwise.

"Excellent, you little wench," I said, smiling, moving toward her. "Hand it over."

She held it out in front of her, high up, and waved it slightly, as if tantalizing me with it. "Why should I?" she asked, slyly. "Do you have something special planned for it?"

I moved closer to her; at the same moment, I snatched the handkerchief from her with one hand, and with the other arm, pulled her body close to mine at the hip. I gave her a knowing wink and kissed her hard. "None of your business," I whispered into her ear, as if it were a lover's promise.

And then, overcome with nervousness that I was once again being disingenuous with my own wife, I let go of her and turned away. I rushed to the far side of the room and stared in distracted fixation on the kerchief. Should I use it? Would that be excessive? Could it be traced to me? Should I leave things as they were and trust that Othello was already distraught enough? No need to overdo anything . . .

"*Iago*," I heard Emilia's voice as from a great distance, behind me. I turned to look at her, feeling my cheeks turning pink. She was frowning. "That is the third time I said your name—what is wrong with you? Why are you staring at it that way?" She gave me a warning look. "I only leant it to you, you understand that? To find somebody to copy the pattern? If you're planning to hold on to it, then give it back to me, I won't have it. She'll notice it's gone soon, and I don't want to upset her. The poor thing already has too much troubling her today."

"Do not worry, I have my plans." I gestured toward the door. "The sooner you leave me alone, the sooner I may act on them." I winked and blew her a kiss.

She looked cautiously pleased. "Very well," she said, heading toward the door. "In case you're wondering, I prefer a slightly pinker tone than is in the original."

I nodded with a knowing smile, and waited until she'd left the room.

I STARED AT the handkerchief. What should I do with it? I had no way to plant it on Cassio's person without his noticing. I could show it to Othello myself and claim I'd found it in Cassio's room, but that was a more blatant, artless lie than I wanted to risk.

I should put it in Cassio's room, now that he had returned to the fortress, and let him find it. So far the gods seemed to be guiding everybody's actions to my ends; perhaps I should trust that Cassio would wield the kerchief in some manner that assisted me. Or perhaps, again—perhaps the kerchief was not really called for. Othello had changed so rapidly in one brief, subtle conversation; perhaps no more was required. Perhaps I really would take the handkerchief into Famagusta and find a seamstress who could make a copy of it for me to give Emilia. It could be a gift to celebrate my lieutenancy.

Shoving the kerchief deep into my jerkin, out of sight, I left the room, heading back through the courtyard for the stairwell to the wall walk. The parapet was a good place to clear my mind and calm my heart.

I was not alone up there. Immediately I saw Othello, pacing in terrible agitation back and forth along a stretch no more than twenty feet long: back, and forth, and back, and forth, talking to himself and waving his hands wildly before him. His agitation was fifty times what it had been an hour earlier. Such a transformation I honestly had not expected.

I approached him quietly; he did not notice.

"False to me? Is that it? Is she really false to me?" he was muttering.

"What are you doing?" I demanded sternly. "We agreed: no more of that!"

He literally jumped, then spun around to see me. For a moment, he just stared.

Then fury rose on his face, and he lunged toward me, arms outstretched toward my neck. "Get out of here, you whoreson! Look what you have done to me! I can't stop thinking about it!"

"General!" I said, jumping back and deflecting his arms with a wrestling move. "Calm yourself!"

His hands were clenched and his arms rigid. "Maybe she is cheating on me, maybe she is not—before I suspected her, it did not matter! It never crossed my mind, and so it never troubled me!" He shouted this at me as if I were to blame for it. Which, technically, I was.

I shook my head and said in a sorrowful voice, "I am sorry to hear this. You should not be so—"

He raged on as if I hadn't spoken. "She could have been sleeping with the entire army and it wouldn't have bothered me, as long as I did not hear about it! But now, whenever I look at my men, I'm going to have to wonder what other officer she's giving herself to—or maybe not an officer! Maybe a common soldier! Maybe all the common soldiers!" He shook his fists, first at the sky, and then at me. "I cannot think about anything else, I cannot calm my mind! I cannot think. I cannot think. I cannot think like a general. So I cannot *be* a general. I won't be able to function, I'll have to turn the army over to Montano until they can send a replacement from Venice—"

This was complete and unexpected madness.

"Are you serious, General?" I demanded. Not an hour had passed since I'd last seen him. If I'd known how potent words could be, I would have used far fewer.

His fists pounded down on both my shoulders, almost dropping me to my knees. I shouted aloud in surprised pain, my hands going protectively to my collarbones, fearing they had both been shattered. Othello grabbed my hands in his and shook them ferociously.

"Villain!" he spat in my face. "You'd better *prove* she's a whore, after tormenting me like this! Be absolutely sure of it, give me *ocular* proof, or I swear to all things holy, I'll make you so miserable, you'll wish you had been born a dog!"

I broke his grip and then immediately grabbed his hands with mine. "Are you *mad*?" I demanded furiously.

"Show me some *proof*!" he shouted, and tried to shake his hands free. I held tighter. "Prove this *thing* you're tormenting me with, or I swear I'll have your life."

"Othello—"

"If I learn that you've just been slandering her—"

"How have I *slandered* her?"

"—and torturing me, you will be damned, not only by heaven but by *me*!" He shook his hands free from my grip and with enraged intensity, began to walk away from me; five steps out, he turned again, and then again, resuming his hysterical pacing.

This, I had not planned: that his anger should turn on me, and not on Cassio. The stakes were changed dramatically. Othello had just made me one of the pieces in the game, and no longer the player controlling the board.

"In the name of *heaven*!" I shouted at his backside when his pacing took him away from me. "Do you have one *jot* of common sense? Othello, you are raving!"

Shocked that I was returning his anger with my own, he whirled around to stare at me.

With a sour, furious glance at Othello, I spat, "So it is not safe to be honest with your best friend? Even when he has *demanded* honesty of you? Thank you for that lesson! Suffer on your own, I can't *risk* caring for you anymore. *Farewell.*" I turned and stormed down the wall walk, my heart beating so fast and loud I was sure it must be audible.

Othello ran up behind me; I readied myself to fend off a blow from behind, but his hand merely came to rest on my shoulder. "No, Iago, stay," he said gruffly. "It's good that you are honest with me."

"I'd rather be wise; being honest gets me beaten," I huffed, coming to a stop and half-facing him.

Othello sighed, and leaned against the low wall. In a confessional tone he said, "Iago, my brother, I am in a terrible state. I think my wife is faithful, then I think she is not. I think you're a good man for warning me, then I think you're not. I need to know one way or the other. This is *torture*, what I am feeling now, it is a physical sensation"—he began to grab at his own body, as if his clothes were biting him—"it feels like I am being knifed and poisoned and burned and drowned all at the same time. I won't endure it, I need *proof!*"

I sighed. "I wish I'd never said anything to you."

I almost meant that now, given how it had turned against me. But we were under way, so I had to stay in charge—or die. Othello had not, in fact, made me a game piece on the board; I had done it myself, by being too good at my enterprise. I had accidentally created for myself an extreme challenge. Seeing what I'd already accomplished, I was confident I could accomplish this as well. "You say you want proof?"

"Want it! No, I'll *have* it," Othello replied with vicious speed. "From *you.*" The threat that had quieted a moment earlier lit up again in his expression.

"I'll do my best," I said. "But . . . how? What are you expecting? If they are having an affair—which I am *not saying* is the case—what do you want me to do? Arrange for you to *see* them, *watch* them, while he mounts her?"

Othello groaned, turned away abruptly, and vomited over the parapet. I tried not to think about whatever or whoever was below us.

"I do not know how to make that happen, General," I pressed on. "Catching them in the act is the only *absolute* proof there is, and how am I to manage that? No matter how hot they may be for each other"—here Othello groaned again, weakly, his forehead resting on the parapet—"if they are hot, which I have not said they are, even if they're rutting like animals"—another groan. I *wanted* to upset him now; the whoreson had *attacked* me—"they would not be fools enough to do the act where we might come across them in the thick of it."

He turned back toward me, looking ill. I continued to chatter as if I didn't notice.

"You are demanding me to prove something that I myself merely suspect. I cannot do that—I *will not* do it. If you require evidence one way or another, you must be satisfied with circumstantial evidence."

"Give me a solid reason to believe she's disloyal," he insisted sourly. "You owe me that at least, for putting this thought in my head."

I shook my head, grimacing. "I do not like that assignment," I said, with absolute sincerity. "But since I am caught up in this affair now—because I was foolish enough to look out for your interests—I suppose I'm stuck with it. All right then." I pursed my lips together and wished I were anywhere but here. A thousand thoughts flashed through my mind before I spoke again.

His fury was too dangerous to let it remain fixed on Desdemona; I had to make this about Cassio and myself. Only one of the two of us could now come out of this well. It had begun as a battle for the lieutenant's sash; suddenly it was a battle for our well-being, possibly our lives. I would never have wished Cassio dead, nor did I now—but if I had to pick one skin to save, naturally it would be mine.

However, no simple hint, or implication, or manipulation of the truth could possibly deflect Othello's astonishing and monstrous passion.

It was time to be a real Venetian: it was time for outright lies.

Chapter 44

"A FEW NIGHTS AGO," I began, "Emilia was not feeling well, and did not want me near her lest I catch her illness. So I stayed in Cassio's room overnight. I had a terrible toothache and I could not sleep. Cassio was dead to the world, but he was also talking in his sleep." This was not the best story to tell, since Emilia could so easily gainsay it, but nothing else came to mind. However skilled I was turning out to be at deception, I was not actually a very able liar.

"Get to the point," Othello said with dull misery.

"Yes. So. In his sleep, I heard him say, *Desdemona, darling, we must be wary and hide our love.*" I said it without any inflection, a dutiful recitation. Othello started; I ignored him. "And then he grabbed my hand in the bed, and said, *sweetheart,* and then he kissed me—" Othello scrambled to his feet and stared at me, horrified. I continued, as if oblivious. "And then he put his leg over mine, and sighed, and kissed me again, and said, *Damn that Moor.*"

Othello looked as if he had been stabbed. He wrapped his thick arms around his middle and turned again to vomit over the parapet. This time it was dry heaves.

"Othello, it was but his *dream,*" I said. That part of me that still loved him wanted to chastise and counsel him: *You fool, why do you believe so easily? When did you become so pathetically credulous?*

"I'll tear her to pieces!" he shrieked abruptly toward the sea.

"No, you will *not*," I said, shocked. "Do not be rash. It's just a dream—dreamers often lie. And it was *his* dream, General, not hers. We have *seen* nothing. Desdemona herself is honest, I am sure." Could I use the handkerchief to damn Cassio but not Desdemona? I had no choice but to hazard it. "Do you recall that strawberry hand-kerchief you gave your wife?"

"Of course."

"That handkerchief—or something very similar to it, but I'm sure it was your wife's—I saw Cassio wipe his face with it this morning."

Something terrible happened to Othello then. His face went slack, and all the light went out of his eyes. He stopped breathing for a long moment, and then gasped, without energy, to take in air. His eyelids drooped, as if they would close without permission.

"If it's that handkerchief—" he said, his voice like gravel, and he could not continue.

The miscalculation on my part had been in thinking Othello's passion would rush through the same channels as mine. But mine was bent on Cassio, and his, on Desdemona. No matter how this enterprise might have unfurled, Desdemona would always have been Othello's target. I could only get to Cassio through Desdemona. Well then, so be it. I sent a passing plea to the patron saint of defenseless women—but I was proving capable of anything, so I could certainly redress the damage later. Somehow. Surely.

"*If* it's that handkerchief," I said somberly, "it speaks against her."

Othello stood bolt upright and shrieked toward the blue sky. "That *whore*! That *bitch*!" I looked around warily—the wind blew his words away, but the guards around the parapet could see that he was raging about something.

"General, please," I said, holding out a steadying arm.

He brushed it aside furiously. "Iago, watch me! All the love I ever felt for her: gone!" He blew into the air. "Blown to heaven! That's it, it's gone!" He pounded the flats of his hands against his chest. "Hate! That's all that is in here now is hate and vengeance! I will be *avenged*!"

"Calm yourself, General," I pleaded, even as I realized where this was going. A wave of dizziness almost knocked me over: that words, mere words, *my* words, could wreak such havoc . . . had I ever known another man with more power than I had right now?

"I want blood!" Othello shouted to the sky. "Blood, do you hear me? *Blood!*"

"I *beg* you, be calm," I said. "You'll change your mind when you are calmer."

"*Never,* Iago!" he declared furiously. "I am unbendable: no looking back, to find a love that has been mocking me from the beginning. There will be blood shed in punishment for this!"

He dropped to his knees on the parapet, as a sudden, terrifying calm washed over him. His placed his right hand over his heart and intoned:

"As the stars are fire, I hereby take a sacred vow to honor the words I have just spoken."

He began to rise as panic poked my gut. I could not believe how quickly this was happening, but it *was* happening, and I had to stay abreast of it. Seeing him in his full rage, I realized: the best way to steer this ship now was to make Othello captain of it. He was more engaged in it than I had ever expected either of us to be. He would not stay this angry—nobody could. And he would repent of this vow when he had calmed. But in the moment, the heady satisfaction of playing Aeolus and putting the winds into those sails . . .

As he began to rise, I pressed down on his shoulder. "Do not rise yet," I said solemnly. I knelt beside him, and took his hands in mine. "As the sun does move, let it witness here that Iago gives up his will, his wit, his hands, and heart, into Othello's service. Let my general command me, and I will obey without remorse, no matter how bloody the business." I said this looking down, as if in prayer. Now I glanced up to see him, and found tears in his eyes. He embraced me with the fervent warmth of an ally and friend. I had not felt so close to him since before Desdemona had plucked him by the sleeve in Brabantio's tile-plated room.

"Iago, do you mean that?" he said quietly.

"Of course I do."

His voice dropped to a whisper. "Then let me hear you say, within three days, that Cassio is not alive."

I knew I would not do it; I knew I would not have to. I knew he would rescind the order later, and so, there was no harm in agreeing to it now—but oh, was there great satisfaction to hear him ask it.

"My friend is dead," I said at once. "It's done at your request." A hesitation, a prick of conscience. Just to be safe: "But let her live."

Othello stood up abruptly and spat to one side. "Damn her, the harlot! Damn her!"

"Damn her, but don't kill her," I pressed.

Othello looked back at me, and held out a hand to help me rise. "Come inside with me, help me decide how to kill her."

"General—" I began, fighting real panic now.

He did not mean this, he did not really mean this, this was insanely irrational, he would calm down. But just as I had brought him so skillfully to this state, it was now my challenge to ease him back to reason—which surely I could do, as slyly as I'd led him here. I had total power over this man, and he had none at all over me.

"General, listen to me when I say—"

"Iago," Othello interrupted passionately, "you are my lieutenant now."

"I am yours forever," I said immediately.

I, Iago

Chapter 45

 was his lieutenant. It was achieved. I had earned it—and most thrillingly, I had achieved it by the exercising of a skill even greater than my military ones. Knowing now my capabilities, I was wholly confident of applying them to any project.

For example, and of greatest urgency: the banishing of all the chaos I'd so deftly summoned, so that the end result of this project was that I would be lieutenant, Cassio would not be, and there would be no evidence that I had made this happen. Before I could afford myself the luxury of gloating righteously, I had to put to bed the demons I had roused.

I knew I could do it. When it came to managing Othello, I knew now I could do anything. Which meant, despite the distraction of Desdemona and the impudent protrusion of Cassio into our lives, I was still the nearest to his soul. Desdemona held his heart, but I claimed a more immortal part of him.

And so, onward, to ensure I maintained that claim. Most importantly, I had to cover my tracks. I had said Cassio had the handkerchief; that meant Cassio had to have the handkerchief. If Othello searched his person or his room, it had to be there, or I would be known as a liar right off.

I did have the passing thought: what if Emilia were to hear that Cassio had the handkerchief, and came to wonder why? That was an easy fix: *oh, dear, I must have dropped it, and Cassio must have picked it up.* As innocent a story as her own.

Beyond that, how best to proceed? Knowing what I could get away with now, the exercise felt like a game of strategy, a living riddle, where I had the upper hand and yet had to learn the rules as I went along. There was no manual, no teacher, as there had been in the military training of my youth.

I had not expected Othello's savageness. He had vowed to kill his wife without having seen a shred of evidence, after repeatedly claiming that visible evidence was required to condemn her. I was certain that I could in time dissuade him; that was not what troubled me. What troubled me was how ripe he'd been for violence. I had never seen that side of him before, even in the midst of battle. It revealed an irrational, unstable quality that shocked me. Yes, I delighted in my ability to coax it from him—but that it was there *to be* coaxed . . . that was a new insight into him, and it troubled me. Genuinely. *Troubled* me. Perhaps a little as his friend, but very deeply as his officer.

I reconsidered what he had said while raging: that he was so distracted now, he would have to leave his post. I had dismissed this as a rant. Perhaps it was not. Perhaps he knew himself well enough to see the truth before I had—and perhaps he was correct. I did not want that to be the case, but if it was . . . if he was proving himself unfit for office, well then . . .

Given that I could will my way into a lieutenancy . . . why not a higher rank?

I WOULD NOT, then, soothe this storm. I would roil it into a tempest. If he had the fortitude of character that I had assumed of him for years, he would emerge victorious, with me beside him as his able lieutenant. If he could not fend off his own madness, then I was doing the Venetian army, and the entire Serene Republic, a service to reveal him. In either case, Cassio was out of my life; in either case, I knew I could prevent actual harm to Desdemona.

312   Nicole Galland

So now it came down to a match between my clearheaded reason and Othello's raging passion. If I took him down, it was for the wider good, as one fells an oak that has just begun to rot, without waiting for it to come crashing down in nature's course without control. But if he triumphed—as I hoped he would, and thought him capable— then he had proven his endurance and his worth, and I would once again respect him as my general and my friend.

I went down to the chamber level, to Cassio's fine, large room, in pretense of seeking him; finding him absent, I left the handkerchief in plain view on a chest there.

RELIEVED OF THE BURDEN, I took in some hours of wrestling and swordsmanship with my fellow officers in the outer yard. At dinner break, I ate with them at mess. Othello usually joined us for this meal; he was not here. Nor was Cassio.

"Is Lieutenant Cassio not eating with us?" I asked an artillery captain near me. I knew him—it was Bucello, the Brawny Lug from my Arsenal days. We had recognized each other our second day here. He looked unchanged with years; we had had very little to say to each other. As with Zanino and even Roderigo, our reunion held more weight for them than for me; for my closeness to Othello, I glowed with an aura of celebrity that made them want to emphasize their closeness to me.

Bucello gave me a strange look. "Of course Cassio is not eating here. He lost his commission."

"He still has access to the barracks. He has his own room."

Bucello snorted. "I doubt he's been sleeping in it much." He gave me a meaningful, slightly leering smile.

"Oh?" I said. "Has he been out carousing, drowning his woes in libation and lasses?"

He grinned. "There's just one lass, and I'm surprised she hasn't drowned *him* yet, the way the talk is going."

Something new and unsavory. Convenient. "Which lass are you speaking of?" I asked.

He smirked. Then his expression softened. "Oh, I'm forgetting you're a married man, so you haven't met the local ladies. This one is named Bianca. She's a pretty thing, a war widow, with her own house, and she rents herself out to the highest bidder. Usually just for an hour or so, or a night at the most—but after his disgrace, Cassio spent *four days* there without stepping out of the house even once!"

"And how exactly do you know this?" I asked, cutting the overcooked lump of goat meat on my plate.

"I was among the several fellows waiting for her to open up, so to speak." He chuckled. How charming to know Bucello was unchanged from adolescence. "Finally we all gave up and went on to a proper brothel. And then," he added, with an almost nostalgic laugh, as if this had happened long ago, "when myself and another, seeing him returned here, went to Bianca's, she said she would not have us, that she was in love with Michele Cassio and was saving herself for him!" He slammed his fist on the table and almost choked on a chuckle.

"Really?" I asked in surprise. "And does Michele know she feels this way?"

"Course he does." Bucello grinned, downing a huge mouthful of watery ale. "He's proud as a cock about it, but I doubt he returns the devotion. He just likes knowing he can move her. She gives it to him free now! And it's her only means of income!"

"So he talks about her," I said, chewing on the goat meat and hoping for Emilia's sake that she received better midday victuals than I did.

"Talks? Boasts, really," Bucello said. "Laughs and brags about it. I suppose when you have ruined your chance to be Othello's right arm, you need *something* to feel smug about."

"Where does the lady live?"

He gave me the leering look again. "You want a little action? Your wife . . ." He saw the look in my eye and immediately dropped that thought. "I can recommend some skirts at a couple of the brothels," he said. "I'm pretty sure Bianca will not take in anyone but Cassio now, at least until she figures out he's playing her."

I did not need reassurance of my moral rectitude in destroying Cassio's career—but it was still pleasing to hear new reasons for it. The fellow was a cur. To a *war widow*.

"I am quite satisfied with my own lady, thank you, but I want to speak to Cassio, and if he's not here, I bet he's dining at her house."

BUCELLO GAVE ME directions to the place. I finished eating as quickly as I could, and headed out of the fortress gate, down to the broad paved road and through the passageway, into the township itself. I had only done this twice over the past week and did not have a very clear sense of direction yet. Bianca lived near the central market, not far from the palace—where Montano lived, and where Othello and Desdemona would probably move within the week, hopefully taking Emilia and myself with them.

Bianca's house was very small. I doubt it's where she lived while her husband was alive. A war widow. Emilia risked that fate; I could not bear to think she risked this consequence of it. It made Cassio that much more disgusting to me that he took advantage of this woman.

I rapped on the door, and a petite, sharp-featured woman opened the door. She was unexpectedly attractive and vibrant, nothing bloated or weary or resentful as so many prostitutes are. Her face was tinged just slightly with cosmetics, something I was not used to, as neither Emilia nor Desdemona used any. She gave me a disdainful look. "Who are you and why've you come?" she asked.

"I'm seeking a Lieutenant Cassio," I said. "I understand he might be here?"

She blushed—with pleasure, anger, or embarrassment, I could not say which. "Normally he would be," she said, "and I'm pleased to hear his fellow soldiers know to look for him at my house. He practically lives here." Given we'd only been on Cyprus for about a week, that struck me as presumptuous, but I kept my counsel. "However," she went on, "I haven't seen him since yesterday morning. If *you* see him, tell him . . . never mind, I'll go find him and tell him myself." She gave me a tight smile. "Excuse me, if that's all?"

"Yes. Sorry to have bothered you." I touched my chest in a wan salute, and turned back toward the fortress.

I had walked halfway through the market square when I almost literally bumped into Cassio, who looked extremely grim.

"Ensign!" he said in surprise, pulling up abruptly.

I smiled benignly at him and did not correct him. In fact, I greeted him heartily: "Lieutenant! I have just been seeking you out!"

He registered mild surprise. "Here in t— Oh, did you go to Bianca's?" he asked, with a sheepish yet saucy grin that very nearly made me slap him.

"Rumor had it you might be there."

He reddened slightly, and yet looked pleased with himself. "Wine and women. The ancient weakness of the Florentines," he said.

"Quite," I said. "Come back with me to the fortress. Impress upon Desdemona how important it is for you to speak to Othello. I've tried telling him myself, but he won't listen, he thinks I am too partial to you."

"I already asked her this morning," Cassio said. "You were there. You sent Emilia out to me. I'm sure the lady is already doing all she can."

"*She* might be, but *you're* not. Do you recall how you left her? You snuck away, as if you were guilty of a crime. Othello saw that and did not like it, so no matter what she said, you left a bad taste in Othello's mouth."

He grimaced. "Oh."

"Exactly. Oh. So come back with me now and try again. Your lady friend can wait; she seems entirely devoted to you."

A lascivious grin as I'd never seen before spread across his face. "Oh, yes," he said, and chuckled. Truly. A Florentine, chuckling. "She's devoted." He nudged me with his elbow. "Poor thing's besotted, actually."

"As besotted as you were your first night here?" I demanded crisply.

He wilted in reply.

"I'm only trying to keep you focused on your goal," I said. "I assume your goal is to be reinstated in Othello's good graces, and not to burrow yourself into a widow's nether regions?"

Now he reddened. "I forgot myself, Iago, forgive me. I embarrass myself."

"I'm only after your good name," I said, softening slightly. "So come back to the castle with me and help me to help you get it back."

TOGETHER, WITHOUT FURTHER conversation, we walked back up to the fortress, and straight to the scraggly lawn in front of Desdemona's dayrooms.

Here we found Desdemona and Emilia standing in the afternoon sun, staring into the darkness of their parlor with unhappy expressions.

"Is something wrong?" I asked on approach. The women turned toward us, and Cassio instantly went down on one knee, doffing the ostrich-plumed hat.

"My husband . . . ," Desdemona began, still staring into the building. She was paler than usual, and looked frightened. "My husband is not pleased just now. With me, I think."

"Is he angry?" I asked with stunning disingenuousness.

"He was just with us," Emilia said, sounding equally shaken. "He left, he went inside, and he seemed . . . very strange. Unsettled. He spoke rudely to her. Angry, yes, maybe."

I shook my head. "I did not know that man could *get* angry. It must be serious, perhaps a message from Venice? I'll go find him and see what's wrong."

Desdemona took a deep sigh. "Thank you, Iago, do so."

"I'll leave you to it," I said to Cassio and went inside. I did not even exchange glances with Emilia; I could not risk her reading anything amiss in my expression.

* * *

"DO KEEP IN MIND," I urged, "that there are acceptable circumstances for a man and a woman to be alone in private, and kiss each other—"

"This would not be one of them!" Othello snapped. "This would be an *unauthorized* kiss."

"But we do not know that such a thing even *happened*. You should ask your wife! I would ask Emilia, if I suspected anything. You have seen no proof at all, and I have only seen a handkerchief. And if I give my wife a handkerchief . . ."

We were standing almost exactly where we had all met up the day of arrival in Cyprus, on the small stone piazza between the Citadel, the passageway to town, and the harbor road.

After delivering Cassio back to Desdemona, I had sought Othello out within the walls of the fortress. I had not found him; I had gone into the town, and not found him; I had gone down to the port and seen him standing on the slope, staring out to sea. And so I had gone down to him and was coaxing him now back toward the fortress.

Lying by commission was uncomfortable and distasteful to me, and so I decided to sail a different tack, which I thought of as "the Venetian approach." Unlike outright lying (which I had previously thought of as the Venetian approach), this one pecked and clawed while pretending to massage and soothe. Just like the backhanded compliments and veiled slurs so common among the better circles of Venetian society.

"ONCE I GIVE the handkerchief to her, it's hers," I concluded. "And since it is hers, she may give it to anyone she likes."

"Her honor is hers too; does that mean she may just give *that* away?" he snapped.

I shook my head. "That metaphor does not hold. Honor is abstract, it's an unseen essence. You cannot tell by looking if somebody still has it or not," I said, dismissing him. "Whereas a handkerchief—"

"He had my handkerchief," Othello growled, his hands curling into fists.

"So what?" I demanded. "You do not know what that means."

He glared at me. "It means more than just his having my hand-kerchief, you know that, Iago, do not play the fool with me."

"You haven't seen it for yourself," I argued. "You're just going on what you've heard me say. What if I am lying to you? What if I am mistaken? What if I said I had seen him do you wrong? Or if I said I'd heard him say—I don't know, the things men say when they're having an affair—"

"Has he said something?" Othello demanded, eyes wide.

I released a reluctant sigh. "Even if he has, General, of course if he's put to it, he'll swear he never did."

"What has he said?" Othello demanded.

"Well, he said . . ." Oh no, more outright lying. I much preferred to tell the truth deceitfully. "I have no idea what he said."

He grabbed my arm and shook it. "What did he say? What?"

"Something about a lie, about lying—"

"With her?"

"With her, on her, something like that." I sounded flustered, and it was not greatly an act. My whole body rebelled against the act of lying, just as it thrilled happily at all these other newfound skills. In contrast to the other ways I had of getting a result, actually lying by commission was so crude.

Othello started breathing heavily. A sweat broke out on his face, and he waved his hands in small, nervous flutters, pacing around me. His anger turning inward, he muttered to himself more than to me. "Lie with her! Lie on her!" he growled. "And the confession . . . and the handkerchief . . . he'll confess, I'll make him confess all right, and then I'll hang him for it . . ." He smashed his hands together, as if smashing Cassio's brain between them.

I realized what was happening a heartbeat before it began: he was falling into another fit, as he had that day back in the Senate, years ago. By his own reckoning, I had saved his career then. I felt, among the growing morass of other emotions, a strange nostalgia for those early days.

I grabbed him to offer physical support; he was down a moment later, his body twitching, his eyes rolling back in his head.

I stepped back to take a look at him. Suddenly I felt exhausted. I wanted him to wake from this fit with no memory at all of what had happened over the course of the day. Good heavens, was this all one day? Had all this madness, all this dangerous ecstasy, happened over the course of this one day?

It was not even sunset.

"Othello!" I shouted. "Othello, can you hear me?"

At that moment, Cassio appeared.

IN MY ABSENCE, Cassio must have repetitioned Desdemona and then gone straight back into Famagusta to sweeten his woes in the arms of Bianca. Given how little time had passed, I surmised he had been sweetened very rapidly. "Michele!" I cried out, desperately trying to think of a way to prevent Cassio and Othello from meeting face-to-face, especially at this moment.

Cassio gawked to see Othello in this state. He ran close to us, crying out, "What's the matter?"

I held out an arm to restrain him going closer. "The general has fallen into an epilepsy."

Cassio grimaced awkwardly. "Should we do something? Rub his temples?"

Oh, he wanted so badly to be useful. He wanted to be present, the concerned healer, as Othello opened his eyes. *Not for your life*, I thought. Aloud, I replied, with casual authority, "You mustn't touch him, it has to run its own course. If you try to help him, it makes him worse, he foams at the mouth and rants."

That worked; Cassio backed right off. Othello groaned a little on the ground.

"Look," I said. "He's recovering already. I'd disappear if I were you, he'll wake in a moment, but you will not advance your cause by gaping at him when he's like this. I'll get him back inside to safety, but then I want to talk to you, so stay nearby."

He looked around worriedly. "I'll walk down to the bottom of the hill and then come back when he's gone—will that do?"

"Go just around the bend. I'll whistle for you when it's safe."

As he hurried down the roadway, I turned my full attention on Othello. His eyes were open; he was drenched in sweat. "How are you, Othello? I tried to break your fall—I hope you haven't hurt your head?"

He stared up at me. "Are you mocking me?"

"Am I mocking you? *Me?* Of course not," I said impatiently, helping him to sit up. "But with all respect, I wish you'd learn to take your fortune like a man."

"Did he say those things you said he said?" Othello demanded.

I sighed impatiently. "Be a *man*, sir! Do you know how many thousands of cuckolds have no idea they're cuckolds? Wouldn't it be better to know? I'd rather know, then at least I could take action."

"Smart man," Othello said grimly as I helped him to stand. He sighed heavily, straightened his clothes, and glanced back up to the fortress.

"Do not go back in yet," I said, on an impulse. He gave me a questioning look. "While you were lying here, Cassio came by. I convinced him to leave and made excuses for you. Honestly, it bothers me that you'd let your passion get the better of you so severely, but never mind," I added, when he glared wearily. "Anyway, I told him I wanted to speak alone with him once you were gone. I want to determine if he is having an affair based on a conversation with him while he is awake, not talking in his dreams, which does not count. So hide yourself over there"—I pointed to the gate where Roderigo had hidden, the day of our arrival—"and watch him as he talks to me about your wife."

"You cannot be serious," he said, appalled. "Do you think he will do that? Just . . . talk openly about how he is cuckolding me? The whoreson! The damned whoreson!"

"Calm yourself, General," I said sternly. "I do not *know* that he will do it. I would like, for your sake, to *find out.* But I can't do that if he knows you're here. Keep control of your emotions. Are you a man or a spleen?"

He shook his head with annoyance. "Only you have the allowance to talk to me that way, Iago."

"Well I'm glad somebody does, because you need it." I pointed at the gate. "Go over there, Cassio will be right back. Watch him. However much you trust me, you should not be relying on my word. I might be mistaken, or misunderstanding. You must only take as proof what you see with your own eyes. Yes?"

He nodded.

"So be patient, and just watch."

"I'll be patient, but when the time comes, Iago, I'll be murderous as well."

This was no temperament for an army general. It scared me to imagine what would happen—not right away, but over years, as this hidden serpent grew within him—if the army remained under the control of such a man. I had never seen this side of him. I did not believe that I could have drawn from him, so quickly and effortlessly, what was not already there within him. He was failing the test of character.

Perhaps it would be merciful of me to let him see that for himself. I would push him a little harder. This morning, he had declared himself unfit to rule the army—perhaps he had been right. If he continued in this vein, then he was *definitely* right—and it was a service to everyone, including him, to make that plain.

"Do everything as it is timely," I said vaguely. "Will you withdraw?" I pointed to the opened city gate behind which Roderigo must have spent the better part of three hours just yesterday. Othello crossed to it and disappeared between it and the wall.

I whistled through my teeth. A moment later, I saw Cassio's tall, stately form appear around the bend as he walked briskly toward me. For some reason I thought of the first moment I had seen him, back in Venice. It had been annoying then, how very handsome and dapper he looked. He still looked handsome, but no longer dapper. Even the ostrich feather seemed to droop at its master's fortunes. Well, he should not have had those drinks. He was too weak-willed, and he paid the price for it. The revelation of that too I now considered my duty to the army and the state.

"Lieutenant!" I called to him as he approached. "How are you?"

"I feel even worse for being called lieutenant, when I'm not one," he replied, moping beside me now.

"Push Desdemona and you'll be sure," I advised.

"I doubt she's trying very hard, and I cannot blame her," he muttered.

I lowered my voice and whispered to him, slyly, "Too bad it's not up to this Bianca of yours to plead on your behalf."

He smiled then, in that knowing way a man smiles when he knows a woman wants him. "That's true enough, poor thing. I think she's in love with me."

"I heard a rumor in the officers' mess yesterday that she's telling everyone you'll marry her. Is that your intention?"

Cassio immediately burst into laughter. There was a swagger in the laugh, which suited my purposes and also made me more disgusted with him.

"She thinks I'd marry her? I'm just a customer! I'm a Florentine gentleman, Iago, do you really think I'd marry a whore?"

"I'm just telling you what I heard," I protested.

"You did not hear that." He chuckled.

"I swear I did, or call me villain," I said, smiling along with him.

"The little monkey made that up herself." He grinned. "She thinks herself higher than she is, and more desirable too—I certainly never gave her any cause to think that I would *marry* her. That's too much. But you know, everything she does is too much—"

His tone was dropping again, into a confidential one implying he was about to share a naughty yarn. I shuffled a few steps closer to where Othello was hiding, hoping he would hear. Cassio followed my movement without even realizing it, so I took a few more steps closer to the wall.

"If I'm out of her sight for more than an hour, she follows me," Cassio began. "Everywhere. She's even threatened to come up to the fortress, like the common women! A few days ago, I was down by the port, talking to some Venetians, and she appeared out of nowhere, just walked right up to me while I was in the middle of a conversation, and did *this*—"

Laughing lightly, he threw his arm around my neck and sagged his weight against my body. I stepped back in surprise. "Michele—" I said delicately.

"I'm not exaggerating." He chuckled. "She threw all her weight on me, and started weeping and sighing and taking huge deep breaths, pushing her tits right against me." He laughed again. "I could not believe the scene she made! But good heaven, if she's telling people I want to marry her, I'd better cut the whole thing off. It's getting out of hand."

"Indeed it is," I said, looking over his shoulder and hardly believing what I saw. "Here she comes now."

Chapter 46

CASSIO SPUN AROUND to look into the passageway. It was the woman I'd seen in the house, but with more cosmetic embellishment on her face now, and dressed to reveal far more of her slight form. She very nearly had steam coming out of her nostrils, and she was marching through the underpass as if she were a soldier.

For Cassio, this was an inconvenience. For me, it spelled potential catastrophe: Once Othello saw her, and her behavior toward Cassio, he would probably realize this, not Desdemona, was the woman Cassio was speaking of. And then I'd be in trouble for trying to convince him otherwise.

So the attractive young woman walking toward us was my undoing. And I could not think what to do.

"Look at her," Cassio muttered to me. "I, marry *that*?" He raised his voice as she exited the passageway and approached us. "What are you up to, shadowing me everywhere?"

This monkey might be a prostitute, but she had the backbone of a warrior. And she was furious. "The devil take you!" she shouted.

And then she did something I could not have expected, something that once again assured me the gods themselves were overseeing my enterprise:

From her bodice, she pulled out Desdemona's handkerchief, with the little strawberries on it, and waved it furiously in Cassio's face. "Where did this really come from? I am such a *fool*! That was a likely story about your finding it in your chamber and bringing it to me. This handkerchief comes from some finer mistress of yours, and you want *me* to copy it, so you can make a gift of it to someone else? That's it, isn't it! Well, I do not want it. There!" She smacked it so hard against his stomach that he nearly doubled over. "Give it to your hobbyhorse, I'll none of it."

The mocking Florentine had vanished; in his place was a simpering lover wanting to make his mistress happy. "Sweet Bianca," he crooned, reaching down to grab the handkerchief where it had fallen. "Calm down, sweetheart. Calm down!" He straightened, took her face between his hands, and kissed her on each cheek, and then her lips.

Bianca pulled away from his kiss, still glaring. "That's better. A *little*," she said in a steely voice. She gave him an appraising look; she had yet to acknowledge my presence, although she seemed highly aware of me as spectator. "I *suppose* you're welcome to come to supper tonight." The steel softened, and she graced him with a coquettish look. "If not tonight, whenever you're prepared to." She snatched the handkerchief from his limp grasp and marched back through the passageway.

Emilia and I had our differences, certainly, but from what I could tell, ours was by far the happiest and healthiest coupling on all of Cyprus.

"You might want to go after her," I said.

He sighed. "Yes, I better; she'll start screaming about me in the streets otherwise."

I nudged him in the arm. "Will you sup with her?"

He blushed slightly, and looked sheepish. "I intend to. She makes it worth my while if I stay after."

"Go on then," I counseled. I wanted him out of reach before Othello left his hiding place.

Cassio ran after her; I saw him catch up to her just as she exited the passage and the sunshine lit her brightly again.

That had turned out better than I ever could have devised. I knew the effect it would have on Othello. *Men judge more by appearance than reality, for sight belongs to everyone, but understanding only to a very few.* Machiavelli. Ironically, a Florentine.

I heard Othello step out of his hiding place.

"How shall I murder him, Iago?" he demanded.

I ignored that. Nobody was murdering anyone, any more than we really killed each other in fencing practice.

"He laughed at what he does—did you see that? And did you see the handkerchief?" I added, in genuine amazement.

"Was that mine?"

"Absolutely," I said calmly. "And look what he did with it—he gave it to a whore!" I was about to go on about how clearly Desdemona was as wronged by Cassio as Othello was by both of them—therefore giving Cassio twice as much blame, and putting Desdemona in half as much trouble—but Othello interrupted me:

"I want to kill him slowly. I want to spend nine years doing it." He growled. "A fine woman, my wife! Fair! Sweet! The very model of virtue!"

"Forget about that," I said. "Just let that go."

"I will let it go, and her too—I'll let her go to rot and perish and be damned! She will not live the night! I tell you, Iago, my heart is turned to stone." He smacked his palm against his chest. "I strike it and it hurts my hand."

I was about to point out the irony of a stone-hearted man being eaten up with passion. I wanted to see if he had any sense of humor left. If he did, there might be hope for him. But as I opened my mouth, the stony-hearted man crumpled over on himself with a new emotion: grief.

"There is no sweeter creature in the world," he said, his voice cracking.

"Stop this," I begged. "If you love her that much, forgive her. Or at least, *confront* her first."

"I won't! I'll hang her," he announced. "I must not love a loathed enemy. Of course I'll hang her—but the fact that I'll hang her, and rightfully too, does not mean she isn't a remarkable woman. She could charm the savageness out of a bear—"

But can she charm it out of you? I wondered.

"Oh, but the pity of it, Iago. Oh, Iago . . . the pity of it, Iago."

This was getting tiresome. "If you love her despite it all, then let her be. If she *is* unfaithful—*if* she is—you're the only one it touches."

"I'll chop her into pieces!" he shouted to the sky. He grabbed both my arms above the elbows, his face inflamed with passion. He was frightening. "Get me poison, Iago," he said. "I'll do it tonight. I'll do it before we're alone together in a room, I won't let her near me, she is so charming she'll unman me. It will be tonight, Iago."

I stared at him a moment in amazement. I had never once wished Desdemona dead, but I had wished her out of my life, and here he was, offering exactly that. By *heaven, I'm talented,* I thought. This ability of mine was some new weapon that no army had ever thought to nurture and exploit. I was the most valuable man the army had. I could make this man, unflappable in battle and besotted with affection, determined to kill his wife on mere suspicion, and I'd achieved it in less than a day. That was extraordinary. I could do anything. Anything. I could bend any living creature to my will. The world was my oyster: Othello was intent on killing Desdemona.

Which did not mean I wanted Desdemona to die. I did not. So I could not give him poison; he would use it.

"Do not do it with poison," I said, thinking fast. He himself had said—and it was obvious to anyone who'd seen them—that her presence, her proximity, her touch, still had the power to undo his will. In my omnipotence, I would give her the power to save herself: "Strangle her in her bed," I said.

He would touch her, and he would melt; she might not come out of it unbruised, but she would survive it. He could never touch, actually *hold,* that flesh he was so enamored of, and destroy it. I had not realized it until today, but he was a man ruled entirely by his passions—and sexual passion burns hottest of them all. The very thing that made him want to kill her would be the thing that saved her: how sensuous he found her.

"In her bed," I insisted. "The very bed she has contaminated."

Othello blinked. "Good," he said approvingly. "I like the justice of it. Very good."

An alarm sounded from the fortress walls, announcing a ship approaching the port below.

A loud cannon shot exploded from the water in response.

We looked at each other with the same horrifying thought: *the Turks.*

And to myself, I thought, *Thank God.* My experiment, but a day old, was wearying and maddening; the harsh reality of war would slam everything back into perspective, and we could leave all this madness behind us.

Othello and I turned and ran up to the Citadel gate together, instinctively reaching for our swords.

Chapter 47

INSIDE THE CITADEL, we rushed together up to the keep tower. We burst out the door onto the very part of the wall walk where Cassio had let himself get so drunk a week earlier.

Outside the harbor bobbed a single light galley, with the lion of San Marco flapping on its pennant.

It was not the Turks.

"An envoy from the doge, Captain," said the watch, saluting Othello.

Othello almost sagged with relief.

"Thank you," Othello said, returning the salute. "Iago, I need you." He turned on his heel and headed back into the tower stairwell. I followed.

AN HOUR LATER I was in my bedroom, freshly shaved, in a new shirt and military dress. I stood before Emilia. Her eyes sparkled with tears. The lieutenant's sash was draped across my chest, from left shoulder to right hip.

"You look handsome," she said proudly. She held her hand out toward me and delicately stroked the sash. "It is a pity for Michele, but it should have been yours anyhow."

"Yes," I said. The sash sat well on me. How unfortunate so much madness had been required for this to come out right. I smiled at my wife and held my hands out in invitation. She moved toward me, pressed herself against me, and when I folded my arms tight about her, she embraced me too. Emilia's embrace was the best feeling in the world. "I love you like life," I whispered.

WE MET THE Venetian envoy in a formal audience above the sleeping quarters. The room was devoid of furniture but hung with tapestries made of the best silk I have ever seen outside of Venice. There were three to a wall, depicting glorified European images of the twelve months of the year. They were completely out of place here. February and August were both on rods and could be pushed open to lead into other chambers. I never learned where February led, but August opened up into the general's dining room.

The party that greeted us was six in number: two officials with two attendants each. Their outfits looked almost painfully gaudy and impractical compared to the military dress of the Citadel and the simple peasant garb of the city population.

Whether by design or coincidence, one of the envoys was Desdemona's uncle, Gratiano; not a senator but certainly a patrician, and one who could not have been pleased that his niece had run off with a foreigner. But he greeted Othello with all signs of good regard, almost more so than his own kinswoman. I could see from Desdemona's face that she was expecting greater warmth from Uncle Gratiano than she received. *Well honestly,* I thought, *you trick the man's brother and run off into danger with a savage. What did you expect?*

With Gratiano was a man named Lodovico, another patrician I remembered chiefly from gossip and parties.

Having greeted and kissed the cheeks of, saluted, or ignored all of us in the chamber, the party from Venice now turned to business. Lodovico held out a gloved hand, and an attendant opened a leather file, took out a sealed letter, and handed it to Lodovico, who then handed it to Othello. "The doge and senators of Venice greet you. This is the letter we were told to give you if you had defeated the Turks by our arrival."

Othello took the letter and ceremoniously pressed it to his lips. "I kiss the instrument of their pleasure," he said with exaggerated formality. His eyes flickered slyly in my direction, and the poignancy pained me: not so long ago, I had taught him to use that very phrase, and we had laughed like brothers. Now I was horrified to think myself kith to such a madman.

He broke the seal and unfolded the paper. We all watched him, spellbound. His eyes blinked, slowly, once. Then rapidly, several times. Holding the letter out with unbent arms, he pointedly turned away from the rest of us as he studied it. I willed myself to look away from him, and turned toward the visitors, intending to make conversation; Desdemona managed to do so first.

"What's the news from home, cousin?" she asked. She looked even paler than she had this afternoon, and slightly shaken.

"Welcome to Cyprus, sir," I said. "I'm very glad to see you."

"Thank you," Gratiano said, speaking to me rather than to her. She was crestfallen at being shunned. "How is Lieutenant Cassio?"

Desdemona and I, unexpectedly, exchanged uncomfortable glances.

"He lives, sir," I said, as neutrally as I could.

Both Venetians gave me a curious look; I allowed Desdemona the chance to address her kinsman: "Cousin," she said, taking a step toward Gratiano and laying one hand tentatively on his arm. He looked at it as if it were a small animal. She lowered her voice. "There's been a breach between him and my husband. But you will surely fix it."

"Are you sure of that?" we all heard Othello mutter, his back still to us.

"Excuse me?" Desdemona said tentatively

Othello immediately began to recite formal greetings from the letter.

"He's just reading something," Lodovico pointed out unnecessarily. "You were saying? A division between him and Cassio?"

She shook her head. "A terrible one. I wish I could fix it, poor Cassio is—"

Othello swore abruptly, his eyes still on the letter, his back still to us.

"Husband?" Desdemona said, notably more nervous. Othello ignored us all. "Is he angry?" she said quietly to me, sounding desperate.

"I think the letter has upset him," Lodovico said, almost off-handedly. "The Senate is commanding him home, deputing Cassio to stay in his place."

This was either the worst news or the best news for my plans; in the surprise of the moment, I could not work out which.

Desdemona breathed an enormous sigh of relief. "I'm glad to hear it," she said in a confessional tone.

Something snapped in Othello. He turned abruptly on his heels, threw down the letter, and stared furiously at his wife. "Indeed?" he demanded, as if he were accusing her of something.

"My lord?" Desdemona said, taking a step back on reflex. She looked down, and I could see the fabric of her sleeve tremble.

He took three slow menacing steps toward her. "I am glad to see you mad," he said, mockingly.

She tried to smile but looked near tears. "My sweet Othello, you mistake—"

He smacked her.

It was very abrupt, and very harsh, without warning—his arm came up, and he backhanded her against her right cheek with all the strength he would apply to a boxing strike. "Devil," he said under his breath, almost casually, and turned away.

Desdemona dropped, too stunned at first to make a sound; I knelt to help her up, out of instinct; Lodovico knelt beside her too.

I put an arm around her, and at my touch, she began weeping. "I did not deserve that," she said.

No, she did not. I felt righteous indignation toward the brute that hit her, that he should be so easily moved to strike out.

Lodovico, seeing I had her weight, stood up sharply and turned to follow Othello, who had crossed the room. "Good sir," he said, trying to keep himself civil. "Nobody in Venice would believe what I just saw." Othello shrugged, insolently meeting Lodovico's gaze. The patrician was astounded. "Apologize to her," he insisted, "she's crying."

"Crocodile tears," Othello replied contemptuously. Desdemona squeezed my arm to thank me, and then, not quite steady on her feet, took a few embarrassed steps toward her husband, holding her arms out hopefully. "*Out of my sight,*" he said viciously, and turned away.

She took a ragged breath, and then tearfully, almost in a whisper, responded, "I will not stay to offend you." She turned to leave.

Lodovico looked at me in amazement, as if for help; I shook my head and glanced away. "General, I beg you, call her back," he urged as Desdemona reached to part the curtain into the stairwell.

"Madam," Othello said sharply, not looking at her.

Desdemona immediately turned around with a pleading, hopeful expression. "Yes, m'lord?"

He did not look at her; he looked rather at Lodovico, with an expectant expression. "Well?" Othello demanded after a moment. "What do you want with her?"

Lodovico blinked. "Who?" he asked. "I?"

"Yes," Othello said, both ponderous and impatiently. "You. You're the one who wanted me to have her turn back. As you see, sir, she can turn. And she can weep, yes, sir, she can certainly weep, and my goodness, but she's obedient. Go on, then, keep weeping," he said, glancing briefly at her and then back to Lodovico. "So I am commanded home." With a brief, withering glance at Desdemona, he ordered, "Go away, I'll send for you later." Back to Lodovico, entirely civil: "Sir, I will obey the mandate from the Senate, and return home immediately." And back to Desdemona, viciously: "*Get out of here!*"

Everyone in the room shifted their weight away from him. Des-

demona dissolved into fresh sobs and turned back to the heavy curtain; she nearly tore it off its rod as she pushed it away and ran into
the darkened stairwell beyond. Immediately civil again, Othello
again returned his eyes to Lodovico. "And yes, Cassio shall replace
me. Please dine with me tonight, Lodovico, and welcome to Cyprus."

He stormed out of the room through the same curtain Desdemona had exited, muttering to himself in a frightening tone.

A FEW ATTENDANTS nervously trailed after him; everyone left in
the room looked immediately to me, as if it were my job to make
everything all right. I was as stunned as they were. Words had done
this. My words. It is terrible to see a woman cry, but her tears would
dry soon; the import of the moment would last far longer than her
tears.

After a full breath of silence, Gratiano finally burst out, "I cannot
believe what I just saw. Is *this* the noble Moor the entire Venetian
Senate is so enamored of? The general who's famous for his calm in
the most dire circumstances?"

"He is much changed," I said diplomatically.

"Has he lost his mind?" Gratiano demanded. He almost seemed
angry that I was not showing more distress.

"It's not for me to judge that, sir," I demurred.

"Iago, he just struck his wife! My kinswoman! In front of all
of us!"

I nodded, grimly, my hands clasped together low before me,
looking down. "That was not good," I admitted.

"Does he do this all the time?" Lodovico demanded, horrified.
Trying to calm himself: "Or did the letter so upset him that he has
just lost reason, this moment?"

The dutiful lieutenant, I declined to meet his gaze. "It's not for
me to say, sir. I suggest you observe him and see his actions for yourself."

My delivery was perfect; the tone condemned Othello while the
words committed me to nothing. I glanced up when I heard Gra-

tiano sigh; he was staring in the direction Othello had departed, and he looked, above all, saddened.

"I was an admirer of his, despite the upset with my niece. I'm sorry I was so deceived in him," he said.

I turned to one of the gape-eyed attendants. "Show the gentlemen their rooms," I said. "If you will excuse me, sirs," I said, and headed through the curtain both Othello and Desdemona had taken. I went a few steps down the stairway, then stopped and leaned against the wall, pressing my cheek against the cooling stone, troubled.

Until that moment, I did not think it was possible for Othello to actually hurt his wife. I had assumed his vows were all passionate hyperbole, with no danger of execution. I was still confident he would not actually try to *murder* her, but my assumption that she was immune to danger . . . I was wrong. It further proved to me that a man of such extreme passion was a danger to everyone around him, including those he loved; but I did not like to see a woman weep, and I suspected there'd be more tears, and even wailing, before this ended.

And I knew now how it had to end.

When I began my project, it had been to exercise my sense of vengeful indignation, but the only outcome I had been attached to was the lieutenant's sash. Along the way, however—truly to my shock, absolutely unanticipated—I had uncloaked a demon lurking within my friend and general, and that demon, once revealed, had to be removed. I had genuinely hoped Othello could defeat the beast, but he was falling hourly more under its control. A man who cannot rule himself surely must not be allowed to rule an army. Already Lodovico was musing on that, I could tell. Othello risked demotion upon his return to Venice—rightfully so. I could never take public credit for unmasking his dangerous animus, but I could nonetheless benefit from it, and I intended to. I would be, from this moment until the moment a new general was invested, the perfect lieutenant.

And then I'd be the first Venetian-born general of the army in at least a century.

While my brother remained nothing but a silk merchant.

* * *

THE PLEASURE OF that thought allayed my bruised conscience for making Desdemona teary. I continued down the steps. At the bottom, I heard Emilia's familiar tread coming from the direction of Othello's room, and realized I had been expecting it.

"Iago," she said breathlessly when she saw me, and hurried to me. She threw her arms around me; I could feel her trembling. "You will not believe what—"

"I do believe it. I was there, I saw it," I said.

She shook her head, clutching me, pressing her face against my neck. "Not the slap. She told me about that. It's worse. He came storming into her room afterward, and the way he spoke to her . . . Please help her." She released me, grabbed my hand, and rushed me into Desdemona's room.

There were candles lit all around the periphery of the room. It was large, but spare; a bed, a few chests to hold her gowns, pegs on the walls for Othello's clothes; a table for her jewelry. Emilia had lit incense, the soothing smell of sandalwood and jasmine intended to calm the lady, but it was not working.

Desdemona's pale face was splotchy red and wet, and a bruise was reddening where Othello had struck her. It was the least attractive I had ever seen her. She sat on the floor, her back against the bed, knees drawn up toward her face like a frightened child.

"Lady," I said, moving toward her. "Are you all right?"

"I do not know." She sniffed. "I've never been spoken to that way." Emilia knelt down beside her on the other side, and stroked her hair.

"What's the matter?" I asked, gently laying a hand on her arm.

"Iago, you will not believe how he just spoke to her, he called her a whore. It was atrocious, it was heartbreaking," Emilia declared.

"Am I? Iago?" Desdemona asked between hiccupping tears.

" . . . Are you what, sweetheart?" I said, voicing more affection toward her than I had ever felt. It was an instinctual reaction to a fragile girl in pain; I'd have been as kind to a stranger on the street in need of solace.

She looked sickened. "The . . . the word she said my husband said I was."

"He called her a whore," Emilia repeated with brisk disgust. "A drunk beggar would not use that kind of language to his mistress."

Had I said anything to Emilia that would get me in trouble right now? I didn't think so. "Why did he do that?" I demanded, looking shocked.

"I do not know," Desdemona said, tearing up again. "I'm sure I'm not one." She turned to rest her head against Emilia's bosom for comfort.

"Don't weep," I said solicitously, patting her head. "Please don't weep. Oh, heaven," I muttered under my breath. I wished I were anywhere but here. I thought it was only Emilia's tears that undid me; I learned at this moment I was wrong.

I wanted to apologize to her for revealing what a monster her husband really was, but my apology would accomplish nothing; it would not make him less a monster. The truth would have come out eventually in any case; I was doing her a favor to help her see it so quickly, before she had devoted a lifetime to him. Her uncle was here to protect her from Othello's wrath, and she would soon be Venice-bound. How fortunate this happened now, rather than some few years in the future when she might find herself not only far from home but stranded alone with him somewhere.

While I was musing on this, Emilia was fuming: "She turned her back on every gentleman in Venice, she left behind her father and her country and her friends, to be with this man—and now he calls her *whore*?"

"Shame on him," I said with vigor. Did they have any inkling how things had come to this? "What's happened that he'd think that of her?"

"Heaven knows," said Desdemona, moaning. She turned away from Emilia and tried to wipe her face dry with her hands.

"I bet my life," Emilia declared, her face livid with anger, "that some nasty little jabbering sycophant slandered her to get ahead somehow."

I looked at her in bald alarm, my stomach churning with a panic I had not felt once before in all of this. Did she know? Was she accusing me? She stared right at me with fury on her face.

"Do not be ridiculous," I said, feeling faint and sounding, to my own ears, breathless. "There's no such man."

"If there is, God forgive him," Desdemona said mournfully.

"Let the *hangman* forgive him!" Emilia declared. "Let him rot in hell!" She stood up, too agitated to remain seated. She began to pace around the bed. "Why would he call her whore? Who could she possibly be whoring *with*?"

I relaxed a little. If Emilia did not know Cassio was the suspected paramour, then she'd have no reason to associate this with my ascension to lieutenancy. The panic in my stomach lessened slightly.

"He interrogated me about Michele," Emilia went on. The knot of panic tightened again. "But I put that *ridiculous* premise to rest." The knot loosened. "Besides—when does she ever see anyone? Where does she whore herself? And when? And *how*? Othello has been gulled by a villain. And by all the sainted angels," she went on, her voice rising as her righteousness exploded, "if I had a whip I'd lash the whoreson myself!"

"Emilia," I said sternly. "We are indoors; lower your voice."

"Oh, be quiet!" she snapped back. "I'll wager it was the same malcontent who drove you mad thinking I was sleeping with Othello!"

"Do not be stupid," I said brusquely. But she was, in a sense, correct: *I* was the one who'd made myself suspicious then, as much as I'd made Othello suspicious now.

"Please help me, Iago," Desdemona said, grabbing my hand. "What should I do to win him back? Be a good friend and go to him for me. I don't know how I lost him. I've never deceived him, or abused him, I've never even *looked* at another man."

There was another wave of tears. Oh, I wanted to get away from there. She was so pitiful, so desperate, so genuine. I patted her wrist.

"I cannot say"—she took in a loud, rasping breath—"I cannot say . . . whore." She gasped; for a moment I thought she would vomit on me. "It sickens me just to *say* the *word*, I could never do the *deed!*"

I put an arm around her and rocked her slightly. There was nothing I could do, to make any one of us feel any better in this moment. "Please calm yourself," I said gently. "It's just his mood tonight. The business with the letter offended him, and he's taking it out on you."

She sniffed and looked up hopefully at me. "If that's all it is . . ."

"I'm sure that's it," I said, as reassuringly as I could manage. I felt more than saw Emilia give me an appreciative, approving smile. I desperately needed her smile at that moment.

From down the corridor, a cornet sounded the call to supper. "There now," I said. "Go in to eat, your uncle will be there to keep an eye on you, and I'm sure your husband will mend his attitude. Never cry. All things will be well." I kissed her on the crown of the head, and stood up.

Emilia moved swiftly across the room to me; she wrapped her arms around me, squeezed me tightly but briefly to her, and kissed my cheek. "Thank you," she whispered. "God blesses you for that." I felt a wave of unease. *Thank God*, I thought, *thank God you do not realize.*

I FOLLOWED SLOWLY behind the women, needing time, ever more time than I ever had, to sort through my thoughts and plans. That brief moment of fear I'd felt, thinking Emilia suspected me of something nefarious—that had unnerved me. I knew to the depths of my soul that nothing I did was errant, that in the greater sense, I acted out of righteousness, however vengeful and indirect it seemed. But I also knew that I could not explain that to her while she was so emotional, and I hoped I would never have to.

I was ready to end this now. Immediately. Othello had proven himself to be beyond redemption. That happened when he struck his wife. I was content to leave it all to Gratiano now. I trusted him to remove Othello's title, and take his kinswoman home again to safety . . . Othello's behavior was so extreme, so far beyond any wrong that I had done or even schemed of, that truly I no longer considered this my project. The complaints now rested with the state of Venice. Let the Serene Republic put to bed the demons I had waked—

I WENT BACK UP that same stairway and turned a corner that would take me to the officers' dining hall. I was leaning my weight forward to take a step, when a sound well known to any soldier made me stop: somebody to my left had just drawn a dagger from its sheath. Immediately I found myself staring at a new, well-oiled blade, the business edge right at my throat and gleaming in the lamplight. It was held with a notable lack of soldierly confidence, however, which could only mean one thing.

"Good evening, Roderigo," I said. I had entirely forgotten his existence. "Is something wrong?"

The blade was lowered with a jerk, and my childhood friend stepped out of the shadows, into the corridor itself. He was furious. He grabbed my collar with one hand and poked the dagger against my collarbone, hard enough that it hurt even through my leather jerkin.

"You have not been honest with me, Iago," he growled.

I tried to give him a disdainful look. My heart was pounding so hard I could hear it in my ears, as if the sound came from somewhere else. The attack itself hardly accounted for this; I knew I could disarm him easily if I had to. What frightened me was the rude remembrance that I had a rogue actor in my drama, and the realization that he could do a lot of damage.

"What are you talking about?" I asked with incredulity.

"Every day, all week, you've put me off with some excuse or other!" He was so upset, I was reminded of my darling-faced six-year-old friend. But the six-year-old had not been armed. "I'm *sick* of it, I'm *through* with it, you're *obviously*—"

"Will you be quiet a moment and listen to me, Roderigo?" I said urgently, in the voice that had served me so well with him our first decade of friendship.

"I've listened too much already," Roderigo shot back, waving the dagger in my face. He rested it once more against my collarbone. "And your words have precious little to do with your actions, anyhow."

I made a hurt expression. "That is unfair."

"It may be unfair but it's the truth," he spluttered. "The jewels I gave you to deliver to Desdemona would have half corrupted a *nun* by now, but for all your claims that she delighted in them, I've yet to receive one moment of her time or attention."

Well, *yes.* Roderigo's jewels. I was admittedly amoral regarding Roderigo's jewels. I had been stowing them away to give Emilia, on the grounds that Roderigo wouldn't miss them and Desdemona wouldn't want them. In fact, I had afforded Roderigo priceless pleasure by letting him imagine what might become of Desdemona's appreciation.

But I had wanted the jewelry for Emilia because I'd feared I could never afford such finery for her. Now that I was a made man, I did not, in truth, need what Roderigo had so trustingly given me. If I had to, I would just give it all back. But only if I had to.

"Very well," I said, in a placating voice.

"No, it is *not* very well," Roderigo snapped. "If I did not know you better, I'd think you were leading me."

"Very *well*," I repeated, sounding slightly desperate. I glanced down at the dagger with exaggerated nervousness.

"I'm telling you it is *not* very well!" Roderigo nearly shouted in response. I gave him a warning look and gestured at his clothing: he was dressed as a common soldier, and he knew as well as I did that he'd be in trouble if he was found in the general's personal quarters. "Listen to me," he hissed, lowering his voice but pulling my ear nearly to his mouth. "I will make myself known to Desdemona. If she returns my jewels, I will stop hounding her, I'll even apologize for what I've done so far. But if she does not return them"—here again, with a complete lack of confidence, he waved the dagger under my nose—"I will seek satisfaction from *you!*"

"Very well," I repeated, holding up my hands, as if I were afraid he'd have the balls to use the dagger. "You have spoken, and I've heard you!"

"And I mean what I say!" Roderigo announced, shaking the dagger, trying so obviously to feel dangerous.

I could not continue to pretend to be afraid of him when I wasn't. Instead, I chucked him on the shoulder nervously and lowered my voice to speak conspiratorially: "Why, *now* I see there's mettle in you, Roderigo. I really was not sure before. Give me your hand." I gently pushed the dagger down from my clavicle and reached to take it from his grip. "Your complaint is entirely understandable, but I've only acted in your interest here."

"I fail to see any evidence of that," Roderigo said, jerking his hand away from mine and returning the dagger to its very disagreeable spot near my throat. He was a danger because he had no idea what he was doing. He could slit my throat almost without meaning to, if he lost his calm again.

"I agree it does not look like that," I said quickly. "Your suspicion is not without judgment. But, Roderigo, if you have purpose, show me tonight, and if you haven't gotten what you want by tomorrow night, I'm yours to kill."

He frowned and looked uncertain. Then he grabbed me by the collar again and jerked me toward him—nearly impaling me on the dagger without realizing it; I deflected a wound by shifting my body perpendicular to his grasp. "Well, what is it?" he demanded. "Is it reasonable, or is this some new nonsense scheme of yours?"

"Listen to me," I said. "There is a special commission come from Venice, to replace Othello with Cassio."

As soon as I said these words aloud, a horrid realization struck me: the Senate, not knowing Cassio had been demoted and I was his replacement, had promoted him instead of me. What if, because his demotion and my elevation had been ordained by a man who was clearly not rational . . . what if they undid all that I had worked to gain? What if they replaced Cassio as lieutenant and made me once again an ensign? They were in essence doing that already by putting Cassio in charge of Cyprus. Damn that Othello—why could he not maintain a veneer of sanity until the Senate had been properly informed that Cassio was shamed and I was elevated? Now I would have to get Cassio demoted a second time, and the one weapon I had to use against him—drunkenness—well, he would not make that mistake again.

Roderigo was gaping at my news. "Is that true?" he demanded. I nodded. He thought a moment. "That means Othello and Desdemona are heading home to Venice." He gave me a warning look. "If I do not get satisfaction here, I most certainly will when we're all back home."

"No, no, you misunderstand," I said. "Othello's being sent to Mauritania and Desdemona goes with him. The only way to keep him here is by some accident, like the removing of Cassio."

"What do you mean, 'the removing of Cassio'?" Roderigo asked. I felt his grip on my shoulder soften.

"By making him incapable of taking Othello's place," I said. Roderigo still looked cautious. Knowing he would not be capable of it—but that he would be willing to try, and thereby do just enough damage—I explained impatiently, "By knocking his brains out."

Roderigo involuntarily let go of me. "You would have me do that?" he demanded, flustered. I knew the man so well, I could tell exactly what ingredients made up his mood right now: he was morally offended, but this was offset by the manly thrill that I—his soldier friend—would think him capable of such an act. Roderigo was the perfect man to do a job I just this moment realized needed to be done.

"If you want to do yourself a favor, then yes, I think you should consider it," I said dryly. I once again reached for his right hand; he let me take it this time, and I very firmly lowered it so the dagger was nowhere near me. "You should know, Roderigo, I heard something from one of the envoys, something touching your business very directly. I am unclear on all the particulars, but it has something to do with Cassio's family and the pepper trade." Roderigo's eyes widened in alarm. "I just heard it tonight, and I planned to tell you more as soon as I could get better information in private. I know how much of your trade you had suspended to come along to Cyprus—"

Roderigo looked horrified. "The whoreson," he whispered. "I know exactly what it's about. His family must be the one trying to buy the loyalty of my Egyptian connections."

I was grateful to him for so conveniently informing me what lie I was to tell him. "I can get you details within the hour. Speaking of whores, Cassio spends a lot of time with one, named Bianca, and he'll be eating at her house tonight," I said. "He doesn't yet know about the honor the Senate has given him. I can show you the place and you can jump him anywhere between her house and the fortress. I'll follow him and back you up if you need help; between the two of us, he won't stand a chance. All right?" I said it as casually as I could, hoping to impress upon him that it is not such a momentous thing to plot a man's death.

I was confident he would not kill Cassio. I knew he did not have the skill, even if he thought he had the stomach. The goal was not to murder Cassio, but to render him useless as a soldier. "Roderigo," I said, patting him arm briskly. "Do not stand here looking amazed. I'll find the envoy who had the news, and meet you in an hour with the details. But it's suppertime now, and I have to make my excuses at the high table first, so please put away your dagger and let's get on with our evening—time's wasting."

Roderigo gave me a surly look. "I want to hear more about this pepper business."

"And you will," I assured him. He sheathed his dagger.

Chapter 48

I HAD TO HOPE Roderigo's fear of Cassio—that he was secretly en-meshed in the Alexandrine black market in pepper—posed a serious threat to Roderigo's livelihood. Even this would not compel Roderigo to kill Cassio, but it would compel him to think he was up to trying. That's all I needed. Then everything would work itself out well:

If Roderigo distracted Cassio, I could safely attack Cassio from behind, and wound him in some way that would end his soldiering days without endangering his life—a sliced calf tendon, for example. I knew my skills and dexterity, especially in the dark; I could strike and then disappear unseen. Cassio might strike Roderigo and hurt him a little, but I knew I could get to Cassio before he reached Roderigo.

If Roderigo suffered some small wound? That was no catastrophe. First, it would make a good yarn to tell his sons, when he finally managed to sire some; second, he had it coming to him for being foolhardy enough to come along to Cyprus. Nothing he could say against me would be taken seriously when it was revealed he was personating a soldier. He would likely get just a hand-slap from Lodovico, who would be preoccupied with demoting Othello. Roderigo would be furious at me, so I would have to return all his jewels, and try to convince him the story about Cassio trying to buy the loyalty of Roderigo's Egyptian contacts was an honest misconception on my part.

Meanwhile, Cassio would be too wounded to remain in the army, and Othello would prove himself too unstable to remain in office. That left the new Lieutenenat Iago in an enviable position.

Yes, this was most tolerable.

WE MET AT MIDNIGHT, half a block from Bianca's pitiable house; Roderigo, having feasted on his own terror since I'd seen him, had convinced himself he had to put the Florentine down.

"Stay nearby, because you and I both know I'll probably blunder at it," he said, his hand on the sheath of a new sword. It matched the dagger he had used earlier. Roderigo had heavily armed himself since arriving in Cyprus.

"I will be right beside you if you need me, brother," I said and offered him my hand. The memory of our secret childhood hand-shake overtook my muscles, and I found myself initiating the ritual; Roderigo followed along with me, and a light danced briefly into his eyes that made me confident he could go through with this.

I felt myself the most magnificent theater-prompter. All the actors were in their proper places, and all would do exactly as I in-tended, at the moment I intended; then the actors would become the audience, for the desired effect would not be what any one of them expected.

"Do not think too much about it," I said to Roderigo as I slipped away into the shadows. "It's but a man gone."

"But a man gone," Roderigo echoed, trying to look brutishly casual, and failing.

We waited for Bianca's door to open, Roderigo standing in the market square, ghost-lit by candlelight that came from several win-dows of surrounding houses, myself secluded. As we waited, I admit, I had the thought that the most convenient thing for me now would be if by some strange chance, Cassio and Roderigo killed each other off. It would simplify everything. Then I could keep the jewels, and be certain of my military status, and never have to worry about either of them realizing they had been made fools of, and by whom, and plot to take revenge.

Such a fantasy does not mean I *planned* for it to happen that way, or even truly *wished* it to.

"I hear him coming," I whispered loudly toward Roderigo as the door to Bianca's cottage opened. There he was, back-lit, the ostrich feather bobbing.

"I see him!" Roderigo hissed. I prayed he would not make too much a fool of himself. He backed a few steps in the small plaza, as if this would somehow make him invisible.

Cassio, in a chipper mood from dinner, sex, and wine, had his guard down as he strode through the dim campo, in the direction of the fortress. I felt sickened watching him: here even in his deepest disgrace, his pretty face assured that he would have a pleasant enough life, and now *on top of that* he was about to be made the military ruler of Cyprus, for no good reason but that he'd helped a madman and a pretty ingrate to elope. The man could not even *duel* correctly. Oh, I hated him in that moment. I hated him more than I had ever hated anyone. I knew Roderigo would not succeed in even scratching him, but for a moment, I really wished my friend could take the Florentine's head off.

"Die, you villain!" Roderigo screamed. He leapt toward Cassio in the dark and brought his sword down with energy and a complete lack of precision, nowhere near Cassio's body.

Cassio—however much I liked to think of him enfeebled—was a trained soldier. His instincts were quick and accurate, and he had already drawn his own sword, engaged it with Roderigo's, and disarmed the Pepper King. He raised his sword again, prepared to kill.

I leapt out from the shadows and lunged at Cassio from behind. I intended a lengthwise cut down the back of his leg. I had not been in battle for months now, had not actually tried to damage human flesh. Perhaps I hesitated.

In the moment between my leaping forward and my reaching Cassio, Cassio himself raised his sword and then arced it so that it sang through the black night air of the campo to slice with thick, breathless meatiness into Roderigo's midriff. I heard a sickening shriek as my sword began its downward slash at the back of Cassio's knee. I tightened my grip on my hilt and slammed the blade down the length of Cassio's lower leg, somehow skirting all the blood. He fell screaming to the floor of the campo, and I dropped my sword and fled down the small side alley where I'd been hiding, his screams of pain echoing behind me.

I had to find a light and return again immediately, as if I'd just discovered them. And I had to keep them apart. Most of all, I had to see how badly Roderigo was hurt. I could not think clearly what I needed to do beyond that.

I went down the small alley and then followed it into another on the left, which in turn went back to the street that led into the market square. Here was an empty watch-station—the far end of a circuit that featured an alehouse at the other end—and there was a torch lit. I could take this torch and return to the square, as if coming to the aid of both men.

I had not intended Roderigo to be hurt so badly. He was supposed to be able to run off so that I could solicitously look to Cassio, and deliver him to the castle infirmary like the good friend I was. Just as soon as I'd determined that his wound was bad enough to keep him from ever soldiering again.

But now my childhood playmate lay bleeding on the paving stone in excruciating pain, and of course I could not leave him there. I found my feet breaking into a run despite myself, so anxious was I to get back there and keep the situation controlled.

As I approached the square I heard a confusion of voices. Loudest of all was Cassio's, crying out for a surgeon, for help, for a light, crying out that he was being murdered; under his voice was Roderigo's, saying almost exactly the same thing, but far more fearfully and tearful.

But there were other voices, and all of them had Venetian accents. As I approached the square, I saw Lodovico and Gratiano huddling together with their small mute collection of armed attendants. They were all at a distance from the two grasping prostrate figures on the ground, watching them as if they were a disgusting, captivating carnival display.

"Help me!" Cassio shouted at them angrily, holding his hand out; Roderigo lay curled on the ground a few yards off, moaning, "If nobody helps me soon, I'll bleed to death."

"They might be counterfeiting," Lodovico warned his companions. "It's suspicious that they're both lying there as if they're wounded. I don't think we should take a step closer to them until there are more people here to help."

I'd forgotten how contemptible I found Venetian patricians.

"What's going on?" I shouted angrily.

"Look!" Lodovico's companion said, pointing at me as if this were a play and he a child watching it. "Here comes someone now! He's even got a torch!"

"Who's there?" I demanded, holding out the torch in front of me and craning my neck to see around it. "Who is screaming?"

"We have no idea," Lodovico said. "We were just out for an evening constitutional."

"Help! I'm *right here*, for the love of heaven!" Cassio's voice hollered in the darkness. "*Help* me!"

I held the torch toward his voice. "What's the matter?" I called out. "I think that's Othello's ensign, isn't it?" said Gratiano.

"That's right," Lodovico said—they really were behaving as if they were watching a play. "His name is Iago, he's an excellent man."

Ignoring them, I moved closer to the two prone figures and waved the torch around. "Who's there? Who's crying out?"

"Iago?" Michele Cassio gasped. "Oh thank God, Iago, is that you? I'm badly wounded, give me some help!"

I knelt beside him, wondering with a sick feeling in the pit of my stomach how Roderigo was now going to fit into all of this. "Lieutenant!" I gasped, moving the torch to examine the wound I'd given him. Bloody gristle glistened in the light; near the top of the diagonal slash, something stringy—perhaps ligament?—showed. I had done an expert job. He would probably never walk again without a crutch. "What villains did this to you?"

Cassio was grabbing his leg, trying to staunch the flow of blood with his bare hands, which were slick and slippery now. He was weakening quickly. "I don't know," he grunted. "I struck one, I think he's here nearby, couldn't get away." He gestured toward Roderigo, who was lying in a puddle of his own blood.

"Treacherous villain," I spat in his direction, and then turned immediately toward the two patricians, wondering what the devil to do. This had suddenly become a nightmare. "Come over here and help us," I snapped at them.

"Help *me*! Over *here*!" cried Roderigo, in a failing voice.

Cassio grabbed my arm and shook it. "That's one of them!" he said, and with faltering strength, he pushed me toward Roderigo's form.

I resisted, and so I stumbled, slipping on the blood and landing nearly on top of the wounded man. Almost too weak to speak, Roderigo grabbed my arm and pulled me close to him. I still held the torch aloft, and I could see his face. Too well. His expression hurt my very soul. I remembered his face screwing up into tears that morning by the canal, when we were boys, when he could not believe my generosity for giving him my share of Galinarion's bounty. That was among my earliest memories of him, and now here he was making the same expression, in this last moment of our lives together.

He had lost a lot of blood. Battlefields teach you how to assess odds, and wounds. Given how far we'd have to carry him, with the burden of Cassio as well, even with the paunchy patricians' attendants as manpower . . . I closed my eyes and shuddered. He would not make it up to the Citadel alive, and there was no other hospital in Famagusta.

I opened my eyes and shook my head slightly, as if this would somehow calm him. It did not, of course, because he understood the meaning of the gesture. He sobbed, and grabbed my leather jerkin weakly. "No," he begged.

I put a finger to his lips and whispered, "Shshshsh." I would tell his parents some beautiful lie about his death. Over my shoulder, I sensed more than saw or heard the others looking over at us. How could I explain this? What if Roderigo, in the terror of his last moments of conscious life, blurted something out that gave too much away? I couldn't risk that. He was dying anyhow; he need not take me with him.

I tossed the torch away from me; it lay spluttering, but still lit, on the pavement. I reached over to Roderigo's right side, for his new Cyprian sword lying just out of his reach. *He is dying anyhow,* I told myself again. It was the truth. *You cannot murder a dead man.* I grabbed him by the bloody shirtfront and lifted his limp body off the pavement. "I will meet you someday in heaven, and explain why I am doing this," I whispered into his ear.

I STABBED MY oldest friend straight through the heart with his own blade.

I bent over close to him again from the intensity of the thrust, and his last conscious act was to grab the back of my head and pull it closer to his mouth. "Damn you, Iago," he grunted tearfully. "You inhuman dog."

I felt him shudder and then his grip released. I was so glad I could not see his face now, with the torch away from us.

"Kill men in the dark!" I shouted at his inert form, and let him go, trying to ignore how heavily his head smacked back down on the paving stones. I felt a dreadful pressure behind my eyeballs. "Where's the rest of the thieves? Why is this town so quiet? Somebody cry murder! There's murder in the streets!" I shouted, standing up. I spun around, Roderigo's sword in my hand, and pointed it directly at Lodovico and his companions, who were still cowering. "Who are you, anyhow? Are you here for good or evil?" I had not just murdered my oldest friend.

"Don't you know who we are?" Lodovico quailed. I had not just murdered my oldest friend.

I lowered the sword. "Signior Lodovico?" I said. I had not just murdered my oldest friend. You cannot murder a dead man.

"He, sir," Lodovico replied tremulously. "And Signior Gratiano."

"I beg your forgiveness," I said, bowing slightly, awkwardly. With the sword I pointed to the living wounded. "Cassio's here, hurt by villains."

"Cassio!" said Gratiano. "This is Michele Cassio?"

I ignored them both and returned to Cassio's side. I had not just murdered my oldest friend. "How are you, brother?" I asked in a hollow voice, a hand on Cassio's shoulder.

"My leg's cut," he grunted in pained response. "It feels like it has been cut in half."

"God forbid," I said. "Gentleman, light, get the light! I'll bind this with my shirt." As Lodovico scampered around the edges of the bloody scene to retrieve the torch, I reached for my collar to begin to untie my shirt. I had not just murdered my oldest friend. I would bind Cassio's leg. I would carry him myself up to the hospital in the fortress, and later, I would send somebody to collect the corpse of the stranger who had tried to murder him, but whom he—Cassio—had killed in self-defense.

"What's the matter?" a tremulous female voice called out from the far side of the plaza. I stopped untying my shirt collar, and spun around to look. Petite, ferocious Bianca stood silhouetted in her doorway, candle in hand, straining to see what was happening. "Who cried out?"

"Who cried out?" I echoed her sarcastically. "Don't you know your lover's voice?"

She gasped and darted barefoot across the plaza like a swallow. She skirted the growing pools of blood, circling halfway around Cassio, and then practically throwing herself down on top of him, screaming, "Oh, Cassio. Oh, Cassio, Cassio, Cassio!"

The last thing this situation required was an hysterical woman, especially one I felt both judgmental and protective toward. That was a complication completely uncalled for. How could I get her to go away?

"Be quiet," I said sharply, and tried to pull her off him. "Cassio, do you have any idea who would have come after you?"

"No," the Florentine said limply, growing weaker.

"I was coming after you," Gratiano said idiotically, moving closer in. "But only to send for you to the castle."

I heard a shuffling noise in the background; glancing around the plaza quickly, I saw that all the yelling had finally garnered some attention. The town watch in livery, and other men in cloaks thrown over bedclothes, were gathering around the edges of the campo, most with lamps or torches, perhaps a score in all. I elbowed Bianca away from Cassio so that she knocked into Gratiano. "My shirt won't do it, we need a tourniquet. Does anybody have a garter?" I called out to the newcomers. "Is there a sedan chair anywhere? We need a sedan chair to get him up to the hospital."

"He's fainted," Bianca lamented, as if he had just died. She tried to reach over me to get back to him. My clothes were stained with Roderigo's blood, and now her gown was smeared too. "Oh, *Cassio!*"

"I think this strumpet protests too much," I said warningly. "It's enough to make me suspect her involvement in his injury." I pushed her away and reached to slap Cassio's face sharply. "Stay with us, Michele! Hold on yet!" I looked around, aware that I was the only one in control of the situation, but equally aware the situation was beyond my control. I stood up and stepped toward the corpse. "The torch," I commanded, holding out my hand. Lodovico immediately moved to give it to me. "Does anyone here know this face?"

I could hardly bear to, but I held the torch out so that it illuminated the dead man's face. When I saw him, so clearly dead and so clearly—despite the absent tresses—Roderigo, I groaned involuntarily. "Roderigo," I grunted. "Oh, God, no—but yes, it is, it's Roderigo."

Gratiano took a timid step closer. "What, Roderigo Rosso, of Venice?" he cried out, amazed. "The spice trader?"

I held the light closer to the corpse but allowed myself to look away. He was dead because Cassio had wounded him past help. You cannot murder a dead man. "Did you know him?" I asked. I would write his mother a letter, telling a beautiful lie of how he met his end. I knew how to lie now; I could at least use that skill for kindness.

"Know him? Of course I knew him! He was my neighbor!"

I blinked several times quickly, stalling for time. If they were neighbors, was there any possibility Gratiano might know something damning about my involvement in Roderigo's life? "Signior Gratiano, is it?" I said, as if Lodovico had not already mentioned him by name. I bowed. "I beg your pardon, sir, this bloody accident has deprived me of my manners, I'm very sorry. I'm Iago, Othello's new lieutenant." It was the first time I had made the claim aloud.

"I'm glad to see you," Gratiano said indulgently. That anyone could sound indulgent in these circumstances was ridiculous, but the poor frightened noble was clinging desperately to what he knew.

I pressed passed him and back to Cassio. "How are you, Cassio? Stay awake! A chair," I called to the air at large—and to my amazement, Lodovico was suddenly beside me, with a sedan chair he had dragged into the plaza. It must have come from the slowly growing crowd of watching men. It was primitive by Venetian standards, but nicer than anything I'd seen upon a battlefield: an actual chair strapped to two long poles, but at least the chair had arms to hold on to for balance.

None of the Cypriots dared to move in close to us within the piazza; they all stood warily on the outskirts, including the men of the watch, some of them Venetian. Even the patricians' attendants stood gawking. As Lodovico awkwardly helped me to raise up Cassio, Gratiano kept gaping at the corpse beside him. "Roderigo," he said, sighing mournfully.

"Yes," I said brusquely, wanting him to shut up. "Yes, it's him. Might you help us with the chair, sir?"

Between the three of us—mostly me—we pulled Cassio onto the sedan chair; he was in a twilight state as I curled his fingers around each arm. We were impeded in this process by Bianca's sobbing hysterically and trying to pull us away from his body so she could throw herself against him. Remembering how he'd spoken of her earlier, I was sickened for her sake—he did not deserve such devotion from a dog, let alone a human being. Between the blood still on my jerkin and the blood smeared onto her, we rendered almost everybody bloodstained.

"Where are my men? Get him up to the fortress," Gratiano called out, suddenly in charge. His two attendants stepped from the crowd—now perhaps three dozen men—and lifted the sedan to carry it out of the campo. "I'll go with them and fetch the general's surgeon," Gratiano announced. He turned next to Cassio, who was struggling to retain consciousness, and was impeded, once again, by the sobbing prostitute. "Calm down, madam," he said. "Save your energy." I took her by the shoulders and pulled her, sobbing, away from the sedan chair as

Gratiano pressed, "Cassio, the man you killed tonight was a very dear friend of mine. What malice was between you?"

Michele Cassio was barely hanging on to this world. "Nothing," he said feebly. "I do not know the man."

Bianca tried to pull away from me, her slender outstretched grasping arms toward Cassio. "What are you up to?" I asked her sharply. "Gentlemen, take him up. Somebody take that one too," I added, with a gesture. Nobody wanted to touch Roderigo; there was so much blood, on him and around him. Who would have thought a lily-livered merchant to have so much blood in him?

Bianca continued to struggle against my grip. I would have let her free, but she was hysterical, and the evening was mad enough. I had to frighten her to silence. "You look very pale, lady," I said in an accusing tone, shaking her. She stared up at me, teary-eyed and abruptly silent. "What have you got to say for yourself? Where have you been all night? You came along quick enough when Cassio was attacked—did you have anything to do with it?"

Shocked, she stared at me even harder, and I was confident that if I let her go, she'd head straight back to her cottage and not come out till morning. I released her. She took one step back toward her home, but then a movement on the opposite side of the plaza caught her eye; she paused, turning to look, and I turned with her.

Pushing through the growing crowd of Cypriot men came a dark-haired beauty whose appearance at this moment made my heart break.

Chapter 49

"WHAT'S THE MATTER HERE?" Emilia cried out. And seeing me, with greater alarm still: "Husband, what's the matter?"

Oh, no. I would sooner anyone appear this moment but Emilia.

As she pushed her way through and came near, I grabbed her to me, to prevent her from seeing Roderigo's corpse.

"Cassio was attacked," I said softly in her ear. "Here in the dark. Roderigo was one of the attackers—"

"Roderigo?" she said, flabbergasted. "*Our* Roderigo? From Venice? Roderigo Rosso?"

"Cassio was very badly wounded," I said, still gently. Tightening my grip on her arms I added, "And Roderigo's dead."

Her entire body shuddered with the shock of it. "Oh no!" she gasped, her hands coming to her face. "Not Roderigo! And poor Cassio! What on earth happened?"

"I'm trying to find out," I said in a louder voice. "Emilia, will you help me find out where Cassio dined this evening?" I saw Bianca start violently at this, and releasing my wife, I turned on the war widow. "What, do you shake at that?"

She drew herself up straight. She was a fiery little thing. "He dined at my house, but I am not shaking."

"Did he really?" I said sharply, and took a step toward her, reaching my hand out. "Come with me, then, harlot, you've got some explaining to do."

Emilia was so shaken that she was not thinking very clearly. "Shame on you, you *whore!*" she snapped at Bianca.

"I am no whore," Bianca said with saucy bravado, hands on her hips. "I am every bit as honest in my life as you are. Which I realize may not be saying much."

There was a titter of nervous laughter among the men watching us. Emilia's eyes widened, and I saw her check an impulse to grab Bianca by the throat. "That's rich!" she snarled back.

I clapped my hands together. "Enough of this. I must get back to the Citadel and see Cassio attended to. You, lady," I said, with a threatening look at Bianca, "you better have a story for how you come to know Cassio so well, unless you were part of some plot to take him down. Emilia," I went on briskly, before Bianca could reply, "run ahead to the Citadel, tell Othello and Desdemona what's happened here."

She nodded and after a quick squeeze to my hand, immediately ran back the way she'd come. Lodovico followed her, not so quick on his feet. Bianca turned and ran back into her cottage, slamming the door.

I looked around the square. Everyone still here now and still living was unknown to me. "Go on," I said angrily to all of them. I did not know how many of them even spoke Italian. "The show is over. Go home, leave."

They did. There was nothing left to see but blood and one dead body. After a few moments, there is little satisfaction to be got from staring at death.

Unless the death is that of your oldest friend. I stood over Roderigo's dead body and felt angry grief wash over me. The poor fool. I would find something wonderful to say in the letter to his mother. I'd make sure she could mourn for him with dignity.

I turned and looked up toward the fortress above. I could not imagine what was happening up there. Othello seemed to me to be half a world away. Was he still raging like a madman? Had he struck his wife again? Had Lodovico already removed him from his office but not had a chance to say so in the upset of our encounter just now? I sensed I had already done all that was required of me to bring justice to the universe. I had nothing left to do but see how it unfolded. This night would either make me or destroy me: it was out of my hands now.

Chapter 50

I RETURNED TO a fortress full of chaos. First I heard the noise— general shouting, people crying out to one another, servants and lords and soldiers alike. Othello must be on a rampage. What should I do now? How would honest Iago behave?

He would check on the well-being of his wounded colleague Michele Cassio.

I crossed the courtyard diagonally, toward the infirmary stairwell, but I did not reach it: Lodovico and Gratiano came tripping down those same stairs, as lightly as old Venetian gentlemen can trip, and nearly ran into me. "Iago," Lodovico said, ashen faced, "something has happened in Othello's chambers, the servants have called us to come. Please help Montano—" He pointed up the stairs, and I saw Montano, still weak from Cassio's drunken attack, on a stool. He sat upright, but he kept his left arm protectively pressed against the wound in his side.

"Come, Governor," I said, concerned and urgent. "Lean on me while you walk." I ran up the steps and offered him my arm. He took it, gratefully, and I helped him to stand.

"Something has happened in Othello's rooms," he repeated as we descended the stairs together back into the courtyard. "I heard a woman screaming."

My blood chilled. Emilia? "Was it the general's wife?" I asked, and began to pull him across the courtyard.

"I could not tell whose voice it was," said Montano. I glanced back to make sure Lodovico and Gratiano—who did not know the layout here—were following after. "There was one shriek so loud it echoed around the courtyard, and then everyone else began to shout in alarm and there were too many voices, coming from too many places, to understand what was going on. Finally a servant came into my room and said Cassio had been attacked, and I must come at once. So . . ." He was already out of breath, but I could not slow down; I tightened my grip around his rib cage and walked faster, letting more of his weight rest across my shoulder as he stumbled to keep up. Behind me I could hear Lodovico and Gratiano clucking like worried hens. *Useless politicans*, I thought. "So I managed to get to the infirmary, and there was Cassio, and badly wounded. He begged me to forgive him for my injury, in case he did not live the night. I was . . . may we slow down?"

"No," I said. "But I'll take more of your weight." I shifted so that his armpit was directly above my shoulder, and my right arm moved from his rib to his midriff. He groaned with pain. I relented. "All right, we'll slow down," I said. "But not by much."

"He came into the infirmary," said Gratiano, upset but clearly relishing the role of storyteller. "Montano did. He saw Cassio and spoke to him and then was going to go back to bed, because he's weak."

"But he heard the shriek before he started down the steps," Lodovico said, taking up the story. "He hadn't the energy to take the stairs alone. I helped him down to the stool, where he could rest, while I saw how Cassio was doing."

By now we were across the courtyard and inside the wing of private rooms. Voices were piling toward us in the air—especially a woman's voice. The outermost and smallest room was the one in which Emilia and I had been staying; the door was open. "Emilia?" I cried out worriedly as we went by it. "Emilia, are you in there?"

"I think she must be in Othello's room," said one of the Venetians, I could not tell which one, I was far too distressed and terrified at the notion that Othello had done some violence to my wife. Ahead of us I heard the woman's voice, Emilia's voice, wailing on in pain. I almost could not see straight I was so desperate to get to her.

We rushed next past the lieutenant's room, which I would or would not sleep in tonight, depending on what awaited us ahead. Then guest rooms set aside for the visiting noblemen; then the corridor that ended in Othello's private quarters.

A group of servants huddled before it, pounding at the door and begging to be let in. "Out of the way!" I shouted. They jumped, and entangled us in their rush to move away from the door.

With most of Montano's weight upon me, I leaned back and furiously kicked the door. It flew open, and the crowd of us rushed into the room in alarm.

I saw my wife and my general standing some five paces apart, staring at each other with bloodshot, shining eyes, each looking ready to tear the other one apart.

Chapter 51

EMILIA'S FACE WAS whiter than I'd ever seen it. What had we interrupted? Where was Desdemona? What had I saved Emilia from by my appearance? *That whoreson lunatic!*

"Emilia!" I shouted. Both of them started violently and turned to face us.

"What's happened?" Montano said as I released him. "General?"

Emilia glared at me. I had never seen such rage on that face. "Oh, are you here too, Iago?" she asked, her voice sharp with sarcasm. "What in hell have you been up to, that men must lay their murders on your neck?"

"What murders?" I asked as Gratiano, entering behind me, demanded, "What's the matter?"

Emilia ignored the nobleman, her enraged attention entirely on me. "Disprove this villain," she demanded, pointing at Othello. "He claims you told him his wife was unfaithful. I know you never said such a thing. *So tell me what you really told him.*"

A sinking feeling pulled my stomach to my ankles. I could not lie to her. If my very life depended on it, I could not do it. "I only told him what I thought," I said. "That's all I did. He demanded me to tell my thoughts. He took from that what he himself considered to be true."

"But did you ever tell him she was *false*?" Emilia demanded impatiently, her outstretched hand still pointing furiously toward Othello.

There was no way out of it, then. She commanded, I obeyed. *Please, for the love of the angels,* I thought, *let me get her alone somewhere to explain all this. She will understand why it was necessary, and also why it does not put Othello's sins upon my shoulders.*

"I did—" I said, as if I were about to add a modifying thought. But she cut me off with rising, vengeful fury:

"You told a lie, Iago!" she screeched, sounding as much confused as furious. "You told an odious, damned, wicked *lie.*" Her arm still limply held out toward Othello, she shook her head at me. "With Cassio? Did you say *with Cassio?*"

Othello was invisible to me; so were the men beside me and behind me; so were the walls and candles of this chamber; so was the rumpled bed. Emilia knew that I was lying; Emilia did not understand the significance, the importance, the brilliance and genius of what I had been up to. All she saw was a single, simple lie, and she was ready to condemn me for it. She would not condemn me so if she understood the bigger history here. How could I distract her until I had the chance to explain it all to her alone?

"With Cassio, yes," I said calmly. I could not lie to her. I could only beg her to stop asking questions I didn't want to answer. "Emilia, enough of this, leave now. Stop your tongue."

I thought I'd seen her rage at its worst already; I was wrong. A dozen times as much fury and the grief reddened her face. "I will *not* stop my tongue!" she shouted at me, spittle flying with each consonant. "I am honor bound to speak now!" She ran to the crumpled bedsheets and with a billowing gesture, she swept them all off of the bed—

—to reveal Desdemona, lying utterly still upon the mattress. There were bruises on her neck and cheek; her lips were colorless. "My lady has been murdered in her bed!"

I almost vomited. I heard the men around me cry with shock; I don't know if I made any sound. I could not make sense of what I looked on. With Roderigo, there had been a fight, and blood, and dying; this was simply death, pale and sudden and silent.

Involuntarily I took a step toward the body. There was so little to her being; not enough to justify such outrageous wrath. Just some flesh and bones and hair encased within a nightgown. The spirit of Desdemona had departed from this earth. So suddenly. With so little warning.

"Iago," Emilia was still shouting at me, "Iago, he did this because of what you told him! Can you deny it?"

Now there was another cry of shock, and I realized, as if through a haze, that every person in the room was staring at me. I could not look away from Emilia. I could not speak.

"It is true." I heard Othello's voice. I could not look away from my wife. I wanted to scream out, *What kind of man reacts this way to words without proof? Why are you not the one to blame for this?*

Gratiano and Montano were speaking over each other; I did not know if they were condemning the general or me, and I did not care. The only person in the room who seemed real to me in this endless moment was my wife, my love, the first person ever who believed wholly in my goodness, the one person who had never wavered in her faith in me, who was now staring at me as if I were a fiend.

"This is an act of villainy," she announced, sounding as if her gorge rose to think of me this way. "Villainy. How could I not have smelled it earlier—when I think back, Iago, oh my God, when I think back—" Her eyes widened and widened, filling with tears, the color draining from her face until it was almost as pale as Desdemona's. "I should have *seen* this, when I think about it, all the signs were right in front of me, oh my God, I could never have thought you capable of such villainy, I never suspected this was happening right under my nose because I thought you were a good man—but you are not—I'll kill myself with grief—"

I felt my pulse beating in my neck, behind my ear, within my stomach. I was trembling. I could not let myself tremble. I tried to will the trembling to stop. I trembled more. "What are you talking about, Emilia?" I said, trying to sound condescending and parental. "You're very upset about what's happened here, understandably so, but I want you to leave here, and go back to our room and wait for me."

Emilia took a moment. She looked at me in silence, and shook her head. Then she turned to face the others in the room. "Gentlemen," she said somberly, suddenly deadly calm. "Give me leave to speak."

"Go home, Emilia," I said in a low, urgent voice.

Her attention snapped back to me. "It is possible, Iago, that I will never go home to you again."

In my peripheral vision I saw Othello crumple to the bed and begin to sob over the woman he had just strangled. Emilia's fury for a moment turned from me to him. "Sobbing is not enough, you whoreson—lay down and *roar* at your own actions! You have killed the sweetest innocent that ever walked this earth!"

Othello immediately stood again, and shouted back at Emilia, "She was not innocent! She deserved to die! Gratiano, I admit it, I killed your niece, I stopped her breath with these hands, I know this must appear horrific, but if you knew what she had done—"

Gratiano was unable even to speak. My eye had barely flickered from Emilia, and now she looked again at me, the accusation mounting in her expression. I had to get her alone, somewhere, somehow, I had to explain all of this, right away, make her understand how little I had done, and the little that I did I'd done with good cause, and the great undoing that came out of this was not an expression of my malevolence but of my misjudging how mad Othello really was. I had to do it right away.

She could not read my thoughts, but she saw something going on behind my eyes. We knew each other so well, so well; she understood there was something I had to tell her, and her expression softened slightly, as if to say, *You may have a chance yet to win me back.*

I could do nothing but focus on getting her away from here. *A man killed his wife in this room, let that be the end of it; arrest him and let the rest of us go and mourn in our own private ways.* How could I make that plea without sounding suspicious?

"It broke my heart to do it, but she was sinful and required it," Othello was saying, in a choked voice, to the horrified Venetians. "Iago knows that she shamed herself with Cassio, over and over again—Cassio confessed it himself!" There was no relenting in the faces of the men he addressed; suddenly on the defensive, Othello pressed on, sounding less confident and almost childish, "There is proof! Proof I've seen with my own eyes! She gave Cassio a pledge of love that I had given her—an old handkerchief my father gave my mother when they married—"

"*What?*" Emilia shrieked. She turned back toward me and with both hands pointing at me, stammered, "Heavenly powers—"

"Come," I said warningly. "Hold your peace."

This was bad, this was very bad. She did not realize Othello was a madman and had sworn to do this dreadful deed before seeing any proof at all; she thought the handkerchief had led to Desdemona's death, and now she thought I'd had a hand in it, and worse, that she did too. *You cannot kill a dead woman,* I wanted to tell her; Desdemona was doomed before the handkerchief came into play. Everything was still salvageable, if I could somehow communicate to her that there was a rationale to all I did. "Hold your peace," I repeated, almost pleading.

She was beyond reason. "The truth will out, Iago! It will out! I will speak if the heavens and the devils together conspired to shut me up, I'll speak, you *evil creature!*" she shrieked at me. Her eyes raged so full of horror, shame, and anger, I could not bear to meet her gaze. I looked down.

"Be wise, and leave here now," I growled.

"I will not," she retorted. She was breathing heavily and fast and looked disoriented. She ran toward me and slapped me hard across the face. I stood there like an idiot without responding. "You stupid man!" she said, turning back toward Othello. "That handkerchief you speak of? *I found it,* by chance, and I gave it to my husband, because he said he wanted it for something." She gave me a disgusted look. "Now I know, now I know why you wanted it, you *demon*, how could you use me to accomplish so much evil? I cannot believe I'm married to such a *demon!*" Her hands spread out before her, shaking violently, she broke into harsh sobs. "How could you have done this? *Nothing* can justify this—and you are an *abomination* if you think otherwise."

IT WAS MORE than a slap, it was a door slamming closed. Understanding nothing, Emilia was condemning me. Not just judging, but condemning, casting out. She was wrong to do it. Emilia had never been wrong about me ever before; she knew enough to give a situation consideration before judging, especially where I was concerned; how could she so swiftly see me out of tune now? She was betraying the most vital, spiritual, profoundest aspect of our marriage vows. She was betraying me. Of course she was upset about Desdemona—even I was upset about that—but there must be something broken in her soul if she would let her emotions overrule her reason. Her reason knew I was not evil. She was rebelling against her own nature to think otherwise. She was failing herself, and therefore me.

"Whore," I blurted harshly, heartbroken.

"She gave it to Cassio?" Emilia said, and now turned her attention to the patricians in the room. "No, *I* found it. I gave it to *my husband*, sirs, and he—"

"You're a filthy liar!" I shouted at her, desperate to shut her up.

She turned to look at me.

Everything within her, all the rage and fear and upset, calmed. Everyone around us disappeared. Everything around us disappeared. We were in some other world. She had just ruined everything I'd undertaken—I would not be lieutenant now, no matter what befell Cassio or Othello. I would probably be demoted, or cast out of the army altogether, perhaps even fined, imprisoned . . . none of that mattered in this moment. In this moment all that mattered was Emilia. I held out my hands helplessly before me, a plea for understanding.

All I could see were Emilia's eyes, and the deeper I looked into them, the more clearly I saw myself within them. I saw not a determined, deserving soldier earning his right to the lieutenancy by demonstrating his rival's unfitness for office; not a slighted confidant testing his friend's mental clarity and finding it alarmingly cloudy; not a doting husband trying to better himself to be deserving of a cherished wife. I saw only a man of a vindictive and violent nature, hell-bent on doing whatever it took to get whatever he wanted, no matter the cost; I saw a man so twisted up with jealousy and envy that he would sacrifice and demean anyone to tear others down; worst of all, a man of tremendous capabilities who would not hesitate to let those capabilities lead to the death of innocents. All this I saw. She was wrong, of course, but she was locked in to her misperceptions; she would not be budged, no matter what I said to her. And now I would have to spend the rest of our lives knowing those beautiful eyes and that brilliant mind were judging me. It was not a judgment I could bare.

"I renounce you," she said under her breath, in a tone of absolute finality. And then she slowly, deliberately, meaningfully turned her back on me, her thoughts full of what an evil man I was.

I could not live with that. That judgment. That condemnation. That unwaveringly harsh misappraisal. Not from her. From anybody else, it would not matter. From Emilia, it was the world's end. It had to be. If only she had not condemned me, not slammed the door between our souls.

I drew the short sword with my right hand as the left one reached up to grab her shoulder from behind.

She hardly resisted, as if she knew her fate and was resigned to it. The blade went in between her lowest ribs, and I shoved upward, slicing through everything I loved, severing her from her ability to make me see my actions with her eyes.

She cried out weakly, once, and then fell slack against me, life oozing from her. I pushed her away, and she fell uncomplaining onto the bed beside Desdemona, the blood spattering and ruining Desdemona's perfect paleness.

I was free. The judging eyes would judge no more.

I fled the room, because it seemed a man should do so in such a situation.

I did not do it to escape punishment or capture.

I COULD HEAR my pursuers in the hallway, and once out in the courtyard, I felt their footsteps as if they were stampeding. I knew I was cornered; the impulse to run was animal, there was no sense or reason to my movements.

Everywhere I saw Emilia's eyes staring at me, although I'd put that light out, although she was not here to stare, still her eyes were staring at me, telling me how villainous I was. *I could have made all clear to you,* I wanted to scream, but the unblinking eyes were unmoved. They were on the walls of the courtyard, they were blinking at me in the dark stairwell of the keep, when I burst out onto the wall walk they held me fixated staring down at me from heaven.

That is when I realized they were not Emilia's eyes. They were my own.

Three innocents lay dead tonight, two by my own hand. No rationale under heaven could mitigate such villainy. My mangling of Othello's reason paled compared to how I had suborned my own. Honest Iago had fooled everyone, but most of all himself.

I stared into the cool night sky and waited for the men pursuing me to grab me.

LODOVICO HAD COME IN during my absence. So had Cassio, looking weak, his leg bandaged, still seated in the sedan chair which two servants had lowered to the ground. The servant who had caught me was very pleased with himself, and he pushed me down to my knees in the bedroom in front of Othello more harshly than he needed to.

Othello looked at me, tears streaming down his face. He drew his short sword and held it up, as if I were an animal about to be slaughtered. Perhaps I was to him: a sacrifice to appease the gods for his credulity and rage. I would accept it. We were both sinners and heaven knew a sacrifice was required here.

"They say you cannot kill a devil," Othello said in quiet disgust, and slashed my left arm with his sword. The pain was terrible, but so was the release; I deserved the wound, I knew it now, and to accept it offered solace.

"Take his sword!" Lodovico shouted in alarm to one of his attendants. The fellow was terrified of the assignment, but Othello yielded with weariness. At Lodovico's gesture, another attendant approached me and wrapped a rag around my arm to staunch the bleeding.

"I bleed, but I'm not killed," I said dully to the general.

"Good," Othello said with tired anger. "I would rather you live. You do not deserve the peace of dying."

I agreed with him, so I said nothing. I gazed on the form of my wife, lying sprawled beside Desdemona's corpse. Othello and I, the shamed malignants, were outsiders once again, like the day we met.

"Othello." Lodovico sighed. "What can I say to such a good man who fell so far so fast?"

"It's not such a mystery," Othello retorted. "I did nothing out of hate, it was all for honor."

"Did you plot Cassio's death with Iago?"

"Yes," Othello said, looking down.

Cassio, weak and feverish, said, "General, I never gave you cause for it."

"I know that now," Othello said, "And I ask your pardon for it."

These two men—the fearfully obsessed and jealous wife-beater, and the boozing womanizer, who had colluded together to defraud a Venetian senator of his only child—had already repaired their love.

I did not care. My soul had run aground while I still thought it was expertly navigating open water. I had not noticed the shipwreck until Emilia forced me to admit it, and I had punished her for that. I was a fiend.

Othello pointed toward me without looking at me, and spoke through gritted teeth. "Cassio, will you ask this devil . . . *why*?"

The only person I admired was my wife, for she led always from her heart, even when it took her into danger. The rest of us—all the rest of us—deserved a whipping or a hanging. All of us. Othello and Cassio were not without sin, they had no right to judge me unless they judged themselves first, and neither of them had the humility or strength to do it. Far easier to make me the single villain.

Very well. I, like them, was far from sinless. But now I understood and owned my sins, in a way I would not have done an hour earlier, before I had to see myself as Emilia did. She had given me the greatest and most terrible of gifts: unflinching honesty. Exactly the thing I'd prized myself for, before I'd abandoned the true path without noticing. Othello and Cassio had both fallen off their own true paths but did not know it, and would not be forced to know it, ever. Othello, maybe. Cassio, most definitely not.

I could not explain this to them. They would not understand. "Ask me nothing," I said calmly. "What you know, you know. From this time forth I will not speak another word."

"Not even to pray?" Lodovico demanded warningly. This man had no idea he was not sinless; I had nothing to say to him.

"Torment will make you open your mouth," Gratiano warned, as if he had the right to torture anyone. To him also, I did not try to explain myself.

Othello, unexpectedly, squatted down to look me full in the face. He gave me a look of anguish—not only grief and anger but a soul-wrenching desperation that was very nearly envy.

He understood. He alone among them understood. "You do best not to speak," he said.

I knew then he meant to take his life. And I knew that none of them would understand why. The others argued and accused me and produced evidence—my directions to Roderigo found tucked into the corpse's belt about where the campo was that we should meet to attack Cassio, for example. The whole time, Othello remained kneeling upright, gazing into my eyes with almost all the understanding of Emilia's stare. He would not survive the night. He did not want to. They might later say he killed himself for grief, or shame, but it would not be that. He had seen the truth in Emilia's look as clearly as I had; if I had not killed her, he surely would have, and for the same reason. But killing the truth-teller does not kill the truth. In that moment of understanding, as furious as he was at me, he was my brother once again. He would leave this mortal coil understood by nobody but me. Is that not a kind of love?

"OTHELLO." LODOVICO'S VOICE broke into our shared silence. "You are removed from office. We'll keep you imprisoned until we can present your crimes to the Venetian Senate. Cassio will rule in Cyprus. For this villain"—and of course by that he meant me—"he will be tortured for as long as he survives it." He snapped his fingers at the attendants who were warily watching all of this unfold. "Come, bring Othello away."

Othello glanced at me a final time. I nodded slightly, in farewell. I knew he had a dagger in his boot; I was the only one in this room who knew that—not even Cassio had inkling of it. If I really hated Othello, I would have warned them that he had a weapon, I would have forced him to remain alive with me, and go out into the world, and be judged by others who would never judge themselves. I had the power to do that to him. If I hated him, I would have told them.

I did not say a word. I watched him rise, and ask them for the favor of their patience as he gave what they supposed would be his final speech before imprisonment. The words he spoke washed right over me; I did not hear them. I was saying my own silent farewell, offering and asking redemption of a soul about to be unfettered.

He startled all of them by pulling out the dagger from his boot and shoving it hard into his own breastbone. Unsurprised but heartbroken, I lowered my head with a prayer of deliverance. As the self-important men around us cried out in shock and dismay, Othello fell onto the bed between the women. He kissed Desdemona's lifeless body tenderly, before falling into silence.

"I was afraid of that, but I did not think he had a weapon," said Cassio in a hollow voice. "He was too great of heart to remain a captive all his life."

That's not it at all, you stupid fool, I thought, but kept my lips sealed.

THE DEAD ARE buried now, and the news is being told and told and told again. In each telling, I am certain, there is an insidious rounding of rough edges, a subtle simplifying, a massaging of the tale into one of deliberate villain and hapless victims. It is easy to call someone a villain; the title allows dismissal and more important, distance: as long as you know somebody else is the villain, then you are not one, and you may rest snugly in your own nest of good intentions, no need for vigilance or self-reflection. You mean well, and even when you act in anger, your actions are justified—somehow, surely, they are justified, they must be, and you have done nothing wrong, because you are not evil. This is the comfort of the smug.

I am honest Iago, and I ask you: might not you be dishonest with yourself?

Acknowledgments

Thanks, and thanks, and ever thanks:

Above all to Chelsea McCarthy, the best of coconspirators, for declaring, "I want us to do *Othello*—but only if Billy Meleady plays Iago."

To the immensely generous and joyful Seccombe-Martin clan, for being a home away from home, and then a home, and then a home away from home.

To those earth-angels who were still there for me after I had absented myself from felicity awhile: my agent Liz Darhansoff, my editor Jennifer Brehl, and Marc H. Glick, Esq.

To Jeremy Bornstein, Kate Feiffer, Laura Roosevelt, Cathy Walthers, and Melissa Hackney, for being the first to greet these characters.

To innumerable others who helped, inspired, or sometimes challenged, in ways direct or indirect, deliberate or unintended. Among them: Michele Mortimer, Mac Young, Eowyn Mader, Todd Follansbee, Nick Walker, Sheryl Dagostino, and William Shakespeare.

P.S.

Insights,
Interviews
& More . . .

Meet Nicole Galland

Eli Dagostino

NICOLE GALLAND is the author of three previous novels: *The Fool's Tale*, *Revenge of the Rose*, and *Crossed: A Tale of the Fourth Crusade*. After growing up on Martha's Vineyard and graduating with honors from Harvard, she divided most of the next sixteen years between California and New York City before returning to the Vineyard to stay. She is the cofounder of Shakespeare for the Masses, a project that irreverently makes the Bard accessible to the Bardophobics of the world. She is married to actor Billy Meleady. ⌒

The Story Behind the Story of *I, Iago*

A FEW YEARS AGO, my friend Chelsea McCarthy and I started a project to keep ourselves out of trouble during the long winters on Martha's Vineyard. (Even resort communities have winters, and real people live through them.) We began irreverently adapting Shakespeare's plays by creating script-in-hand performances that needed one day (or thereabouts) to rehearse and one hour (or thereabouts) to perform. With a talented group of local actors and occasional guest artists donating their time, we staged these performances free of charge at the Vineyard Playhouse. The Playhouse's artistic director, MJ Bruder Munafo, dubbed us "Shakespeare for the Masses."

We were a surprise hit our first season, staging seven plays between October and May. We had stage combat and love scenes and dumb-shows. (A dumb-show is a pantomime of sorts.) We had fun, and so did our audiences.

When Chelsea and I met over the summer to talk about our second season, she made a request that would have a profound impact on my life. She wanted us to do *Othello*, and specified she wanted Billy Meleady to play Iago. ▶

The Story Behind the Story of *I, Iago*
(continued)

Billy was a Boston-based Irish actor, phenomenally talented, and especially adept at villains and comedic roles. He'd worked with each of us on several plays over the past couple of years. I asked if he'd come down to play the role. I offered him our fold-out couch to sleep on. (Ayad Akhtar was coming from New York to play Othello and had dibs on the guest room.) I could not offer him any money or even travel expenses; he'd have to do it as a favor.

Billy said he'd love to play Iago. I'd sent him the script ahead of time, but when he arrived, he admitted sheepishly that he hadn't had a chance to look at it.

"Oh, don't worry," I said. "We didn't change much, we're basically just doing a shorter version of the original."

"You don't understand," said Billy. "I haven't read the play."

"*Othello*? You haven't read *Othello*?" I asked.

He shook his head. "No, I haven't."

I repressed my wave of panic. We had one day of rehearsal, and the actor *for whom we had specifically selected the play* wasn't familiar with the role.

"Why did you say you wanted to

play Iago if you don't know the part?"
I asked.

"Every actor I know wants to
play Iago," he said. "There has to
be a reason."

So Billy and I stayed up until
two in the morning, reading and
analyzing our way through the script,
playing around with different ideas,
motivations, interpretations. The
more we delved, the more fascinated
we each became with Iago. It was
a treat for me—most actors playing
Iago already know what they want
to do with the part, so it's rare for a
director to help shape the character
so much.

We had a day of rehearsal with
the cast, and then the next evening
we continued our crash course in
Iagosity. Lights up, on with the show:
Billy was a fine Iago the first night, a
brilliant Iago the second night—and
then the show was over. (Shakespeare
for the Masses only puts on two
performances per play.)

So that was that. Billy went back
to Boston, now hungry to play the
part "for real." The questions he'd
raised and the ideas we'd played
with haunted me. Other tantalizing
questions had surfaced as well,
especially regarding Iago's
relationship with his wife, ▶

The Story Behind the Story of *I, Iago*
(continued)

Emilia (whom Chelsea had played).
I could not stop thinking about this.
I believe Iago loves Emilia, which
makes her death a different *kind*
of crime than any of his others.

I was also fascinated (as many
people are) with Iago's sudden
silence near the end of the play.
He has more lines than Othello;
he talks incessantly not only to
other characters but also to the
audience, to whom he gleefully
boasts why and how he intends to
cause mischief. He uses words as both
weapon and shield. All his power lies
in his words. Then suddenly, having
been found out, he declares he will
not say another word—and he
doesn't. What changes to make
him stop talking? Is it merely
that he's been unmasked? That's
such a simplistic answer for such
a complicated character.

After that weekend, I took my
dog for long morning walks in the
autumnal woods and hardly noticed
the glory of the beech trees turning
gold; my attention was focused
inwardly on Iago's behavior.
One morning, I had an epiphany.
I remember the very step I was
taking, the exact moment in space
I was inhabiting, when a tumble
of thoughts brought me to a

standstill. Maybe *that's* why he does *that*, I thought. And *that's* why he does *that*! And *that*! And *that*!

I rushed home and began to write like a woman possessed.

Here is a happy little epilogue:

Cut to the following summer. My life was greatly altered: I was newly divorced, living in a small cottage I shared with my new landlords, and I was halfway through the first draft of "the Iago novel." It was late July on Martha's Vineyard, and Billy Meleady—whom I had not seen and barely spoken to since *Othello*—came down to the island for vacation. We had a few friendly meals together. To our shared surprise, a chemistry developed between us that neither of us had ever felt before, not even when we were wrestling with Iago the previous year. The attraction proved too strong to resist. To borrow from Brontë for a moment: Reader, I married him. ❧

Dramatis Personae
A Character Reference, of Sorts

WHEN CREATING THE CHARACTERS in *I, Iago*, I relied on information in the original *Othello* text. Although the play appears to be about innocent people being tragically duped and destroyed by a villain, a closer look reveals that there are few real innocents in this story. Here is a brief introduction to some of the major characters. (I have elected not to introduce Iago or Emilia here—that would give too much away.)

Othello

The heroic, trusting, good-natured, passionate general of the Venetian forces. He elopes with his beloved Desdemona. He is cruelly, fatally duped by his ensign Iago, who single-handedly brings about Othello's downfall through cunning and deceit.

On the Other Hand

Othello betrays his patron, Brabantio, by running off with his only child. Later, despite the absence of any proof, Othello is so gullible that over the course of one scene, Iago convinces him that his bride might be having an affair; and only a few hours later, Othello has histrionically vowed to murder both his bride and her supposed lover. (He makes this vow *before* he sees the infamous handkerchief—so he vows to kill her without any "ocular proof" at all.)

Cassio

Othello's innocent, honorable young lieutenant who becomes the dupe in Iago's scheme to drive Othello mad with jealousy. Cassio beat out Iago for the position of lieutenant, which accounts for Iago's hatred of him.

On the Other Hand

An alcoholic, Cassio becomes extremely violent when drunk. He has a prostitute mistress who dotes on him, but whom he mocks and belittles behind her back. Although he has less military experience than Iago does, Othello has made Cassio lieutenant at about the same time that Cassio helps Othello to carry out his affair with Desdemona. Is that timing really a coincidence?

Desdemona

The spirited young daughter of Senator Brabantio; she elopes with Othello and goes with him to Cyprus, where her husband murders her because he believes she is having an affair with Cassio. ▶

Dramatis Personae *(continued)*

On the Other Hand

She carries out a secret affair with a man her father knows, trusts, and likes. This isn't *Romeo and Juliet.* There is no need for her to keep her feelings secret from her father—they love each other, and he has indulged her disinterest of Venetian youths. She shouldn't marry Othello because he isn't a member of the Venetian patriciate, but given the understanding, supportive nature of her father regarding affairs of her heart, she might at least have *discussed* the situation with him first. Her father literally dies of grief after his daughter goes to Cyprus.

Roderigo

A wealthy, hapless Venetian, hopelessly in love with Desdemona. Iago steals from him and puts him in harm's way to carry out his plans against Cassio, then cold-heartedly murders him when the plan to kill Cassio goes awry.

On the Other Hand

The play opens with Roderigo and Iago commiserating—possibly the only moment Iago is ever sincere with another character. At the start of the play, Roderigo already has a trusting enough relationship with Iago that he continually puts himself, and his money, in Iago's hands. He would (he claims) have drowned himself for grief, had Iago not distracted him with other plans. Even when he begins to suspect those "other plans" are not in his interest, he tries to kill an innocent man in the hope of winning the married woman for whom he lusts. ⁓

Questions for Discussion

1. Have you (or anyone you've known) ever acted out of anger that you believed was justified— and then realized you were in error? If so, how did you handle the realization?

2. What is the worst lie you have ever told? Was it a lie of omission or commission? What were the consequences of the lie? How did you feel at the time you were lying, and how do you feel about it now, thinking back on it?

3. Is there such a thing as "a little white lie?" Who and what defines it? What is the worst kind of lie? Why?

4. Do people's behaviors in dire circumstances reveal the truth about their character, or a warped version of their character?

5. Are people's tendencies toward honesty or deceit more informed by nature or by nurture— by innate character or by circumstance?

6. If your partner were cheating on you or if someone you love were being deceitful, would you rather know about it or remain completely oblivious? Why?

7. At what point in the story do you feel Iago loses his way?

8. If you know the play *Othello:* Which of the characters in *I, Iago* feel most familiar to you, and which ones feel most like deviations from the original play? What do you most enjoy or miss in this interpretation?

9. If you do not know the play *Othello:* Does the novel make you curious to see it? Why or why not? What characters are you most curious to see in their original form? ∾

Read on

Have You Read?
More from Nicole Galland

For more books by Nicole Galland check out

THE FOOL'S TALE

Wales, 1198. A time of treachery, passion, and uncertainty. Maelgwyn ap Cadwallon struggles to protect his small kingdom from foes outside and inside his borders. Pressured into a marriage of political convenience, he weds the headstrong young Isabel Mortimer, niece of his powerful English nemesis. Gwirion, the king's oldest and oddest friend, has a particular reason to hate Mortimers and immediately employs his royally sanctioned mischief to disquiet the new queen.

Through strength of character, Isabel wins her husband's grudging respect but finds the Welsh court backward and barbaric—especially Gwirion, against whom she engages in a relentless battle of wills. When Gwirion and Isabel's mutual animosity is abruptly transformed, the king finds himself as threatened by loved ones as he is threatened by the many enemies who menace his crown.

A masterful debut by a gifted

storyteller, *The Fool's Tale* combines vivid historical fiction, compelling political intrigue, and passionate romance to create an intimate drama of three individuals bound—and undone—by love and loyalty.

REVENGE OF THE ROSE

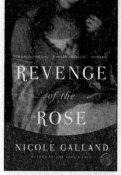

An impoverished, idealistic young knight in rural Burgundy, Willem of Dole greets with astonishment his summons to the court of Konrad, Holy Roman Emperor, whose realm spans half of Europe. Immediately overwhelmed by court affairs, Willem submits to the relentless tutelage of Konrad's minstrel—the mischievous, mysterious Jouglet. With Jouglet's help, Willem quickly rises in the emperor's esteem . . .

. . . But when Willem's sister, Lienor, becomes a prospect for the role of empress, the sudden elevation of two sibling "nobodies" causes panic in a royal court fueled by gossip, secrets, treachery, and lies. Three desperate men in Konrad's inner circle frantically vie to control the game of politics, yet Jouglet the minstrel is somehow always one step ahead of them.

Inspired by an actual thirteenth-century satire of courtly life, *Revenge of the Rose* is a novel rich in irony and wit that revels in the politics, passions, and peccadilloes of the medieval court.

CROSSED: A TALE OF THE FOURTH CRUSADE

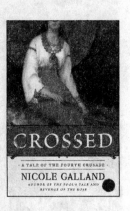

In the year 1202, thousands of crusaders gather in Venice, preparing to embark for Jerusalem to free the Holy City from Muslim rule. Among them is an irreverent British vagabond who has literally lost his way, rescued from damnation by a pious German knight. Despite the vagabond's objections, they set sail with dedicated companions and a beautiful, mysterious Arab "princess."

But the divine light guiding this "righteous" campaign soon darkens as the mission sinks ever deeper into disgrace, moral turpitude, and almost farcical catastrophe. As Christians murder Christians in the Adriatic port city of Zara, tragic events are set in motion that will ultimately lead to the shocking and shameful fall of Constantinople.

Impeccably researched and beautifully told, Nicole Galland's *Crossed* is a sly tale of the disastrous Fourth Crusade—and of the hopeful, brave, and driven people who were trapped by a corrupt cause and a furious battle that were beyond their comprehension or control.

Don't miss the next book by your favorite author. Sign up now for AuthorTracker by visiting www.AuthorTracker.com.